Rowena Through the Wall

Melodie Campbell

ROWENA THROUGH THE WALL
Book 1 in the Land's End series

http://www.melodiecampbell.com

SECOND EDITION TRADE PAPERBACK

Imajin Books

March 25, 2012

ISBN: 978-1-926997-52-0

Cover designed by Sapphire Designs:
http://www.designs.sapphiredreams.org

Praise for Melodie Campbell

"A hot, hilarious, romantic fantasy that enthralls you from the first line. If you enjoy Diana Gabaldon's *Outlander* series, you'll adore Rowena and her riotous romps in an alternate world..." —*Midwest Book Review*, Betty Dravis, author of *Dream Reachers*

"Filled with plenty of fun, action, and a main character that takes no prisoners, *Rowena Through the Wall* is an exciting romp through a fantasy world that will leave you completely and utterly satisfied." —*Allbooks Review*

"This raunchy romp transports us to an alternate reality where being a woman presents unique challenges. Luckily, Rowena is equal to both challenge and challengers and never loses her sharp intelligence or sense of humor. She'll need both to survive! Fun and surprising." —Mary Jane Maffini, award-winning author of *The Busy Woman's Guide to Murder*

"Time-travel romance with a rollicking sense of humor...A new dimension of romance in a parallel universe." —Lou Allin, author of *She Felt No Pain*

"Filled with brutal, sword-swinging danger, yet sexy and funny, you'll be rooting for Row as she uses her head to stay alive and her heart to find love." —Kelsey Lewis, author of *Hot and Bothered*

"Multi-published author, Melodie Campbell is a talented story teller. Her award-winning short stories pack a powerful punch and her alternate world fantasy novel, *Rowena Through the Wall*, is a rollicking, sexy romp through time." —Dee Lloyd, award-winning author of *Out of Her Dreams*

"*Rowena through the Wall* is a wild ride of fantasy, with a lusty lady who male readers will wish had walked through a wall to them." —Mark Alldis, former editor *Distant Suns* fantasy magazine

"Rowena is the most interesting, unique fictional character to come along since Lisbeth Salander. She is smart, witty and down to earth...I can't wait for Book Two!" —Cathy Astolfo, author of *Seventh Fire*

For my family, who has good-naturedly tolerated the "black hole of writing" that often extends into the night.

Acknowledgments

Thank you, Alison, for keeping me sane at work and sharing this grand adventure with me. Cathy, your sparkling enthusiasm has truly guided and inspired me this year.

Special thanks to my earliest readers—Angela, Cindy, Cheryl, Marilyn and Grace—who were always there for me with encouragement; Janet, Helen and my other "Sisters in Crime" from the Toronto branch; Lynda Simmons, first a student, then the teacher—how life comes around.

And everyone needs a Mark, the best friend a girl could have, who has pushed me to keep writing for nineteen years.

Cheryl Tardif of Imajin Books and Jennifer Johnson of Sapphire Dreams, thank you for making dreams come true.

Dear Reader,

Imagine my delight when the first reviews of *Rowena Through the Wall* began to be posted from readers on Amazon. "Hot and hilarious!" said one. "A character you can truly love!" said another.

Readers from all over the continent and as far away as Estonia were telling me how much they loved my spunky character Rowena and her sexy warrior suitors. They embraced the medieval world of Land's End and giggled at the wacky predicaments Rowena got herself into.

But one thing seemed to be common in all reader responses. They wanted a happy ending for Rowena, and they wanted it immediately, not in future books.

I've been writing fiction since 1991. Here is one thing I can tell you about authors, and about me in particular: when it comes to our books, there is no one more important to us than our readers.

I talked to my esteemed publisher, who is always ready to listen. Together, we agreed to give readers what they wanted: a happy ending for Rowena.

Hence this expanded edition of **Rowena Through the Wall**. Rowena has a ton of rollicking adventures, but in the end…

I won't give away the ending. But I can assure you that Rowena is happy with it.

I hope you will be too.

Thank you for reading!

Melodie

Please follow my blog: www.funnygirlmelodie.blogspot.com

Chapter 1

I saw the first one right after class. It was late April and already hot as a Swedish sauna in my home town of Scottsdale, Arizona. Kendra Perkins had stopped me to ask about a mark on her undergrad veterinary assignment, and while I was moving my hair away from my neck and longing stupidly for winter, I looked over her shoulder and there he was.

The man was extremely large and very blond. He wore a banded tunic with leggings and had leather bands on both his wrists.

My first thought was, how the heck had he gotten to the back of the classroom without me seeing him? Especially with that long gunmetal-gray sword that was hanging from a belt at his waist.

I blinked twice and stared. He didn't move.

Crap. He appeared to be real.

"Is there a medieval festival in town?" I asked with a little skip in my voice.

Tunic-man looked right at me, startled. His eyes were ice blue.

Not one of my students, I realized. I'd never seen the guy before. And believe me, I would have remembered. Scary and way too attractive. Well, let's just say scary.

I'd only taught for one term and I'd only been out of veterinary school for a year, but the impetus to protect my students was automatic.

I stepped around Kendra. "Hello—can I help you?"

I managed a smile and that seemed to surprise the stranger. He frowned and bent his head slightly as if to bow. Then he swung around, walked through the wall and was gone.

Bloody Hell.

"Row, who are you talking to?" Kendra asked behind me.

I turned, my mouth gaping. "Didn't you see that guy dressed up as...as..." What, some sort of warrior?

Kendra shook her head. "I didn't see nothing."

"*Any*thing," I corrected.

Somebody was playing tricks. I walked to the classroom door and peered out. The hall was empty. No pranksters jumped out at me. No Derrick, Mark or any other of the motley crew in my first year class.

Kendra eyed me. "You're kinda weird, you know. But in a nice way." This, coming from an eighteen-year-old with spiky black hair, black leather boots, armbands and a complete assortment of Goth piercings.

Shaking my head, I let the whole thing drop.

That night, I had peculiar dreams. I was in a world where the sky was azure, the sun was orange instead of yellow and the green was too dark for normal foliage. The edge of the forest looked over a verdant valley. I scanned the sky for birds, as I always do, and saw none. Where were they?

From behind a split tree trunk, a little ground squirrel peeped out at me. It wanted to know what I was doing here, but before I could answer, I heard the pounding of hooves. Whether guided by instinct or by something more powerful, the squirrel and I slipped back into the foliage just in time to miss being seen by the riders. Horses whipped by us, frenzied mounts with riders clinging to their backs.

I waited until the last animal had swept past us. Waited until the air was clear of pounding. Then I stepped into the clearing.

Down the meadow I drifted, past Queen Anne's lace and clover. No bees hovered over the delectable menu of wildflowers. I called silently and nothing responded.

How could that be? This valley should be teeming with life.

I headed down to the river's edge and tried to get the attention of any frogs or fish that might be swimming in the turquoise water. Two clear eyes looked up at me and I smiled, reaching down to cup the small fish in my hands.

A deep male voice thundered behind me. "Who are you? And what in Hades are you wearing?"

As I turned, the scene faded and I awoke in a sweat.

Chapter 2

The second time I saw Tunic-man, he wasn't alone. It was the same classroom, two days later. I was alone, marking papers at my desk. I heard a sound and looked up.

There they were in front of me.

I dropped my pen. "Holy crap, you scared me."

The blond one wore the same tunic and leather get-up. This close, I put his age at mid-thirties, a little old for this sort of play-acting. His companion was blond as well, but younger, shorter and just as bulky.

They looked right at me.

"She's a comely lass," Tunic-man said in an unusual accent. "And she has the look of the Huel women."

The younger man's eyes lit up with excitement. "Astonishing. But is she fertile?"

My mouth gaped. Fertile?

"Excuse me," I said. "I'm right here, you know."

They stared back at me, shocked.

I sighed. "I'm not deaf and that is rather a personal question. Don't be rude." It's always best to talk plainly with students, I find, especially since I'm not much older than they are.

The younger one spoke first. "She can hear us?"

Tunic-man nodded. "Apparently so. Woman, what is your name?"

"Woman?" I pushed back the chair and jumped to my feet. "Are you fucking out of your mind?"

"You don't have a name?"

I was almost speechless. Almost, but not quite.

"I don't know what fraternity you guys are from" I said, "but if you don't tell me what is going on this very minute, I will personally see that you two never *ever* graduate from anything other than obedience school."

Tunic-man looked at his friend. "They have schools for the obedient here, Janus. We should think about such things."

"This one doesn't look very obedient."

"Perhaps they don't send their women."

I picked up *Epidemiology for Veterinary 1* and slammed it on the desk. "This has gone far enough. Leave my classroom immediately."

To my surprise, Tunic-man grabbed Janus by the shoulder and pulled him though the wall.

I watched the empty space for a good thirty seconds before reaching for the cell phone on my desk. I called a coworker.

"Debbie, it's Row," I said. "Have there been any strangers hanging around lately? Strangers in weird medieval costumes like extras from Lord of the Rings?"

Debbie, of course, laughed and said I was crazy.

My name is Rowena Revel, but everyone calls me Row. Except for Dad, who calls me Red. It's the hair, which is a true auburn and reaches nearly to my waist. It's my one vanity, and by God, I deserve it. I'm not especially tall and I'm not slim. They invented underwire for women like me.

There are worse things though. I may look sloppy in pants and a tailored shirt, but I look pretty darn good in slinky evening wear and satin nightgowns.

That night, I slipped into one of my favorite nightgowns—a Natori—in a sapphire blue. It had spaghetti straps and came with a matching full-length dressing gown with lace edging. I had planned to wear it on my honeymoon. That didn't happen.

If I had to tell the story of my life, it would be through the dogs I have known, not the men. I've loved animals all my life. I became a vet so I could care for them. I find, as most animal lovers do, that little creatures give back a lot more than they take. I can't say my experience with men has been the same.

My expression in the bedroom mirror was sad, but the nightgown was as beautiful as the day I first set eyes on it.

Piper, my West Highland white terrier pup, yipped and I looked down at his sweet furry face. "Come on, little one. Time for bed."

We settled into the four-poster bed…and into our dreams.

The sky was azure, the sun was orange and the air was as still as it had been the last time.

How could I be back in the same dream?

"Who are you? And what the Hades are you wearing?"

I turned, perplexed.

A dark-haired man in a tunic hovered over me. "Well, speak!"

I opened my mouth, then closed it, floundering for words. "It's a Natori. I got it for seventy-five percent off at Saks."

His anger turned to puzzlement. "What is this *Natori* and where do you hail from that maidens wear such flimsy items of finery? Where are your undergarments?" He crossed his brawny arms in disapproval. "You are obviously not from here. That much is certain."

I took a deep breath. "I 'hail'—as you so quaintly put it—from Scottsdale, and I don't wear undergarments to bed. Besides, I wasn't expecting to be here."

"Wasn't expecting to be where?"

"Oh, for Pete's sake, in this dream."

This was getting absurd. I was starting to feel like Alice.

"So you're a Scot."

Good Grief. "No, I'm American. Scottsdale is in Arizona."

That seemed to stump him, so I took the opportunity to look him over. He was worthy of it. With the sun behind him, his hair looked black, but I could see now it was really a rich brown. Yup, he was wearing the same sort of tunic as Tunic-man and friend, with the leather bracelet thingies. This dream was becoming predictable.

He frowned. "Are you a witch?"

"No," I said slowly, as if talking to a dull-witted child. "I'm a vet."

His brows drew together. "What is your name, vet?"

I smiled with pride. "Dr. Revel. I qualified last year."

He didn't seem impressed. "You shouldn't be out here alone, clad in only a Natori. It's not safe. Who is your father?"

"Tom Revel. And although it's none of your business, my mother was Rowena Revel, nee Trefusus, if that makes a difference. What's this all about, anyway?"

His dark face turned white. "Rowena?"

"It's my first name too, actually. Rowena Revel. But everyone calls me Row."

He sat down. "Rowena Trefusus?"

I nodded. Oh boy. This didn't have a good feel. I wasn't liking this dream at all.

"What about you?" I asked.

"My name is Jon. Jon Trefusus."

I stared at him, my heart hammering. "And that would mean what exactly?"

Before he could answer, we heard hooves pounding over the ground, approaching with great speed. Jon grabbed me, threw me to the ground and covered my mouth with his enormous hand.

He needn't have bothered. I wasn't going to say a peep.

I could tell from the horses that this wasn't a group I wanted to meet. Images of fear and loathing invaded my mind. I sensed pain caused by the lashing of a whip. I tried to tune them out.

Jon held me down. Don't make a sound, his hard gaze commanded. I tried to reassure him with my mind, but my *gift* never works on people. Especially in dreams.

We were so close I could smell him. Fresh hay, leather and something rather musky. It shocked me to be that close to a man I didn't know. It shocked me even more to find my body reacting so primitively. I squirmed, but he moved his leg over my hips and pinned me down.

After a few minutes, the meadow returned to silence.

Jon pulled his hand away from my mouth, then put his index finger to his lips. He lifted his head and looked swiftly about. Then he smiled an 'all clear.' He was about to say something when I saw him glance down.

I followed his gaze. Oh, crap. My nightgown had twisted, and the top, which had been somewhat daring before, was serving absolutely no purpose now.

I saw the hunger in Jon's eyes and tried to roll away. His leg held me down and his hands pinned mine to the soft grass. I heard him groan as his mouth moved down to my throat.

I struggled as he pulled down the strap of my nightgown and bared my breast. When his mouth latched onto my nipple and sucked hard, I gasped.

Jon tugged at my skirt and I tried to push him away. It was like pushing against a rock face.

"Stop," I cried.

I awoke in a sweat, my heart racing. The light of dawn filtered through a crack in the blinds. It was hot in the bedroom and the thin strap of my nightgown had slipped off one shoulder in the night, baring one breast.

My nipple was damp.

Chapter 3

Next evening at the animal clinic, I asked Debbie, who had done her undergrad in psych, what she knew about dreams. She was a 'brainer' with short brown hair and an athletic body.

"Do you mean clinically?" she asked. "Dogs have dreams, I know. You see them shake and twitch sometimes in their sleep."

"Actually, I meant *people* dreams. Did you learn about them at all?"

"Yeah, sure. What do you want to know?"

"Have you ever had a dream that felt so real that you swear it actually happened?"

She looked at me, curious. "No, but I've had dreams that I wish would keep on going." She grinned. "Some dreams are better than reality, you know?"

I knew. But I wasn't getting closer to understanding.

"Actually, it's quite interesting, Row. There is a lot of reality in dreams. Your mind latches on to some thread of unfinished emotional business from the day. Then in REM sleep—you know, the rapid eye movement sleep when most dreaming occurs—it calls up bits of older memories that are somehow related and melds them together. That's why dreams look so peculiar. You have old memories and new memories woven into each other."

Okay, this was beginning to sound scary. Old memories?

"They are emotional connections," Debbie said, "rather than logical ones. The latest research shows that usually people work through the most negative emotions first. Their dreams become more positive as the night goes on. But nightmares interrupt that process. People often wake up before the frightening emotion is resolved, so the dream keeps repeating."

I gulped. My fantasy dream world of intense color had some place in my past?

"Speaking of reality," she said, "Steve called."

My heart skipped.

"Are you ever going to see him again, Row? I think he really wants a chance to explain."

How can you explain cruelty? Steve was my ex. Or would have been, if I'd actually married him. Two months before the wedding, I saw him kick a stray cat across the pavement at the Biltmore Shopping Plaza, and that was it. I left the ring on the restaurant patio table. It was a full carat and it killed me to leave that ring.

I shook my head firmly. "No, that's over for good. He's a jerk."

"Too bad." Debbie sighed. "He sure was gorgeous. Are all investment bankers rich and handsome?"

Handsome maybe, but in light of the men dominating my mind lately, Steve was scrawny. He was probably still sane, though, and I wasn't so sure about myself. Had I been daydreaming? Were the heat and the disappointment getting to me? Did I imagine those guys walking through the wall of my classroom? Or—

I shook my head. Of course I imagined it. I was just feeling deprived. No more Steve in my life. No new man on the horizon. No sex in forever.

Besides, gorgeous men don't walk through walls.

Debbie was looking at me funny. "What did you say?"

"Nothing."

"You said something like 'gorgeous men don't walk through walls.'"

I said that out loud?

"Wouldn't it be grand if they did though?" Debbie mused.

As soon as I fell asleep that night, my eyes opened to the azure sky and to a man with his hungry mouth on my breast.

"Please," I whimpered. "Please don't."

Jon raised his head. I held him in my gaze for a long time until he moved off me and sat down at my side, a dazed expression on his face.

"Forgive me," he said hoarsely. "God forgive me. I can't imagine what came over me."

I made a small sound of relief and tried to straighten the bodice of my Natori. Once adjusted, I glanced anxiously at Jon. He sat with his knees drawn up, his head resting against them.

"Rowena Trefusus, can you ever forgive me?"

I sighed. "Actually, it's Rowena Revel."

"Not here. We take the mater's name, if it be the greater. Though Rowena Revel is pretty. And maybe safer." He lifted his head, gazed at me and started to shake.

I said nothing and he looked away.

"I am bewitched," he said in a bitter tone.

I waited, not moving.

He leapt to his feet and held out his hand. I took it and he pulled me up. "Are you sure you are not a witch?"

"Not even a bit," I replied. "I'm a vet."

"And what is this *vet*?

"The full word is *veterinarian*. It comes from the Latin. I help animals that get hurt. I also teach younger students how to help animals."

"Ah, a healer," he said, nodding in comprehension. "You use spells?"

"No. I use medicine."

"Potions?" That seemed to upset him.

"No, no! More like..." I searched for the word. "Elixirs."

Time to change the subject.

"But tell me, sir, what you were going to tell me before. Who am I to you and to this place?" Good grief. Where did that stilted language come from?

Jon had moved down to the stream and was cupping water into his hands. "Your grandfather and mine were cousins. That makes us distant kin. Your mother disappeared many years ago—when I was a babe—never to be seen again."

"Ah," I said softly. So that's the connection. I was missing my mother again and it was showing up in this subliminal way in a very weird dream.

"Her father—your grandfather—is the Earl of Huel. He lives still."

I'd never known any of my grandparents. "And my grandmother?"

"All the women of Huel are dead."

That can't be good. "What happened?"

Jon left the riverbank and returned to my side. "A witch put a curse on the land, that all babies of my generation would be male. It didn't seem so bad at the time because all the families wanted male heirs. They didn't think it through to the next generation."

No female children. Therefore, no fertile women.

"Holy crap," I said. "That's slow suicide."

"Yes." His expression was bitter. "And so we die out."

I didn't know what to say. We sat in silence as I tried to imagine a world with no children and few women.

"You can't get the witch to take back the curse?"

"No, she's dead. We burnt her."

Well that's pretty final, I thought. Of all the stupid things to do.

"Wait a minute," I said. "Surely you could intermarry with females from other lands."

"There aren't many on this island. In war, the weak are vanquished. And women are weak. We've been at war for decades and there's been retribution. Hardly any have survived, and none with royal blood."

He paused and I could feel his sadness.

"The last great battle was four years ago. Now, there is nothing left to fight for. If you don't have women and children, nothing else matters. Who cares about grabbing more land?"

This was definitely a horror story for the men of Huel, I realized. Good thing it was only a dream.

"Jon, what about me?" My stomach turned over in knots. "Tell me. Did my mother leave Huel before the curse?"

He looked away.

"Is that why Tunic-man and his blond brother were scoping me out?"

"I don't understand you. What is this *scoping out*?"

I took a deep breath. "Two men—very big and blond, wearing tunics just like you do—popped into my classroom. They seemed surprised that I could hear and see them. I think one was named Janus."

"Dear God in Heaven." He stood suddenly. "I need to get you to your grandfather."

Panic rose within me. "They wondered if I was fertile."

"I expect you are." Jon helped me to my feet. "You smell…intoxicating. That's what drove me crazy."

It was half-past three in the morning when I awoke. Piper slept soundly beside me. I stayed in bed for awhile. Then I slipped on the matching sapphire dressing gown and went to the bathroom.

When I returned to the bed, I stripped off the dressing gown and tossed it at the end of the bed. I lay down on top of the covers, amazed at how deliciously cool the desert could be at night.

I closed my eyes.

"Is this yours?" Jon held my dressing gown in his hand.

"Where did you find that?"

"On the grass, over there. Put it on, please. Somehow, I've got to get you to Castle Huel without starting a battle." He scowled. "Where are your sandals?"

I looked down at my bare feet. "Is it a long way?"

Jon sighed. "Maybe I should leave you here. I can be quicker on my own. Look, stay right here, below the crest of the bank. Don't move. I'll only be a short while."

I nodded like a good girl. Really, what choice did I have?

Jon moved swiftly along the riverbank. When he was out of sight, I sat back in the clover and opened my mind.

A squeak sounded beside me. It was my squirrel friend.

"Hello, little one. Can I hold you?"

The squirrel scrambled into my left hand. I stroked it gently.

It was warm under the orange sun, with the babbling of the river behind me. What a lovely, perfect place to sit and escape from the world. Maybe doze off.

Hoofbeats warned me of Jon's return. He wasn't alone. Four horses galloped toward us at a breathtaking pace.

Holy crap, I've walked right into a *Bonanza* rerun—only with better clothes. Any minute now, the theme song would start to pipe through hidden speakers in the hills.

Idiot.

I rose to my feet with as much grace as I could manage. The squirrel scampered away.

The first man to dismount was Jon. With ease, he swung off the side of a big bay. "Sorry to leave you this long." He pointed to the man on the black. "This is your grandfather, the Earl of Huel. And these are my cousins, your distant kin, Ivan and Richard."

The sun was in my eyes, but I could see a tall, elderly man flanked by two larger riders.

"Rowena, you've come home?" the old man asked, a tremor in his voice. The earl stared at me as though he couldn't believe what he was seeing.

"I think you mean my mother." I paused. "My name *is* Rowena though."

"Rowena's daughter?" the older rider said in disbelief. "Can that be?"

"It might be a trick," the other said.

"Silence!" The old man dismounted stiffly and approached me. "Look at her. She's Rowena through and through. Where did you come from, child?"

I nearly said Kansas, but that would have been too wicked.

"Scottsdale, sir. In Arizona."

I watched him mouth the word *Arizona*. "And is your mother there too, child?"

This part I didn't like. I shook my head slowly and fought tears. "My mother is dead. She died when I was sixteen."

The old man sagged, his hopes dashed. I felt awful. When he moved closer to peer at my face, I saw the lines on his. They were deep and vertical along his cheekbones. His hair was white and coarse, and his eyes were the same color as mine. He was thin now, but I could tell that he had been powerful in the past. He had the family shoulders.

He reached out to touch my hair, as if to prove that I was real.

"What is this you are wearing, dear one? It seems inadequate."

"It's a Natori," Jon announced.

"Ivan! Your cloak."

Immediately, one man slid off his black steed and was at my side in four strides. He carefully wrapped a short black riding cloak around my shoulders and fastened it at the neck. Then he moved back and I was able to study him. Ivan was a good-looking man with thick black hair and warm brown eyes. Damn, he was big. He towered over me—and I'm not exactly a peanut.

The earl stepped closer and reached around to lift my hair on top of the cloak. It was an intimate thing to do and oddly familiar. That surprised me.

"And how did you come to be here, child?"

"I don't know. I went to sleep and awoke in this forest. I walked down to the river and Jon found me."

"Did he guard you well and with respect?"

I sought Jon's eyes and saw the fear there. "Yes."

The earl turned to Jon. "You did well, Jon. I am in your debt."

Jon looked relieved. He owed me one, that's for sure.

"Maybe there's a portal?" the younger man—Richard—said.

I looked at him for the first time. He had the appearance of a young Greek god. He was tall like his brother Ivan, but much thinner, with dark golden hair.

"This may be," the earl said. "But we can look for a portal later. It's not safe for her here." He turned to me. "Rowena, we must take you back to the castle. You can ride with Ivan." He touched my cheek with the back of his hand. "Do not be afraid of us." With that, he returned to his horse.

Ivan mounted the black stallion, prodded it forward and leaned down. In one swift move, he grabbed me under the arms and swept me up in front of him, sidesaddle. He kept one arm around me and then nudged the black with his boot. We shot forward to a gallop, and I was very glad that he held me so tightly.

The experience was exhilarating. I wanted so badly to hike up my gown and ride the black between my legs. But that wouldn't have been a good idea at all in this company. As it was, I was battling a cadre of feelings. My face was only inches from Ivan's chest and the strong scent of male was inescapable. It made my brain foggy. I wanted to distance myself. At the same time, I wanted to close the distance. In the back of my mind, I wondered if Ivan was equally bothered.

When we slowed, I tried to make conversation.

"Grandfather seems a good man."

"He's clever and ruthless. But fair."

I thought about that.

"I should warn you," Ivan said. "He will want to marry you off quickly. You have royal blood and we need an heir."

"Good thing I'm not married already then."

"I didn't think of that."

I could sense there was more to come. "Will I have a choice?"

"Probably." He paused. "He will want to keep it in the family. There's me and Richard, although he's rather young. You've already met Jon, though I don't know if the earl will include him. And there is Cedric, the oldest. He's scouting down along the southern border right now."

I sensed that Ivan didn't like his older brother.

"What's wrong with Cedric?"

"He's even more ruthless than your grandfather."

I shivered and wrapped the cloak tightly around me. Something told me I wasn't going to like Cedric at all.

But before I could analyze those feelings, the dream began to fade.

Chapter 4

The next day after class, I stayed late. I waited until the last student had left and then walked to the back of the room. I felt along the wall, starting at the top left, moving down in a grid pattern and shifting slowly to the right. I had covered about five feet of wall when I heard a noise.

"What are you doing?"

Kendra stood in the doorway, staring at me.

My mouth shot open, then closed again. I could tell her that Tunic-man walked right through that wall and I was trying to find out how he did it. Or if he did it. Or if I had only imagined it. I could tell her that, but it probably wouldn't improve my reputation.

So I lied. "I was doing balance exercises."

"Wicked," she said, nodding her spiky head. "I do that all the time in martial arts." She left me to my balancing.

I found nothing but a damn wall.

When I got home that night, the answering machine was blinking. I listened to the messages.

"Rowena, it's Steve. I want to see you. Call me." Click.

"Rowena, Steve here. Call me as soon as you get this." Click.

"Rowena, I know you're there. Stop acting like a child. Call me." Slam.

Delete, delete, delete.

I went to bed feeling powerful.

Under a night sky, we rode over a dry moat, then through iron gates into an empty courtyard. The castle was gray stone and quite pretty with turrets on all four corners. Later, I would come to know that rounded turrets were harder to knock down than walls with sharp corners. I would come to know a lot about war.

As I entered the great hall, an enormous Irish wolfhound rose to his feet and moved forward to greet me.

"Duke, halt!" Grandfather commanded.

The beast ignored him.

I held out my palm and Duke walked right up to me. He sat and I scratched his ears.

"You're a gorgeous fellow," I murmured. "I'm sure we will get along just fine."

Duke rolled on his back so I could scratch his belly.

My companions were stunned into silence.

"She has her mother's gift with animals," Grandfather said.

I heard the satisfaction in his voice. There would be no doubting who I was now.

I took a moment to survey the cold hall. The walls were dull gray stone, as was the floor. Tapestries of red and gold lined the inner walls, and a great wooden staircase rose up to the right, leading to another floor. In the middle of the hall, a long wooden table was ready to seat forty. Candles lit the room like a hundred stars as a fire blazed in the huge fireplace at the far end of the room. I could have walked into the hearth, it was so tall.

"Are you hungry, child?"

I shook my head. "Just weary."

"Let me take you upstairs. You will have your mother's room. Ivan, Jon—wait here."

He took a lighted candle from the table and I followed him up the staircase and along a long corridor. He led me to a corner room at the end and stood back so I could enter.

The first thing I noticed was the windows. Two on each exterior wall. And they were open. Heavy draperies were pulled back to each side. A high wooden bed stood in the center, its head against one wall, a tapestry above it. The bed was already made up with fresh linens. Across from it, an unlit fireplace segmented the wall.

It was as if my mother had left for a long weekend and was expected back at any moment.

"I have always kept it waiting for her," Grandfather said, facing a large oak wardrobe. "I've left all her garments as they were. They can be yours now, if they fit." He opened the wardrobe doors and I fell in love.

First, there was my mother's sweet scent. It drifted from her clothing and enveloped me in the tenderest of memories. Tears came to my eyes. I missed her now, even more than in those early days after her death.

Then—those clothes. All her favorite colors. Greens and burgundies, silks and velvets.

I pulled out a beautiful ivory form-fitting gown. My heart broke. There was no way I would fit it. Back it went.

There were a few exquisite formal gowns in a different style that I thought might work. I pulled out an emerald green silk with a high waist and fully gathered skirt. The bodice might need letting out, but the skirt would be perfect for my generous hips.

"I remember when she last wore that," Grandfather said. "It was a feast night not long before she left."

I could feel his sadness all about me.

"Goodnight, dear one," he said from the door. "I hope you'll be happy here."

I hoped so too.

It was a warm night and my poor nightgown had gone through enough. I pulled down both straps and let it slide to the floor. Naked, I reached to pick it up and felt a little puff of air sweep past me.

"Is anyone there?"

No one answered.

With a shrug, I moved to the window and peered outside. How strange and yet how beautiful the evening was in this world. Two moons dazzled against a cloudless black velvet night sky. For several moments, I was transfixed by the twin moons. This is what my mother had seen every night of her young life.

At last, I pulled away. Leaving the window open to let in fresh air, I blew out the candle and climbed into bed.

Sometime in the night, I awoke. It was still dark and it took me a moment to take in the stone walls and the tapestry—and to place where I was.

Ivan was sitting in a chair by the door. A striped orange tabby lay curled on his lap.

I sat up in surprise, holding the bed linens closely to me.

"We're taking turns guarding you," he said. "I have tonight." He calmly stroked the cat.

Ivan seemed to be the most stable of the three boys who would be my suitors. The middle brother, he was built like a chariot and I didn't doubt that he could protect me very well. His arms were knotted with bulky muscles and I could see scars running down both forearms. He had a clever wit, and in the great hall, I had concluded that he seemed very in control of himself—which only goes to show how wrong a girl can be.

Richard, the youngest, had looked barely eighteen. But people aged early in this primitive world. He was probably at least twenty. He had seemed wiry, on edge, as if anxious to prove himself among men.

Cedric hadn't yet made an appearance, but from everything I'd heard, that was a good thing.

Ivan shifted the cat carefully off his lap and stood up. I could see beads of sweat on his forehead. He focused on my eyes and held them. A strange, calming warmth seeped through my mind.

How odd, I thought. How did he do that?

"I want to protect you, and I can only think of one way to do that," Ivan said, his eyes drifting over the sheets that covered my nakedness.

"Are you suggesting what I think you're suggesting?"

"If we wait until tomorrow, Cedric will find a way to disarm me."

I didn't doubt him. Even the name *Cedric* gave me the creeps.

"Rowena, will you let me?"

My mouth shot open. Protection, my size seven foot. I didn't pretend not to know what he meant, but I hardly knew what to say or even think.

"I don't even know you!"

"You know I'm your grandfather's kin." His warm brown eyes never left my face. "You know I would never hurt you."

I was caving under his gaze. "Is this customary here? I'm not exactly a prude, but isn't this rushing things a bit?"

"I am thinking of your own protection."

My cheeks were flaming hot. Protection from what? Other randy males like the one in front of me?

Time was ticking. What to do?

This was a dream and I was over twenty-one. I wasn't usually promiscuous—like *never*— but I wouldn't have to live with it in the morning, metaphorically speaking, since this *was* a dream.

Still, I hesitated, because who wants to bring on a nightmare?

I glanced at Ivan and shuddered. Then to both of our surprise, I nodded. "Okay. For my protection."

Ivan's eyes widened. He took off his hefty leather belt and scabbard. He hesitated a minute. The next thing I knew he was on the bed, pushing me back against the pillow and dragging the sheet away. His eyes lingered on my breasts, as if trying to decide where to start.

He kissed me quickly, once on the mouth. "I need to tie your hands in case we're interrupted," he said, working quickly. "This is so they know you didn't agree to this. I have a soft cord. See this? I'm going to wrap it around both your wrists like so and tie it lightly to the iron rail at the top of the bed here."

I watched, spellbound. I had never done anything like this before, never even considered it. But this was a dream, right? A safe place to try all the things you had always wondered about, but never wanted to chance in real life.

"Are you comfortable, Rowena?"

I nodded slowly. The rope wasn't tight. I could bend my elbows easily.

"Forgive my speed. I don't know how long we have." He shot to the foot of the bed. "Rowena, look at me." He pulled up his tunic. "I'll try not to hurt you."

He spread my legs apart and raised my hips with both hands. He positioned himself and pushed forward slowly. I gasped. It was all I could do. I swear I could feel everything as though it were real and not some crazy sex dream.

He pulled back a bit and I made a small noise. He began to move. The dream didn't save me from any of the physical sensations. He moved over me, holding his weight on his hands. He picked up the pace.

Oh. My. God.

I moved with him as much as I could with my arms held captive. Overwhelmed by a fierce heat, I tried to focus on Ivan's face. It seemed he was gone and a beast with fiery eyes and black body hair was moving over me instead. I struggled to cry out. I'm sure I did. But the beast continued to rage inside me. I felt smothered, captive. There was no escape from his relentless pounding. And God help me, I loved it.

Ivan shifted slightly and the room burst into streams of light, flying through my mind, lifting me out of the bed and into the night sky. He called out in an ancient language, but I was floating, helpless, as his movements became less frenetic and finally slowed.

My panting subsided and I opened my eyes.

Grandfather stood in the doorway.

"Ivan," he said coldly. "What have you done?"

Ivan was off me in a flash. He instinctively reached for his sword. It wasn't at his side. It was somewhere on the floor.

"I've impregnated her." Ivan's voice was wild.

"I can see that, you idiot." Grandfather's rage was tangible.

"I was protecting her from Cedric," Ivan said with a shrug. "You know it had to be done."

Grandfather was furious. He glanced at my tied hands, at my naked upper body. Clenching his hands, he spat, "Cover her, boy! And for God's sake, untie her."

Ivan obeyed.

It felt good to have my wrists free, but I dreaded the rage to come. Was there any way we could fast forward through this scene?

"Is this the way we treat our valued guests?" Grandfather seethed. "Our own blood? We ravish them against their will on the first night they stay with us?" His voice rose to a crescendo.

"I had to. You know it's best." Ivan stood firm, his face composed.

"You had no right! It is not up to you. She is *my* granddaughter and *your* kin. You have disgraced me and the memory of your mother. God help you."

Grandfather gave me a tortured look. "Rowena, I am in despair at how we have treated you. But there is no other way to fix this. You will be married at noon. Forgive us all."

Looking a hundred years old, he strode out the door. All the air seemed to whoosh out of the room with him.

I was so embarrassed, I wanted to die. Or at least wake up.

"That went rather well," Ivan said with satisfaction.

I stared at him in disbelief. "You wanted us to be found?"

Fastening his belt and looking too darn pleased with himself, he said, "It's better this way, with him as witness. There can be no doubting the word of the Earl of Huel. And best that it wasn't Cedric, because then there would have been a fight. Although I wouldn't mind having a good go at him."

He leapt onto the bed and drew me to him. "Rowena, we are so good together, even better than I could imagine. You are beautiful, too beautiful to be real, and I worship you. We will be married at noon. I will protect you forever." He kissed me, a deep languorous kiss that reached right down into my womb.

"Dawn is breaking," he said, pulling away. "Get dressed, my love, and I shall see you downstairs in one hour. There is something I must do." He blew me a kiss from the doorway and then he was gone.

I sat up, clutching the sheets to my neck. How did that man have so much energy after all we had been through? Honestly, I could've slept for days. I looked around for the cat and found her pawing at the drapes beside the window. Below the drapes, the toes of two dirty boots moved slightly.

Great. There had been another witness to the night's activities.

I sighed. "You can come out now."

The boots stopped moving.

"Any time now," I said dryly.

The drapes parted, revealing a red-faced Richard.

"How long have you been hiding there?"

He looked away. "Before Ivan arrived to *protect* you."

"Damn," I said, recalling that faint breeze earlier. "Well, I hope you got an eyeful."

"Yes, Ma'am."

"Richard, I—" To my horror, tears rolled down my face.

"Please don't cry, Rowena. I didn't mean you any harm. I only wanted to make sure you were safe. I didn't mean to watch, but ..." His voice trailed off. "The men talk all the time about being with a woman, and I have never..."

To my despair, the tears continued to fall.

"Ivan's a good man," Richard said. "The best. I know it was wrong of him, but he loves you, I'm certain. He'll make you a good husband."

I wiped my nose on the sheet. "I'm so embarrassed. What must you think of me?"

Wanton hussy was the phrase that came to mind.

"I think you're wonderful. I only wish I were five years older, like Ivan."

My heart gave a tug. "That's sweet."

"Please don't tell anyone I was here. Ivan would kill me."

"I won't. But don't you ever do that again."

He nodded, his face still red. "You look like her, you know."

"My mother?"

"Yes, according to the painting in the Earl's bedroom. Except your hair is redder. Hers was more bronze."

"And I'm a little bigger," I said in a flat tone.

Richard blushed again. "Maybe, but in a good way."

"Turn around while I get up. I need to get dressed."

He did so, and I climbed out of bed. I'd already set out my mother's emerald dress the night before. It seemed fitting for today. I slipped it over my head. It barely fit. I sure wouldn't need a pushup bra.

"Here, can you do me a favor and lace up the back?"

I could feel Richard's warm fingers pulling, drawing the two laces together at the top.

"It won't quite close," he said.

"That's okay. My hair will cover it."

I turned to look at my reflection in the long mirror. The dress fit snugly under my breasts and flared out in a flattering circle to the ground. The arms were long, bell shaped, and the neckline was a deep U, almost too deep. I couldn't bend over without spilling out.

"I'm glad we're friends, Richard."

God knows, I needed a friend.

As I reached up to pat his shoulder, I heard a small *rrrip.*

Uh-oh.

Moving toward to the door, I bit my lip, nervous. "What will Cedric say about all this?"

Richard winced. "I don't know what he'll say. But I can imagine a whole lot of things he might do."

The hallway blurred as we headed to the stairs.

This time it was harder to pull out of the dream. As the hallway dimmed, I fought against it, struggling to keep the images from fading. It was a dream, I reminded myself. Life is real.

Something licked my face and I blinked. Piper stared at me, then jumped up and down with happiness.

"Animals are better than men," I assured him.

I took Piper to the clinic with me that morning and he played with the boarding animals, while I worked at trying to forget the steamy dream. And my night with Ivan.

On the way home, we picked up take-out chicken—Piper's favorite. Then we settled in to watch *Dog Whisperer*.

After dark, Dad phoned.

"How's Rome?" I asked.

"Noisy. Can't wait to get back to the desert."

Dad is an airline pilot on the international circuit.

"Dad, can you remember much about Mom's parents?"

A pause. "She wouldn't talk about them. They lived in England somewhere and there was some sort of estrangement."

"How did she manage to pay for vet school?"

He sighed. "She worked part time at an animal clinic through school. And I remember her saying she sold some old jewelry." Another pause. "Are you okay about Steven, sweetheart? I worry about you."

"I did the right thing, Dad. You don't need to worry about me."

Except that I might be going crazy. Frankly, Steve was the least of my worries.

"I love you, Dad."

"Love you too, Red. And don't forget, one day you'll meet the man of your dreams."

If Dad only knew.

Chapter 5

The wedding took place in a small stone chapel attached to Huel Castle. Grandfather wanted my arrival kept secret until after the ceremony, so the only attendees were Grandfather, Richard, the priest, and of course Ivan.

At least eighty years old, the priest wasn't happy. He frowned at me as if he'd seen a ghost. Maybe he hadn't liked my mother. Or perhaps he didn't approve of the amount of cleavage I was showing.

There was a lot of passing of goblets back and forth, and chanting in a language that sounded very old and primitive. I didn't actually have to say or do anything, except drink the wine when it was passed to me. I knew my wedding was over when Ivan pulled me to him and kissed me.

Grandfather exhaled with relief. "We'll go back to the hall to sup and I'll make the announcement."

Duke whined beside me. I stroked his soft head.

A great commotion sounded from the square outside. The chapel door burst open, slamming into the stone wall behind. An enormous hulk of a man with long copper hair strode inside. He wore an angry scowl and full warrior gear.

Did I mention he didn't look happy?

"You bastard," the stranger hissed as he approached. "I'll kill you for this."

Ivan stepped in front of me. "You can try."

"I'd be happy—"

"Cedric!" Grandfather yelled. "It's done. Accept it."

"I don't accept it! I wouldn't even have known if Jon's groom hadn't ridden to tell me. So when were you going to tell me, Sire?" Sarcasm dripped from his voice. "Or did you plan it this way when you sent me off on a fool's errand to the south?"

"Cedric, stop this!"

"I'm the eldest. She should be *mine*. You always favor him. You and mother. I should have killed him at birth."

Cedric's whole body shook. In front of me, Ivan stood stone-still. It occurred to me that I was witnessing a perfect demonstration of hot anger versus cold fury.

"You will still rule here after I'm gone, Cedric," Grandfather said, touching the man's sleeve. "You'll rule until you die. That doesn't change."

"But Ivan's offspring will take over then." He spat the words. "I won't have any prodigy."

"Progeny," I said automatically. "The word is progeny."

God help me, where did that come from?

Everyone stared at me. I think it was the first time Cedric actually saw me. I met his eyes and the world seemed to pause for a minute. I heard a sharp intake of breath. Cedric reached out to touch my hair, but Ivan slapped his hand away.

This didn't go down well.

Cedric hissed like a snake. "Stupid old man! Why didn't you let me challenge? Why didn't you wait the ceremony for me?"

Grandfather gazed at the floor. He was so solemn it almost broke my heart. "Ivan made it necessary."

Oh crap.

I saw the dawn of understanding cross Cedric's face. A swift movement and a dagger materialized in his hand. Ivan backed away, pushing me behind Grandfather. They circled each other, one armed, one defenseless.

"Stop!" Grandfather ordered. "If you do this, I'll have you quartered."

Cedric glared at him. Then he flung the dagger with all his might across the room. It hit the back of the door and stuck there.

"I'll see you in Hell," he roared, storming out of the chapel.

Silence.

But that didn't last long. Ivan tore out after Cedric.

"Gods above," Grandfather said. "Richard, go after them."

Richard charged outside, the old man following slowly. Even the priest shuffled to the door, not wanting to miss the action.

Alone with Duke, who was mentally exhausted by yet another family fight, I called out to an empty room. "Hello! I'm still here, people. Does anyone care?"

Apparently, they didn't.

Men! They're all nuts.

I could hear yelling from the courtyard. I was curious, but my dress was bothering me and I couldn't breathe. I reached around to loosen the back laces. Rrrrip.

Bloody hell.

Maybe if I could slip off to the castle, I could change and get back here before anyone noticed.

Since nobody was watching me, I was able to sneak out the door and hide behind a pillar. Men were on their feet, stomping and cheering, while Ivan and Cedric duked it out in the middle. Cedric's nose was clearly broken, while Ivan's ceremonial tunic was torn and bloody.

As I slipped around the side of the chapel, I saw both brothers hit the ground in a wrestling clench. It was a full bare-knuckle fight. I hoped it wasn't to the death.

I picked up my skirt and prepared to run. Unfortunately, I neglected to turn at the sound behind me and a heavy black cloth was thrown over my head and shoulders. I cried out as strong arms swung me over a wide shoulder.

"Don't scream," a deep voice said. "They won't hear you anyway."

"Go to hell," I shot back.

A hand whacked me hard on the butt. I struggled, but my arms were caught up in the fabric.

"She's a hellcat," my captor said with a chuckle.

Another voice said, "Good luck to you, brother."

They laughed.

I was flung across a horse, my hands tied in front and roped at the waist to something firm. My captor mounted the horse and settled in behind me. Then we were off at a gallop, my dress lifting in the wind.

It was *not* comfortable. The cloth over my head was hot and stuffy. Riding on my stomach left me no room for air, not to mention it made me nauseous. I tried to read the horse, but it wouldn't open its mind to me.

We rode hard for several minutes. I spent the time trying to get one hand free. When I succeeded, I reached out and jabbed my captor's leg, trying to get his attention.

"Hold up, Janus," he yelled.

He nudged me. "What's the matter?"

"Can't breathe."

"You have to promise not to scream."

"I promise." My fingers were crossed.

Instantly, three things happened. The suffocating cloth was removed from my head, the rope around my waist was loosened and I began to slide down the side of the horse. I landed on the ground in a heap.

At least I could breathe. Glorious air. I tried to stand up, but dizziness swept over me. I stumbled.

"Whoa there." A hand caught my arm. Then an arm reached around to hold me steady.

I gazed into ice blue eyes. "Tunic-man."

"What?"

My captor's friend pulled alongside us. "What did she say?"

"She called me 'tunic-man,' Janus."

I took a deep breath. "You came to my classroom. Twice."

"Did I?"

He seemed to be preoccupied with something on my dress.

I glanced down. Oh hell.

Sometime during the ride, the bodice lace had broken. A deep V of skin ran to my waist.

"Gareth, we need to move on," Janus said.

"Right," Gareth said, drawing his eyes away.

Finally. The identity of my captor was known. But who was this Gareth anyway? And why had he kidnapped me?

"I can ride," I said. "The normal way."

Gareth frowned. "As you please."

"Cup your hand. I'll mount my way."

That puzzled him, but he did it.

I pulled my skirt up above my knees, used his hand to balance and then swung my leg over the beast. To hell with modesty. It felt good—really good—to feel the horse between my legs.

Gareth's eyes widened. "You ride like a man?"

"Of course." I gestured with my hand. "Come up."

Janus laughed, while Gareth shook his head in disbelief. He mounted easily, put his arms around me and we were off again.

It was a wild ride. I leaned forward, holding the palomino's mane. My hair whipped behind me, probably blinding my captor. We galloped along the river's edge for many miles, then Janus took the lead and we followed him up a hill. There was a forest ahead. I recognized it from my first dream. We slowed to a walk as the palomino picked its way through a narrow trail.

Finally, we arrived at a small camp in a clearing.

Gareth dismounted first. He helped me down and roped the horse to a tree.

"We'll be safe here," he said, more to Janus than to me.

"I'll meet with Roderick," Janus said, looking from Gareth to me and back again. He pitched back his blond head and roared with laughter, then disappeared into the night.

"So what happens now," I said sharply.

Gareth's eyes went to my chest. "You're hanging out."

"Oops." I straightened my bodice. "All fixed."

"Not that it matters, because that's coming off."

Oh brother, not again. Okay, I was definitely getting the theme of these dreams. Too little love in my real life, so my subconscious mind was making up for it at night.

Gareth's expression was determined. He didn't have a bad face. And he had let me ride freely. Besides, this was a dream. Wasn't it? I mean, do you need to be worried about your own behavior in a dream?

"Shouldn't we at least exchange names or something?" I said.

Gareth smiled. "I'm Gareth and you're Rowena, granddaughter to the Earl of Huel. I'm the Earl of Norland. My castle is north of Huel. You'll see it tomorrow."

When he moved closer, I backed away.

"So...where are all the rest of your men?" I asked, stalling.

He crossed his arms. "I sent most of them north, so that Ivan's men will follow the trail. They'll expect me to head north toward my own land. We went southwest. They won't expect that. It will take them at least two days to figure out where we went. We'll be gone by then." He gave a smug chuckle. "A small band of my men are in the trees here, keeping guard."

Got to admit, Gareth was well organized. But I was still sort of miffed at being kidnapped.

"I'm married, you know. I was married to Ivan this morning."

"It wasn't consummated."

Not if you don't count that little episode last night, I thought.

"And besides," he continued, "we don't recognize the laws of Huel. We have our own laws."

I sighed. "Then I must obey them." The laws of dream land.

I headed for the tent. Gareth followed.

"This damned dress," I said, floundering. "Help me with the back."

He moved behind me, unhooking the laces. "Are you always this pragmatic?"

"Well, if it's gonna happen, it's gonna happen. Dreams are funny things. Doesn't seem to be much I can do about it, so why fight."

"What an extremely wise lass you are. And lovely too."

Gareth reached out, ripping my dress down to my waist.

"Wait!" I cried.

His mouth was on my breast. I gasped in shock. He worked my skirt free and it slid down my hips. He whipped off his belt and tunic, and undid his britches. His body was covered in fine white-gold hair. He was magnificent.

We slid to the bed of fur on the floor of the tent and I reached up with both hands to touch his massive chest.

"First time, gently," he said.

He covered my mouth with his. It was a deep, slow kiss. My legs opened automatically for him. He was over me, then on me and in me so gently that it felt like a caress. He balanced on one hand, holding me up with the other.

I groaned in pleasure and grabbed his shoulders. His mouth licked my ear and I started to move. Sweet waves of pleasure washed over me.

Then Gareth fell on top of me.

"Damn." I could feel him inside me. "I really like this dream."

"Dream?"

"Yes. Why is sex is always better in dreams?"

Gareth's long blond hair lay across my face in a tangle.

"Off," I said. "You're too heavy."

He chuckled and moved away.

We shared the bed, his arm draped across my waist, until darkness came. Then we slept.

Chapter 6

I awoke—still in the tent in the twin moon world—with one thought on my mind. "God, I'm hungry."

Gareth was already dressed and on his feet. He smiled down at me. "Come on, lady-mine. We have a feast to go to."

He flipped back the tent flap as I searched for my bodice and skirt. We managed to get the laces tied loosely at the back. For the front, I found that the broken lace was enough to do up the top. If it gapped a bit, so be it. There was nothing I could do about the ripped shoulders, so I tucked the loose pieces into the bodice.

Gareth stepped outside first. He said something to someone, then turned back to the tent and gestured for me. When I emerged, he took my hand.

Six men stood around a campfire. Something roasted on a spit. It smelled wonderful.

"This is my lady, Rowena," Gareth said.

The men nodded.

"Janus is my brother," Gareth added. He pointed to a dark-haired man. "My cousin Roderick." He introduced three red-haired men—more cousins—also tall, but of slender build. "And this is Collin." Collin was an older man with curly gray-blond hair and a beard.

An elite team, I surmised. The group closest to Gareth.

Somebody shoved a tankard in my hands and told me to drink. I sipped immediately. Rough ale, but not unpleasant. I gulped it back with gusto. God, I was starving.

Gareth approached with a plank-load of meat. I reached for some, ravenous. It was delicious. Venison, I think. The tankard reappeared, miraculously filled, and I drank that down too.

Sometime later, Gareth was talking with the eldest red-haired cousin—I forget his name—and I was seated on Janus's lap, singing a song. The men had started off with an old ballad. Afterward, I regaled them with "Barbara Allen." It seemed to go over well. I tried to think of the songs from *Brigadoon,* which seemed appropriate. My audience loved "Go Home with Bonnie Jean," especially when I taught them the chorus. When I finished "Come to Me," Roderick had tears running down his face.

"Haven't heard a woman sing in four years," he mumbled.

Somebody handed me another tankard. As I drank, it occurred to me that Janus might be enjoying our current position a little too much. His hands were starting to wander. But there didn't seem to be anything I could do about it, 'cause I was having a hard time sitting upright. In fact, the whole campsite was whirling.

Whoa. I closed my eyes, slumping to one side.

"That's it," I heard Gareth say. "She's had enough. Time for bed." He picked me up and swung me over his shoulder.

"But *has* she had enough?" someone asked.

The campsite erupted in snickers.

I heard the tent flap close. It was the last thing I heard.

Many hours later, I awoke to an empty tent. The strange orange sun shot beams of light through the seams. I attempted to sit up, but was hit with something unexpected. I was sore. God, I was sore.

Who does it three times in one night?

I rolled over to my stomach. Rising on my hands and knees like a dog, I shuddered. Gareth stepped into the tent, looking hale and hearty. I scowled at him with loathing.

"If you stay like that, I'm going to have to undress again," he said.

I groaned at the thought.

I must have looked ridiculous, with my breasts swinging freely and pointing to the ground. But it didn't matter, because I wasn't sure if I was going to live through the next hour. My head was pounding like fury.

"Ow," I moaned.

"Ah, too much ale. It will soon pass. Come on, my lovely wife, you have to get dressed. We have things to do."

"Wife?"

He crouched in front of me. "Three times in one nightfall makes you mine. Under our law." He smiled. "And we did it four."

"We did?"

Oh, right—I remembered now. The last time, I was half asleep on my side and had barely moved.

"In our land, you'll be safe. No one will harass the wife of the Earl."

Oh great. Only an earl messes with the wife of the earl. When was this bloody dream ever going to end?

"Leave me," I managed to say. "I'll get dressed myself."

I could feel his eyes on me. "Be swift."

My wedding dress was a rag. I pieced it around me as best as I could and looked for something to brush my hair. Gareth had thoughtfully laid out a few things for me. A cup of water, a soft washcloth and a rough comb lying on a black bag. I drank half the water, then used the rest to dampen the cloth. It wasn't much of a wash, but it would have to do.

When I reached for the brush, I noticed a jeweled pin. It was about three inches square with a beautiful, sparkling blue-and-green Celtic design. I could use it to fasten the front of my gown. That accomplished, I did what I could with the comb.

One step outside, I stopped dead. My hand dashed up to shelter my eyes. "Why the heck is it so bright?"

"Rowena, we have visitors." Gareth's voice was cold, dangerous.

Ivan, Richard and Jon sat on horseback, not twenty feet off. Their swords were out.

"Oh, hi," I said with a wave. "You didn't happen to bring another dress with you."

Everyone looked at me as if I had spoken Swahili.

"I guess not."

"You've hurt her," Ivan growled at Gareth.

"I have not!"

"Stop shouting," I pleaded.

"A little too much ale," Gareth explained.

Ivan's scowl widened. "Enough of this! Rowena, come over here right now."

I didn't like his tone.

"Don't move," Gareth said to me. To Ivan, he said, "You can try to take her, Huel. But you'll have to go through all seven of us to do it. And there are only three of you."

"She's my wife!" Ivan roared.

"You don't deserve her. You couldn't even protect her on your own castle grounds. I was the one who took the trouble to find her. I paid the wizard to locate the portal to the other world. And I was the one who went through it."

All this was interesting. Trouble was, my head was exploding.

Ivan had murder in his eyes. "Rowena, what say you?"

"Does anyone have any aspirin?" I asked with a whimper.

There was more arguing back and forth. Gareth's men moved forward with their weapons drawn.

I had to get out of there. It was far too loud.

I stumbled back to the tent. Holding onto the side of it for balance, I stared at the peaceful valley to the east. I had seen this sight before. In fact, I had stood very close to this spot in an earlier dream.

As the men continued to rage behind me, I walked toward the forest. I saw the place where the trees met the side of the hill and I followed the line, trying to remember the exact spot where the squirrel had come to meet me. Approaching the tree line, I headed toward the split tree trunk.

Not far.

I took two steps into the forest and walked through the classroom wall.

Chapter 7

The clock on my classroom wall read 8:40. It was morning, judging by the light streaming through the windows. Gorgeous, comforting yellow sunlight, not orange.

I looked down. I was still wearing the blasted green silk dress, with Gareth's jeweled pin holding the bodice together.

How could that be? I was awake now. Wasn't I? My dreams and reality had never merged like this before.

I tried to recall waking up and going to the university.

I couldn't.

If this were a dream, then why was I now in my classroom?

Wait a minute! Isn't that what Gareth did? He walked through the wall of my classroom twice. When I was awake.

Like I am now.

If that were the case, then I hadn't been dreaming after all. The world with the two moons was real—as real as my tattered dress. An alternate world beyond the wall.

In the hall, a locker door slammed. I peered out the door and saw Kendra. "Can you come here a minute?"

She smiled through black lipstick and followed me into the classroom.

"Do you have any aspirin?" I asked.

"Ibuprofen. Will that do?"

I nodded. "Give it to me quickly. I'm dying."

She handed me two tablets and I swallowed them without water.

"Wicked dress," she said. "I didn't know you were into anachronism."

I took a deep breath. "Kendra, I need you as a witness. You really did see me here in this dress, in this classroom on—what's the day?"

"Friday."

"Friday," I repeated.

"Yup, I'll remember. You in some kinda trouble?"

"You could say that."

Her black-lined eyes lit up. "Need an alibi?"

"Not that kind of trouble. More like man trouble."

"No shit. What's his name?"

"Ivan. I sort of married him by mistake." That wasn't the half of it, of course, but at least it was partially true.

"Wow. Sounds heavy."

"The thing is..." How could I put this? "I lost my purse getting away from him and I need a lift home."

"I can drive you. We can go right now."

I sighed. "Thank you so much."

Five minutes later, Kendra pulled a beat up Cavalier to the side door of B wing. I snuck out of the university without attracting attention. I gave directions and we were off.

"How did your dress get wrecked?" she asked. She shifted to third and the car shuddered.

"A lot of weird things went down last night," I said as explanation.

"That's totally rad. Nothing ever happens to me." There was envy in her voice.

Are you kidding me? With that Goth thing going on?

We pulled up in front of my townhouse.

"Thanks, Kendra. You don't know how much I appreciate this."

"No problem. Look, if you ever need me, let me know. I'm into martial arts in a big way." She waved as she drove away.

I reached for the key behind the potted geranium. Piper wagged his tail when I opened the door. I let him out to pee, then locked up after him. He followed me to the bedroom, where I took off the green dress and laid it on the chair. The broach winked at me under the artificial lights. If I hadn't gotten it in Huel, where the heck had it come from?

I grabbed my pink dressing gown and sat down on the bed.

Wait a minute...*dressing gown.*

I had worn the sapphire Natori nightgown the first time I set foot in Huel and I'd left it there. So it made sense that if the nightgown was still here in my room, the dream was just a dream.

Terrific. I felt much better.

I went to the left side of the closet, where I always hung my good nightgowns.

The Natori wasn't there.

I searched the floor of the closet, in all my dresser drawers and in the dirty clothes hamper.

Nothing.

This wasn't good.

"Okay," I said to Piper. "What we have here is a theory, one I need to test." But first I needed to arrange for Piper's care.

I reached for the phone and called Debbie at the clinic.

"I need to go away for the weekend," I said when she picked up. "Can you possibly look after Piper?"

"I'll come by this aft. What's up?"

"I'm not sure. But it involves two large men and potential sex."

I knew that would seal the deal.

"I'll want all the details on Monday," Debbie replied.

After she hung up, I pondered the clothing situation. The green dress was toast. I needed something that could be worn on the other side of the wall. Something that would pass for decent.

Time to inventory the closet.

Something long, to the ground if possible. That meant an evening dress. I nixed the silver sequin. Too much bling. The black was too witchy. Not a good idea at all. They burned witches in Huel.

My eye caught a new outfit, one I hadn't worn—a stretchy two-piece in stunning turquoise that had also been destined for the honeymoon.

I grimaced. I'd been getting a different kind of honeymoon the last few nights, one without Steve. Frankly, I'd never had so much sex in my life and it was amazing. Those startling orgasms I had with Ivan. And even more delicious ones with Gareth. That simply did not happen in real life—at least not with Steve.

Back to the outfit. The skirt flared out from the waist, so I could walk easily. The midriff top was tight-fitting with three quarter sleeves and a wide square neck. A silver zipper ran down the front of it. And it had a built-in bra, which was a bonus. Pewter walking sandals would finish it. I wouldn't be without footwear this time.

I took a long, hot shower. It felt so good to wash my hair. I dressed quickly and took a last glance around the room. The Celtic broach. I should take that with me. I pulled a heavy silver chain from the jewel box and slipped it through the broach pin. I placed it around my neck. It sparkled like it had been made for my outfit.

I gave Piper fresh water and food, and blew him a kiss. "Bye, sweetie."

It took me ten minutes to drive to campus. There were few cars in the staff lot. I hurried to B wing and my classroom, as I had hoped, was empty. Closing the door behind me, I ran to the desk and put my car keys in the top drawer.

I walked to the back of the room.

After one last look around, I held my breath and stepped through the wall.

The orange sun blazed across the valley. I peered left and right to see if anyone was around, but the camp in the clearing had been vacated.

Okay, so what do I do now?

A beefy hand clamped over my mouth. "Don't say a word," Gareth whispered. "There are men in the valley below."

He pulled me back into the forest where it was dark and still. When I turned, he took my hand and led me through a path dense with ferns. We walked for some time until we reached a cave.

"We can talk here," he said, pulling me inside.

It was dark in the cave and the air smelled sweet and damp.

"You waited for me," I said.

"I knew you had gone through the wall. The others don't know where it is. It killed me not to follow you, but I didn't want to show the location."

"How long would you have waited?" My voice held something close to awe.

"I don't know. Until the others left the valley. I would have followed you to the other side and waited there." He leaned down to kiss my throat.

I pushed him away. "There's no time."

"You're right." He straightened. "We need to leave for Norland immediately. Janus left two horses. Come, I have a present for you."

He led me out of the cave and into the light.

Looking down at me, he took in my new attire. "Is this something you wear at home? I like it."

I was distracted by a gorgeous roan filly with soft eyes. She sought me out immediately and I reached with delight into her mind.

Pure joy swept over me. "She's beautiful!"

"This is Lightning," he said with pride. "She's three years old, from my stables. She's very sweet and fast like the wind. I thought you'd be perfect for each other. She's yours to keep."

Lightning nuzzled my side as I stroked her. "Gareth, this is the sweetest thing ever. Thank you so much."

"It is my pleasure. Indeed, I can't believe the pleasure it brings me to see you happy." He seemed pleased, though somewhat perplexed by his own reaction.

I cooed to Lightning as he brought over a stocky bay gelding.

"We should mount now," he said. "I sent my men ahead."

"To Norland? Is that a long way?"

He nodded. "We should make it by nightfall."

What was I getting into?

"Just a minute. Gareth, I need to know more. If I go with you, what happens next?"

There was an uneasy pause.

"Huel will be gathering his men from the south. He'll move to the northern border."

I didn't need to ask what that meant. "And if I go with Ivan and Grandfather? What happens then?"

He gave me a fierce look. "Then I take my men to Castle Huel and burn it."

"They are my family, Gareth."

He was silent.

"Maybe I should walk back through the wall."

He grabbed my arm. "Don't even think of it. I'll just go through and bring you back."

I suddenly felt trapped. "If you cared for me, you'd let me go."

Gareth snorted. "What kind of fool notion is that? I *do* care about you. And because of that, I will never let you go." He pulled me close and sought my mouth. "I'll die before I let you go."

Oh heck, I thought. This was a lot better than dying.

I remember reading years ago that most medieval castles in Britain were a twenty-mile ride from each other. A horse could only cover so many miles in one day, so that was the measure used since Roman times.

It was dark when we arrived at Norland Fortress. Even in the pitch black of night, I could tell that Gareth's home was not a fairy-tale castle. It was a fortress through and through, with a soaring stone wall surrounding the property and a keep that served as central quarters. The fortress stood on the highest hill, the land around it rough and wild, and there were no flowering meadows anywhere.

Two great wooden doors opened to an inner yard, where an elderly groom helped me dismount. Gareth took my hand and we entered the center hall of the keep. It was nothing like the great hall at Huel. There was a fire, but no grand table, and the walls were bare. Men stood or sat on stone benches.

I really hoped there would be beds upstairs.

Janus, Roderick and the rest of the men were already there, making plans for defense. They nodded at me, then carried on with their business.

"Collin and I will ride to the northern fortresses tomorrow to gather the men," Janus said. "Argyle should stand with us. Plenham too."

"I know the Danes at Eastfork," Roderick added. "They love to fight and it's not two days from here."

"Do it, then. Take Wilfred with you."

"And to the west?"

Gareth frowned. "I don't want to include Sargon unless I have to. Not yet."

Janus raised an eyebrow. "Why not?"

Gareth glanced at me. "I don't trust him."

"But he is the king," Roderick said.

"Exactly."

So this land had a king. I hadn't known that. Surely a king outranked the Earls.

Gareth scowled. "Sargon doesn't know about her yet. I want to keep it that way."

Collin nodded.

"We'll see first who stands with us."

They moved on to discuss weaponry. Since I wasn't really needed, I asked to be excused.

"I'll show you our room," Gareth said.

He took me to a room at the top of the keep. The walls and floor were stone, and a mattress of straw lay on the floor. It was covered with layers of fur.

I sighed. I was going to miss those soft linens at Huel.

I removed my clothing and shivered in the cool night air, realizing that I once again had nothing to wear to bed. I snuggled into the skins and tried to get comfortable.

Gareth joined me sometime in the night.

Chapter 8

The men rode at dawn. We were left with a skeleton crew, enough to perform essential chores until the others returned with reinforcements the next day.

I had nothing to do except think.

Gareth and I were in the small anteroom next to the bedroom. He was sharpening his sword, while I gazed out the window into the fog. Every now and then, it would clear enough so that I could see a few ghostly shapes moving beyond the gates. This rough, misty land was cool and confining. I longed for the sunny skies of Arizona.

"This isn't a dream," I said.

Gareth sheathed the sword. "What do you mean?"

I hesitated, trying to put my thoughts into words. "The first time I saw this land was in a dream. I'd pass the night in *this* land and wake up back at home in Scottsdale. But I'm not waking up in Scottsdale anymore."

"Ah," he said, nodding. "No, not since you went through the portal."

The portal.

Gareth's words confirmed it. I couldn't bury my head in the sand any longer. In a dream, you can try all sorts of things you wouldn't try in real life, even those dark, erotic desires. The kind you don't talk about, where civilization is stripped away. But this wasn't a dream anymore. I was responsible for my own actions.

How had my dreamworld become reality?

My eyes searched his face. "What do you know about this, Gareth? I heard you tell Ivan that you paid a wizard to build the portal."

He shifted uncomfortably. "The wizard is a Dreamweaver. I expect that is why you first saw our world in your dreams. He can't resist planting seeds of what is to come. That's how I found you."

I raised an eyebrow.

"I was looking for a way to find your mother. Then I saw you in my dreams."

"This wizard is quite a businessman. He plants dreams in your head and then gets you to pay him to make them come true."

Gareth frowned. "I never thought of it that way. But you're right. The clever bastard."

"I'd like to meet him some day."

"You will. I'm taking you north very soon."

"You're preparing for war, aren't you?"

He nodded, then turned away.

"I don't want there to be a war over me." Or my womb. "I don't want people killed."

"Too late. The die is cast." He seemed excited, as though he were looking forward to it.

"This is exactly like the Trojan War," I said suddenly. "I'm Helen."

"What war is this?"

I told him about ancient Greece and Troy. How Paris had lusted for the wife of Menelaus, and how he had abducted her. And how Menelaus and Agamemnon, his brother, had responded, with the launch of the Trojan War.

Gareth seemed entranced. "She was beautiful then."

I nodded. "'The face that launched a thousand ships.'"

"Like you."

A chill swept through me. I heard the whiz of the arrow right before it slammed into Gareth's right shoulder. He jerked back and slumped to the floor.

I screamed as Ivan's men charged into the room.

Gareth lay on the floor, groaning in pain. Jon had a sword to his throat.

"Save him for me," Ivan roared from across the room.

"Don't kill him!" I yelled. "There's been enough killing."

Ivan glared at me. "You are *my* wife!"

"I'll go back through the portal," I warned.

No idle threat, and he knew it.

His wild brown eyes rested on Gareth. "Get him out of here." He signaled to Jon. Two archers came forward. I couldn't watch, but I heard moans as they dragged Gareth from the room.

Ivan was already undoing his britches. "Leave the room," he said to Richard, who was frozen to the spot.

"No!" I cried.

"You smell like him," he said with disgust as he moved toward me with one thing on his mind.

This couldn't be happening. This is what happened to captured women in wartime, not beloved wives.

He grabbed me by the hair and dragged me to the desk.

"Not here!" I cried. "Not like this."

He hauled me onto the desk. "Yes, like this."

"You do this in front of your men," I said, shaking with fear, "and I'll never come willingly again."

Ivan froze. The darkness in his eyes changed, as if he suddenly realized who I was and where we were. He braced his hands against the desk, his head hung in shame.

No one said a word.

Moments later, he spread my skirt carefully over my hips. He wouldn't meet my eyes.

"We'll go now," he said, grabbing my arm.

Richard followed us, white faced and breathless.

Out in the corridor, Gareth was sprawled on his back. Jon withdrew his sword and moved aside. Ivan kicked Gareth hard in the ribs and I heard a cry of pain.

Without a word, Ivan hustled me down the hall.

The courtyard was grim, gray and silent as a tomb. Two bodies lay lifeless by the stable. They both had red hair.

I looked away.

Five horses were tied to a rail. Ivan steered me over to his, but I broke his grip. Placing two fingers to my mouth, I whistled softly. Lightning trotted out of the stable and nuzzled my arm.

"Good girl."

With my foot in the stirrup, I swung gracefully onto her back.

Mouths gaped in disbelief.

"I've been riding since I was five," I said to my stunned audience. "She's mine, by the way. A little present from Gareth."

Ivan's mouth turned into a sneer.

"What have you ever given me?" I said nastily.

There was no reply, only intense anger.

"I hope you can keep up," I said, giving Lightning a swift kick.

I heard yelling and hoofbeats as Ivan and his men followed.

Sometime toward mid-afternoon, we stopped to water the horses. Richard shyly ventured over, uncertain of his welcome.

"Where did you learn to ride like that?" he asked.

"In Wickenburg. My parents had friends with a ranch. I spent all my summers there as a kid. You should see me rope a cow."

His eyes widened with a whole new level of awe.

"There's blood on your tunic," I said.

A pause. "I got lucky," he replied.

The fog had lifted and the orange sun beamed overhead.

"Gareth wasn't expecting you so soon," I said after a short while.

Richard shrugged. "It was my idea, actually. The Northman would expect us to round up troops for a full battle. He'd be doing the same. That could take days. I figured if we could leave immediately with a small band of men, we could take him unawares."

"A stealth attack."

He smiled. "Yes."

"And Cedric was absent from this mission?"

"He hasn't been seen since the wedding. We think he's gone south."

Just as well. The very thought of Cedric witnessing me with Gareth gave me shivers.

"Why do you dislike him so?" I asked.

"Cedric has abandoned God. Sometimes I think he has made a pact with the devil himself."

A dark cloud passed over the sun.

Lightning came back to me for a muzzle rub.

'How do you do that thing with animals?" Richard asked. "What do you hear?"

I'd never tried to describe my gift before.

"I don't *hear* anything. Animals don't have language like we do. It's more like I sense shapes of emotion, like fear and pain. Or I catch a glimpse of fleeting images. Memories. Sometimes I can calm them down by reaching out with my mind."

"Jon has that affect on me sometimes. I wonder if it is a family gift."

We stood in companionable silence.

"What do you call this land," I asked.

"We're back in Huel now."

"No, I mean the whole land. Your country."

He grinned. "Land's End."

How fitting.

"And why are there no birds and bees here?"

His smile faded. "They went with the witch's curse."

Well, holy crap. No birds and bees for a barren people. What a perfect metaphor. That witch had a wicked sense of humor.

"Why did she curse you all?"

"Because we burnt her sister."

This didn't sound good. "And why did you burn her sister?"

"Because she was a witch."

I shook my head. *Men.*

"It's time," Jon said, interrupting us.

I avoided Ivan's eyes as we mounted and set off again. We didn't stop until we reached the gates of Castle Huel.

Chapter 9

We rode hard into the castle courtyard and pulled up quickly. The dust was wild about us. Ivan sprang from his horse and came over to help me, but I was already slipping off the far side of Lightning. Richard swung from his horse and Jon hitched his mare to the post. The other men were behind us.

Grandfather stood not ten paces away. I took a step toward him and his hard expression stopped me.

He turned to Ivan. "Is he dead?"

"Wounded. Probably mortally." He dunked his head in the water trough and then shook his head.

"Did he use her?" The old man's voice was gruff.

"Oh yes. Most definitely."

The silence in the square was ominous.

"Did she come back willingly?"

Ivan looked at me. "Yes, she did that."

Grandfather turned to me, stepping forward. "Rowena, are you hurt?"

"No."

"We are a pathetic lot that we can't keep one woman safe between us."

"It won't happen again," Ivan growled.

"You can't keep me chained to the castle forever," I retorted. "We'll have to negotiate something."

Jon snorted. "Negotiate?"

"Negotiate?" Ivan roared. "Are you out of your mind? I don't negotiate with barbarians."

"Stop yelling at me!" I closed my eyes and clenched my hands. "All you do is bully me."

"Ivan, cease this," Grandfather said. "Can't you see she's exhausted?" He moved closer. "Where is the rest of your dress, child?"

I shrugged.

"What strange garments they wear up north." He reached for the chain around my neck. "Ivan, look here. Did you see this?" My broach caught the light and it sparkled in the sun. "This is the jewel of Tintagel. It is said to keep the wearer safe from mortal danger. Rowena, did Norland give this to you?"

It took me a moment to realize that by *Norland,* he meant Gareth. I nodded.

There was an awed hush in the courtyard.

"He must value you greatly to give up his own guard against destruction," Grandfather said. "He puts you above his own life. This Earl of Norland is a man of honor. I didn't expect that."

"He is still a barbarian," Ivan snapped.

"A barbarian who won't give up. You should have killed him when you had the chance. He'll be back to take her. If he lives."

A cold wind blew across my heart.

Grandfather took a deep breath. "Richard, escort Rowena to her bedroom, then go to the Great Hall. Ivan, come now. We need to talk."

In my cool, dark room, I undressed and slipped into bed.

Both moons were high when Ivan came into the bedroom.

"Wake up," he said, taking off his belt. "I want to make love to you."

"Ivan, you may be my husband in this world, but it is hardly *love* you offer. All you do is abuse me."

This was probably unfair, but I was bone-weary and still angry for the way he had behaved in the fortress.

He froze. "You must forgive that. It was in the heat of battle."

"You would have taken me in front of all the men," I shot back. "How could you even think to do that?"

"I was provoked! You are my wife. And he—"

His next words were cut off and we stared at each other in fury, remembering.

Tears welled in my eyes. "I was mortified."

He sat on the edge of the bed. "You can't begin to understand what I was feeling. I could have killed every single living thing in that room."

Taking me would have been the lesser evil, he was saying. And that was supposed to make me feel better?

We sat in awkward silence. I tried to imagine what was happening in Norland now. Did Gareth live or did he die?

"I can't do this now," I said bitterly, looking away. "I can't do this tonight. Can you understand that?"

He picked up his belt and turned away. "Sleep well" His voice was thick.

For the first time since the beginning of this adventure, I wanted to go home. Could I find the portal again and go through the wall? Even more, could I leave Grandfather now that I'd found him? I stewed over these options until the moons drifted behind a cloud.

Finally, I fell asleep.

A short time after sunrise, I went down to the great hall. I had selected a different dress to wear—a deep lavender one. The round neck was high and prim, but the bodice was about two sizes too small so I had to leave it loosely laced in the back. I'd bust through the armholes in no time, but it couldn't be helped. It had a matching vest to the ground, trimmed in white fur.

The atmosphere in the hall was so frosty that I nearly turned back at the door.

"I order you to tell me," Grandfather said coldly.

Richard stared at the stone floor. Ivan stood to his left with his back to me and Jon leaned against the outer wall, his arms crossed.

Grandfather saw me first. "Rowena, come here."

I hesitated.

"Come here, child."

I moved forward a few steps.

"Something happened yesterday, something terrible, and these wretched fools won't tell me what it was."

I closed my eyes, positive that my face was white.

"Tell me, Rowena. I know you know."

I looked from one to the other. Do I obey my grandfather—or my husband? Interesting dilemma. Not one I'd ever considered facing before.

Ivan shook his head. "Rowena, don't!"

"You dare to countermand me?" Grandfather was close to fury. "I know something happened. The three of you will hardly look at each other. And the poor girl is terrified. What went on yesterday that you so fear to tell me? What did you do?" He whirled around, facing the other men. "Richard? Jon?"

Jon made a face of disgust, pushed away from the wall and strode out the room.

"Richard! Tell me!"

Richard continued to look at the floor.

"Rowena?" Grandfather's voice softened, but there was still an edge to it.

I snapped my head around and met Ivan's eyes. They were deep pools of anguish, and so help me, I fell into them.

"I can't," I said, helpless.

Grandfather let out an exasperated breath. "I admire your loyalty to your husband. That is as should be. I won't press you further." To Ivan, he said, "You push me too far. I am still Earl! Their first loyalty must be to me, not you. Remember that. There will be no next time."

I fled the room.

Richard was waiting for me on the front step. "Are you okay?" His eyes were soft and full of care.

I nodded and pulled him toward the courtyard.

"Thank you for not telling him," he said. "It would have gone very badly for us."

I walked a few paces, then let out the breath I had been holding. "For Ivan."

"No, for Jon and me too."

I could feel his discomfort.

"I should have done something," he said bitterly. "I wanted to do something to stop him. I hated myself for being there. I didn't even leave the room."

I stood still. There didn't seem to be anything to say.

"I've thought of nothing else since," he said. "I won't forgive myself. Ever."

His golden head hung down in shame. I thought of Apollo, so young and beautiful.

"Oh, Richard. You are a good man, whether you think so or not."

"You don't understand." He lifted his head and swallowed hard. "That was the way my own mother died."

I felt a lightning bolt of clarity run through me.

"Others." His voice was low and hushed. "When the castle was breached and our men were south fighting with Sargon. They left her for dead. I was a child. I couldn't do anything. And I did nothing yesterday either."

Oh Lord in heaven, no wonder the old earl had been so enraged in the hall and the others so stricken. This was like a nightmare repeating, with Ivan as the villain and Richard so clearly fascinated that he stood and watched.

What a primitive world it was here. Every emotion seemed heightened and out of control.

I closed my eyes and sought calm. "Thank you for telling me this, Richard. I understand now. Let it be over. We need this to be over."

We walked through the courtyard toward the main gate.

"Will you forgive him?" Richard asked.

"He's my family," I said, as though this solved everything. Maybe it did in this world. Richard seemed to accept it.

We looked out the main gate together. How I longed to run away across the fields. But it would only get Richard in further trouble.

"There is something you could do for me," I said with unease. "A way you could pay me back."

He looked hopeful.

"Find out whether the Earl of Norland lives or if he is dead. I know you have scouts."

"I don't think—"

"He was good to me, Richard. And that's more than can be said for the men of this house."

No kidding. Ravished on the first night here, married without a choice, nearly taken like an animal in the heat of battle...

I heard a sharp intake of breath.

"I'll find out," he said finally.

There was something more left to ask, something that had been haunting me.

"Richard, what will happen if I have child?"

He looked out upon the fields. "If it's a girl, there will be rejoicing."

"And if it's a boy?"

"I don't know. I think they will want you to try again."

"And what will our enemies do?"

He fell silent.

"I think I know," I said. "If it is a girl, they'll try to take her. They won't care about a boy. But if it's a girl—I'm right, aren't I?" I felt cold fear. "And if I prove I'm fertile? What happens to me?"

I already knew the answer. They would take me too. It would start all over again. It would never be over. *Never.* That much was certain.

"Let's go back to the castle," he said.

I followed willingly, but all the time a plan was forming in my head. I had to get home. I didn't want to have a baby here in this primitive world. I wanted hospitals and doctors and modern medicine. And the chance to raise a child in relative safety.

As soon as I could, I would leave through the wall.

That night, the moons were full. Sleepless, I had been laying in bed watching them for a long while.

Ivan came to me and sat on the edge of the mattress.

"Please talk with me," he said. "We need to talk."

I sat up and looked at him. He didn't meet my eyes, but stared out the window at the moons.

"Understand when I am with you," he said, "I am made mad with desire all the time. When we are apart, I am consumed with worry for your safely. It is tearing me apart."

"I need you to be gentle."

"I want to be gentle, but when we are alone, it is like a beast takes over me. I cannot control it." He sounded bitter. "When another man looks at you, I want to kill him. Even my own kin."

That sounded grim.

"Jon told me about feeling bewitched when he first encountered you by the river."

I bet Jon didn't tell him everything.

"Let me sleep with you tonight. Let me lie with you and hold you, and I will not bother you for sex this night. I give my word."

The flow of moonlight blanketed the room in a soft embrace. I settled down upon the bed and moved the covers back to make room.

Ivan removed his clothes and slipped silently in beside me, gathering my back to his chest. His arms held me loosely. I felt him hard behind me, but true to his word, he made no move. Before long, I felt him relax and fall to sleep.

I silently made plans for my escape.

It started to rain midway through the night. I had to close the shutters since Ivan was sleeping like a log.

When I woke at dawn, the place beside me was empty.

As the rain subsided to a gentle sprinkle, I dressed quickly, determined to reach the stable undetected. Making no sound, I found my way down the stairs, past the great hall and through the side door.

Pools of water lay in the yard. As I walked, mud gathered along my skirt bottom. I didn't care. I was going home.

I hurried across the courtyard.

"Where are you going in this rain?" Ivan called behind me.

I hesitated. "I'm going to visit my horse." I turned toward the stables.

"No, you're not. You're lying." He grabbed my arm.

"Let go of me!"

"You're not going anywhere."

He grabbed my other arm and pulled me around. I tried to smack him with my hand, but I slipped and landed on my knees in the mud. He grabbed me around the waist and I struck out with my right leg.

Down he went on his back, into a mixture of mud and manure.

Someone yelled. Someone else laughed.

I attempted to crawl away on hands and knees, but kept kneeling on my skirt.

Then Ivan was upon me again. We rolled over and over in the muck, like two mud-wrestlers on cable TV. I slipped out of his grasp twice, then yelled like a banshee and called him all sorts of names. He pinned me to the ground.

A roaring, cheering crowd had gathered around us. Not a single man missed our debacle.

"You're like a greased pig," Ivan said, lurching to his feet. "That was a whole lot of fun, but let's do it without clothes next time."

I tried to kick him, but fell flat on my chest.

"Ivan! Rowena!" Grandfather bellowed from the top of the steps. "Stop this. Stop this at once."

Ivan reached out to help me up. I grabbed a handful of mud and threw it in his face. He gagged and someone whooped. Jon and Richard grabbed my arms and dragged me away.

Not the most elegant exit I've ever made.

"Holy hell, you can fight," Jon said with a snicker. "Have pity on the poor man."

Richard was panting hard, but whether in laughter or outrage, I wasn't sure.

Grandfather was livid. "Rowena, look at you! What is it with you two? Why can't you get along like civilized married people?"

Okay, so I wasn't a perfect example of grace and decorum. My beautiful lavender gown was ripped down the side and slathered with mud. My hair was caked and I could hardly see out my left eye.

Richard picked up a piece of my vest—the pretty one with fur trim that now looked black—and I could see his eyes were full of mirth.

Damn, this place was hell on clothes.

Ivan had fared no better. Mud ran down his front, in his face and in his hair. He appeared to have ingested some of it.

"Get to the showers, both of you. I despair of you."

Poor Grandfather. He really did sound at the end of his wits.

Rising with caution, I brushed off as much muck as I could with one hand and walked past the men with my head held high.

The showers were at the side of the castle by the kitchen. They were outdoor wooden stalls and operated by a pulley system.

I stomped into the first stall and locked the door behind me.

Ivan entered the next one.

I shucked off my tattered, dirty gown and pulled the cord to release the stream of water. "Yikes!"

The water was bloody cold. They had a kind of soap made from—well, best not to think about that. It worked well on mud, which was the important thing. I scrubbed until I finally felt clean.

This presented a new dilemma.

"Ivan?" I said.

"Yes, dear one?"

"They haven't brought us any towels."

"No, my love, they haven't."

Silence.

"Then how are we going to get back to our rooms?"

Ivan chuckled. "We'll have to run."

I swore, then heard his door swing shut. I opened mine and peeked out.

"Up you go," he said, hefting me over one shoulder.

"Help!"

I let out a feeble cry while he raced across to the kitchen door and through to the great room, laughing all the way. He took to the stairs and I whacked his back, yelling obscenities as I bounced along.

For a brief second, I saw Jon and Richard in the hall, their eyes widening with shock. Then we turned the corner and stumbled into my room.

Ivan tossed me on the bed and flopped down on his back.

I started to giggle.

"Lord, you are a lot of trouble," he said, panting hard. "But a whole lot of fun."

We both whooped hysterically. I was laughing so hard that tears streamed down my face and I could hardly breathe.

"I'm exhausted," he said at last.

"You gave the cousins quite a show."

He laughed again.

"Do you think Grandfather saw?" I asked.

He shook his head. "Didn't see him there."

We stared at the ceiling, while our heartbeats and breath returned to normal.

Ivan rolled to his side and looked at me. His eyes were a tender rich warm brown. He picked up a lock of my wet hair with his hand. "I can be gentle," he said, his voice soft.

"Prove it," I whispered.

He gave me a kiss that would always remain in my memory as one of the most delicious moments of my life. He kissed every bit of me, my hair and every inch of skin that was visible—and some that was not.

"That was the main course," he said. "Here comes dessert."

Chapter 10

We slept in each other's arms until a knock on the door woke us. Jon was on the other side.

"Ivan, Rowena. Wake up. The old man wants to see you both in the hall."

Ivan sprung out of bed. He hesitated, then remembered that he had come in with no clothes on. He looked back at me and smiled. "I'll go get dressed." He left the room in his natural state.

I climbed out of bed, stretching and taking my time. "Time to find another dress to wear—*and* face the music."

The wardrobe was looking bare, but I picked out a pretty muslin day dress in virginal white and attempted to hoist myself into it. It was a tad too tight across the hips and as usual, the back gaped. Tomorrow I would have to look into altering the remaining three dresses. I could sacrifice one to get the scraps I needed to let out the others.

My hair was almost dry. I brushed it into a high ponytail and used a soft white sash to make a bow. Then I grabbed a pair of plain leather slippers and hurried down to the hall.

Grandfather waited at the long table with Jon, Richard and two men I didn't know well. Ivan strode into the room after me.

Grandfather smiled at me and pointed to the chair next to his. "Sit here, my dear. You look very pretty."

I smiled back.

Duke plodded to my side and put his head in my lap.

"We have some questions about the Earl of Norland," Grandfather began.

My heart leapt to my throat.

"We know Norland's mobilizing forces and I thought you may have learned something of his plans during your stay there."

I looked down at Duke and continued to stroke his head.

"Yes, sir, he is," I said.

Or he *was*. I had to find out if he lived.

They waited.

I let out a sigh. "He sent his brother to the northern fortresses to gather their traditional allies. His cousin Roderick rode east to barter with the Danes."

Jon cursed, while Ivan frowned.

"And west, child?" Grandfather prodded.

"Janus wanted to ride to the west, but Gareth stopped him. He'd rather not let the king know I existed."

Grandfather let out a sigh of relief. "Smart man. The king is our ally, but I fear he has his own interests at heart."

Ivan snorted.

"Thank you for telling us this, Rowena," Grandfather said. "You're a good granddaughter."

"I will always help you, Grandfather. You must know that."

He reached over and held me close.

In truth, I didn't feel that I had betrayed a trust. I owed my grandfather loyalty, and in these circumstances, Gareth would expect me to pass on what I knew.

"Norland planned for defense," Jon said. "Do you think he'll move his forces south to attack?"

"He'll come," Ivan said, unsmiling. "I would."

Grandfather nodded. "If he lives. Even then, Janus might take it up without him. We have some days to plan, I think. They'll wait until Norland can ride."

I couldn't bear to hear this. "May I be excused? I feel a little faint."

"Of course, my dear," Grandfather said. "Forgive me for keeping you here while we talk of...defense."

I hurried to the door. "Come, Duke."

The dog followed me outside where the day was still gray. The rain had stopped, but nothing could remove the solemn mist that settled around me. I sat on the stone steps at the castle entrance and put my arms around Duke, holding him close. The dog panted happily, free of all the worry that was heavy in my heart.

As I stroked Duke's soft fur, I imagined the tragic fate that awaited my barbarian lover. Gareth would come down from the hills and he would kill my husband or be killed by him. More would die. And there was little I could do to stop it.

Sometime later, Richard interrupted me.

"He lives," he said, sitting down beside me. "But he won't live long if he comes to Huel."

I trembled.

The next afternoon, I heard horses approaching. I was in the stable visiting with Lightning when a band of riders thundered into the courtyard. I moved to the door, peeking out as the men dismounted.

It was easy to tell their leader. Imposing, regal and dressed in black with a silver-trimmed cape, the man dismounted with grace. When he pointed left and then right, his men flanked him. Then he moved forward, one hand resting on the hilt of his sword.

Grandfather, Ivan and Jon waited with grim expressions on the front step.

"Hail, men of Huel." The visitor's voice was deep.

"Sargon," Grandfather lowered his head to a short bow. "Welcome."

Wow, I thought. So this is the king.

"What brings you, Sire?" Grandfather asked with a politeness I'd never heard before.

Sargon didn't waste any time.

"Word has reached us that you have a prize of great worth."

Grandfather frowned. "You heard correctly."

"And your daughter's daughter now resides within your walls."

"That is so."

A pause.

"Where is the Lady Rowena?"

I stepped out from the shadow of the stables. "Here."

Sargon spun around.

I caught his dark eyes with mine and moved to a deep curtsey.

Hey, where had I learned to do that?

"Rise," he said, stepping forward and taking my hand. "They did not exaggerate." He touched his lips to my hand. "By Zeus, I thought they must have."

I did not pretend to be coy, but looked him straight in the eyes. There was a challenge in them. I held my head high.

The man before me was not as tall as Ivan, but he was more compact and fierce looking all the same. He had more years, as evidenced by the strands of salt that mingled in his short, peppered locks. His eyes were black as obsidian, his nose Roman and his expression intelligent.

I feared—yes, *feared*—this was a very clever man.

"I hear you have been married recently, m'lady," Sargon said, smiling. "Your husband is a lucky man."

The intensity of his gaze flustered me and made me rather hot.

"You honor me," I replied. "For as you know, he did not have many from which to choose."

Sargon barked a laugh. "What fresh wit! Why, Huel, she has a quick mind within that lovely form. What a rarity in a woman."

"No rarer, surely, than I find in men," I shot back.

His eyes widened.

For a moment I thought I had gone too far. But no, he threw back his head and laughed again, the only sound in the courtyard.

"Well said, fair lady. I'll spar with you later and look forward to it. But for now, business."

With a brief nod, he turned to Grandfather. He strode to the stone steps, his black cape flapping behind him, and took the steps two at a time.

Then Sargon, Grandfather and Ivan went inside the castle.

"Well, rock my socks," I muttered beneath my breath. "That was kinda fun."

"Are you out of your mind, Rowena?" Richard hissed behind me. "Do you have any idea how dangerous he is?"

I stared at the horses being brought into the stable.

Yes, I had a very good idea how dangerous Sargon might be.

Chapter 11

We were to meet in the great hall for dinner. Ivan came into my bedroom and flopped down on the bed.

"Things aren't good, are they?" I said, turning from the wardrobe. Things weren't good in my wardrobe either, but that was another story.

Ivan stared at the ceiling. "No, they're not."

I sat down on the edge of the bed and waited.

"There are rumors of a takeover coming from the south. Sargon's here to confirm alliances and take stock of the remaining men."

I remembered something. "Jon told me there was nothing left to fight for since the fertile women and children are gone."

Ivan rubbed his weary eyes. "It seemed that way when everyone was grieving. But now you have a lot of men with nothing to occupy their time but petty grievances. There is nothing to do *but* drink and fight. Even though there is no obvious reward."

"You're saying men fight because it's their nature?"

"Exactly."

This was a new development in our relationship. Ivan was *sharing*. He had come to my room to talk things over with me, a real a turning point, and I was happy to play my part.

"What does this mean for Grandfather," I asked, surprised at how much I really cared.

"Durham, the castle south of here, was razed in the last battle. It's a ruin. We're first in line for a southern attack. I can't see how we can defend this castle and stand with Sargon at his. There aren't enough men. He'll pull us from here, I fear, and leave Huel defenseless."

A chill ran down my back. This beautiful castle left defenseless to enemies who might burn it?

"You don't like Sargon, do you?"

"He's devious, Rowena. I don't trust him an inch."

I thought that was a fair assessment, and probably the very reason Sargon was still king.

"'Uneasy lies the head that wears the crown,'" I quoted.

"What did you say?"

I repeated it.

"I like that." Ivan smiled. "It speaks the truth. Tell your grandfather that one."

I didn't like to think about what my family faced in the near future. It was hard enough coping with what I had to face tonight.

"How did Sargon know about me?" I asked.

"The man has scouts everywhere. He probably knew the exact hour you set foot in the castle." He stood and stretched. "You had better get dressed. I said I'd be down early to sort out the sleeping arrangements for our guests." The disdain in his voice was clear.

When Ivan was gone, I turned back to the wardrobe. Dinner was a problem. My last good dress had been wrecked in the mud fight and I still hadn't completed the alterations on the few remaining gowns that didn't fit. I had two muslin day dresses, but to wear them at dinner would be an insult to our esteemed guest.

The only thing left was the turquoise two-piece from home. I didn't like the fact that it was bare in the middle. When I slipped it on I realized I'd lost a little weight because the skirt now hung lower on my hips. But it was a shimmery fabric and not a color found in this world, so that made it special.

I draped Gareth's jewel around my neck. "When in doubt, add jewelry." That was my motto.

My mother's beaded slippers were a snug fit, but doable. I did as much with my hair as I could, but it would have to stay down. I didn't have the tools for anything more elaborate.

Noise erupted from the corridor. Male voices and laughter.

Now or never, I thought as I left the sanctuary of my room.

As I descended the stairway, there was a hush. All eyes turned toward me, mouths gaping. Sargon's murky stare held mine as I paused on the bottom step.

Ivan rushed forward and held out a hand. "Allow me."

"We have a Goddess in our midst," Sargon said, crossing his arms.

There was appreciation in his eyes as they trailed from my bosom across the expanse of bare skin to my hips. His eyes veered upward and latched onto the jewel. He scowled. "May I?"

Without waiting for an answer, he grabbed the jewel and turned it in his hand, the candlelight casting beams of blue across the room.

"This was Norland's, last I saw." His eyes narrowed. "A gift?"

I nodded.

He grinned with wolf teeth. "You become more and more interesting. There must be a story there."

I gave him a tight smile in return. Ivan stiffened beside me.

"This is my brother Thane," Sargon said, introducing me to a man standing nearby.

Thane was a softer version of his older brother. Was it possible to use the word *soft* with respect to any of these men? There was no softness in his strong, hard body. He was a similar height to his brother, about six feet, and his face reflected the same chiseled features as Sargon's. The softness was in his eyes, which were a friendly blue instead of black. And the mouth, although thin, smiled with kindness, not contempt. He had the most beautiful black hair that curled over his forehead and ears.

When I caught Thane's eye, there was a *zing* of electricity.

I shrugged it off.

Beside Thane stood Rhys, a man of few words. Next to him was Logan, who was even taller, but younger, with hair as auburn as mine. There were more men behind them, all well built, all respectful, and—I noted—still armed. You might leave your sword at the door in this world, but never your dagger.

In the dining hall, two places were set at the head of the table. Grandfather took a seat and I sat to his right. Sargon chose a middle seat along the left side, opposite Ivan. His men filled in beside him. Our men took places along the right side of the long table. It was an odd arrangement, but I expect it had something to do with defensive positioning.

One thing I noticed at these meals, there was a lot of meat. We had chicken, venison, wild duck and every variation of game. They used a bland flatbread to soak up juices. No one seemed to have heard of vegetables. Or salad. The thing I missed most in this world was coffee.

And table manners.

As far as I could tell, there were none. Men reached for food and discarded bones with little finesse. I was used to ranch life and the way of cowboys, so this didn't shock me completely, but the loud chewing and talking with mouths full of food did little to appease my sense of proper etiquette.

I took my modest serving and tried to stay out of their way.

Partway through dinner, I noticed a curious thing. The men were drinking far too much as usual, but not Sargon. He made the motions, but did not sip every time he raised the tankard to his lips. His ominous glance would catch me now and then, measuring. This made me wary.

Why was he intent on not drinking?

The room grew hotter, noisy. Smoke from the candles gave the air a ghostly haze. Through it, I could see something being passed about. A dagger.

I had a bad feeling, a sense of dread.

"You like this blade?" Sargon asked Ivan.

Ivan nodded, mesmerized.

"It is perfectly balanced," Sargon said. "Here. Touch it. Try it in your hand."

He held the sharp blade across the table. Ivan took it eagerly.

"I will make you a trade." Sargon's mouth curled in a sinister smile. "You may have it in return for something else. I want one night with your wife."

Gasps hissed through the room.

Ivan roared and pushed back from the table. The dagger was in his hand.

"Stop, Ivan!" I jumped to my feet. "Can't you see he's maneuvering for an excuse to kill you?"

And then I would be conveniently without a husband, no doubt the purpose of this plan.

Sargon rose smoothly and took a determined step toward me. "A woman who can strategize." His eyes blazed. "How fascinating."

We stared at each other across the short space. It was like being mesmerized by a snake.

"I studied Tacitus at school," I said in a cool voice.

"Remarkable."

Sargon took another step and reached out to touch my hair. I heard Ivan growl. Jon held him firmly by the shoulders.

I stepped back. "I am not a chattel to be passed around. I'm not Ygraine."

"Take care, Rowena," Grandfather said, meeting my gaze with a worried look.

We both knew we were at some balance point where things could turn nasty at the flash of a flame and he would be unable to defend me.

"Who is this Ygraine?" Sargon demanded.

Perhaps I could play Scheherezade and defuse the room with words.

I turned to address the king. "Ygraine was wife of the Duke of Cornwall in ancient times. She was beautiful and a talented entertainer and Cornwall liked to show her off. One night there was a banquet very much like this," I swept my hand across the table, "with lots of ale flowing freely. Too much ale. Uther the king of Britton was a guest, and his whole entourage supped along with Cornwall's men." I scowled at the men of Huel. "The men got bawdy, as they will. Toward the end of the night, Cornwall ordered Ygraine to dance and when she did, Uther the king was filled with lust."

Surveying the audience to see how my story was going down, I noticed the drinking had stopped. They were spellbound.

"Uther demanded to have Ygraine," I continued. "Fighting broke out in the hall and the men went out to gather arms. Uther raised his mighty forces to meet Cornwall on the battlefield, but at nightfall before the first day of battle, the wizard Merlin cast a spell for his king. Uther was a man possessed. He could wait for Ygraine no longer."

I paused to take a breath. Even Sargon was caught in the web of my voice. He seemed transfixed.

"While Cornwall slept with his troops on the field, Uther took the form of Ygraine's husband and walked right into the Castle Cornwall. He went to Ygraine's room and lay with her that night. All night he took her, wearing the face and body of his enemy so that Ygraine would think she was submitting to her own husband."

There was a collective gasp.

I looked off in the distance. "He left Ygraine at dawn. Cornwall died on the battlefield that day and Uther rode back to claim Ygraine for his queen." I paused for effect. "There was a child from that night. His name was Arthur. He became ruler of Camelot, the greatest kingdom our world has seen."

I stopped there. The story of Arthur and Lancelot was a sad one full of betrayal. It wouldn't help the atmosphere in this room tonight.

"I think I need you at my court," Sargon said, his voice thick.

Grandfather moved to my side. "But, Sire—"

"You will *all* come," Sargon commanded, his intense gaze directed at Ivan. "She can be kept safer there, you must agree."

He smiled, the look of a famished wolf.

When he turned back to me, his expression changed. I had a horrid feeling of inevitability.

Oh, bloody hell, I thought.

The guests had bedded down for the night in another area of the castle far from my room, but I could hear voices in the corridor outside.

"What are our choices?" I heard Jon say.

"Not many." Ivan sounded bitter. "To refuse would mean we'd have to stand. And I don't know if any would stand with us."

"If we can call back Cedric, would his southern connections join with us?"

Ivan's laugh wasn't pleasant. "Cedric will be glad to see me go down."

"Norland will wait for us to kill each other off and then descend like a vulture."

So Gareth was recovering well. God help me, I was relieved.

"We go then," Jon said after a while.

"And I wait helpless for him to lay his claim?" There was fury in Ivan's voice. "No. I'll not stomach that. I want it out here."

"We have no other choice," Jon insisted.

"We do. I can challenge him outright."

"Are you out of your mind, Ivan? You can't challenge the king. That's treason. Even if you did win—which is unlikely for he is a master—you would stand trial."

"I hate this. There must be some way."

"Of course, if he were to challenge you..."

They moved down the hall, out of hearing.

I thought about what I'd overheard. Ivan was right. There was another way. A way that would solve everything.

I could leave this world and go back through the wall.

Chapter 12

I got up at dawn and dressed in rose muslin. It was a fair day, a good day to make time on a horse. I dashed down the staircase, and left by the side door

A man I didn't know blocked the door to the stables. He was as big as a bar room bouncer and just as formidable.

"Orders," he said, without apologizing. "No one to enter until Sargon arrives."

I turned and ran to the far gate. It had two guards on it.

Rats, I thought. The blasted man thinks of everything. There would be no escape to the wall today.

The square was getting busy. Men were piling small animals, boxes of food and weapons on carts. I opened my mind to the animals. The chickens and ducks were squawking and frightened. I tried to sooth them, but it's hard to calm birds because their brains are so small. The horses were in good temper, excited and eager to run.

But I didn't want to travel on one of those carts. So I ran back up the steps of the castle to find Grandfather.

"Ah, there you are," a deep voice said. "You see we make arrangements."

I bobbed a quick curtsey to Sargon and veered past him.

"Hold on there." He sounded amused. "We need to talk."

With a resigned sigh, I faced him.

The king looked good in the morning light—less frightening. I saw he wasn't as old as I had first thought—maybe mid-thirties. He was clean-shaven, which must have been tough with that thick black hair. A scar jagged down the left side of his face from under the eye to his mouth.

"How did you get this?" I murmured, reaching out.

He seized my arm before I touched him. "The usual way. I was careless."

"I'm sorry. I don't know what came over me."

He looked at me with those black eyes. I saw them soften. "Rowena, I—"

"We're almost ready, Sire," one of his men interrupted.

Sargon released my arm. "Good. Collect the men." To me, he said, "They tell me you can ride, Lady. I will let you take your horse if you promise to stay close." His hand rested on the hilt of his sword. "You are to stay with your grandfather. You must promise."

"I promise."

"Good. Now go and pack. I'll see you shortly."

I rushed up the steps, knowing he watched me all the while.

Grandfather waited in my room. He held a large satchel.

"Put your clothes in here, child. Pack everything you have. I don't know what we'll find at the other end. Come to my room when you're done." He kissed me on the forehead, then left.

There wasn't much to pack. I had one spare day dress and two gowns that were too small for me, plus the turquoise two-piece from home.

Mustn't forget that.

I'd pack the good slippers and wear my sandals for the ride. At least they had a short heel for stirrups.

Darn, what I would give for my cowboy boots back home.

The soft blue dress I wore now had a full skirt that would do for riding. Over it, I'd wear a split apron made from spare fabric.

Very clever of me, I thought. I could spread my legs around a horse and tie the apron to my waist so that it would drape on both sides to cover bare skin.

The broach I carried within a deep skirt pocket. I laced the pocket shut, just to be sure.

Ivan came to get me.

"Sargon has already set out with his knights," he said.

In the yard, the carts were pulling out while our men mounted their horses. Lightning pranced over to my side.

"We can ride ahead of the carts," Grandfather said from his own great horse. "I've told the men to go on as they like. We can travel at our own pace, you and me."

We took turns galloping and walking our horses to give them a break. Lightning was a darling and she loved to do my bidding.

"Did your mother teach you to ride?" Grandfather asked.

We had been traveling for over an hour.

"Actually, I taught *her*," I said with a smile. "I've been riding since I could walk. My father came from a ranch and I was always messing around in the stables. Mom rode, but not hard, if you know what I mean."

"Was she a good mother to you?" His voice broke.

"Oh yes, the best. She was pretty, always laughing and I adored her. So did Dad. I miss her every day."

"You are so like her."

"And so are you in many ways. Everything about you reminds me of her and makes me feel comfortable." I recalled a memory. "She loved to dress me up in long dresses. I guess she was missing the ways of back home, but I didn't know it then."

We had nearly reached the river. We dismounted for a bit to give the horses water. I scrutinized the spot, taking in every detail. I needed to remember the point where the river went north along the forest to the split tree.

"Why did she leave here?"

Grandfather sighed. "She was the youngest girl left in the valley—the last female born before the curse took effect. Already the predators were circling. You have experience of that and she was younger than you, not more than fifteen. I meant to marry her to someone I had chosen, but she didn't want that."

She had never told me this. My poor, dear mom.

"I think she made a bargain with a sympathetic witch, but I don't know for sure," Grandfather said. "She disappeared one day with all her jewelry. We never saw her again. We would have known if she had been taken by a man from this island."

Lightning nuzzled me and we mounted again.

"Child, how did she die?"

I'd been expecting this question.

"Her heart stopped. She had a weak heart. None of us knew it. She died one night in her sleep."

How fitting that the woman who was all heart should die of a weak heart.

It was dusk when we arrived at the great castle of Sargonia. And *great* it was. The walls were at least ten feet thick and topped with crenellations and merlons. Atop them, a line of archers stood ready. Gray towers rose into the sky on all four sides. A huge dry moat ran around the periphery.

The iron gates were open and the drawbridge down. As we approached, I could see many men in the yard—perhaps a hundred. Chickens and ducks ran wild across the dirt. Everything and everyone was in frantic motion, readying for battle.

Men of all ages stopped and stared as we passed. A few bowed their heads, but most just gaped.

It was eerie to have so many eyes on me. Uncomfortable, I scanned for the stables that ran alongside one great wall.

Ivan crossed the courtyard to help me dismount.

"This is quite a place," he said. "At least two hundred live within these walls. And another two hundred close by."

"We're weary," Grandfather said, groaning and dismounting stiffly. "Are there activities planned that we must attend tonight?"

"No." Ivan handed off my horse to a groom. "I'm to show you to our rooms and food will be brought up there."

"Thank the Gods," Grandfather murmured.

We had been riding so long that I found it difficult to walk up the steps to the castle entrance. My legs didn't want to work.

Inside, we found ourselves in a long entrance hall.

"The great hall is beyond those double doors," Ivan said. "It's three times the size of Huel. Everything here is enormous." I could hear the reluctant awe in his voice.

He guided us up a massive wooden staircase and along a dark stone corridor with slits for windows. These would be for defense, I realized. Our rooms were next to each other. Mine and Ivan's first, Richard's next and then Grandfather's. Jon was further down the hall.

Our room had a window to an inner courtyard, but best of all it had a real bed like the one at Huel. Beside it was a tray of cheese and bread. I leapt upon it, ravenous.

As I stuffed my face, Ivan said, "I have to leave you now. There's a meeting. You should be safe until I return." He seemed reluctant to leave, as if he didn't quite believe his own words, but eventually he left.

Soon after, young Logan arrived at the door. He handed me my satchel. I thanked him and he blushed.

After he had gone, I took off my riding dress and snuggled into the bed. A steady breeze blew in through the courtyard window. Exhausted by the arduous trek across the island, I soon was whisked off to sleep.

Chapter 13

It was late the next morning when I wandered into the stables, looking for Lightning. She was relieved to see me and nuzzled up to my side. I stroked her, reading her. Apparently, some stallion was giving her trouble. I sought to ease her mind, but she rubbed against me skittishly.

Then I saw the problem male.

Sargon, mounted on a beautiful black stallion, approached from the far door. It was the first time I had seen him since we arrived at Sargonia.

"Ah, Rowena. You are a lover of horses?"

"Yes, Sire." I nodded my head in a short bow. "In my own land, I am an animal healer."

His eyes widened and he flashed a smile. "Is there no end to your mysteries, woman?"

Lightning pranced nervously, so I hushed her.

"Your filly is a beautiful animal," Sargon said. "She looks fast."

"She's small but swift. Arabian blood, I suspect. We have mustangs like this that have returned to the wild in Arizona."

His eyes bore a hole in me. "Does she come from the Huel stables?"

I hesitated. "Norland stock."

What would he make of that?

"Come ride with me," he said. "I've a mind to show you something."

My breath caught. It was another challenge, a delicious one. Excitement soared within me. I'd play with fate today and meet her head on.

"Lead the way," I said.

He backed the stallion away to give me room. I reached for Lightning's leather saddle, tightened it and fastened the bridle.

All the while, Sargon's eyes never left me.

I led Lightning from the stable, hiked up my white muslin skirt and mounted her in one graceful sweep. Sargon watched me adjust the fabric to cover my knees. It was brazenly immodest to ride like this, but I wasn't going back for my riding apron.

Sargon was off on a canter out the far gate. He glanced over his shoulder, judging my speed. Then he kicked the stallion. I put my heel to Lightning and she rose to the challenge. Together, we raced across the fields.

Lightning lived up to her name, dear girl, and I laughed with joy as we rode the wind. I felt like a kid again, riding through the wilds of the Arizona desert...back when mom was alive, the world was sweet and I had no worries.

When Sargon pulled up, his smile was as wide as mine.

We stopped at a high plateau. Sargon leapt from the stallion's back and rushed to help me down. I brushed him away, sliding to the ground on my own. The horses panted as hard as we did.

Sargon strode to the edge of the cliff top.

"This land is mine," he said. "From the borders of Huel to this great cliff. Come closer, see the view from here. Land's End goes to the sea. To the edge of the world."

The cliff gave way to a rocky shore with boulders as big as boats. The surf pounded below us. Beyond, the ocean was a dark raging blue. White terns soared and swooped in the sky above the water, not venturing as far as land.

"'Beyond this point, there be monsters,'" I quoted.

We stood side by side with the wind raging and the sound of the waves crashing below us. My hair whipped around my face. I put my face into the sea breeze and closed my eyes, drinking in the energy.

"Rowena, I mean to take you and I want to discuss terms."

I was so shocked I stumbled. "Terms?"

"You will submit." He shrugged. "I am the king and I hold power over those you love." His eyes gleamed with danger. "I can have your husband killed if you have scruples."

"No," I squeaked. "Not necessary."

Dear God, he would kill a man to make me feel okay about this betrayal?

He walked to the very edge of the cliff. It was a cool and arrogant thing to do. For one wild moment, I thought I could rush him and he would plummet over the edge. But I couldn't kill a man. Not even Sargon.

"You will submit," he said, eyeing me, "but will you respond to me? I don't know."

Respond?

A choking sound erupted from my throat. I turned away.

This was real. This was not a dream I could hide behind. Sargon would kill my husband if that's what it took to have me. Would he kill me as well if I refused to cooperate? Could that strangled laugh be coming from my mouth?

I could hear the hysteria rising.

"Rowena!"

He grabbed my arm and swung me around. Then his arms were around me, his mouth on mine and there was madness. I clung to him like a drowning swimmer fighting to stay above water. His fingers twisted in my hair, pulling me closer. I fell into him, his coal black eyes, his strong embrace, the fire in his body, in his kiss.

He laughed when we broke apart. "It's as I thought."

He put his mouth to the place where my neck meets my shoulder. And then—dear God—he bit down hard. I cried out in shock. His hands ripped my dress from the neckline, yanking it down my arms, frantic to get it off my hips.

My breath came in gasps. "Wait, I—"

We were on the bare ground. His mouth found my breast, taking as much of it as he could. His right hand cupped the other one, kneading it, rolling the nipple between his thumb and finger. Then his lips latched onto that breast and I roiled beneath him, my legs already apart.

His mouth was on mine again, demanding more, and I felt him moving against me. Heat surged over me, through me. He raised his face, looked into my eyes and then arched over me. He took me swiftly, his control slipping, changing to frenzy.

This was no dream, but something more sinister, wild and frightening. I fell into a world of ghostly images, envisioning the pounding of waves and the roaring of men in battle. A broadsword appeared in my hand.

Then I heard the growling, savage need of the man inside me.

I cried out.

He yelled a triumphant, haunting roar. Then the ground melted away from me. The only thing keeping me from sinking down into the bowels of the earth were his arms around me.

I slept.

When I awoke, Sargon stood over me, fully dressed, his eyes smoldering. "I'll have to kill Ivan now."

We argued all the way back to the castle.

"It's not your choice," he said. "You can't ignore the customs of our land. They have governed us for a thousand years."

"You and I were together only one time. Can't you pay him off?"

He gave a derisive laugh. "One time? You think that?"

Sargon reined in and I did the same. Leaning over, he pulled me from Lightning's back and gathered me close. His mouth sought mine and I was plunged into the madness once more. I clung to him as a strange and unwanted lust built up inside.

When he released me, I slid to the ground, my legs shaking as I remounted Lightning.

Sargon's eyes narrowed. "Not one time, I think. Not one lifetime either."

We rode at a calm walk.

"I know him," Sargon said. "Huel is a man of honor, if somewhat simple. I've been with his wife and will do so again. Honor demands this to be settled."

"Settled," I repeated in a faint voice.

A pause.

"We've been destined for this from that first night at Huel. You know it. I may have settled for one night then, but not now. There is no going back. I don't *want* to go back."

Was there nothing I could say to stop this madness?

"You could be killed."

His black eyes flashed. "Unlikely."

The ride was nearly over. I had little idea of what to expect and I dreaded the welcome we would receive.

The horses slowed at the gate.

There were men everywhere in the courtyard. Grandfather and Richard stood beside the stable. Ivan was across the court with Jon. Thane waited on the castle steps, his arms crossed.

As we advanced, voices swelled in outrage.

Then all was silent.

There was no disguising where we had been and what we had done. My gown was marked with streaks of dirt and the bodice was ripped. I held it together with one hand.

If I could have crawled into a hole in the earth, I would have.

Sargon helped me from my horse.

I ran to Grandfather. He embraced me and I let out a sob.

Could I be any more ashamed?

Sargon turned to Ivan. "Huel, I challenge you. Now."

Chapter 14

This is what I have learned about fights with broadswords. It is *not* like the movies. People don't leap around like Orlando Bloom and Johnny Depp in pirate gear. Broadswords are heavy, unwieldy things that can kill on contact. Battles are usually very short and always lethal.

Ivan rushed forward, sword in hand, as though he were waiting for this, almost relishing the opportunity. He was the bigger man, but Sargon held a sword with practiced ease.

The king smiled his demented wolf smile. "To the death."

All these Land's End men were mad.

I clung to Grandfather and buried my face in his tunic. There was no cheering with this fight, only deadly silence and the sound of clashing metal.

God, how I hated that sound.

As the swords clanged once, then twice, a man cried out.

Grandfather stiffened and I spun around.

Ivan was on his feet, his sword on the ground. This should have been the end of him, but Sargon did the most extraordinary thing. He threw away his sword.

The crowd gasped.

"No!" I cried out.

Sargon drew his dagger and waited for Ivan to reach for his. It was arrogant, crazy and somewhat gallant. He was giving Ivan a second chance.

Dismay was on every face around me and disbelief on Ivan's.

In a blink, he lunged forward.

There was a blur of action that I couldn't see for the dust.

Sargon swung to the right. His left arm hooked Ivan around the neck and the dagger found its spot. A trail of blood ran down Ivan's chest.

"Rowena, your call," Sargon yelled.

"Spare him. For me." And more quietly, "*For* me..."

The emphasis was different. I knew he would understand.

To Ivan, he hissed, "It will be as if you are dead to us. Leave immediately."

He removed the dagger and stepped back, stumbling slightly.

Ivan fell to the ground.

There was no air left in this stifling world. I collapsed to my knees. Grandfather lifted me with Richard's help. I sagged against Richard's chest and closed my eyes.

"Granddaughter, this is not your fault. It was in the fates. I do not blame you." Grandfather sounded defeated and very old.

We all knew what Sargon's words meant for my husband—banishment. Ivan would keep his life, but lose his title and land. *And* wife.

Men were moving in the square again. A shadow crossed in front of me. Sargon. He stood before me, breathing hard.

"Come," he said, reaching for my hand.

I had no choice.

I let him drag me from Richard's arms. When we reached the top of the steps, Sargon paused. He reminded me of a victorious Roman Centurion, one who had proved himself today before all, not once but twice.

He nodded to the crowd. "Thane, see to it that Ivan obeys me. Rhys, to the hall in one hour. Logan, come."

He nudged me inside the castle. I followed him to an unfamiliar room at the back of the castle. Sargon's private chamber. It was on the main floor, which was unusual, and looked very much like the rooms at Huel. There were tapestry walls, a large wooden bed and dense draperies.

He grabbed my wrist and pulled me inside the room.

"Stay at the door," he ordered Logan.

When the door closed, Sargon collapsed on the bed.

"You're hurt," I said.

"A surface wound, I think."

I raised his tunic. It was black, of course, so the blood didn't show. Nor the gaping wound. Ivan must have caught him with the dagger in that first lunge. The wound was in the side of his chest, missing the rib and not too deep. Any deeper and it would have pierced a lung.

I ran to the door and flung it open. "Logan! I need boiling water and clean cloths. Hurry! Don't tell a soul."

Startled, Logan gave a quick nod and went to do my bidding.

It counted for something, being the consort of the king.

I returned to the bed.

"You're making a fuss for nothing, Rowena."

I felt his head. It was hot and sweaty.

"All men are fools," I said, tugging the tunic over his head.

Scars ran up and down his body. I couldn't count them all.

"How could you do that?" I snapped. "How could you walk from the battle, stride up those steps and wave to the crowd, with a bleeding wound in your chest?"

"Never show weakness."

He gritted his teeth as I probed around the gash. I wanted to kill him. And save him.

"I wish I had my vet bag here," I said.

"Your what?"

"My healer's kit," I explained. "I have medicines that would take away your pain and clean the wound so it won't become infected."

"You can do this in your world?"

"I could do it here, if I had my bag."

Dammit! Getting the bag was next to impossible. Sargon would probably place guards on me now. He wouldn't permit me to go for as much as a pleasure ride alone. And he certainly wouldn't let me go home. I'd never be allowed to venture back through the wall.

Logan rushed into the room. He set a pot of water on a table.

"Thank you," I said, gesturing for him to stay. "I could use your help."

"Of course."

The poor boy was frightened to death, but held the water vessel as I dipped the cloths and cleaned the wound.

Sargon watched me work. "Do you love him?"

"Ivan?" I shrugged.

We'd had one good night together and one really bad day.

"No," I said.

"And Norland?"

I hesitated. "I don't know."

Again I was honest. He seemed to appreciate that, as much as he didn't like it.

"You're free now," my patient said with satisfaction. "He'll not be back."

I glared at him. "Ivan may not come back, but I am hardly free."

It was dusk when I awoke alone in Sargon's room. I remembered bandaging him as best I could and then stretching out beside him on the bed.

Someone knocked on the door.

I sat up. "Come in."

The door creaked and I could see a chair in the hallway. Logan stepped inside, a half dozen dresses flung over his arm. "Sargon said you might want a change of attire." He gave me a shy smile. "I've brought a few dresses from my late aunt's wardrobe. I hope they fit. There's more if these don't suit." He laid them on the bed.

Logan had picked the prettiest of gowns, not necessarily the most elegant, and I certainly needed a change of clothes. My old white muslin was ready for the fire.

"Can you leave the room for a minute, please?"

Logan nodded and closed the door behind him.

I plucked the mint gown from the pile. It might be a little loose in parts, but the high waist would snug in nicely with lacing. It had a low square neck with pretty rows of white lace around the neck and cuffs.

I slid the dress over my head and smoothed it over my hips. Logan's aunt and I were of a similar size, though the dress was short by several inches. So what if my ankles showed? I could put lace on the bottom later.

Logan returned.

He'd been given the task of guard for the day. I felt sorry for him, being left out of the men's meeting to babysit a woman. If he minded, he certainly didn't show it to me. He was thoughtful and charming, as well as dead cute with those freckles. A gentle giant.

"Logan, will you take me to my Grandfather?"

It seemed this was a reasonable request for a lady to make because Logan nodded and escorted me up the grand oak stairs to the second floor. When we crossed a long corridor and passed the room that Ivan and I had shared, I shivered.

Grandfather was lying on his bed. Next to him, Richard sat in a chair. They both clambered to their feet when I paused in the doorway.

"May I come in?" I asked.

"Of course, child," Grandfather said.

Logan waited outside the room.

Grandfather hugged me and kissed my hair. "My poor child, you must think that all men are beasts. I would not have you harmed for the world."

"Please don't worry," I said into his chest. "I'm pretty tough, you know. But I'm so very sorry—"

"I know, child. We all are."

When Grandfather relaxed, I left his arms and went to Richard. "I'm so glad you're here, cousin."

I gave him a hug and he moved awkwardly into my arms. I wondered if this was the first time he had ever embraced a woman.

"Where will Ivan go?" I asked when he released me.

Grandfather frowned and quickly closed the door.

I'd forgotten about Logan, who would serve not only as guard, but also as Sargon's spy.

"South, to find Cedric," Richard said. "That's what I would do."

Cedric. The name always gave me a chill.

"He doesn't blame you," Grandfather said. "He knows what sacrifice you made to save his life. We all were there. He loathes himself for failing you and leaving you to that wolf."

Wolf?

"I acted rashly commanding you to marry Ivan," he added. "I should have waited, knowing what the others might do." He sighed. "We could have saved a lot of trouble if I'd thought that through. Sargon should have had his chance at the start. It was his right, as king."

"I know you were acting in my best interests, Grandfather. Don't blame yourself for this."

"Oh, but I do. It is a bitter alliance now, with you a carnal prize. How I have failed you."

So that was how they saw me—as a carnal prize.

This annoyed me, but I also saw the irony. Here I was, a modern woman shocked that I had been with three men in such a short time, yet my own kin seemed to think this was perfectly understandable. Maybe it was, under the circumstances. They didn't blame me for my actions, nor think that I should feel shame.

Values were different here.

But a prize?

Gareth had never thought of me that way. As much as it distressed me, I knew that Sargon saw me as more than a prize to be won. I was the future of this world.

"Grandfather, I am not fragile," I assured him. "I don't faint at the sight of a naked man. Never fear. I come from a long line of strong women."

I averted my eyes. Best he not see my fear.

"Good girl," he said, his voice stronger. "My pride in you grows and grows. Now brace yourself, my dear. I have more bad news."

My heart sank. "What?"

"Tonight is for grieving. The king allows us that. But tomorrow there will be a celebration, a feast. You must prepare yourself and behave with poise and deference." He paused a moment, searching for the right words. "You must respond to his call."

I nodded, not trusting my voice. How could I remain with a man who insisted on complete control of me?

I sensed discomfort in the room. "There's something more?"

Richard cleared his throat. "Jon rode away with Ivan this afternoon."

"No," I cried, sitting on the bed.

"We are a house divided," Grandfather said, a tear rolling down his wrinkled cheek.

When I left the room, I said to Logan, "Can we visit my horse?"

He shook his head and gave an uncomfortable grimace. "I've been given orders to keep you inside the castle at night. You can go to the royal chambers or return to your old room, if you want."

"Can you give me a tour of the castle instead? I'd love to see the kitchens and the public rooms."

He brightened. "And I could take you to my aunt's wardrobe, so you can choose more clothing."

"Let's do that first." Perhaps new garments would cheer me up.

We climbed the third floor stairs and walked a short distance to another room like mine. It appeared to be unoccupied. There was a full-length mirror at one end and a wardrobe beside it.

"Look here," Logan said. He opened the doors.

"Yes!" I clapped my hands.

There were at least ten dresses—simple day dresses in cotton and wool, and at least three stunning dinner gowns in silks and velvets.

My eyes went immediately to a sapphire silk with blue fox trim on the cuffs and hem. The neckline plunged to a deep U in front and the waist was high. It would suit me well.

"Turn around," I said. "I'll try this on."

Logan spun around and I whipped off my rose dress. The sapphire gown popped over my head. It seemed to be made for me, minus the few extra inches on the bottom.

"What do you think?"

Logan turned around, his face growing beet red. "You're beautiful."

I gazed past him and realized the reason for his blushing. A mirror had been right in front of him while I changed, reflecting my every motion.

I blushed. "Help me carry these to my wardrobe."

"Your old room?"

I couldn't bear to return to the room I had shared with Ivan.

"No, the royal suite."

He breathed in relief. "Allow me, m'lady." He swept the dresses into his arms and proceeded through the doorway.

When we finished delivering the dresses, Logan went to my old room and gathered my belongings.

"Thank you," I said when he returned. "Have a good evening."

"You too."

I suspected he'd resume his position outside the door.

For the next two hours, I played dress-up with my new clothes. The two moons were high when I finally settled down to sleep.

Sargon came in late that night. If he was surprised to see me in his bed, he didn't say so. I feigned sleep as he slid beneath the covers beside me. Thankfully, he fell asleep within minutes.

In the morning, he was gone when I woke up.

Chapter 15

Logan came for me after breakfast. Sargon had summoned me to the great hall. I dressed carefully in the new rose day dress—well, new to me anyway—and lost no time making my way to the hall entrance. I stood there in awe for a minute, looking around. The ceiling had to be three stories high and there were four mammoth tables in the room.

Sargon gestured to me. "Ah, Rowena, come here."

He sat at the end of the center table, about ten men flanking him on either side. I recognized a few from the feast at Huel. Most stared, but a few men frowned. This didn't seem a place for me.

"Maybe I should leave," I murmured.

Sargon shook his head. "Come."

Thane gave me an encouraging smile and Rhys nodded once.

Reluctant, I made my way toward Sargon, facing him at a respectable distance.

"We were discussing strategy," he said, his eyes blazing. "I am wondering if you might like to give your opinion on our situation."

A collective gasp emitted from the table. Someone guffawed.

"Silence!" Sargon snapped. "You must hear this. I think it will surprise you. The lady has studied Tacitus." He smiled.

What a sneaky bastard! He was setting me another test. And a tough one.

"Do you have a map?" I said.

He frowned, perplexed. "Map?"

Oh rats! I tried to recall when the first European maps had been created. Not yet in Land's End, it seemed.

I approached the head table, which was already set for dinner.

"Here, I'll demonstrate. Help me clear these plates and spoons to one side."

No one moved.

Then Thane stepped forward and cleared the table. I took the spoons and ran them down the center of the table and off to the right. That would be the river. I took one plate and put it at the top of the river. Another I placed to the bottom right of the river. The third went to the very left of the table, parallel to the second plate.

I went for tankards next. I put three above the highest plate, two to the right of it and another two at the very bottom of the table.

The men gathered around, watching me.

I eyed Sargon. He nodded.

"See here," I began, pointing to my makeshift map, "I've made a drawing of the layout of Land's End. It's not to scale, but it will do for now. This plate is Castle Sargon, this one Huel and this one up here Norland. These spoons represent the river. I don't know what you call it."

"River Sargon," Thane said.

I raised a mocking brow at the king. Of course.

Picking up a spoon to use as a pointer, I said, "These tankards at the top are the fortresses north of Norland. I don't know how many there are, but they ally with Norland, I am told."

"There are four still standing that we know of," Sargon said.

I pointed with the spoon. "Janus has gone to the northern allies to gather troops. His cousin has gone east to meet with the Danes."

"What?"

A rumble of noise rose around the table. I had their attention now.

"He was already preparing for war before you came to Huel, Sire." Sargon frowned. "How do you know this?"

That's when I hesitated. "I was there when he gave the orders."

"At Norland's fortress?"

"Yes," I said, meeting his eyes. "War with Huel, not you."

Sargon smiled, but it was a grim one. "And I can easily guess why."

The testosterone in the room was growing.

I flushed and turned back to my crude map. "Cedric is somewhere down in the south. I don't know how far your island goes. These tankards represent the southern forts. Ivan will join with him there."

"Do you know this for sure?"

I glanced at Thane. "No, but it's what I would do. He can't go to Norland. They hate each other. And Gareth would kill him on sight. Ivan wounded him last week and would have killed him if—" I didn't finish the sentence.

"You know this is true?" Sargon asked, his mouth curled in a scowl.

"I was there," I said.

He cursed.

"So you've got Cedric, Ivan and Jon," I said, ignoring him. "Yes, Jon went with him and Cedric. They're roaring for a fight. Castle Huel you left unattended and it is his by right. I expect they'll head there with the men from the south. I don't know anything about them—or how many they are."

Murmurs coursed around the table.

"Gareth will come south for sure," I said. "He promised the allies a fight and they'll have it. But he needs time to heal. That may take a month or more. He'll want Ivan's head, I know. Will he challenge you?" I shrugged. "It depends."

"He'll know you're here," Sargon said. "He has scouts too."

"Then you have three choices, as I see it." I scanned the men. Hoo boy! Except for Thane, this was a rough crowd. "You can wait for Norland and Huel to engage in battle. Then attack when their troops are decimated. Or you can wait for Norland to attack from the north and hit him from the other side."

"And the third choice?"

I cleared my throat, nervous. "You can sit this out and negotiate with the winner. I expect you would need to release me, as terms. Honor would demand it."

The rumbling grew louder.

"What would you do?" Sargon challenged above the din.

"I would go home if I could, because I want no part of this."

Sargon barked a laugh, then turned to his men. "Now you see of what I speak." He looked as proud as if he had just hatched me himself. "We have our own Minerva, here in the flesh."

I really wished he hadn't used that word. I didn't like the feel of all those eyes on me.

"May I go now, Sire?" I asked.

He waved a hand in the air. "Yes, go."

I moved as gracefully as possible to the door. Thane and Logan followed a few steps behind. I left the hall and walked outside into the sunlight. Leaning against the outer wall, I let out a long sigh, thankful for the wall holding me up.

"You were magnificent back there," Thane said, his voice thick with emotion.

I drew a breath. "Do *you* think it would make any difference if I left?"

He was silent for a long moment. "It might be worse. I think they would be even angrier that we let you go or did not protect you."

I absorbed the warm sunlight. "I thought as much."

So there would be war. Men would get hurt—killed—and there was nothing I could do about it.

Or maybe there was…

"I'd best get back," Thane said, interrupting my thoughts. "Logan, can you…?"

"I'll take her back."

Thane studied me. "I'd like to think if I were Sargon that I would act differently."

"About war?"

"About you. But I greatly fear I wouldn't." His finely shaped lips formed a brilliant smile. "Take care, brave lady."

I watched him leave through the great wooden door and disappear into the castle. A sense of loneliness swept over me. And a yearning.

For Thane.

It occurred to me that I really liked this calm and intelligent man. For the first time, I felt a surge of regret that he wasn't the older brother.

I gave myself a mental shake. Best not to think that way. Best to do what I could.

"Logan, I need my healer's bag. I left it at home. If there's going to be war, I should have all my medicines here so I can help our men when they get wounded." I lifted my chin. "Will you come with me to get it?"

"Of course," he said without hesitation. "It is a good plan."

"We'll have to ride. You've got your weapons, I see."

"I do, m'lady."

"Let's go now. We can be back before anyone notices."

"I think we should tell Sargon," Logan said.

"I wouldn't bother him now when he is working on important plans. Besides, he trusts you completely with my safety."

Logan swelled with pride. Young men and their vanity. This was almost too easy. If I hadn't been acting with such good intentions, I would have hated myself.

Heading to the stables, I saddled Lightning. Logan did the same with his horse.

Soon we were off at a gallop through the gates.

When we reached the river, I turned Lightning north.

"I thought we were going to Castle Huel," Logan called out.

I slowed Lightning and shook my head. "That's not my home. Follow me. It's not far now."

I led him along the river, then to the forest. Up the hill we went, into the clearing where Gareth's tent had been set.

I dismounted and gestured for Logan to do the same. Alarmed and somewhat pale, he dismounted and opened his mouth to argue.

"Come now," I said, taking his hand. "We're almost there."

I guided him along the path to the split oak tree. Then I faced the forest and yanked him through the wall.

Chapter 16

Kendra gasped. "How did you do that?"

"Do what?"

"I saw you walk right through that wall!"

"Oh, that," I said, brushing myself off. "Look, sweetie, not to change the subject, but I don't have a whole lot of time. I—"

"And who is *that*?"

Kendra gaped at Logan, who stood at least a foot taller than her. He, in turn, gazed down at her as though he'd just discovered the meaning of life, the universe and everything that might possibly be in it.

"Damn," I mumbled. "Logan, this is Kendra. Kendra, Logan. Now that we're all introduced, I really have to hustle."

Kendra's eyes widened. "Is he for real?"

"Yes, yes, he's real," I said, trying to speed things along. "He's a cousin of my fiancé."

Kendra stared at me, mouth open. "He's Ivan's cousin?"

"Not Ivan. Sargon." I sighed. "It's complicated."

She crossed her arms. "I can follow."

As a very curious Logan watched us, I sucked in air. "Okay, here goes. I was married to Ivan the first day I got there, but then I got kidnapped. Gareth's land doesn't recognize the laws of Huel, but if you have sex with the same guy three times in one day in this place, you're considered pledged. So I'm kind of married to Gareth too. Except then Ivan got banished—long story, not nice—and now I'm affianced to the king."

"The king?" Kendra frowned. "You're hitched to two of these bozos and engaged to another?"

"Kind of. It wasn't my fault."

"What is this *bozos*?" Logan interjected.

I ignored him. But I had an idea.

"Kendra," I said, lowering my voice, "I have to whip home for my vet bag. It would be easier without Logan along. Can you keep him here? I'll only be twenty minutes."

"Sure, but how?" She could hardly take her eyes off Logan.

"I don't know." I snorted. "Flirt with him or something. But don't let him leave this classroom. Got it?"

She gulped. "Okay."

Paying no attention to Logan's concerned shout, I ran to the desk and grabbed my car keys. As I reached the exit, I heard Kendra say, "So…is that a broadsword on your belt or are you just glad to see me?"

I made it home in five minutes, breaking all sorts of traffic rules. I tore through the front door, raced up to my bedroom and grabbed the leather vet bag. I took a box of supplies from the closet and emptied every container of drugs and serum I could find into that bag. Then I ran to the bathroom for aspirin, ibuprofen and Tylenol 3. Next, I went to the bookshelves in the spare bedroom.

There it was—my book on herbal medicines.

"I hope they have the same herbs in Land's End."

Back in the bedroom, I grabbed a pair of jeans, a T-shirt and one more item. I stuffed everything, along with the book, into a pink designer backpack.

What had ever possessed me to buy pink leather?

I searched for my hiking fanny pack. It held a first aid kit and miscellaneous stuff. Finally, I returned to the closet for my cowboy boots. Yes, there they were! I threw them in a shopping bag.

On the top shelf, I spotted a box that sent a chill through me. It had been a gift from Dad, after the university had been broken into and ransacked one night. Since he knew I often worked late, he wanted me to feel safe, protected. So he'd given me a gun.

I slid the box from the shelf and opened it. The small Derringer pistol gleamed back at me. The only time I'd used it was for the gun lessons Dad insisted on.

There were two bullets beside the gun.

I dumped the contents of the box in my fanny pack.

Hurrying into my office, I booted up the computer and left Debbie an email. "I may be a little longer than I thought. Can you please look after Piper for the rest of the week? Owe you big time. I'm fine and the sex is astounding. Talk soon. Row."

I signed off and shut down the computer.

When I turned around, I let out a startled gasp.

Steve stood in the doorway, looking smug in a dark gray suit and tie.

"How did you get in?" I asked, trembling.

"I still have your key." He held it up. "Where have you been? And why are you wearing that silly dress?"

My mouth opened and then snapped shut. "None of your business."

I pushed past him and stepped into the hall.

"You're going somewhere?" he asked. "Where?"

I marched past him and headed for the bedroom, ignoring his irritating though gorgeous presence. I strapped on the fanny pack, slung the backpack to my shoulder and picked up the shopping bag.

"What did you do to your neck?"

My heart stopped. "What are you talking about?

"Your neck. It's all bruised and purple, like a vampire bit you or something." He moved closer. "Who did that to you?"

I looked in the mirror. Holy crap, he was right.

"I can't talk now," I said, frantic. "I'll call you."

He followed me downstairs. "No, you won't. You're lying!"

"Yes, I will. I promise." I had nearly reached the door.

"When?"

I groaned. "Tuesday."

Tuesday? Why had I said that?

"Row, stop this. Come back here!"

But I was running for the car.

When I reached the classroom, Logan was demonstrating how to wield a broadsword. Those things are heavy, and even with both hands, Kendra couldn't get it above her knees. Logan was showing off, of course, and my star student watched him, smitten.

"Sweetie, I'm so sorry," I said, hurrying toward them, "but we have to leave right now. Steve is right on my tail."

I crossed the room and threw my backpack at Logan.

"Who's Steve," he asked.

"No one."

"Where are you going now?" Kendra demanded.

"I promise I'll tell you everything when I come back."

I shoved my hand through the wall to make sure the portal was still open. "Hurry, Logan."

"Can't I come too?" Kendra wailed.

Without waiting for my reply, Logan grabbed her arm and pulled her through the wall.

Chapter 17

Kendra landed on her knees.

"Oh poop," I said, vexed at this new complication. "Okay. Well, Kendra, here are the rules. You've got to do everything I say. And by the way, I'm your *cousin*. Got that?"

"Cousin," she mumbled. "Where are we?"

I made for the clearing where Gareth's men had been camped—that seemed like months ago—and where Logan and I had left our horses. I'd no sooner turned the corner when a dozen bows were aimed at me.

"Go back!" I cried out.

Men dropped from trees. Two seized Kendra by the arms.

Sargon emerged from the bushes. "Logan, you idiot, you captured a boy."

"I'm not a boy," Kendra yelled. "I'm a Goth."

As she continued to struggle, I scowled at the king. "Sargon, she's a girl. Tell them to stop hurting her."

Frankly, Kendra seemed to be hurting the men more. She kneed one in the crotch and he rolled on the ground. The other man, Rhys, had a bloody nose. She got in a last kick before they backed off.

"Who are these nut-bars, Row?"

I was about to answer her when Sargon grasped my shoulders.

"I'm Sargon," he told Kendra. "This disobedient wench is to be my queen."

I winced. Oh crap, here we go again.

One of the older men stepped forward and peered curiously at Kendra. "So you're a Goth. I heard tell of Goths from way east across the sea."

The crowd was hushed.

"Beyond the island, out of reach of the curse?" Thane asked.

Kendra glanced at me. "What curse?"

"You really don't want to know about that right now." I shook my head. "Trust me."

"Nice armbands," one man said.

"Thanks," Kendra said. "They match my boots. See?"

"Do all Goth's have funny black hair like that?" Sargon asked, disapproval in his voice.

Kendra glared at him, her fists clenched.

"He has rather antiquated ideas about how females should look," I told her.

"I like your hair," Logan said. "And the ring in your eyebrow looks...fierce."

Kendra glowed. "Thanks."

Uh-oh. She was going to be trouble.

Sargon's men made a small camp. They built a fire and tethered the horses close by. After a while, I noticed Kendra chatting with Logan and Rhys by the fire, so when Sargon motioned me toward the trees, I felt it was safe to follow.

I had some explaining to do.

Sargon clenched his teeth. "I don't know whether to kill you or love you to death."

A hysterical sound left my throat. "Do I get a choice?"

Would I ever have a choice?

"Why?" he demanded. "Why did you leave?"

"I went back for my medicine bag. I have antibiotics for your wound now. We would have been back by dusk."

His eyes bore into me. "One of the grooms saw you leave and got Thane, who reported your defection to me. I'll have Logan's hide for this."

"Don't you dare! It's not his fault. You told him not to leave my side and he didn't."

"That boy doesn't stand a chance. You could charm the spots off a leopard." Sargon's mood was lifting.

"How is your wound?"

"Mending."

We glared at each other.

"This Kendra," he said. "She will be a good companion for you?"

"She's my cousin and one of my students."

"Ah, you are a teacher as well as a healer." He pushed me against a tree trunk. "I like that."

"Can you keep the men off her?"

He laughed hoarsely. "From what I have seen, she can do that herself. Don't worry, my love, I will find her a suitable mate."

If she doesn't select one first, I thought.

When we strolled out from the trees, the men were sitting in a circle and Kendra was demonstrating how to do a judo move. She gave one wild yell, then tossed Logan neatly over her back. He landed on the ground with a thump and gazed up at her in adoration.

My worst fears were allayed. Kendra *could* take care of herself.

The ride back to Sargonia was uneventful, except that Kendra rode with Logan, and I had issues about Sargon's wandering hands. Black leather with pink snakeskin will have that affect on some men, and I'd caused a bit of a scene when I put on the cowboy boots.

Kendra said they were "sick," so I guess she approved.

When we got to the castle, it was very late.

Sargon took me straight to his bedchamber.

"I will be gone a short while to make arrangements," he said.

The chair outside the door remained empty.

Still dressed in my rose gown, I was sitting on a chair when he returned an hour later.

"You look thoughtful," he said, undoing his belt and dropping it.

"So," I drawled, "I passed the quick-wit test, the riding test, the strategic-intelligence test and presumably the carnal test. Are we done now? Or do you have any more tests in store for me?"

He burst out laughing, until the tears ran down his face and he had to stop in order to resume breathing.

"Caught, fair lady! I do believe that is the most I have laughed in my entire life. But still, you cannot blame a man for wondering how intelligent his children might be."

I allowed myself a small smile. "No more tests, please. At least not in front of others. You don't have to marry me, you know."

"Don't be absurd. I would *want* my children to be illegitimate?"

"There is that," I said quietly.

So the die was cast.

My heart was heavy. Surely there was some way I could get out of this?

"I should tell you right now that we are being married tomorrow," he said. "That's where I went just now. To see the priest."

I almost swore.

He frowned. "Do not think you can wiggle out of this, Rowena. I fought hard for you. And I plan to keep you." He lifted my chin with one finger. "Mark my words. Woe betides the man who tries to come between us. I'll show no mercy."

I quivered with fear.

"I'm not a bad man, Lady. I am a hard man, though."

"Really?" God, what was I doing?

Sargon threw his tunic on the floor. "Come and see, fair maiden."

He led me to the bed and I allowed him to unfasten my dress. He raised the fabric over my head and tossed it on the chair. Standing behind me, he wrapped his arms around me and cradled my breasts in his hands.

"These," he whispered, "drive me insane. You are so very beautiful."

He kissed my neck and rested his head on my shoulder. His hands continued to play with my breasts.

He released a deep sigh. "I want to take you, but I'm so tired I can't stay upright."

The relief I felt was palpable.

"Lay down," I ordered. "Let me see your wound. Is it hurting?"

He had ridden hard all day with a wound in his side.

"Like the fires of hell," he admitted, lying down on the bed.

I retrieved my bag, took out two pill containers and grabbed a tankard. "Here. Swallow these. One is a painkiller and the other is an antibiotic. It fights infection."

He did as he was told—probably the first time ever—and then settled back, exhausted. Closing his eyes, he said, "I'm sorry."

I crawled onto the other side of the bed and lifted the bandage. The wound looked raw, but not infected.

"Tell me something," I said. "This land is Sargonia. The river is the River Sargon and this is Castle Sargon, so it occurs to me that Sargon must be your family name. Am I right?"

"Yes. So?"

"So you must have another name—a first name. What did your mother call you when she was alive?"

"Wolf," he said in a faint voice. "My name is Wolf."

I nearly rolled off the bed. Before I could think of a fitting response, soft snoring filled the room. After a while, I fell asleep too.

Hours later, I awoke.

Sargon was sitting on the edge of the bed.

"Where's Kendra?" I asked.

"She's fine. I've put her in your old room. Logan is guarding her door."

I shot out of bed. "You *what*?"

"He's completely loyal and very skilled with a sword. He won't let anyone harass her."

"Oh my God." I was pulling on clothes faster than a Florida matron at a designer sale. "Have you no sense?"

"There's nothing to worry about."

"You might as well have put a fox in charge of the hen house."

And I didn't mean Logan.

I was out of the room before Sargon was dressed. Racing down the corridor, I took the stairs up to my old room. Sargon was hot on my tail.

Sure enough, no Logan guarding the door.

Laughter came from the room.

I pounded on the door until my fist hurt. "Kendra Perkins! If you have been corrupting that poor young man, so help me God, I will fry you like a chicken."

The giggles stopped.

"I'm fine," Logan said from behind the door.

"We're both fine," Kendra called out.

"You're both toast," I yelled.

I turned to Sargon, who was looking rather pale. "Crap."

About mid-morning, Kendra skipped into my bedroom.

I hugged her. "Are you okay?"

"I'm fine," she said, her eyes widening at my physical affection.

I studied her face. It was clean of makeup and she looked like a cute little pixie.

"In fact, I'm terrific," she said, smiling.

I drew back and fought for control. "You little idiot. Have you any idea—?" I started to pace. "You can't mess around with guys here. These men are dangerous. They have antiquated rules about honor and stuff. They *kill* people, for Pete's sake."

"I'm not messing around with Logan."

"Look," I said. "Gareth—that's my second husband—was going to burn Castle Huel to the ground if I didn't go back with him. And Ivan would have slaughtered Gareth—and I do mean *slaughtered*—if I hadn't intervened. And Sargon? Don't even get me started on him. You missed the whole moronic duel thing. And believe me, it wasn't pretty."

Kendra shrugged. "Logan told me."

"And about Logan," I was on a roll, "that poor young man is going to consider you *his*, and there's nothing you are going to be able to do about that."

"That's okay. I don't mind."

I glared at her as if she had suddenly sprouted elf ears.

"That's nuts," I said, outraged. "I can't believe this. I'm responsible for you. How old are you anyway?"

"Nineteen next month." Kendra raised her head with pride.

"Well, at least you're of age," I muttered.

She sat on my bed with her knees up and her arms around them.

"Kendra, I'm being serious here. You so much as flirt with another man and Logan will have to challenge him. And that will end badly, I can assure you."

"I won't do anything stupid." Her eyes looked dreamy.

"And another thing..." I was starting to sound like her mother. "That boy is smitten. Have you thought of how it will tear Logan apart when you go?"

A pause. "Go where?"

"Back to Scottsdale, of course."

Another pause.

"But I'm not going back, Rowena. We talked about it last night. Logan says that since the king is his cousin, there won't be any problem. I can be pledged to him—whatever *that* means. I can stay here and help you with the animals."

"The animals..." I must be going insane.

"Yeah. Logan has gone down to speak to Sargon right now, to get it all arranged."

My mouth was dry. "You're going to help me with the animals."

"Sure." Kendra grinned. "And when you have children, I can help with that too. I love kids."

Something in my face must have given me away.

"Oh my God," she said, her gray eyes large. "I get it now. You aren't planning to stay yourself."

I hesitated. "I haven't made up my mind."

"Does Sargon know?"

"Of course not. I'm not a complete idiot. He'd chain me to the bloody wall."

"That's not fair. This whole war thing is all about you. And you're just going to leave?"

I stood with my mouth open. I didn't know what to say, but that was okay because apparently Kendra hadn't finished yet.

"And you accuse *me* of leading Logan on?"

Damn. I hate it when my own words are thrown back at me.

I sucked in air. "Look, Kendra, I don't know what I'm going to do. This place scares the crap out of me." I plunked down on the bed beside her. "You know about the curse?"

She nodded.

"Then you know what I'm up against. My mother was the Earl's daughter and that makes me a bloody heir factory."

"A what?"

"A vessel for producing royal babies."

"Sounds gross when you put it that way." She wrinkled her nose.

This was better. She was getting it.

"My mother left here because she didn't want that sort of life. I don't want it either. I'm a practicing vet, for Pete's sake. I don't want to have a baby here in this primitive place. Did you know fifty percent of women died in childbirth before 1920?"

"But how can you leave? Don't you love him?"

She meant Sargon, of course.

Did I love him? I almost laughed out loud. No, I didn't. I was sure of that.

Sargon intrigued me, it's true. The scientist in me wanted to explore what I was seeing when we were in the throes of passion. He scared the dickens out of me in other ways though.

I didn't like that he had power over my body and restricted my movements. The rational side of me said I needed to do his bidding in order to survive. But I was used to complete freedom—or at least the freedom to choose my own actions. This loss of control was terrifying. I feared the way he so often leapt to violence and seemed to relish it.

"Look at this pragmatically," I said. "If I loved him, I wouldn't be able to leave him. Since I'm thinking of leaving him, that ought to mean something."

"But you didn't leave the guy yesterday when you had the chance," Kendra countered. "You could have stayed in Scottsdale and not gone back through the wall. I think you care a lot more than you admit."

Poor Kendra. I hated to burst her dream of romantic love.

"The thing is, I love Grandfather and I know it would break his heart if I left like my mom did. Especially now that Ivan and Jon have gone. For now, I guess I'm staying for Grandfather. But I don't know what I'm going to do in the long run. Honest. I'll tell you when I figure it out so you can make a choice too." I eyed her with frustration. "But what about you? Don't you have family that will miss you or something?"

Kendra shook her head. "Mom and Dad split years ago. They each have new families and live in Memphis. I hardly ever see them."

I wondered if the Goth phase was a bid to fit in somewhere, anywhere.

"Why were you in the classroom yesterday when I went through the wall?"

"To get my final mark. You were going to hand them out."

"Of course!" I'd forgotten all about end of term. "Ninety-two."

She clapped her hands. "Awesome!"

"Yes, it was top mark." I smiled.

Kendra had such promise, if only she would go back and finish school. Ah well, I didn't want to make her sad.

"Let's talk about something else for a while," I said.

"Okay. How about the feast tonight? What are you wearing?"

Now *that* was a happier subject.

"I've got a choice. Let me show you." I headed for the closet. "Oh, before I do that, I've got something for you. Four things, actually. Two day dresses and two gowns. They're too small for me, but they should fit you fine."

When I pulled the two gowns from the closet, Kendra squealed. One was deep red velvet with black trim. The other was copper brown.

"The red one!" She held it against her. "I've always wanted to dress like they do at those medieval festivals. This is perfect."

"Try it on."

She whipped off her Goth garb—no modesty there—flung the dress over her head and smoothed it down.

What a transformation.

"Kendra, you look amazing."

Her smile was radiant. "It's pretty, isn't it? Do you think Logan will like it?"

I snorted. "He'll have to fight the other men off. It fits you perfectly. You don't even need a bra."

"I'm not stacked like you," she said with good-natured envy.

"Well, there are disadvantages to that, let me tell you."

She raised a brow.

"They get in the way a lot," I said.

"What are you going to wear?"

"This."

I showed her the blue gown with fox trim. I held up a second dress. It was burgundy-cherry silk, with off-the-shoulder sleeves, high gathered waist, a low-cut sweetheart neckline, and an underskirt of silver satin. "Or this. Which do you think?"

"That one." She pointed to the cherry silk. "That's the most beautiful thing I have ever seen."

"I don't usually wear these colors because of my hair. But this one is probably dark enough."

"It'll be awesome with your hair. Honest. I wouldn't lie." She twirled, playing with her skirt.

I put both gowns away in the wardrobe.

Kendra stopped twirling. "Where are we, Row? What is this place? It seems like ancient Britain, but it's not."

"Why do you say that?"

"I would put the culture here as early Saxon. After the Romans. But the clothes are all wrong and so are the fabrics. These dresses are more neoclassical. Or even Renaissance—from centuries later. And these lavender colors? Mauve dye wasn't even available until around 1830." She glanced out the window. "It's more than that, though. The sun isn't right. The colors here are wrong for England."

I nodded. "It's not the Britain we know. It's an alternate world with a different history. They have adopted some Roman customs like cleanliness, thank goodness, and the men wear tunics that look more Roman than dark ages. The church seems a form of early Christianity, but it isn't our world."

"Spooky," she said. "So we haven't so much as gone back in time, but traveled across to some other place."

"As far as I can figure out," I said. "I get dizzy thinking about it."

How my mother must have felt walking into twentieth century America.

"Kendra, we better get our story straight. You're my cousin from my father's side, okay? Let's say your mother was my father's sister. That will explain the different last names."

"Sure, but why are we lying?"

Hard to put into words what I was thinking. "It's a precaution. If you are related to me, it protects you more. Sargon will have an obligation to you that he wouldn't have otherwise."

"Fine with me."

"And you're originally from New York, which is why we don't know all that much about each other. We can catch up on details as we go along."

"Sounds good."

"As a matter of fact..." I was scheming. "Let's test it out now on my Grandfather. I should introduce you to him before anyone else."

"Okay." Kendra stroked her gown. "Can I wear this?"

I smiled. "No, sweetie. That's for tonight. Try on this one here. It's a day dress."

I tossed her a dusty pink muslin. It would be pretty with her hair, not to mention comfortable.

Once she had changed—and I was right, it was great on her—we made our way to Grandfather's room.

He was resting in bed, but stood when we entered. "Rowena, child. I was so worried."

I hugged him. "I'm fine, Grandfather. I went home for my medicine bag. Surely they told you."

"They did, but I worry anyway."

I laughed and stepped back. "Grandfather, this is my cousin Kendra. Kendra, my Grandfather, the Earl of Huel."

Grandfather bowed. "Enchanted."

Kendra had the quickness of mind to nod her head. Then she smiled. "Pleased to meet you."

Dang, I was proud of her.

"Grandfather, Kendra is my cousin and my apprentice. She wanted to come back through the portal with me. I thought it would be okay with you."

"I'm honored. So truly honored to have you in our family. Are you ortho-cousins?"

"Cross-cousins," I replied. "Kendra's mother is my father's sister."

"I'm from New York," Kendra said, grinning.

Grandfather smiled in return. "Then I shall be very pleased to know you better, Kendra from New York."

Well, hot damn. The old man was taken big time. I was inordinately pleased that he had refrained from commenting on her hair and piercings. I was sure he'd hit me up for that story later.

Grandfather turned to me. "Rest assured your cousin will have my complete protection."

I could see that having Kendra around was going to have a sunny effect on the house of Huel.

"Thank you, Grandfather. And you should know in return that Logan has asked for her."

I heard his sharp intake of air. "Already? Does she accept this?"

I rolled my eyes. "You try talking to her. I can't do a thing."

Grandfather sighed and patted the bed. "Sit down, Kendra, and tell me all about New York."

At midday, we took a tour of the stables. We caused a near riot crossing the yard. Everyone stopped and stared. To Kendra's credit, she held her head high and didn't make eye contact.

I caught a sense of mild distress when we entered the stables. I immediately went to the animal in question.

"This mare here is almost ready," I said. "One, maybe two weeks."

Kendra stroked the mare's muzzle. "I thought you were a small animal vet."

I shook my head. "Horses mainly, but I do my time in the university clinic. I love dogs. It will be lambing time here soon. You'll like that—it's quite life-affirming."

"M'lady, can you look at this gelding here?" the old groom asked in a shy voice.

"Sure. Is he limping?"

I knelt down in the straw and felt down the right foreleg.

"Aye, a bit," the groom replied.

"Not a break. Probably just a strain. Keep him off it for a few days. Kendra, feel along here."

A shadow blocked the light. Logan.

He fidgeted, anxious. "Could you come, m'lady? The king has requested your presence immediately. He needs you."

I sprang to my feet. "Of course. Is he unwell, Logan? Is the wound bothering him? You come too, Kendra."

We rushed from the stables and crossed the courtyard.

"He said for you to come quickly," Logan warned.

I hiked up my skirt and ran up the steps to the castle, into the entrance hall and down the corridor that led to his private chamber.

"M'lady!" Logan called behind me.

I burst into the room.

Sargon wasn't there, but I could hear voices around the corner. I dashed into the next room, which served as an office and library, as evidenced by the rows of books on wall high shelves.

Beside Sargon stood Thane and an older man.

I jerked to a halt, confused. "Is it your wound? Has it reopened?"

There was merriment in Sargon's eyes. "You can put your skirt down now, Rowena."

"Oh." I glanced down. "Logan said to come quickly."

"You have something here." He plucked a piece of straw from my hair.

"I was with the mare," I said, panting. "She's due to foal."

Logan and Kendra had followed me into the room.

Thane shifted in discomfort as though he'd rather be somewhere else. He wouldn't even look at me.

"What's going on?" I asked, nervous.

Sargon chuckled, then waved a hand.

The older man stepped forward, holding an open book. "We are gathered here today—"

"Oh crap," I said. "Not now. Not in these clothes."

Sargon's eyes danced as he clasped my hands. "I'm not taking any chances, Rowena. I want this done now, in secret, so that none can interfere. We will celebrate with the others tonight."

And that is how I became the reluctant queen of Land's End, in a rose muslin dress, with straw in my hair and smelling of horse.

Chapter 18

At dusk, I stood in front of the long mirror. The image reflected there was serene and quite unlike the quivering that went on inside me.

The dark cherry dress was stunning, as Kendra had predicted. It clung to me like a second skin. The only thing to mar this regal look was the angry purple bruise that showed on the left side of my neck. I pulled my hair forward to cover it.

Sargon came up behind me and caught my eye in the mirror.

"So beautiful," he murmured. "I have something for you."

A necklace wrapped around my throat, sparkling amethysts embedded in an ornate silver band. A choker, we called it back home.

"This was my mother's," he said, "and her mother's before her."

He kissed my bare shoulder. I trembled. Every time he touched me, a shiver ran up my spine.

"Thank you," I whispered.

He draped his arms around me. "I want to get you something else. A wedding present for you. Can you think of a special gift?"

I put my hand up to my neck. "This is more than enough."

"We'll wait on that then."

I glanced back to the mirror and saw his image reflected there. A full head taller than me, with curly black hair and bright black eyes, he looked like a well-built Roman in his black ceremonial cape with the silver trim. Or perhaps a dashing pirate with that scar running down the side of his face.

"Come. It's time." He led me from the room.

The great hall was rollicking with men. Each table held a hundred and there were four tables within the room. Candles beamed and tankards clinked.

As we made our way to the head table platform, Sargon held my hand and my heart was beating wildly. All eyes were on us and the noisy hall grew quiet. I tried to smile, but I'm sure I looked more like a stricken child. He squeezed my hand.

"Men of Sargonia and Huel." Sargon paused to let the din die down. "Today is a great day for both our lands. I introduce you to your queen, Rowena, daughter of Huel. We were married this day at noon, in the sight of our Lord."

Everyone stared, speechless.

I hardly knew what to do. Then the clapping started. Some men stomped, some yelled and the hall echoed with such a deafening racket that I feared the walls would come down like those of Jericho.

Solemn and resigned, Grandfather stepped forward and kissed my cheek. He gave me a gentle hug, then placed his hand on Sargon's shoulder. "Treat her well."

My husband nodded. "I shall."

Richard, my next nearest male relative, approached the platform. His eyes caught sight of the bruise on my neck and his expression turned grim. When he hugged me, I could hardly breathe.

He moved beside Sargon and held out his hand. Sargon took it and squeezed hard. I think there was some sort of contest going on.

I heard Richard whisper, "You bastard."

Sargon smiled in return—that demented wolf smile of his.

He turned to give one more speech about our lands being united, there being a true blood alliance—yada, yada, yada—and he proclaimed the start of the celebration.

Sargon sat to the right of me, Thane to my left. The latter still seemed unable to look at me. Grandfather and Richard had chosen seats at the very end of the head table, as far away as custom would allow.

Kendra was being well protected by Logan. As a matter of fact, his hands never left her, one arm always around her shoulder or waist. He was making a solid and indisputable demonstration of claim to all the other young men that this girl was his. *Come no further.*

Kendra didn't seem to mind.

Heaps of different meats were carried in on platters—game, poultry and a suckling pig, which I couldn't look at. Other platters of cheese and dried fruit were next to reach the table. Ale flowed freely, our tankards kept filled by the elderly men who did the serving.

We ate our fill and drank too much. At least I did. I was going to have to drink a lot to get through the night.

I flicked a look down the table to see how Kendra was doing. She was sitting on Logan's lap. When she caught my eye, she winked. I smiled back.

Candlelight beamed across the room, creating giant moving

shadows against the stone walls.

I turned to Thane. "I noticed there were several books in the room where we had the ceremony. Are they Sargon's?"

Thane set down his tankard. "My father's. Sargon doesn't have much use for books."

"And *you*? Do you like to read?"

He smiled. "If this castle were to burn, I would rescue the books first, Lady. They have a value to me beyond anything."

Finally, a man who thought of something other than battle and sex.

The ale caused me to be a little devilish.

"You love books that much, Thane? More so than a lover? Then you're no Omar Khayyam."

Puzzled, he frowned. "Explain."

"'Here with a loaf of bread beneath the bough,'" I quoted, "a flask of wine, a book of verse—and thou, beside me singing in the wilderness—and wilderness is paradise enow.'"

He stared at me as if he were seeing me for the first time. The startling blue of his eyes penetrated my own green ones and left me breathless.

"Who is this Omar?"

I was about to answer him when we were interrupted by a young man, who tapped Thane on the shoulder. The page whispered something in Thane's ear. Thane nodded, signaled to Sargon, then turned back to me. "Duty calls. Back soon."

After Sargon and Thane departed, Rhys moved over to keep me company. He was a middle cousin—a great warrior and horseman, I'd heard. We had a grand time talking equine matters. I told him about my training and the riding I had done.

"Come to the stables tomorrow, Lady Rowena," he said. "You can see the mare I'm thinking of breeding."

After dinner, we played a drinking game. Every time someone said a certain word and clinked a glass, we all stood and drank. I didn't quite understand the rules, but I wanted to be a good sport so that the men would think me approachable and not too proud.

So drink I did.

"Drink, you bastard!" I heard one man yell.

When the other man didn't drink enough, or quickly enough, the first fellow threw his ale in the other's face. This caused a minor rumble. The men jumped to their feet, stomping and cheering.

I didn't know whether to cheer for the man with ale on his face or the other one, so I yelled like I was at a WWF match. Beside me, Rhys hollered too.

It was all great fun, except for one thing. I couldn't raise my arm to cheer. The shoulder of my gown had slipped dangerously low and the whole bodice would be down to my waist before long.

I wondered how Kendra was faring.

When I spotted my wayward student, Logan had her in a firm hold, out of the way. He seemed prepared to run if things got rough.

"Okay, that's enough," Sargon said when he returned. Standing behind me, he gathered me in his arms, which was a good thing as I was having trouble staying upright.

"Well, my wanton bride, are you prepared to do your wifely duty?"

I leaned back against his chest and sighed. The drink would make this easier, I hoped.

"Not too much ale, I hope," he said. "I want you wide awake for me. Up you come." He lifted me in his arms as easily as he would a child. "Thane, take care of the celebration."

This time I couldn't meet Thane's gaze.

Sargon carried me out of the room. Raucous cheering followed us down the corridor.

Two candles burned in our bedroom. Sargon must have lit them before returning to the hall.

He set me down by the bed and closed the door.

The rest of the world went away.

With rough hands, Sargon unlaced my dress.

"Don't rip it," I pleaded.

Slowing, he slipped my gown over my head.

I crawled onto the bed, stretching out on my back.

Sargon undressed with haste. I couldn't see his scars in the dim candlelight, just the illumination of his strong body.

Think like a scientist, I willed myself. You are conducting an experiment. Play the part and all will be well.

I reached up with one arm.

"Impatient, aren't you?" he murmured, holding my hand down. "We'll start when I'm ready. I am the king."

He leaned over and kissed me. A light kiss on the mouth, sweet and unexpected. Then he kissed my chin, my neck. His mouth traveled down my body, his lips caressing each breast, my tummy and down further. Then lower still…

I gasped.

"Alright," he growled. "I'm ready."

His body moved over mine. I tried to meet his mouth. There was no small movement this time, no gentle rocking to start, but a hard, determined surge. I was breathless. I rolled beneath him, fighting the vortex that sucked us down into a burning fire.

In blinding color, I saw myself through his eyes—the brightness that he saw, the beauty that left him breathless, a carnal beauty, not untouchable. I saw the relentless loneliness break free, the pure joy released within his soul. I swam to it, joining him, breathing in his air, living in his mind.

His mind.

Dear God, I was in his mind. How could that be? I had one special talent and one only. I could see into the minds of *animals*, not men.

Like the flick of a remote control, the vision was gone.

I hardly noticed when he stopped moving.

"Good God, wife."

Panting, he rolled to one side, but kept his hand cupped on my breast. We lay like that for several moments.

"My wife," he whispered. "My love."

He took me twice more that night, once in the middle and once more at dawn. I guess that made me his in the most traditional laws of the land.

But my mind was absorbed with other things.

Awake in the dark, I relived the visions I had seen, the terror there and the pure animal power.

Sargon slept soundly beside me.

Finally, I slept.

The sun was high when I awoke the following morning. Sargon was dressed and seated on the bed. He stared at me and I tried to smile. Taking my hands, he eased me into his arms.

"It is the most amazing thing," he said. "I understand what the world is all about now. Why we live. Why we breathe. And why we fight. It is not a game. It is as though God has cleared my mind and given me this tremendous wisdom."

His black eyes glowed. "I understand why Huel came willingly to meet his death. I know for certain that Norland will come south to fight me. You are worth it. Our children will be worth it. Nothing else matters."

Sunlight streamed through the window.

Like a Roman god, Sargon stood with his back to the light.

"I must go now," he said. "There are things I must do. Wait dinner for me."

He strode out the doorway.

Chapter 19

When Kendra came to wake me, it was midday. She bounced in and settled at the end of the bed.

"Well?" she said, grinning. "Still in bed, I see. That was quite a night, huh? Spill it!"

How good could I act? We were about to find out.

I rose up on one elbow. "Kendra, you're my student. I shouldn't be telling you gory details of my love life."

Her mouth turned down in disappointment.

I winked at her and she clapped her hands in delight.

"I knew it, Row! I knew you had a hot night. Everyone's talking about it."

"Oh no! What are they saying?" I shot up in bed, forgetting the sheet.

"Man, you really are stacked, aren't you? Lucky king."

I hit her with the pillow.

"Okay." She let out a snort. "They're saying he was at you all night and he can't keep his eyes open now. They say he is walking two feet off the ground. They say if you want something from him, go today 'cause he's in such a good mood."

"Nuts." I held my head. "This is embarrassing. How am I going to face everybody?"

"You'll face them with me. I am your cousin after all. And you really should see Gramps. He's waiting anxiously for you."

So Kendra was calling Grandfather "Gramps" now? I wonder what he thought of that.

"You're right," I said, sliding out of bed. "Hand me the rose dress over there."

"Shouldn't you wear fancier outfits now that you're queen?"

I nearly choked. "Kendra, don't ever call me that. I can't get my head around it. Besides, it scares me half to death."

She swung her feet off the side of the bed. "Gramps has already told me how to behave. I don't have to curtsey because you're my cousin, but I need to nod my head in public."

"That's crazy. Absolutely insane."

"I don't mind. After all, you are a lot older than me."

I reached for the pillow again and she squealed.

"But to answer your question, Kendra, you wear a day dress during the day and the fancy ones for dinner. We don't have that many good ones. This one is my favorite."

My wedding dress. How many women get to wear their wedding dress again?

"It *is* pretty," she said. "That U neckline suits you and the ruffle is cute. I always feel stupid in ruffles."

"Nonsense, sweetie." I ran the brush through my hair several times. "Okay, I'm ready. Oh—just a sec."

I grabbed a package from the pink leather backpack.

We dashed through the corridors. Eyes were on us, but I tried not to think about it. At one point, Kendra grabbed my hand to keep me focused.

Grandfather wasn't in his room, so I deposited the parcel on the table by the window. Looking out, I saw him in the center courtyard, enjoying the sun.

"Grandfather!" I waved.

"Wait there," he called, smiling. "I'll be right there."

It was a sweet reunion.

He held me close and I melted into him. Then he moved away and stared at me. "You are well, child? You have been treated well?" His dear face was stressed with concern.

"Yes, Grandfather. I'm content." I faked a contented smile.

Sitting on the edge of the bed, he sighed. "I swear the two of you will be my death. I worry every moment now. It is so much easier with sons."

"Oh, that reminds me." I picked up the parcel that I had placed on the table. "I have something for you. A present." I handed it to him.

It was a framed photo, taken about ten years ago. I was a teenager with long auburn hair. A woman with shoulder length hair the same color stood behind me, her arms around me. My mother. We were both smiling widely.

I heard Grandfather's sharp intake of air.

"It's mom," I said. "Taken right before she died. See how similar we are?"

Tears welled in his eyes. "What is this image? How did you get this?"

"It's a photo, a true image taken right on the spot. It's something we can do in my land. And I brought it with me when I went back for my medicine bag. I wanted to give it to you."

He could not take his eyes from the photo. After a while, he kissed my forehead. "This is the best thing ever given to me."

Kendra stood on tiptoes, trying to see. "You really are alike."

Grandfather put his arms around both of us. "My two lovely girls."

In the afternoon, Kendra and I kept busy in the kitchen. It was situated at the back of the castle in a separate building for fire reasons. Smart. If the kitchen caught fire, it wouldn't burn the whole castle down.

There was a spacious open fireplace and a large stone oven. Herbs and spices dried on hanging strings. Shelves of preserves lined the walls. Ralph, the kitchen mutt, sprawled on the floor, happily panting. He liked the company—especially the treats we dropped.

Logan arrived. "They said you were here. I couldn't imagine why."

"I'm checking supplies." I smiled. "To see if I could bake a cake."

"A cake?"

"I'm a really good cook," I insisted. "And Kendra can cook too."

His brows scrunched. "But we have a cook."

"I don't mean I can cook like George."

George glanced up from the pot he was stirring. He was a big, sturdy fellow with no hair and a jolly disposition.

"I bake sweet things," I said. "For special. Like fruit pies and sweet cakes."

"And George doesn't mind us here," Kendra said. "He likes us."

There was no question that George liked Kendra. He beamed at her like a benevolent uncle.

Logan looked from me to Kendra and back again. She giggled, and that brought him back to his mission.

"Sargon wants you," he said to me. "In the chamber library."

I left them with George and hurried to the library.

Sargon sat at the table with Thane and Rhys.

I peeked at Thane. He smiled, then looked away.

"Rowena," Sargon said. "You remember the three options that you suggested not two days ago? I've thought of a fourth and I'd like you to hear it."

He leaned back in the chair and linked his hands behind his neck. I shivered, remembering those hands.

"Not another test," I said warily.

He laughed. "Not at all, Lady. I truly want your opinion. I'm thinking to announce a tournament."

"A tournament?" I turned that over in my mind. "You mean with jousting and archery?"

"Yes," Thane said. "We used to have them here each year, before the wars. Men would come from every land to test their skills against each other."

"I thought it might diffuse some tension," Sargon said, "and provide distraction. Men like to win in competition. And they like others watching when they win, especially women. We have two here now."

I sighed. "Keep your friends close and your enemies closer."

"Ha! Exactly."

"She does have a way of seeing clear to the heart of a matter," Thane agreed.

"When?" I asked.

"A fortnight hence," Sargon said. "Enough time to allow for travel. And soon enough to offer a distraction from our present difficulties."

Anything was better than war, in my mind.

"You hope to force alliances," I guessed. "Forge some and pry apart others. A tournament is gutsy. They will be mighty curious and I bet the northern men would welcome it. But it is dangerous, Sire. They could turn on you within your gates."

The wolf grinned. "I'll be ready if they do."

Chapter 20

Next morning at early light, the courtyard was already bustling. Without electric power, the people in this world took advantage of every single minute of daylight. They rose with the sun and worked until the light was gone.

I went to the stables.

"Good morning, Avery," I said to the groom.

He brightened when he saw me. "Good morning, m'lady." He bowed deeply, which was a struggle for his back.

"Avery, please. A nod is sufficient when the king isn't around. I feel rather silly about it actually. We don't bow and curtsey where I come from. Not even for kings."

Well, not for presidents, anyway.

He smiled. "As you please, m'lady. Would you like me to saddle Lightning?"

"Yes, please. Do you know of a wood carver who would take on a small commission for me? A fellow who can do fine work?"

"Of course. I will send for him this morning."

Avery brought Lightning from her stall. I sensed that she already knew I was there. She whinnied as she pranced up to me.

Happy, I inhaled. "How I love the smell of hay and horses. It's like a drug for me, signaling that all is right with the world."

"Me also, m'lady."

We shared a companionable moment.

"Avery, do you know of a quiet field where I could do some training with her? Close by so the king doesn't have a fit."

He held back a chuckle. "Yes."

"And do you have a long rope? Not too heavy, but the longest you can find."

He scratched his chin, baffled by that request. But he was quick to do my bidding. As I mounted Lightning, he returned with a coil of rope.

Avery's directions were good. The field I rode to was south of the castle, but still within sight. And it was unoccupied. The men practiced their weaponry to the east and north, where the grass had been cleared for games.

I don't think I had ever seen a sweeter day in Land's End. The sun shone orange—I was getting used to that—and the air was warm. The seasons followed the same as those at home. I wondered if the days did too, if one day here was the same as one day there.

I dismounted and removed my dress. Under it, I wore the pink t-shirt and my blue jeans. A brilliant move, I thought. No one had known. I folded the dress and set it next to my bag.

Lightning was frisky, so I started her with easy stuff. She needed to learn to obey my commands at an instant. I moved her into a gallop, then signaled her to turn. She seemed confused at first, but after a few tries she caught on. I ran her around in a circle. Man, she was quick. Then I began to teach her the cutting moves.

After a long while, I let her rest. Sliding from her back, I went over to my bag. The rope was inside. I touched it.

"Not as pliable as I'd like." But that could be fixed.

The pounding of hooves signaled an approaching rider.

Sargon rode into the pasture. "What are you doing?"

"I'm training Lightning." I shaded my eyes with a hand. "I can do it best when wearing my riding gear. That's why I came here where no one can see me."

"Not so. The lookouts can see you from the parapet. One came to find me."

Rats. There was no privacy here at all.

"I'm sorry if I alarmed you," I said with a tentative smile. "As you can see, we were taking a break before going back."

Sargon dismounted and took in my ponytail, jeans and t-shirt.

"What is this you are wearing? And where is your dress?"

"I put it over there." I pointed. "Of course, I'll wear it back to the castle. And these are jeans." I patted my legs.

"These jeans you wear are obscene, woman. But I like this soft thing." He touched my T-shirt. "It shows your breasts, but not fully, if you understand me." He moved his hands down to demonstrate and I hissed in air.

"So tell me," I said, trying to be calm. "How is it there are no women here and yet you know so much?"

He didn't pretend to misinterpret me. "There has always been a shortage of women in this land because so many died during childbirth. Until the war four years ago, there were some women here. The youngest would have been your mother's age. Older women can teach a lot."

Ah, so that was it. How nice for the older women to have young lovers. I was careful not to ask what had become of these women. Whenever I had shown curiosity about this, no one would speak of it.

"Is this writing on your shirt?" he asked.

I nodded.

"What does it say?"

I hesitated. "Cowgirls do it sitting astride."

"What does that mean? What is a cowgirl?"

Without waiting for an answer, his hands moved down to my bottom. He drew me closer and his mouth found mine. I clung to him and we were off on that raging sea of longing, riding the rolling surf until he pulled back and cursed.

"We can't do this here. They can see from the battlements."

I trembled. Amazing how my mind got muddled so quickly.

He went to get my dress. Silent, I slipped into it and we mounted our horses and headed for the castle.

"I don't mind you coming here," Sargon said, "but tell me when you intend to, and go no further. I'll make sure someone keeps an eye on you from afar."

"Thank you."

Funny how I felt the need to thank him for giving me any freedom at all. This irked me.

"You wanted to give me a wedding present," I reminded him. "I've thought of something."

"Tell me."

"I'd like a puppy. At home, I have a little white terrier. I miss him. Also, I had to leave Duke, an Irish wolfhound, behind at Huel."

Sargon's expression shifted to rage and he almost growled. "I hate dogs. I won't have them in the castle. Pick something else."

I was so shocked, I could scarcely breathe. It was as if the sun had suddenly turned to gray stone and had no warmth at all.

Was it the word *wolfhound*? Had that been the trigger?

Obviously, he didn't know about Ralph, the kitchen mutt. But then, what reason would Sargon ever have to visit the kitchen?

It seemed safer to change the subject.

"Well, perhaps I could have a new saddle," I said. "One that fits me well and is more styled the way I am accustomed."

He nodded, satisfied. "That is a perfect gift. I will speak to Avery immediately."

He eyed me with curiosity. "Only one in a million women—if

that—would ever ask for a saddle. How different you are."

Damn straight, I thought.

At least I had gotten my way on one thing. I could train in the field and hopefully regain my former skills as a horsewoman.

Sargon led me to the stables.

"This interlude has interrupted my own training," he said before leaving. "I'll join you at dinner."

As soon as he was gone, Avery arrived with a message. "I have the carver here, m'lady. You can meet with him in the back."

"Thank you."

He introduced me to an elderly man with no front teeth. The man gave me a shy nod and I explained what I wanted. He seemed quite bright and anxious to get started, but I wondered if he would get the instructions right. He didn't write anything down. He couldn't. Most of these men were illiterate.

I thought about the library full of books and Thane's love of them.

"What would you like in a saddle?" Avery asked.

I explained the difficulty of getting up and down, and the fact that a horn—I described it—would be of much help as I would have something to hold on to.

When I got back to the castle, I went straight to the royal suite. I heard a sound in the room next door, so I peeked around the corner.

Thane sat in a chair, reading a book.

For some reason, my heart felt lighter.

"Hello," I said. "May I come in?"

He jumped to his feet. "Of course, Lady."

There was an awkward silence.

I turned to the shelf beside me and read the book spines.

Thane watched me, saying nothing.

"What are you reading?" I asked.

"It's about the Gods."

When I looked up, he passed the book to me.

"You have Hesiod's *Theogony*." I opened it. "But it's in Greek."

He nodded.

"I don't read Greek," I said with a sad sigh.

"You don't?"

"No. Only English, Spanish and some Latin. I can recognize ancient Greek when I see it, but that's about it."

"You read three languages?"

"But not Greek."

He smiled and it reached his eyes, which were that startling blue—so unlike his brother's.

"Most of the books in the library are Greek," he said. "I can teach you."

"Would you?" I could hardly contain my excitement.

"It can be my wedding present to you."

"When can we start?"

He thought a moment. "After the tournament."

I must have looked disappointed because Thane hurried to explain. "I don't think Sargon would appreciate me taking your time in these early days. It would not be...wise."

I felt that little heart tug again. There was always something dark about my time with Sargon. Yet, here in the library, I felt quiet joy.

I touched his hand. "Thank you."

I heard his sharp intake of breath. He pulled his hand away and stepped back. I felt an inexplicable loss and turned away, embarrassed.

Why did I long for Thane's company so much?

"At first, I thought you looked exactly like your brother," I said. "But your eyes are different."

"I have my mother's eyes."

"So your father's eyes were black?"

"No, blue as well, but lighter."

I was struck still. Very carefully, I worded the next bit.

"Did you both have the same parents?"

"Yes. Mother died when I was born. Father never quite got over that, I think. He loved her dearly."

"That's sad. I am so sorry."

A young page knocked on the open door.

"Excuse me, Lady," Thane said.

My mind was elsewhere.

Sargon's mother had blue eyes. So did his father. Yet Sargon had black eyes. This was so improbable it could only mean one thing. But they wouldn't know that here. They wouldn't know about genetics. Or that it was very rare for two blue-eyed parents to produce a child with black eyes.

Sargon had inherited his father's eyes, all right.

And I'd bet my last dollar his father hadn't been the king.

Chapter 21

The next morning, Richard found me in the stables.

"Rowena, can you come now? Your grandfather wants you."

"Of course," I said. "Kendra?"

She shook her head. "I'm meeting Logan for training, so I'll see you at dinner. I'm showing him how to fight with sticks."

I grinned and followed Richard into the castle.

"Cedric is here," he said. "He's come to meet with the king to officially establish his claim to Huel Castle. Or so he says."

This was disturbing news. Grandfather wasn't dead yet, so wasn't this premature? I wondered if the eldest male in the family automatically took control when the existing earl could no longer fight with his men.

Grandfather met me at the door to his room. He wasn't smiling.

"Go speak with Cedric," he told me. "I'll be in the courtyard."

Cedric was sitting on the chair by the window. His feet were propped up on the bed. I could see him clearly now, unlike that first time in the church when things were so rushed. He appeared to be about thirty, although his face seemed older. His tunic was dusty from riding. A Roman coin hung from a silver chain around his neck. His arms were huge, banded with muscle, and the gold hair on them bothered me.

So this was my eldest second cousin—or was it third?

"Ah, cousin," he said in a tenor voice. "Come sit here on the bed."

I didn't see any good reason not to. "Choose your battles" is my motto.

Cedric leaned forward. "So my worthless brother lost the most important battle of his life and now you sleep with Sargon. How does he treat you?"

Before I could answer, he was on his feet. He yanked my hair back and stared at my throat. "Richard was right. I see that it is true then.

Sargon is part wolf."

I pulled back, startled.

Cedric's red-gold hair swung in front of me. "Did you not know that some beasts bite the female, to hold her in place for mating?"

A cold wind crept down my spine.

"It is rumored that Sargon's mother was a witch, who slept with wolves," Cedric said, sneering. "Or at least one wolf-god. And so she called him Wolf."

"Take care," I warned. "Do not try to say this to him."

He snorted. "I'm not a fool." He pointed to the bruise. "This angers me. Do you want me to do something about it? I will if you say so."

"No!" I cried.

I hardly knew what to think. Cedric was protecting me?

He frowned. "You know I have been preparing for war. I am pondering which path to take. The old man is finished. He'll stay here with you and young Richard for now. I have command of Huel and all the men. We'll attend this tournament. Then I will decide my course of action."

"Is Ivan with you?"

"Yes and no." He gave me an enigmatic smile. "Your ties with him are severed now in any case."

I didn't know what to say.

"How interesting this is." He reached out. "Your hair is a darker red than mine and your eyes a lighter green. We look like kin, that is certain. Distant cousins, which makes it acceptable, although I hardly care about that. If you were not a prize for the king, then you would come under my protection. I wonder if you are worth it."

Outraged, I clambered to my feet. I was halfway across the room when he caught my shoulders. Then he did the strangest thing. He leaned in close to my cheek and inhaled deeply.

"Jon was right. You *do* smell good. I wonder how you taste."

He put his mouth to mine.

I trembled, but he surprised me. His lips were gentle against mine. I relaxed. That startled him, but he drew me closer and kissed me deeply. So help me, I responded with eagerness. That lit a fuse in him. He grabbed me and I felt him grow hard against me.

I shoved him away.

Wow, oh wow. What was this?

"Great Thor, you are astonishing." His voice was hoarse. "You're ready for it even now. Does the king not keep you satisfied? By God, I would."

I blushed. "Stay back."

"I begin to see what all the fuss is about. And I love a fight."

I fled through the door. His laughter followed me.

I hurried along the corridor, down the stairs and into the Royal suite. Slamming the door, I leaned against it, panting.

My jeans were folded in the bottom of the wardrobe. I slipped them on under my dress, pulled on my boots and scurried to the stables. Lightning would save my sanity, as she had before.

Avery saddled my horse and I mounted with haste. I took the gate at a gallop and reached my secret field in minutes.

But I longed to go further, out of reach.

I turned Lightning west, toward the coastline where Sargon first took me. We traveled this route at a slower pace since the ground was unknown to me. I wasn't taking chances with my feisty filly.

We approached the cliff. The midnight sea rose up in the distance, meeting the azure sky. I dismounted, walked closer to the edge and listened to the surf roar. It matched my thoughts.

What was wrong with me? Why was I responding this way to every man who kissed me? Or was it just these powerful men who seemed to live on testosterone, the men of Land's End?

I was pretty sure I loathed Cedric. And yet the electricity that had coursed between us was like wildfire. What did this make me?

Some names came to mind that made me blush.

Thing is, I hadn't responded to Steve this way. Or any previous boyfriends. Sex had been nice, but not fundamentally necessary. Not an essential like eating and breathing, the way it was here.

I might as well admit to being a bad girl and be done with it, I thought bitterly. What point is there in denying your true nature—once you know what that is?

Cedric's words were clear in my mind.

"Sargon's mother was a witch, who slept with wolves."

Could Sargon be part wolf? Was such a thing possible?

It would explain his aversion to dogs. It would explain why I could see into his mind when he made love to me. I can touch the minds of animals.

There *was* magic in this world, heaven knows. Magic that I couldn't begin to understand.

The wind raced through my hair as I looked out to sea. I embraced the raw energy, let it coarse right though me.

In the distance, I thought I saw a ship. Now *that* was different. I squinted. The ship sailed behind a wave and out of sight.

"Time to go back," I murmured. "Before they came looking for me."

Lightning was ready. We rode like the furies. When the castle was in sight, I slowed my horse and she trotted daintily through the gates—like the lady she is. I, on the other hand, looked wild and windblown, like the creature I had become.

Much later, Sargon returned to the suite and we dressed for dinner. I wasn't looking forward to it. Cedric was still here and that meant that we would dine *en famille*, with both his relatives and mine at the table. This meant dressing with care.

I removed the sapphire gown from the wardrobe and slipped it on in front of the mirror. It was simply beautiful.

"Good God, wife, you take my breath away."

Sargon wrapped his arms around me and I tried to relax.

"I like this one too," I said. "It is a lovely gown."

He kissed my hair. "That color against your skin is most alluring. I'll need to keep you close tonight."

Through the window I could see the sun setting on the horizon.

"Why do you have your chambers on the main floor, Wolf? It seems unusual."

"Come," he said. "I'll show you."

Guiding me to the library next door, he pushed aside a set of shelves on wheels and revealed a hidden door. "I love that I can enter and exit without anyone knowing."

We stepped through the doorway, which led outside to a private courtyard hidden by a flying buttress.

"I come out here to think at night," he said. "My private shower is over there. You may use it. And these are not the only suites I have. When the tournament starts, we'll move to the tower."

I studied the side of the castle up to the battlements. "I was thinking that this castle is in the wrong location."

Sargon's brow raised in question. "Why is that?"

"If I were building a castle, I would locate one side against a seawall. That way I could see the enemy coming by sea and also have a way to escape if attacked."

He frowned. "What makes you think I would ever abandon this place if attacked?"

Oh yeah, there was that. This man would fight to the death rather than run.

"But what you say makes sense," he admitted. "I think this fortress was built before the threat of attack by sea. We've never had a sea advance. It's always been by land."

We walked back through the hidden door.

"I shall think about this," he said. "Maybe we should plan for a lookout tower by the coast."

I thought of the ship I'd seen, the one I couldn't tell him about lest I revealed my ride to the coast.

"If so, do it soon. Who knows what we may face shortly."

We entered the great hall at dusk and gathered at the center table. Rhys and Thane were already seated. Thane sat many seats away from mine, I noticed with disappointment. When he glanced my way, a hot flush swept through me.

"You look ethereally beautiful, my child," Grandfather said.

"Thank you." We hugged and he kissed my hand.

Kendra danced in, wearing the golden-brown dress. Logan was at her side. He still had the duty of bodyguard and took it most seriously. A pry bar between them would do no good.

Richard entered the hall and sat down beside Logan and Kendra. The three of them seemed fast friends.

Kendra smiled at me and gave Cedric a wary nod.

As my eldest cousin and guest of honor, he was placed next to me at the table. It was disturbing. I was aware of his every move next to me all night. I was also conscious of his intense stare.

I wondered if Sargon was aware of this too.

Our meal was the usual roasted meat and flatbread. I had introduced vegetables like asparagus to our cook and was planning more additions to the kitchen in the future.

Candlelight glowed and the ale flowed freely.

Partway through our meal, Cedric nudged me. "You ride like a Valkyrie racing across the sky to Valhalla."

I gasped. "You saw me?"

His smile was cryptic. "When will you realize that I see everything about you, Rowena?"

What exactly did he mean by that?

I scanned his face and he met me gaze for gaze.

Zap!

His eyes drifted lower, deliberately slow, so that I would see him linger on my curves.

My face grew warm and I lowered my eyes.

Talk around the table turned to the tournament and which contenders were likely to make the final cut. This led to many heated opinions.

I found my mind drifting.

During the discussion, Cedric leaned forward and his arm brushed mine. I sprang back. Shortly after, his thigh pressed against mine below the table and I could feel heat raging inside me.

When there was a lull in the conversation, Cedric turned to Sargon. "So what do you have planned as grand prize for the Champion of the tournament, Sire—a tryst with the queen?"

There was a communal gasp in the room. Richard and Thane cursed, while Kendra went chalk white.

I thought my heart had stopped.

Grandfather spoke first. "Cedric, you go too far."

I glanced at Sargon. His finger slowly traced the rim of his tankard. His expression was forbidding yet tempered.

"I would not joke about such things," he said coldly. "You would not care to share your brother's fate."

"My apologies, Sire—and to you, fair cousin," Cedric said in a smooth voice. "No offense was intended. I merely sought to point out the greatest prize in the kingdom."

I wanted to leave the room and would have given anything to disappear right then. I could not look anywhere but at my plate.

The room defused, but the atmosphere was poisoned by animosity. A messenger came to the door to speak with Sargon, who rose and signaled for Thane and Rhys. They talked briefly, standing out of earshot.

"Forgive me," Cedric said to me.

"Why do you do that?" I whispered.

A pause. "I don't really know. I find it amusing. Don't you?"

I gawked at him. "You must have a death wish."

He laughed.

Sargon crossed the room. "They have discovered a scout, my queen. I must go now and could be away until the morrow."

I nodded.

When they left, I excused myself and rushed to the royal suite.

The night was hot and there were no moons in the sky as I slept on top of the bed sheets, on my side with one knee up.

I had a luscious dream.

I felt a presence in the room, but my eyes were heavy from too much ale and would not open. A shadowed figure joined me, curling into my back. A gentle touch and soft stroking between my legs made a sigh escape my throat.

Someone breathed in my ear and a tenor voice whispered, "Shhh...enjoy this."

Something hot and hard entered me, sliding, moving ever so slowly, filling me, while a warm hand fondled my breast.

My dream lover moved out of me.

"No..." I pleaded.

He returned and I sought to take him deeper. Now I was moving with him in a sweet, melodic rhythm, breathless, feeling his breath at my ear. I wanted more. When I bucked against him, I heard soft laughter. I grabbed his hand and bit it hard to keep from crying out. For one brief moment, he held me tight and then my dream faded as I slipped into a deeper sleep.

When I awoke, the shutters were open. The sun streamed in, glinting off something near my eyes.

A Roman coin was in my hand.

Chapter 22

I was still frozen to the bed when Kendra bounced in, looking pretty in light blue muslin. She plunked down beside me.

"Are you alright, Row? You look sick."

I shook my head.

"Ah! You're missing him, aren't you? He hasn't come back yet."

I let out a squeak, then a few strangled chortles, which was not bad considering the rampant hysteria I fought to control.

Inhale deeply. One…two…

"Row, what's wrong? Did you have a bad dream?"

That set me off. I laughed like a manic fool, gasping as tears rolled down my face.

"Sweetie, you don't know how funny you are," I said between breaths.

Kendra gave me a wounded pout. "I worry about you. This is all pretty heavy stuff we've been going through. Especially you. I never had an older sister. Or even much of a mother."

"Oh, honey," I said, hugging her. "If I could have any sister in the world, she would be you. I already feel prouder of you than if I had hatched you myself. And what you have done for Grandfather—God bless you for that."

"It's so nice to have a family now. How can you imagine I would ever leave this for Scottsdale?"

I frowned. "Kendra, do you have a cell phone?"

"Sure, in my fanny pack. I didn't even think to try it here."

"Go get it, will you? And don't let a soul see it."

She was off.

I looked at the coin still in my hand. Last night...I'd swear it was a dream. A rather daring dream, but all the same, not real.

Except for the coin, which was very real.

"So let's look at this pragmatically," I murmured.

There was only one man who wore a coin around his neck. That coin was in my hand. I could think of only two ways that could be possible. One—last night was real and *not* a dream. Or two—there was magic happening here and Cedric was messing with my head.

I shuddered with guilt.

But if I had thought it was a dream while it was really happening, did that exonerate me? If only I could talk to Thane about it.

That caught me up short. Why Thane?

Kendra entered with the cell phone. "You won't believe this, but I have a signal."

"Give it to me. I need to leave a message for my Dad or he'll be worried sick. Cross your fingers."

I punched numbers and was astounded to hear the connection go through. The answering machine picked up.

"Hi, Dad," I said. "It's Red. You won't believe this. I've found Mom's family in…uh, England. They want me to come over, so I'm hopping a plane tonight. I'm so happy. I'll tell you all about it next week when I get back. Love you. Bye." I flipped the phone shut.

Kendra was quiet.

Sadness overwhelmed me. I missed my dad.

"That should keep him satisfied for another week," I said.

When would I see him next?

I gave her back the cell phone. "Amazing that this worked here. We must be connected to our world somehow. Thank you for that. It means a lot to me. What about you?"

Kendra shrugged. "There's nobody I need to call."

My mind took an unexpected detour.

"Kendra, are you using birth control?"

Her head jerked. "I'm on that new patch, but it's nearly due. And I'm going to be desperate in a week for you-know-what."

"I'm not on any birth control," I said, sighing. "I get migraines on the pill, so we always used—you know."

"Not much chance of *that* here."

"I know. However, I was thinking we should make a quick trip to the pharmacy on campus to load up on monthly supplies."

"That's a good idea, Row. How soon?"

"Let's go now." I chewed my bottom lip. "The men are still out somewhere with this scout person. I don't think they'd miss us. Empty your backpack and I'll empty mine. We can load up on the other side. Oh—and you might want to wear your Goth gear for riding. I'll wear jeans underneath my skirt." I paused. "I forgot to ask. Can you ride?"

"A horse?" Kendra grinned. "How can you live in Arizona and not ride?"

We had no trouble leaving on horseback. We were two ladies out for a morning ride together. It was a typical day in Land's End. The sun shone brightly and the temperature was near perfect. We rode hard to the river and made it by midday.

I showed Kendra the landmarks and how to find her way to the split tree so she would be able to find her own way back—if something were to happen to me.

This was her first time going back through the wall. I think she was nervous. I gave her a big smile, took her hand in mine and through the wall we went.

There were no lights on in the classroom. Classes were over until next fall. I pulled the ivory muslin dress over my head and put on the pink T-shirt.

Kendra rushed to her locker in the hall and worked the combination of the lock. "I have my debit card in here. I can take five hundred out at once."

"Good idea," I said, stuffing the dress in her locker. "I didn't think to bring mine. And who knows when we'll get back here again."

Or when they'll cancel our cards, I thought, or clean out her locker. But I saw no reason to worry her about that right now. We had enough to deal with.

The campus pharmacy was like one great big candy store. So many things I had not seen in weeks. We picked up several packages of tampons, enough for months. I bought a good hairbrush, some hair combs and elastics. Kendra got her birth control and I snuck in some chocolate.

I used the payphone to call Debbie at the clinic. She didn't answer, so I left a message. I left the same story that I gave my Dad and asked her to keep Piper for another two weeks. I'd owe her big-time.

"Hey, Row, where have you been?"

I turned and forced a smile. "Hi, Ted."

Ted was the program head for veterinary medicine. "I've been trying to get you for days. I'm planning a meeting for next Wednesday at nine, about the new regulations for lab safety. Can you make it?"

"I think so," I said.

"Good. I see you've been riding."

I followed his eyes to my boots. Uh-oh. It was a darn good thing I'd taken off the dress.

"Got your horse parked outside?" he quipped.

I smiled again. "Pretty close by."

He squinted at my T-shirt. "'Cowgirls do it sitting astride.'" He chuckled. "Do they really?"

I blushed. "See you Wednesday."

"What a hunk," Kendra said after Ted had left. "And he really likes you."

"He's married. And a little too thin for me."

Interesting how my tastes had changed.

"Come on, Kendra, let's get going before we run into anyone else."

After she paid for the items, we hurried back to B wing. I got my dress out of her locker and she grabbed all her own clothing. A black sweater, a long black T-shirt and gladiator sandals, black of course.

We dashed to the classroom where I took off the pink T-shirt and donned the dress. Meanwhile, Kendra stuffed both our backpacks with all the pharmacy purchases.

"What about the plastic bags?" she asked.

"Better leave them. We want as little trace to this world as possible."

I stuffed my shirt in the backpack and stood. We stared at each other for a moment.

"You don't have to go back with me," I said softly.

"*You're* going back."

"You have a choice. I don't. Gareth will come through the wall if I don't go back. He's done it before."

She shook her head. "I'm going with you."

I smiled and took her hand.

The orange sun shone just as brightly. The valley was a verdant green below.

"How beautiful it is here," Kendra said in awe. "It looks like a painting by that guy. What's his name—the one who does the amazing things with light?"

"It's truly is a magical world," I admitted, "which is fine if you happen to like magic."

I called to Lightning and both horses trotted toward us. We fastened our backpacks to the saddles and walked the horses to the clearing to mount.

Without warning, men dropped from the trees and surrounded us. Kendra was beyond my reach, a dagger to her neck.

I counted six rough men of varying ages. They all were armed and their eyes gleamed with hunger. I looked for their leader to see if he might be the bargaining type. He wasn't. When I saw his leering gaze, my hopes fell.

"What have we here?" he sneered. "A comely lass dropped from the skies into my lap. 'Tis my lucky day."

A tall, thin man stepped forward. "She's Sargon's new queen. I've heard of her."

"The wife of Sargon?" Their leader laughed. "Oh, this is quite a treat." He held a dagger to my chin. "Your name, Lady?"

I willed myself not to shake. "Rowena."

He scowled at Kendra. "And the queen's page. How old are you?"

"Fifteen, sir." Kendra said.

Her eyes shot to me and I nodded my relief. They took her for a boy.

"You must be the youngest in the land," he said. "Boy, you will get a show tonight. An education."

Kendra gasped.

No, I sought to tell her with my eyes. Your martial arts can do nothing against so many. Don't interfere. There's nothing you can do.

Kendra cleared her throat. "Sir, the king will pay a handsome ransom for her."

"I'm sure he would," the brigand said with humor. "But I don't intend to collect it."

Oh, no. I felt the blood drain from my face.

"Have you no honor?" I asked, breathless.

"Have I no honor, she asks." He laughed and eyed me. "Lady, I have nothing. *Nothing*. Except a huge price upon my head put there by Sargon. So tell me now why I should not have my fun with you. He'll kill me either way."

I forced myself to look at the man who would decide my fate. It was not a pleasant sight. He was of average height, stocky, with stringy brown hair, an unkempt beard, black teeth and a crazy smile. His clothes were covered in dirt and he smelled as if he hadn't bathed in weeks. They all did.

The Derringer was in my fanny pack. I had two sure shots. If I could get it out, I could shoot at least one of them. I wouldn't miss. The pistol would be like magic to them. Maybe they'd back off.

I needed to get my gun out, but how?

"Shall I brand her first?" the leader asked his men. "How 'bout I make her mine, boys? We'll give her the stamp of the band, right on her pretty arm here."

When he yanked the left sleeve of my dress off my shoulder, I panicked. Especially when I saw that all the men had a triangle brand on their upper arms.

A small, wiry man poked the fire with an iron.

Over my shoulder, I saw Kendra tiptoe toward the trees. She blended in with ease. Thank God. Stay there, I willed.

I tried to work the zipper of the fanny pack with one hand, without being obvious.

"We've just done Benny, our new boy, and he stood it. Let's see how a queen can take it."

The iron was passed. Struggling, I screamed when the searing brand touched my arm. I let out one scream, then I bit my lip and squeezed my eyes shut.

"Not bad, boys. Not bad. Pretty steadfast for a wench. She'll last a while, I think."

My shoulder screamed in agony from third degree burns.

"Shall we see what the king enjoys every night?"

The dagger cut my front lacings and nicked my skin. He grabbed my dress and ripped the bodice to my waist. I closed my eyes, but held my head high. The searing pain had made me strong.

I would *not* sob or beg.

What I needed was a distraction. Something to cause them to look away so I could get at the gun.

I heard a crack of thunder. Then another. The sky darkened, the clouds rumbled. A spear of lightning hit the ground, not fifty paces from the forest edge.

The men cried out and backed away.

Pounding hooves took us all by surprise. I was thrust aside. Falling to my knees, I rolled out of reach, then leaned on my elbows so I could better see.

The Derringer was in my hand.

The clearing was full of men on horseback. I couldn't believe my eyes. Huel men, according to their colors, but I did not know them. They numbered more than a dozen.

The sky split with blinding lightning and thunder roared again.

"The Dark Lord!" someone shouted.

Cedric materialized on a huge palomino. His sword was out. His eyes blazed brilliant green.

"Ah, Willen, you old villain. You have my cousin there."

Willen looked ashen. "Your cousin, Sire? I thought she was the consort of the king."

"And my kin," he said coldly. "My cousin's daughter, under my protection. I see you took the branding iron to her."

"Just a little fun, Sire," Willen said in a strangled voice. "She is not badly hurt."

"And it looks to me as if you were about to rape her."

There was deadly silence now.

"Do you know what Sargon would do to you if he were here?"

Cedric asked, his eyes narrowing.

The man was tongue-tied.

Cedric snorted. "Probably the same as I."

The sword flashed and the brigand's head was severed in one clean cut. I screamed as it rolled across the ground, the eyes still open. Shouts, clangs and cries, the valley filled with horrid sounds amid the rolling thunder. I hid my face and willed the horses to stay back, afraid they'd trample me.

The thunder stopped. A gentle rain was falling now.

Cedric stood over me. "Rowena, come. It's over." He held out his hand, his tunic bloody and his face dirty with sweat and grime.

I got to my knees. One hand held my dress together, while the other deftly dropped the Derringer into my fanny pack.

On my feet, I looked around. The place was a blood bath. There were severed body parts everywhere. Unperturbed, Cedric's men held dripping swords and daggers.

"Kendra!" I called in a panic. "Kendra, where are you?"

"Here." She swung down from a tree.

I ran to her and she clung to me fiercely.

Cedric nodded to her. "Come, ladies. We must leave. It's not safe here." To his men, he said, "Take their weapons and any spoils you want. Go quickly."

He helped me atop Lightning.

"How did you know to find me?" I asked. "And *where* to find me?"

He looked at me sideways. "I was nearby. I followed your fear." He raised a brow. "Where is the Roman coin?"

I hissed in a breath.

So it was true. I hadn't been dreaming. My dream lover had been Cedric.

"I put it in my pocket," I said. "Here, next to me."

"Smart girl. Keep it with you always."

We rode with vigilance out of the forest.

"We go to Huel," Cedric said. "The way back to Sargonia is not safe tonight. That wasn't all of Willen's band."

"Thank you."

With a nod, he kicked the palomino and we galloped away.

Chapter 23

At the castle, I hurried to my old room, with Kendra at my side. I threw myself onto the bed and willed my heart to slow.

"Let me see your burn," Kendra said.

"It hurts like hellfire," I said. "More now than when I was scared."

She bared my shoulder. "I've got antibiotic cream in my backpack."

"Not yet." I groaned. "I don't think I could stand it."

Kendra sat on the bed and crossed her legs. "You were so brave. I could never have acted as you did." Tears ran down her face.

"It's only a burn," I assured her.

"No, I mean what that man was going to do to you."

"Oh, that." I winced.

We both knew there was a good chance I wouldn't have survived the night.

"Good thing Cedric showed up when he did," I said.

Talk about understatement.

Kendra wiped her nose on her sleeve. "I wonder how he knew."

I wondered that myself.

"Did you notice his men and the horses, Row?" Her eyes flared. "I had a good chance to see them from the tree. They looked as though they were all twins. The horses too."

"I don't know these men," I said. "They must be from the south."

"It's funny we didn't hear their approach."

Not so funny to me, since I had been rather distracted.

After a while, Cedric appeared in the doorway with two goblets. "I have something for your pain," he said to me. To Kendra, he ordered, "Leave."

She looked at me, alarmed.

"It's okay. Cedric, can she have the room next door?"

He nodded once.

Kendra leaned over and kissed my cheek. "Call if you need me." She left with reluctance.

Cedric handed me a goblet. "Sip this. It will dull the searing."

"Oh, good," I said, gulping the whole thing down. It tasted like sweet mead. "Bring three more of these and I'll be fine."

"You hide it well," he said with approval.

"Stick a fork in me. I'm done," I quipped, settling back on the bed.

He strode to the door, closed it and watched me with hooded eyes. As he sipped at his goblet, I noted that he had washed and changed.

"What?" I said. "You never seen a woman nearly raped to death before?"

His expression shadowed. "I've seen worse."

I gulped. "I'm sorry. I'm shaking inside really. And trying to cover it by being flippant. You don't want to know how I really feel."

He took my hand and kissed the palm. "You are safe here now with me."

This was a new Cedric—one I hadn't seen before. One I kind of liked.

"Cedric, why are they so wary of you?"

His brow arched.

"There in the forest," I explained. "Everybody. Ivan—even Richard." My mouth felt numb. I was having trouble pronouncing the words.

"They fear me because I practice the dark arts."

Ah, hoo boy! The jigsaw pieces fell into place. Things said by others repeated in my mind.

"The Dark Lord!"

"Sometimes I think he has made a pact with the devil himself."

Cedric stood and removed his belt and tunic. He was wearing nothing underneath—and that *nothing* looked more than plenty.

"Sweet Jesus," I said hoarsely. This was the old Cedric back again.

"You surely knew I'd be with you tonight," he said, taunting me. He put a finger to my chin and lifted it. "So frightened and so sweet. You have nothing to fear from me."

I tried to stand, but stumbled. "Did you put something in my drink?"

He caught me. "Drugs to make the pain subside. And to give you an excuse for Sargon."

"Why do I need an excuse?" My voice was fuzzy. "You drugged me." My head fell onto his chest.

"I didn't expect you to drink it all down at once, foolish girl. Lie down."

"Are you going to—you can't—"

"Of course. Don't you think I deserve a reward for all I did today?" He was lying beside me on the bed now.

"A reward?" I slurred. "The Dark Lord cometh." I giggled at my own joke.

"Ha!" He smiled "And you will too." He unlaced the back of my dress and slid it over my head. I slumped back on the bed.

No, we mustn't. We really mustn't.

Did I say that out loud?

I wiggled my tongue. It wouldn't work.

Minutes passed.

I opened my bleary eyes.

Cedric gazed down at me. "I couldn't see you well that night. I couldn't see these."

He covered my breast with his huge hand, fondling, squeezing. Then he leaned down and his hot mouth covered my nipple.

"Mmm..." I murmured.

I was floating on a sea of pleasure.

His hand trailed down my stomach and between my legs.

"Cedric..." I whispered.

"Yes?"

"Sargon will kill you for this." My legs opened to give him better access.

"Not if you don't tell him," he said.

"I won't if you won't." Why had I said that?

He chuckled. "You are flying like a seagull right now, aren't you?"

"S-stoned." I slurred the word. "That's what we call it." I sighed. "Can you hurry this up?"

He laughed out loud and moved over me. "Not so gently tonight, I think."

Without wasting a moment, he made us one beast in the night. I moaned and was pulled along with him. The drugs were great, except I had no governor on my mouth. As he moved, I cried out, first moans and then animal grunts. Then words I can't remember. I know I screamed.

My fingers clung to his back as he controlled my body and then my mind. Like a demon switch turned on, the world reduced to him, the scent of musk, the feel of his skin, the arms that kept me imprisoned...too much. I wanted to break away, to breathe, but a force kept me there, drowning in his power.

I was gone, rolling with the waves.

Then as abruptly as it had manifested, the switch clicked off. I had my mind back.

He panted beside me.

There was a knock at the door.

"Row? Are you okay? I heard you scream."

Cedric marched to the door and flung it open.

Kendra gaped at him and then at me over his shoulder.

"She's fine," he said, standing there in all his naked splendor.

"Row?"

I nodded, my mouth dry.

Cedric shut the door and he and I were alone.

I tried my mouth to see if it would work. "You didn't even kiss me."

He laughed. "You're right. All we did is mate."

I moaned. "Don't say that word."

"Why not? Too animal?" He was back on the bed again.

"No," I said, yawning. "It gets me going."

Why was I saying these things?"

He grinned. "I like it when you lose your inhibitions."

"And you are going to give me back to Sargon tomorrow."

"Must be done," he said with a shrug. "I'm not ready for war yet and if I don't give you back, I'll have to fight him in the courtyard tomorrow. He's pretty good. So am I. We'd probably kill each other."

"Don't," I said through the haze of drugs. "No more killing."

"Oh, I'll kill him soon. But not tomorrow. And maybe I won't be fair about it."

"The dark arts," I murmured.

"That's right."

"If he wants to make love to me tomorrow night, I'll die," I said in a dream voice.

"Don't say that."

"Why not?"

"Just don't. I don't want to hear it."

"Why would you care? You don't love me."

"Oh, I see," he said, frowning. "Norland loves you. He's raising an army to take you back. Sargon loves you, He fought for you to the death against my worthless brother. I only faced a band of brigands and killed them all like so much rubbish."

"But now you're giving me back to Sargon like a borrowed soup tureen."

"A what?" He snickered.

"Never mind. You don't care."

"You don't know anything," he snapped.

I was nearly asleep.

"How's your shoulder?" he asked.

"Hurts. Can I have some more of that drug stuff?"

"Just a little." He held his goblet up to my mouth. "Whoa! Stop there."

I fell back onto the bed and sighed through the haze. "I don't mind if you don't love me, as long as you do it all over again."

Good God, did I say that?

He snorted. "My own cousin, to talk so randy."

"Distant cousin," I reminded him. Very distant. "I won't be randy when I'm sober."

He stroked my face. "I must say this is a pleasant surprise. I thought women only tolerated sex."

"I'm a bad girl. Very bad. I don't know why."

Guilt. It was there again, haunting me. I shouldn't be enjoying these sexual encounters. I may have to do these things for my own survival, but I shouldn't enjoy it.

Cedric said something strange. "We are uniquely suited. The master has done very well by me indeed."

I drifted off to sleep, one filled with disturbing images. I awoke in the middle of the night, sat up sharply and winced.

Beside me, Cedric moved. "How is your shoulder?"

"Hurts."

"Have another drink." He held the goblet to my mouth and I drank voraciously. "You're a greedy thing."

The air around me swirled darker and I was enveloped in a shroud of heat. Strange noises started to come from Cedric. Chanting in an ancient language, one that sounded familiar but foreign. I couldn't take much more of this dizzying rocking, but the drugs I'd taken sent me off on another voyage, a dark voyage into an unfamiliar place of disturbing dreams and one endless orgasm.

"Don't move," he whispered in my ear. "I need to stay in you."

I didn't move a muscle. I'm not sure I *had* muscles anymore. I moaned. When he withdrew, I was relieved.

"You still haven't kissed me," I murmured.

He did so once.

"You sleep. I've things to do." His green eyes blazed at me and I trembled as I gazed upon the red-gold hair that covered his taut body. "I sent a messenger to Sargon last night. They'll leave at first light and be here with a party by midday."

"Sargon frightens me," I whispered.

"It won't be for long," he said. "I've seen the future. The Rampant Lion will have his mate." He leaned forward for one last kiss. "You may taste another, but you will come back to me."

I hoped not. My drug induced fog made me realize something. I was tired of being passed around from one man to another. Tired of unemotional connections. Hadn't I had that with Steve?

I wanted love, respect. Not sex. *Love!*

But where would I find it? In my world...or this one?

"Keep the coin close," Cedric said before he left me.

Chapter 24

It was mid-morning and I was already dressed when Kendra came into the room. I couldn't look at her.

I moaned. "I feel awful."

"He drugged you," she guessed.

The night came back to me in splendid Technicolor. The drugged wine in the goblet! I drank it down like a desperate creature in the sweltering Arizona desert.

I was stunned, ashamed. How could I have behaved like this? Yes, Cedric saved me from those miserable thugs, but did that mean I owed him?

He'd said the drugs were for pain, but they had the effect of muddling my mind. And Cedric took every advantage of that. Damn and blast. He'd tricked me.

Was every man in this forsaken land determined to take away my control?

I realized Kendra was speaking. She was discussing the merits of Sargon versus Cedric.

"Of the two," she said, "who would you pick if you had the choice?"

"Three, you mean. There's Gareth too."

"Who is he again?"

"The blond Viking fellow from up north. The one who walked through the wall into our classroom. He paid the wizard to open the portal to our world."

"So you'd choose him?

I shook my head, the answer crystal clear to me now. Why had it taken so long to take hold? Physical affection was one thing. A lot of men can give you that, or so I'd learned here. But I longed for something more, something sweeter and lasting.

I longed for love.

Should I tell her the laughable, ironic truth? That the one man who hadn't made love to me was the one whose company I craved?

Thane...

"That's the thing, isn't it?" I said, my mouth curling in disdain. "We don't have the choice in this patriarchal world."

Her dark eyes flashed. "Would you stay with Cedric rather than go back to Sargon?"

"Neither, if I had the choice." I gazed out the window, across the fields of Huel. "I'm not sure I can explain it, but it's been there from the start and I've been terrified. Cedric draws me. Something to do with chemistry I guess. Or maybe magic. I don't even think he's handsome. I can't really be sure how I feel about him, except for this magnetic attraction—like atoms smashing together. Besides, he doesn't love me."

Kendra picked fuzz off her dress. "How do you know that?"

"He's letting me go back to Sargon, isn't he? And he has never said one nice thing about my looks. Not a word." I cringed. "God, my head hurts."

"Withdrawal probably. You're coming off the drugs. Any idea what he gave you?"

"I expect it was an opiate."

She gaped at me. "Row, you surprise me!"

"What? We tested opiates in the lab, fourth year."

Kendra reached into the black leather pouch around her waist. "Here's aspirin for your head." She handed it to me. "And let me bandage that burn. I brought everything with me."

She opened her backpack and took out a first aid kit with gauze and adhesive tape and antibiotic cream.

"You're a lifesaver, Kendra. I don't know what I'd do without you."

She rolled her eyes. "Yeah, right."

"No, truly," I said, meaning every word. "I've never had a friend like you."

A pause.

"You don't judge me," I said, "and goodness knows, I'm one heck of a bad example."

"That's not true. You're kind, brave and very smart. You try to take care of me when no one else ever did."

We sat in companionable silence.

"You also smell a bit," she added. "I think you should have a wash before your husband returns."

"Oh, horse poop," I said. "Bless you for thinking of that."

Later, after I had bathed and Kendra and I had eaten, she found another lace to do up my bodice.

I had a sudden thought. "Where's Duke?"

My canine friend had yet to make an appearance.

"Logan says he went south with Ivan," Kendra replied.

That was sad news. I would miss the gentle beast.

There was a commotion in the courtyard.

We picked up our bags and hurried down the stairs.

Stepping through the great front doors, we were greeted by a line of at least twenty riders on horseback. The front riders held flags—the royal coat of arms in purple and silver. The horses were dressed in colors too.

It was a magnificent sight.

Cedric stood on the bottom step with his hand on the hilt of his sword. When I reached his side, I stood behind him.

Sargon jumped down from his horse, his cape swinging as he strode across the rocky ground.

"Where are the fiends?" he bellowed.

"I killed them," Cedric said.

"Did they hurt her?"

"Willen branded her on the arm. She took it well."

Sargon's face went black. "Did he—"

"No. I got there in time. Just."

Sargon noticed me. "Rowena, are you well?"

"I'm fine."

"Did Cedric treat you with respect?" he asked in a low voice.

"Yes, Sire. He treated me very well."

I caught Kendra's eye. Don't say a word, I willed.

"Huel, it seems I owe you a debt of immense proportion."

It must have cost him dearly to say that. I almost guffawed at the irony. The air defused. I could breathe again.

Cedric stared at me. "She is my flesh and blood and deserves my protection."

"You've changed," Sargon said.

"Perhaps in your eyes." Cedric crossed his muscular arms.

They stared at each other across ten feet. Cedric, a red-blond lion in the sunlight. And Sargon, the older black wolf. They were dangerous opponents.

I vowed right then to do everything I could to keep them apart.

"We go now," Sargon said. "Rowena, to your horse."

"One moment." Cedric turned and placed his hands on my shoulders. "One week," he whispered. "I'll see you then. And never fear, I've found a way to have the things I want."

Logan approached us, calling for Kendra, whose eyes lit up when she saw him.

A groom brought our horses from the stables.

I wore my fanny pack with the Derringer inside. I vowed to keep it close in future. In this world, who knows when I'd need it again? I hooked my pink backpack to the saddle and mounted Lightning. She was ready to race.

As we cantered out the gates, I took one last look behind me.

Cedric stood in the sun, glowing like a fallen angel.

We stopped at the river to water the horses.

"Before you start the lecture," I said to Sargon, "I won't ever do it again. I've had punishment enough and I'm not a fool. I didn't know about those men from the forest. No one ever told me."

He glared. "I don't understand why you went in the first place."

"We needed some things from home," I said. "*Female* things. You don't have them here."

His face reddened.

"We have enough for a long time now—many months," I said. "So you can rest easy. I won't leave the castle grounds again."

"Nor visit the field without an escort."

Well, I expected that.

I mounted Lightning and walked her beside Sargon's horse.

"We finished with the scout this morning," he said. "There are bad times coming."

"You tortured him, didn't you? Then killed him."

His silence told me all.

"Why? Why did you kill him? He was only following orders."

"There's one less spy in the world to worry about," he said with little emotion.

I lost it. "It's barbaric. You talk of the northern men that way, but you're no better in the south."

He reined in his horse. "You will not criticize an order of mine. Not here among others or in private." His tone was menacing. "As much as I might amuse myself by seeking your views on strategy, you will not offer your opinion unless I ask for it. I am the king. You are my wife and you owe me fealty."

I think I started hating him at that moment. It was all I could do not to turn back to Castle Huel.

I slept alone that night.

The next morning, I was awakened by a sparrow singing on the windowsill. *A sparrow...*

Oh my God.

The birds had returned to Land's End.

Chapter 25

Here's what I've learned about men. As long as you continue to have sex with them, they think you love them. The second you deny sex for any reason, they feel rejected in all ways.

I didn't deny Sargon sex. To do so would be dangerous. I submitted to him and tried to tolerate the carnal aspects of our relationship.

Hate is an emotion not so far from love, I found. If one is indifferent, there is no energy. But hate brings its own force and I met Sargon's ardor with a passion just as powerful.

He never knew. I hid it well.

I set a goal for those nightly trysts. To learn the secret of his parentage. Except for that first night back, he didn't leave me alone, so I had a few nights to see the animal that ruled him. I kept my eyes open when I could and sometimes I saw his features change to something not quite human.

On our fourth night back, the moons were full and he bit my shoulder with such ferocity that I bled. I'm sure my scream could be heard clear to the northern fortresses. He licked the wound clean before I could stop him.

After, he seemed shocked and confused. Without speaking, he left the room by the hidden door and wandered the courtyard in the night shadows.

I feared him as I had never feared anyone. And I had a devil of a time keeping my shoulder hidden from curious eyes.

Sargon's days were busy planning for the tournament and strategizing defense. The men spent their time training in the outer fields. Logan and Richard were gone every day and we met only at dinner, which was usually a jocular affair of recounting the day's mock battles.

Thane kept his distance from me.

But I couldn't stop looking at him.

I spent my time with Kendra in the stables, tending animals and doing domestic chores. Together, we helped birth the foal. It was a wondrous event. The grooms shared in our joy and their respect for us grew. Kendra learned quickly. She had a gentle touch with the creatures and I felt their love for her.

Everyone was talking about the birds, of course. The bees had come back too. Somehow the curse had been broken.

I had a horrible feeling I knew why.

I tried not to think of Cedric, but I kept the Roman coin with me as a talisman.

On our fifth day back, I discovered a treasure trove. Thane had mentioned a storage room and suggested we look there for more clothes. Kendra had only four dresses. I had already wrecked as many. Things were getting desperate.

I opened the storage room door and found a dozen or so trunks lining the walls. The first one we opened was filled with capes and furs. The next held a mound of clothing and bolts of fabric, all in pristine condition.

"They must get winter here," Kendra said. "Look at this lovely cape." It was dark red and trimmed with fur.

I pulled out a second, longer cape with a hood trimmed in white fox. "One for each of us. That red will look smashing with your hair."

The next two trunks were filled with summer dresses. Kendra rummaged through one, while I started on the other. In my trunk there were day dresses in muslin and two sleeveless gowns in lightweight silk.

"This is so exciting!" Kendra squealed.

"I love this lilac," I said, lifting it out of the trunk. "And I think it will fit."

I removed the dress I was wearing and heard Kendra gasp.

"What happened to your shoulder?" she asked.

I stood stock still. "It's nothing."

She pushed my hair out of the way. "Jesus. It looks like an animal tried to take a chunk out of you."

I sidestepped out of her reach.

Her eyes were like saucers. "He did this, didn't he?"

"Don't say anything to anybody. Please." My hands shook.

"My God, Row. Has he done this before?"

A pause. I nodded.

"You can't let him do this. It has to stop. He could really hurt you. What if he went for your throat by mistake? Let me get Logan to—"

"No!" I cried. "Don't do anything. You don't understand. It won't help. And above all, don't let on that you've seen this. You wouldn't be safe. I have to tough it out for a while."

Her mouth gaped. "You've got to get away from him."

"I know." Boy, did I know. "But not yet. Cedric's coming. Soon. I can feel it."

Kendra sat down on the floor. "Row, this is awful. Does he really turn into a wolf?"

"Part of him does," I said, clutching the lilac dress to my chest. "I see it in his eyes. They look...vacant sometimes."

"You poor thing. And nobody knew. You've been protecting us all by keeping this to yourself. "

"I can't let Grandfather know. It would kill him. Especially since there's nothing he can do about it until Cedric gets here."

Kendra shook her head. "I never thought I'd say this, but I will be so glad when he gets here."

Me too, I silently agreed.

"What will he do?" she asked.

"Cedric? I'm not sure exactly. He knows magic, so it could be anything."

We sat in chilly silence.

"Maybe we should go back through the wall," she said.

"We can't yet. They won't let me go anywhere. Besides, they know how to find me over there. And I don't want to endanger anyone else." I sighed. "No, I think we have to see this through. Something is going to happen soon. I feel it in my bones."

We replaced the capes in the trunk for safe storage until the winter months. Donning my old dress, I gathered my new gowns and Kendra followed suit. We took them to her room to sort. In all, we each came out with five new day dresses and we split the gowns by size. Two for her and three for me.

"It's only right that I get more," I said, grinning, "because I wreck so many."

Kendra attempted a smile, but her face was full of worry.

Something *did* happen soon.

The following morning, I woke up and was sick to my stomach. Thankfully, I made it to the chamber pot in time.

"What's wrong?" Sargon said, rushing to my side. "Are you ill? What should I do?"

"Get Kendra," I begged, stretching out on the cool floor.

Within minutes, Kendra was bending over me, offering words of encouragement. "I've sent him away. Is this what I think it is?"

I groaned and nodded.

She winced. "Are you sure?"

"I've known since the birds came back. No birds and bees for a barren people."

"Oh my God." She dropped to the floor and sat beside me. "That's why the birds came back. You're pregnant and that breaks the curse. Does this mean it's a girl?"

"I don't know for certain."

Kendra put her head on her knees. "This complicates things."

That was an understatement.

"Any idea who the father is, Row?"

I gave her a wry look.

"Okay," she said, "let's not go there right now."

"I don't want to go anywhere but back to bed," I grumbled.

As she helped me to the bed, she said, "We should tell him."

"Who?"

"Sargon. Your husband."

"No." I moaned and collapsed onto the bed.

"We should," Kendra insisted. "He'll leave you alone then."

"Having sex doesn't harm the baby. You know that."

"But *he* doesn't know that. I can tell him you have to be careful for a while and he'll believe it. He won't want to take a chance, believe me."

I massaged my throbbing head. "Okay. I won't be able to hide it for long anyway. But there's going to be a circus."

I could imagine the reaction here, at Huel and at Norland.

Damn them all.

"Are you happy at all about this, Row?"

I sighed. "I'm not sure. Maybe. If it's not Sargon's. I always wanted to have kids, but I don't want to give birth to a..." I couldn't finish the word. Wolf.

Kendra hugged me. "Any child of yours will be beautiful and loving, just like you are. And I'm going to be right along with you through all of it. I promise."

I started to sniff.

She headed for the door. "I'll go tell him now."

A half hour later, Sargon entered the room, his face beaming with happiness. "You're with child?"

I nodded.

He moved to the bed, took my hand and kissed it. "My beautiful wife. Thank you."

I sobbed a little then. Damn hormones.

"Kendra says we must be careful these first few weeks," Sargon told me. "I will keep you and the babe safe. You mustn't ride your horse."

Right now the thought of bouncing up and down on Lightning made my stomach churn.

"Take all the time you need in bed. We've a feast tonight, remember." He kissed me on the forehead. "I'll be back at dusk to dress." To Kendra, he said, "Stay with her. Take care of her. Don't let her want for anything."

But I *did* want for something. Or someone.

At the door, he turned. "Wear the Tintegal broach, Rowena. Keep it on you at all times from now on. I need you safe."

When we were alone, Kendra said, "You should feel better soon. I remember when my mom had morning sickness. She was usually okay by noon."

Maybe noon in nine months time, I thought, miserable.

Of course, word got around the castle without delay. All day people smirked at me and stared at my stomach. You would almost think Sargon had rented a biplane and had a message towed across the sky, proclaiming, "Red knocked up." Or "Bun in the oven." Or some such thing.

Logan looked as though he'd masterminded the whole thing. He was tickled pink at the prospect of becoming an uncle.

And Thane was particularly sweet. I was to call on him for anything, anytime. Definitely godfather material there—and not the mafia kind. Sadly, I thought about how much better a father he would make than Sargon.

My own kin was less effusive. Richard went red and wished me well. Grandfather worried and scratched his chin, as he so often did. I tried to tell him I was okay with it all, but he knew the odds as well as I did. His own mother had died in childbirth.

Kendra kept me going those next few days. She protected me from too much nosiness and made sure I ate and slept. We spent some happy times in the kitchen with George and Ralph, the dog. George spoiled me with special preserves and treats.

The following day, Avery the groom trotted into the kitchen. He carried a parcel—the chess set I had ordered from the woodcarver.

I clapped my hands in delight. "Thank you." Taking the parcel, I hurried to the library to set up my treasure.

Thane was reading by the window.

He smiled when he saw me.

I was always a little breathless when I saw Thane. With that black curly hair and compact build, he looked so like his older brother that it confused me. Except for his eyes, which were kind and put me at ease.

"What is that you have?" he asked.

"It's a chess set," I said, grinning with pride. "For Sargon. It's a game of strategy with kings, queens and knights. In my world, it is the king of games, for the most intelligent. I had it made for him as a gift."

Thane picked up a queen. "How do you play?"

"I'll teach you," I said.

I explained the different pieces and how they moved about the board. Thane was a quick learner, really keen. Before long, we were playing our first game. I won, of course.

"This is a grand game," he said. "A wonderful gift."

"Do you think Sargon will like it?"

Thane frowned. "He'll like the strategy of it. And the beauty of the pieces. I'm not sure he'll have the patience to play." He paused. "Please don't be disappointed if he doesn't take the time to learn it."

"I thought as much," I said, my smile disappearing.

I was sad for the loss of my innocence. I had ordered the chess set in the early days, when pleasing Sargon was important to me. Now I hoped merely to survive the next month under his authority.

"Let's play again," I said. "I get to go first since I won."

We played in silence for several moves.

My last move was tricky and I bent over the board for some time before moving the piece. When I looked up, Thane was gazing at me with sorrow in his eyes.

"Rowena, are you happy with Sargon?"

He frowned when he saw my shock.

"I expected as much," he said. "I'm trying to word this in such a way that it doesn't sound disloyal." He moved a knight. "Has he been violent to you?"

It took about ten seconds to make up my mind. Thane was a kind man and it would be so good to have someone else know. Someone close to the king. Someone who could perhaps help.

I could answer him without saying a word. Then I could deny I ever told him. I brushed my hair back and pulled down the shoulder of my dress.

Thane flinched and I heard his sharp intake of breath.

"I'm so sorry." His fist clenched and unclenched.

I adjusted my dress, then looked at the chess game and made my next move. "Check."

He sighed. "It's yours again. Thank you for the game."

I started to line up the pieces for next time.

"I don't know what to do," he said. "I want to reassure you that I can help, but I don't know how to do it. I must think."

"Thane, I am grateful that you know and care. I expect—for the time being—I will be safe. Sargon won't risk hurting the child I carry."

"But you're afraid."

I could imagine the struggle he felt. "Very."

He took my hand. "These are restless times. Things are happening in our world that will result in change, I'm sure. Which way? I don't know. It could go badly for us. But there is hope in change, don't you think? Will you hope with me?"

I smiled, nodding. I had a friend in this kind man, who thought before he acted. Just as well he didn't know my feelings for him.

"Tell me about the world you come from," he said. "I've been curious."

This surprised and delighted me. No one else had shown the slightest interest in the fact that I had led a life before coming to Land's End.

"The land itself is very similar, except the sun is more yellow and the sky a lighter blue. We are much more advanced in several fields. We don't use horses anymore, except for sport." I explained our transportation, computers, cell phones and televisions.

Thane's eyes grew wide with amazement.

"Our medicine is much more advanced. We have ways to cure or prevent many diseases. And women don't die in childbirth like they do here."

"Your field is medicine," he said. "Is that a common thing for women?"

"In our world, women have equal rights to men and are educated to the same standard. I am considered a doctor of veterinary medicine." I let my pride show. "It has taken me several years to accomplish."

"To be so educated..." He shook his head. "It must be hard for you here."

He was the first one who had ever considered what it must be like for me, being far from home.

I let out a tired sigh. "It is sometimes. I'm used to complete freedom of my movements and actions. And I miss intellectual pursuits like this one. You are very perceptive to think of that." I paused. "But I have family here. And Kendra and I can't leave Grandfather right now. It is so hard for him, with Ivan gone. If I were to leave too..."

He gazed at me in a way that warmed me all over.

My gaze drifted to the window. "You talk of war coming here. One way in which we have progressed at home—but maybe not really—is warfare. We have tremendous weapons of mass destruction. Not to mention the ability to annihilate entire populations in minutes. It is terrifying."

"Then perhaps our world is not so bad after all."

I stared at him. "Maybe not."

We sat in silence for a moment.

"Could you take me there one day?" he asked.

"What?"

"I'd like to see your world. Could you take me through the portal? For a short time, maybe next time you visit."

I was floored. "Yes, I'd like to do that."

His smile was heart-stopping. I had to leave.

With a hurried excuse, I dashed out the door and down the corridor.

Later that day I learned that my new saddle was complete. I went to the stables, secured the saddle to Lightning and sat on her for a while. The saddle was finely crafted. I couldn't wait until the morning sickness was over so I could test it out.

I'd get around Sargon's claustrophobic control somehow.

Maybe it wouldn't be necessary by then.

Chapter 26

In the morning, I discovered Thane in the library, as I'd expected. I sat down beside him and he smiled.

My heart thudded wildly.

It was my turn to be brave. "Thane, I have a favor to ask. I want to go home to my world for a short time today and I'd like you to accompany me."

I had his attention now.

"You know I'm pregnant. Well, there are things I want from home that I can't get here. With all the warriors coming for the tournament, I'll need someone to watch my back while riding to the portal. Will you take me through and escort me back? I can't go alone. Even I wouldn't try that."

I could see the inner war reflected in his expression. Between the desire to see the world I had talked of and the disapproval that Sargon would extend if he found out, he was conflicted.

Yet, there was excitement in his eyes.

"How far?" he said.

"About two hours to the portal. Then I'd need an hour there. Five hours total." I watched him closely. "Just you and me. I wouldn't bring Kendra this time. As few people as possible should know the exact location of the portal."

That's what did it and I knew it would. Thane couldn't resist actually seeing the portal, knowing where it was and experiencing the travel through the wall. It was *knowledge* that Thane thirsted for, not power.

"I will need to bring some men with me," he said. "For safety. Trusted men, who are loyal to me rather than Sargon. Is there a place close to the portal—but not within sight—where they can wait?"

"By the river. We'd be within calling distance, yet hidden by the trees."

Grinning, he jumped to his feet. "Give me a half hour to get the men. Be ready by the stables. Don't speak to Sargon. I'll talk to him."

I watched his muscular body stride from the room. For an intellectual man, he certainly was well built. To be a man and survive in this world, he had to be fit. Even more so, since he was the king's brother and that king was Sargon.

Kendra was busy with Logan today, marking out the various tournament fields, so I didn't have to worry about her.

The bedroom was empty. I went to the wardrobe and pulled out the pink backpack. I emptied everything from it and placed the contents on the floor of the wardrobe. I'd wear the jeans under my dress, and the cowboy boots. I put the T-shirt in the bag for later.

When I reached the stables, Lightning was ready. This would be the first time I rode her with the new saddle. I swung up, elated.

"See how easy she is to mount with the horn?" I said to Avery.

The old man nodded.

"Where's Thane?"

"He told me to tell you he's by the gate, m'lady."

Sure enough, Thane waited on this side of the iron gates, a smile on his face and anticipation in his warm eyes. Four men sat on horseback not far away.

"I told Sargon you would be under my watch today," Thane said. "He seems to be busy with defensive matters. He thought it wise to keep an eye on you."

I smiled. It wasn't a lie. Thane would surely watch me.

We caught up with the other riders and Thane introduced me. Most of the men were his age, close to thirty I gathered, and all looked tough but respectful. They were well armed and observant.

Our ride to the river was uneventful. To attract little attention, we moved fast and as quietly as possible.

I led the way to the riverbank, where the men and horses could hide. To Thane, I said, "The portal is there, in the trees."

Before we left, he spoke to his men. "If I call, come immediately. You know the signal. If we aren't back in two hours, go into the forest and look for us. Stay until dusk and use caution."

He followed me up the hill to the forest. Seconds later, we rode into the clearing.

Thane cursed. "I should have reasoned it was here."

Of course! Thane had been here the day Logan and I had come back with Kendra.

"Not exactly here, but not far," I said. "We'll leave the horses and go on foot. But first...Thane, in my world you aren't allowed to carry swords and daggers. It could mean trouble for us. And it is a dead giveaway that you are from somewhere else. I don't think we want to advertise this. Can you leave your weapons behind with the horses?"

Without hesitation, he removed both weapons and strapped the belt to his horse.

"Thank you. I appreciate this."

He grinned. "Have no fear. I can fight well without them."

I almost groaned .

Sliding from the saddle, I started down the path. Thane was right behind me.

"See here where the path turns and you can see the valley down below?" I said. "And see that oak with the split trunk?"

Thane nodded.

"It's through there." Grabbing his hand, I smiled. "Come."

Like two children on the verge of a great adventure, we ran hand-in-hand.

Then I pulled Thane through the wall.

The classroom was empty. Light streamed through the windows, illuminating the tables and chairs—and my desk.

I looked at Thane's stunned expression and giggled."Isn't this exciting? We made it, Thane. We're here in my world. *Arizona*. This is my classroom, where I teach."

I made a beeline for my desk and retrieved my car keys from the drawer.

Thane remained rooted to one spot, staring in wonder.

"Come here," I said. "Let me show you things."

With tentative steps, he walked toward me.

"Here are some of my teaching texts." I pointed to the heavy books on my desk. He was awed at their size.

"This is called a white board," I said, picking up a blue marker. "I can write on this to demonstrate things to my students, then erase the writing later. Look."

I wrote *THANE*.

"This is your name in English. And here is mine." I wrote *ROWENA*.

He smiled deeply. "I am enjoying this adventure."

I remembered something. "Hand me the pink backpack. I want to change into my T-shirt." I moved to the side wall. "Can you stand behind me so no one can see through the windows? I'm going to take off my dress and put on this T-shirt."

He did as told. I don't know how much he could see from behind, but when I whipped the dress over my head and reached down for the T-shirt, I heard him suck in a sharp breath. I slipped the T-shirt on, then rolled the dress into a ball and stuffed it in the backpack.

"There," I said, turning. "Now I look like I live here."

His eyes went to my chest. "What you wear here is...different. Quite pleasing in fact."

I blushed.

This was an irony that I couldn't quite get my head around. In Land's End, the dresses were cut so low that I almost fell out of them. Here in Arizona, I was completely covered.

We hurried to the parking lot. At one point, Thane stopped in his tracks and surveyed the scenery. I had to go back, take his hand and lead him like a child.

"The sun is so bright and hot here," he said, shading his eyes.

"Isn't it gorgeous? It's May. Arizona gets even hotter in summer."

I found my car and punched the lock release. I opened the passenger door, but Thane made no move.

"Look, Thane, I've got a lot to tell you and I know you want to see more, but for now you need to sit in here." I pointed to the seat. "I'll explain everything."

A couple of students wandered by at a distance and I did my best to keep Thane out of sight.

When he managed to fold his long legs into the cramped seat, I closed his door and stepped around the car. Climbing inside, I secured my seatbelt and signaled for him to do the same. It took him a few tries, but he got it.

When I started the engine, he jerked and let out a curse.

"What kind of magical beast is this?" he demanded.

"Okay, here's lesson two. This is a car, not a beast. Remember? I explained cars back in the library. These are fueled by a type of oil we get from the earth. They move fast, but I am a good driver, so you don't need to worry."

I eased the car into reverse and slowly backed out of my parking space.

"There are lots of other cars on the roads. Almost all adults have one. But we have rules and we follow them so there aren't as many accidents."

Thane was mesmerized by the dashboard.

"What are all these?"

"They operate the heat and AC. And the music."

I turned on the radio. Aerosmith's "I Don't Want to Miss a Thing" was on and I sang along.

Thane stared at the dashboard as if waiting for people to appear.

"Where do the voices come from?"

"Radio waves. From the sky."

I guess we did have magic in our world.

I sped up as we hit the main road. When I checked to see how Thane was handling the ride, he was grinning from ear to ear.

I answered about a million questions in the ten minutes it took to get to my townhouse. I parked in front and switched off the engine.

"This is my home," I said.

"There is sunshine in your voice when you say that."

I guess there was.

We walked to the front door and I unlocked it.

"I'm very proud that I have my own place. This is an expensive city to live in."

"You live alone here? Does not your father live with you?"

"Dad lives close by, but no, I moved out of his house three years ago. In this world, women can live alone until they get married."

We stepped inside and I switched on a light. Thane's eyes drifted to the switch, which he then tried. The light went out. He flicked it again.

I rolled my eyes. Men with a new toy.

"And you walk around wearing that...T-shirt." He shook his head. "I am astonished that men here have such restraint."

"*You* have such restraint," I blurted without thinking.

Silence.

My face blazed with heat. "Follow me up the stairs to my bedroom so I can get my supplies."

When we entered the room, I let out a sigh of relief. I had made the bed. And I hadn't left a bra draped over the footboard.

Thane froze in the doorway. He took in his surroundings, enthralled. I motioned him to come in, but he hesitated.

Finally, he stepped inside.

"Sit down." I pointed to the bed. "I need to make some phone calls. You can watch."

The answering machine was by the bed. I punched a button.

"Hey, it's Debbie. Got your message. Don't worry, I'll keep Piper for as long as you want. Have a brilliant time. And don't do anything I wouldn't do." Giggle.

"Radio waves?" Thane asked.

"Kind of."

The next message was from Steve. "You didn't call Tuesday. I'm worried. Call me back."

I cringed. Delete.

"Hi, Red, it's Dad. Have a wonderful time and let me know as soon as you get back. We'll do lunch at the Biltmore. Love you."

"My dad," I said to Thane.

Next message.

"Rowena, this is Ted. You didn't make the meeting on Wednesday. Give me a call. Anytime."

There were several hang-ups after that.

"What is that thing called?" Thane asked.

"A telephone or phone. We can talk to each other in different houses. If the person isn't there when we call, we can leave a message on an answering machine. I was listening to messages I've missed."

"Remarkable."

"I'm going to return some calls now. Watch me. Every person has their own unique number."

I punched numbers and waited.

Steve's home answering machine picked up.

"Hi, it's Row," I said. "I'm fine, honest. I've been in England. It's a long story and I'm going back there. I'll be in touch in a few weeks. Bye."

I didn't want him getting so alarmed at my absence that he called Dad or the police. And I did the usual ex-lover trick. I called his home phone rather than his cell because I didn't really want to talk to him in person. He'd figure that out.

"I need to call my boss now," I said.

Thane's brows gathered.

"My commander," I explained. "The person who oversees my work."

He nodded. "Ah, yes. Your commander."

"Hi, Ted," I said when my boss's answering machine picked up. "Sorry to miss the meeting. I've been in England on a family emergency. I'll bring you up to date when I'm back for good. Bye."

"Are you finished?" Thane asked, obviously eager to see more.

"One more."

The hardest one.

"Dad? It's Row. I'm doing great. My English relatives are wonderful. I have so many cousins. Grandfather, in particular, you'd like. I'm staying over for another week or two, so don't worry. For emergencies, you can call my cell phone. Love you."

I hung up and slumped into a chair.

Thane sensed my mood. "You miss him, and he you. You are conflicted about staying in our world."

His deep blue eyes invited honesty.

"I can stay in Land's End, but I need to get back here every once in a while to see my Dad. I need that option in order to be able to stay in your world. Can you understand that?"

He nodded. "I understand. I understand the words you *haven't* said also."

We were silent, uncomfortable in our closeness.

Would I really stay in Land's End? If I had to make a choice and if there was no possibility to return home, I don't know what that choice would be. There was a good chance I would choose home. And not in spite of the baby, but *because* of the baby. A child would be safer in my world. Even Thane sensed that.

For this very reason, I didn't entirely trust him. I had a terrible feeling that he would do all he could to prevent my leaving forever.

"I will help you," he said in a quiet tone. "I will escort you back here when you need to come. I give you my word."

"Thank you," I whispered.

I almost took his hand, but refrained in time.

"Let me pack some things," I said, standing. "You can look around if you like."

For the next five minutes, I was involved with packing. I found a second backpack in the closet. My old one from the Wilderness Store. I opened a drawer and grabbed all the panties there. They would be needed after the birth.

The light kept switching on and off.

I chuckled.

Thane was having fun. Wait until he found the TV.

From the second drawer, I withdrew a stack of T-shirts. I put them in a backpack. I noticed one of Steve's old T-shirts in the drawer. It gave me an idea.

"Thane, can you come here?"

When he moved to my side, I sat on the edge of the bed.

"It might be smart if you took off your tunic and wore this T-shirt instead," I said. "It's what we wear here. Then if someone sees you, it won't matter."

I had no jeans for him, but his britches were a bit like football pants. He'd look like he had just finished practice.

Thane whipped the tunic over his head.

My whole body shuddered in response as he stood there, bare-chested. Curly black hair covered him in all the right places, straight across his chest and trailing down the center of his torso, leading to—hoo boy.

I dragged my eyes to his face.

Within seconds, Thane was smoothing the white shirt over his stomach. It was too small. It clung to every line of his muscles, stretched to the limit. The white cotton against his dark, tanned arms was more than disturbing.

My gaze drifted lower and my mouth went dry.

"This feels good," he said, oblivious to my embarrassment. "May I keep it?"

"Sure," I croaked.

I had learned an important thing about tunics versus T-shirts. The former covered a man's nether regions. The latter didn't. This was especially noticeable since I was sitting down.

Thank God he was wearing britches.

Still, I couldn't help but stare.

His nether regions couldn't always be that size. Could they?

Flopping onto my back, I closed my eyes. It never occurred to me that I was particularly vulnerable lying on my bed, steps away from a barely dressed hunk and protected by a mere T-shirt.

Neither of us spoke or moved.

I heard the ticking of the clock on the wall.

"May I look around, Rowena?"

"Of course," I said.

When he left, I stuffed his tunic into the bag. Then I scooped up my cell phone from the night table. It was fully charged now.

I went to the bathroom to get overnight pads. I was well-acquainted with the messy business of birthing and I wanted to be prepared. The pads filled up half of one backpack. I packed a clean facecloth and a fluffy towel too. What a luxury those would be.

Next, I wanted tea.

I found Thane in my office.

"You have so many books. You must be a wealthy woman."

"Not at all. We make them cheaper here. Although I do spend most of my money on them." I reached up. "Look! Here is my copy of Hesiod's *Theogony* in English. We'll take it back, and you can compare it to your version. I can teach you English from it."

He held the book as if it were the most valuable thing he had ever seen. "Do you have other games like our chess?"

"Good idea. I know just the thing." From the oak desk, I salvaged a deck of playing cards. "I can teach you gin rummy and euchre when we get back."

Thane followed me downstairs. I could see him eyeing the appliances.

"I don't have time to show you everything, but that's the stove, that's a dishwasher and that's the fridge. The fridge is like an icebox. It keeps things cold. As a matter of fact..." I opened the door. "How would you like a beer? I mean, an ale?"

I grabbed two Buds and popped off the tops. I handed him one, watching as he took a swig.

"Cold," he said. "Good, but very light." He gulped the whole thing down in one sitting.

I reached for a Guinness. "Try this one."

He fiddled with the top, trying to open it. When he figured it out, he took a sip. "This one is interesting. More like the drink they make from peat up north."

I took a swig of my Bud, then started packing the pink backpack. I took every packet of tea I could find, including the loose leaf. I added hot chocolate packets and semi-sweet chocolate chips. I moved to the fridge where I cleared out the cheese drawer. This was like the game of "What would you take to a desert island?"

What would I take? The three Cs—cheese, chocolate and cookies.

I threw in some cutlery and a box of tissues.

"I'm done now. Finish your beer so we can go."

My gaze traveled to the floor, where Piper's water dish sat empty. I felt a pang of guilt and sorrow.

"Thane, do you like dogs?"

"I do. There's a sweet little mutt in the kitchens I am quite fond of. Don't tell Sargon. He doesn't know it's there."

The lock on my front door clicked.

"What the—" I rushed toward the door.

Thane jumped to his feet. "Rowena?"

"It's okay." I sighed in resignation. "Only one other person has a key."

The door opened and Steve stepped inside. He looked pissed.

"Rowena! I was at my desk when you called. I could see it was your home number, so I came right over." He froze when he noticed Thane. "Who is *that*?"

"Hi, Steve, nice to see you too."

Hoo boy, I had a bad feeling.

"This is Thane. Thane, Steve."

Thane stood with his hands to each side, ready for a fight.

Steve ignored him. "You didn't call on Tuesday. Where have you been?"

I struggled to hold in my temper. My ex acted like he still had some sort of hold over me.

"In England, visiting my relatives. I have all sorts of cousins over there that I didn't know about."

I was happy that at least something I was saying was true.

I studied the two men. They were exactly the same height, but not the same size. Thane was of a much broader build.

Steve tilted his head at Thane. "Is this one of them?"

"A relative? Yes."

"Brother-in-law" didn't seem like a good thing to say at the moment.

"Who is this scrawny creature, Rowena?"

Before I could answer, Steve said, "Watch your mouth, stranger." He frowned at me. "Okay, I get the Brit accent. You always had a thing for foreign accents."

He glared at Thane, his expression full of contempt. Then eyes went wide. "Hey! Is that my T-shirt he's wearing? Row, what's going on? And why aren't you wearing a bra? Did you just get out of bed? Are you sleeping with this creep already?"

In a blink, Thane pinned Steve against a wall, one hand around his throat, one knee against Steve's groin.

"What a monstrous thing to say, you ignorant peasant. She is virtuous and good."

"Thane, release him," I pleaded. "Please. For me."

I couldn't believe this was happening. Thane was the level-headed brother. If Sargon were here, Steve would be dead by now.

Thane's jaw clenched and unclenched. At last, he stepped back and Steve fell to the floor, gasping and moaning.

"Who is this weakling, Rowena?" Thane said in disdain.

"A former suitor. Emphasis on the former. He's actually quite a good athlete, if you call golf athletic. And he's a scholar."

"He has no honor." Thane crossed his arms, the T-shirt stretching to its limit. "He doesn't even challenge me. He is unworthy of you."

"Yeah, well...I thought so too." I glared at Steve. "That's why I called it off."

"Perhaps we should settle this like men. With daggers."

"Rowena?" Steve whined.

"Don't mind Thane. They talk funny over there. I think you'd better leave now. I'm going back to England." When he didn't move, I leaned down. "Are you okay? Should I call 911?"

Steve shook his head. "I'm leaving. Give me a sec."

Using the wall for support, he clambered to his feet. When Thane made a move to help him, Steve cringed. "Keep that thug away from me."

I almost laughed.

A minute later, he stumbled through the front door and slammed it behind him.

Thane stared at me in disbelief.

"I know, I know!" I said, flinging my arms in the air. "He's a jerk. But I didn't know it at first. And if you saw the size of the diamond ring he gave me..." My voice trailed off.

"He would not have treated you well."

"And you think I'm treated well in Sargonia?"

We stared at each other, sharing the same thoughts. Thane's face turned to stone. He looked tortured.

"We better go, Thane. It's time."

Back in the car, his mood lifted. There was so much to see. I pointed out landmarks as we sped down Scottsdale Road.

But I couldn't help but think of the scene with Steve.

"Thank you for that," I said. "For defending me."

For defending my honor, which seemed such a quaint concept in Arizona, but rather nice just the same.

He nodded once, satisfied.

We stopped at a streetlight.

"A penny for your thoughts," I said.

He eyed me, puzzled.

"It's an expression—an idiom. You looked deep in thought. I was asking to hear them."

"I am trying to decide if I should tell you."

"Surely by now, you know you can trust me."

"I do not fear that. I am trying to decide if it will make things worse."

"Now you've got me curious. You *have* to tell me."

"Very well. I meant what I said earlier. You are a virtuous woman, Rowena. Yet, I know what you were feeling back there when we were alone. I was feeling it too."

My breath let out in a whoosh. I didn't pretend not to know what he meant.

"It's that T-shirt you're wearing, Thane."

"And yours too. But it is far more than that, I think."

We were quiet for the rest of the way back to campus.

We didn't even speak when we rejoined his men on the other side and headed back to Castle Sargon. I can't imagine what the men must have thought.

"But it is far more than that, I think."

He was so right.

At night, Thane did not join us for dinner.

Chapter 27

Day nine, after the birds and bees had returned, dawned bright and warm. We were expecting huge groups of tournament contestants to arrive today. The courtyard bustled as I hurried toward the stables. The grooms scurried around like worker bees.

"Any need for me, Avery?" I asked the groom.

He shook his head and wiped his brow. "Not yet, m'lady. We're busy finding stalls for the guest horses. We're using everything we have. The outbuildings too."

"Come get me at the castle when I can be of use."

Men rode into the courtyard, dismounted and stared at each other as testosterone levels surged.

Trying to stay out of view, I watched them, taking in their brilliant colors and various strange weapons strapped to the horses. Some of the men saw me. They stopped and stared.

Feeling uncomfortable, I looked for Gareth's blue colors. I couldn't see them. But I did see Thane. He was across the square.

"Thane!" I hollered in an unladylike fashion.

He signaled me and I ran to him, too eagerly at first. Self-conscious, I slowed to a walk.

"You shouldn't be here," he said, concern carved into his face. "It's not safe. Too many warriors we can't vouch for."

He *was* watching out for me. Was this his idea or Sargon's?

I hoped it was Thane's.

"I was checking the horses. I'll go back inside the castle."

As he escorted me across the yard, I watched the parade of men and horses. Some came in chainmail, while others wore ceremonial tunics.

"Those are the Danes." Thane pointed to a group of tall blond men in flashy red colors. They seemed to favor longbows.

"So each area or Earldom has a different set of weapon preferences?"

"To some extent. Here, we tend to be swordsmen. Though I compete in longbow."

"I would have thought you were a wrestler." I smiled, remembering his quick moves with Steve.

He shrugged. "I've done that as well."

"I'm sure you do a lot of things well."

He leaned toward me, his warm breath on my ear. "Be careful, Lady, or you may find out."

I blushed, happy with his teasing.

"The southerners are skilled with horses," he continued, "so the best jousters come from there. They have the finest horses. See, over there."

We watched in awe at the spectacle of horse and riders in armor. Each jouster had a groom to help him dismount as the armor was very heavy and awkward. The jousting sticks were several yards long and extremely sharp.

Deadly...

I quaked at the thought.

"In the far north," he said, "they value feats of strength, like mace and caber toss." He steered me away. "Be careful where you wander these next few days, Rowena. Stay with one of us at all times. Every room in the castle will be taken tonight and men will be drinking heavily."

What a good man Thane was.

"Thank you for the advice," I said. I took a deep breath. "Are the Norland men here yet?"

"They've camped in the northern fields. They won't venture in here."

That sounded ominous.

"Will they be here for the opening feast tonight?"

Thane guided me up the castle steps. "Not the regular men. Only the leaders have been invited."

My heart pounded furiously as I watched him leave. Gareth would be here tonight. With Janus and Cedric.

With trepidation, I touched my stomach.

Before the feast, I went looking for Kendra. She wasn't in her own room. I decided to check Grandfather's room. He wasn't there either.

But Cedric was.

With his back to me, he looked magnificent, masculine and fit. The ceremonial tunic he wore was in the Huel colors of green and gold.

I felt that magnetic pull again.

Cedric spun around, his green eyes meeting mine. *Zing!*

"I've just arrived," he said. "Jon is with me."

"I'm glad he's here."

He met me in three strides. "You carry our child." There was wonder in his voice.

"I can't be sure."

"I can."

He embraced me and I cried out in pain.

Jerking back, Cedric yanked my dress from the shoulder, exposing the raw wound. "Bastard," he hissed. "That bastard wolf-child of a demented witch. He can't be human. Not one more night does he deserve to live on this earth. I'll kill him."

"No," I cried, terrified.

"You think I'd risk you now, seeing this? You think I'll allow him to touch you again? You carry my child. Mine!" He paced the floor. "I should have been quicker. I didn't know. I should have realized his nature would lead to such violence."

"I'm safe for now," I insisted. "He doesn't touch me now because of the babe. Kendra told him it was risky."

"Is it?"

"Not at all. She told him that to protect me from him."

"Smart girl. I'm beginning to like this strange cousin of yours."

"You'll be at the feast tonight?" I asked, knowing he'd protect me from all the others—whether I liked it or not.

"I need one more night to work my plan."

"What plan?" I heard footsteps. "Someone's coming!"

Cedric didn't move, his mind was elsewhere, so I fled.

There was no one in hall.

Maybe I'd imagined the footsteps.

As I ran down the stairs, men poured in through the main doors. When they noticed me, their unruly chatter stopped. I lifted my skirt so I wouldn't trip and as I rushed past, one man tried to touch my hair. Gritting my teeth, I hurried down the side corridor toward the royal suite.

A strange little man blocked my way. He was old, wise looking and very thin, but he didn't seem threatening.

"Hello," I said, smiling.

Wordlessly, he held out a small wrinkled hand, his fist closed.

"You want to give me something?" I asked, surprised.

He grinned, nodded and dropped something small and cool into my outstretched hand. Then the man darted down the corridor.

I opened my hand and stared at the man's gift. It was a ring of blue stones. And it matched the Tintegal broach.

That could only mean one thing. Gareth was near.

The champions were gathering.

Kendra and Logan were waiting in the royal suite.

"I was looking everywhere for you, Row." Kendra blew out a relieved breath. "We're moving you to the top floor. Logan's already transported most of your belongings."

"Can you do it without me?" I asked, yawning. "I'm sort of weary and could do without all those steps."

"Of course we can," Logan said.

Kendra nodded. "Do you want to lie down for a bit?"

"Not really. I'll sit by the window and keep out of your way. Come get me when you're done."

While they packed and chatted, I gazed out the window. The square was busy with activity.

A tall, blond man caught my eye. Gareth.

His eyes found mine and he gave a brief nod of recognition. He held up one finger and I nodded. Then I waited.

Moments later, Gareth materialized outside my window.

"Rowena," he said in a strangled voice.

It tugged at my heart. This was the first time I had seen him since that fateful day of the arrow. I remembered how he had appeared that first time in my classroom, like a Viking prince from some dramatic opera. I recalled his strapping body and the muscled arms that would put any weightlifter to shame.

One arm was useless now, cradled in a sling.

"Your shoulder," I said, my eyes never leaving his face. "How is it?"

"It heals. I won't be competing this week."

"I'm sorry. For everything."

Ivan had done that to him. And Ivan had suffered for it. We both knew that and left it unsaid.

"You look beautiful." His blue eyes gleamed. "Like in my dreams."

It was hardly a beautiful dress I was wearing, the green muslin. But I thanked him all the same.

"You're with child, I hear."

I sucked in a breath. "Word gets around."

"Could it be mine?"

"It's possible."

He cursed. "Does the wolf-king treat you well?"

Fear must have been evident in my eyes because he cursed again. His whole body shook with anger.

"I cannot apologize enough for our last minutes together, Rowena. If I ever meet Ivan again, it will be his death."

"He was banished," I said. "That is as good as dead."

"He shamed the woman I love. Death is too good for him. I have something much better in mind."

"Gareth, leave it alone. There is enough violence around us."

"Damn this arm," he muttered. "I hate being helpless. If I were well, this would all be settled."

Gareth would not be my savior this week. And I was loath to tell him how long it would take for his arm to fully recover. Those muscles would atrophy from disuse, as I knew from my medical training. It would take at least three months to regain his former strength.

"When I am well, it *will* be settled. My forces are almost ready and they are formidable, believe me."

I shuddered. "Gareth, no. Please…don't start a war over me."

"What better reason could there be?"

What living, breathing woman would not respond to such a sentiment? This big blond Viking would always own a corner of my heart. But the rest was reserved for Thane.

"Don't do anything foolish this week," I pleaded. "It's too dangerous with all these strange warriors about. We don't know their true allegiances."

"I see you wear my broach." He touched it. "How that pleases me. It will protect you, my love."

"Then I should give it to you so you will be safe."

He laughed. "You lovely thing. It's you who needs protecting. You and your child. Please me by wearing it always."

I reached into the pocket of my dress. "I must give you back this ring. I don't want Sargon to see it."

He reached for me, but I heard footsteps and backed away.

"Hail, Norland," Sargon said over my shoulder. "You have met my wife, I see."

Gareth nodded in courtesy. "We were previously acquainted, Sire, as you may have noticed from the broach."

"Ah yes! I had meant to ask about that. Somehow it slipped my mind."

Oh no, I thought. Not now.

"Your arm does well?" I asked again, as a distraction.

"It mends," Gareth said. "But far too slowly to suit me."

Sargon's mouth twisted into a scornful smile."You grow old, Norland. Old men don't heal as quickly. We will see you tonight. Come, Rowena."

He steered me away from the window. I resisted the urge to look back at Gareth, suspecting he was already gone.

I followed Sargon down the hall to the tower staircase.

"That wasn't a very nice thing to say," I said.

"I don't like the way he looks at you. He makes it plain, his regard for you."

There was nothing I could say to that, so I said nothing.

I spotted Kendra skipping down the back stairs. She greeted me with a wave and curtsied in Sargon's direction.

He left me with her.

As soon as he was gone, I said, "Kendra, I'm starving. Let's go to the kitchen and rustle something up."

"Now? Shouldn't we be getting ready?"

"Can't wait. I threw up everything this morning. I could eat a horse and a half now. Come on."

When we got to the kitchen courtyard, George was busy with the roasting spits. The fragrance of roasted pork and wild duck smelled delicious.

"Go on in the kitchen and help yourselves," George said.

Even Ralph was happy to see us. He wagged his tail nonstop.

I spotted a bowl of steamed shrimp. "Look, Kendra. Seafood."

"Yum. The southern folk must have brought it. And mussels. And real buns and fresh churned butter."

Without waiting for a plate, I started stuffing my face.

One for Ralph, five for me.

I heard a noise.

Ivan's groom stood in the doorway. He was a creepy fellow with stringy hair and bad breath. He should be down south with Ivan.

"Patrick." I nodded. "What are you doing here? Is Ivan okay?"

"You can see that for yourself. I'm taking you to him now."

"I don't think so."

Kendra straightened, immediately alert.

"He's right around the corner," Patrick insisted. "He's come to take you south."

I sighed. This day sucked.

"Nope. Not going. A whole lot of people have been trying to rescue me all day long. Frankly, I'm getting a bit tired of it. So you go back to Ivan and tell him thanks but no thanks. Nothing personal. I hope he's doing well."

Patrick stared at me as if I were some sort of weird sea monster. Then he vanished.

"I handled that pretty well, I think," I said to Kendra, who was feeding Ralph shrimp tails.

"What is it with you and the men here?"

"Maybe they don't have enough to do," I said, shoving a thick slice of pork into my mouth.

Ivan strode into the kitchen.

My jaw dropped. "Are you completely out of your mind coming here? Sargon will string you up like a Peking duck if he finds you."

"I came to get you."

He reached for me, but I jumped back. "I'm not going anywhere, Ivan. I'm very sorry, but I can't leave Grandfather. And where would you take me anyway? You've been banished. Besides, I have the baby to think of now."

"I want you with me." His mouth pursed in determination. "So you're coming with me."

"Stop bullying me!" I yelled, backing up into the shelves. "You're always bullying me."

"I haven't time for this!"

He grabbed my arm and dragged me across the kitchen.

"Let go of her!" Kendra demanded. "Or I'll bust your balls."

He glared at her. "I'll bust more than that if you try."

"Ivan!" I snapped. "You're hurting me."

He twisted my arm behind my back. I screamed.

"Be quiet," he said between clenched teeth. "You're coming now."

"She's not going anywhere."

The room went still.

Cedric blocked the doorway to the kitchen. "You heard the lady. Let go of her now."

Seeing them face off like this made me realize how incredibly well matched they were. One was light and the other dark, but in all other ways and in height and build, they looked like brothers.

Ivan scowled. "Cedric, get out of my way or I'll kill you."

"I'll put you in hell myself!"

Ivan released my arm and charged across the room. The dog followed, barking furiously. Ralph launched into the air and knocked Cedric to the floor, then proceeded to jump on Cedric's back.

Cedric growled. "Will somebody get the damn—"

Ivan hauled back, preparing a vicious kick to Cedric's head.

"Stop it!" I screeched like a banshee. "Stop it!"

I had to do something, so I acted on instinct. I jumped Ivan from behind, circling my legs around his waist. He hollered, but I had his head in a double armlock, and he couldn't see.

"Satan's whore!" he yelled.

We swung around, glued together like a rodeo cowboy on the back of a bucking bronco in a really bad western. Round and round we lurched, me holding on like a boa constrictor and Ivan trying to tear my arms off his head.

From the corner of my eye, I saw Kendra reach casually for the cauldron on the stove. Hot meat stew hit Ivan square in the chest and face, and me on his back.

"What the devil was that?" he roared.

We went down sideways in a slithery tangle of arms and legs, meat chunks and cooked carrots. I gasped for breath and tried to get up on my knees, but the stew was everywhere. I slipped and fell on my face.

"Bollocks!" Ivan bellowed, clawing at his eyes.

Kendra let out a whoop. "Food fight!"

"Woof!" Ralph apparently agreed with her and decided to clamber off Cedric, who was now also swimming in meat, vegetables and gravy.

As the dog skidded past me on a sea of stew, a bun hit the back of my head. Then another. And another. The air was suddenly filled with flying buns, vegetables and platters of antipasto.

I yelped and scrambled under the table.

Cedric crawled over to Ivan, slipping and sliding and cursing like a sailor. Ivan pushed up on one knee and opened his mouth to speak. A plate of marinated octopus landed on his head and slithered down his face.

He roared, clawing with his hands.

Down he went again.

"Get him, Kendra!" I screeched with all the class of a gangster moll. "Get Ivan!"

Shrieking and hollering, I remained under my table of safety, while Kendra continued to pelt Ivan with seafood antipasto. The dog barked, excited by the feeding frenzy, and leapt in the air to catch tasty bits before they hit the floor. Cedric reached Ivan and they rolled on the slate floor, food mashing beneath them.

"Geronimo!" Kendra hurled a plate of lethal asparagus spears.

None of us had noticed the crowd gathering.

"Holy Mother of God," Grandfather said from the doorway.

Richard and Logan stood at his side like stone statues.

Silence.

Cedric and Ivan stopped swiping at each other. Kendra froze, a plate of fruit in her hands. Even Ralph stopped eating.

"What are you doing?" Grandfather demanded.

I poked my head out from under the table and wiped a shrimp from my hair. "We couldn't wait for dinner."

We might as well have sold tickets for the audience our food fight had attracted. Everyone was there—even Thane. He smiled widely and shook his head at me. Gareth and Janus were laughing their stupid heads off.

Sargon, who missed the first act, turned up for the applause. I think he was miffed, but it was hard to tell because he was also splitting his gut. I think it was the collection of seafood I kept pulling out of my bodice that got him going.

"Ick," I said, removing another shrimp.

Sargon rubbed his forehead. "I don't even know why you bother to get dressed in the morning. You ruin everything you put on."

He escorted me past the snickering unwashed hoards to the showers. They weren't wearing entire food groups like I was.

"What started this?" he asked.

"Ivan came with his henchman to carry me off. Cedric stopped him and Kendra helped."

He cursed. "I hate being indebted to Cedric. Where is Ivan now?"

"Don't know, don't care." I picked a baby carrot out of my hair. "He can rot like a bat in hell, for all I care."

Later, I heard that Richard and Grandfather managed to get Ivan out of the castle and squirreled away to a safe place. Patrick didn't make it. The king's men caught him with the getaway horses. Sargon beheaded him personally to set an example for any others who might want to abscond with the queen. I didn't like Patrick. But to be killed in such a fashion? The poor man.

How could Sargon be so cold blooded?

I despised him all the more.

I went to Kendra's room to get ready for tonight. I wore the sapphire blue because that was the only good gown I had that would cover my wounded shoulder. I loved the dress. It was cut too low for somebody wanting to blend into the woodwork, but I didn't tend to blend well anyway as a rule. I wore the Tintegal broach around my neck.

Kendra wore her red dress and looked very sweet.

"That's a real stunner," she said, surveying my gown. "Don't wreck it."

I groaned. "At the rate I'm going, I'll be completely out of clothes by Sunday."

The men came to get us an hour later, which was great because I wasn't going into the hall without them. No sir, no way. I was through with men today. There was a whole pack of them I could do without seeing. Sargon, Cedric and Gareth, all in one room?

Gulp. Talk about nightmares. The ghosts of lovers past...

The mood in the great hall was boisterous. Nothing like a good beheading to set the tone.

I stepped into the room, trying to make as little commotion as possible. The men began to cheer. Kendra moved to my side as they whooped and hollered.

One man yelled, "The shrimp's here."

"Oh, horse poop," I muttered.

Everybody who hadn't been at the food fight had at least heard about it. It was the talk of the castle.

Kendra waved to the men and I smacked her hand. "Don't encourage them."

"We should take up mud wrestling here." She giggled. "We'd make a fortune."

We made a beeline for the head table and sat quickly.

A fist raised in the air, Sargon silenced the room. "Welcome, friends. Tonight we celebrate a double victory. Our enemy, who sought to abduct the queen today, was vanquished—"

"By the queen!" some idiot yelled.

The hall exploded in laughter.

Sargon raised his fist again, but even he cracked a smile. "And tonight we celebrate the revival of our annual Games of Skill, the Tournament of Sargonia. Men from far across the island have traveled here for fame and glory. We honor you. Enjoy the feast tonight. And may God give you strength tomorrow." He raised his goblet. "A toast!"

Everyone stood, including Kendra and me.

"To glory!" Sargon said.

"To glory!" the crowd echoed.

"And to the queen!" someone said.

"To the queen!"

"To the queen's knickers!" another idiot added.

Someone dumped a tankard on the moron's head and the place roared with laughter and profanity.

Thane was positioned behind the drunken fool. I watched as he lifted the man out of his chair as easily as he might a child. Out the doors they went.

Things calmed down a bit and we actually got to eat. Since the birds had come back, I was always starving. I ate everything within reach, including a few pieces of chicken I pinched from Kendra's plate. I had to drink two goblets of ale to wash everything down.

At the corner table with Grandfather, Jon, Richard and men from the far south, Cedric watched me with hooded eyes. He had cleaned up pretty well and didn't show any injury from the food fight. I noted that he always sat with his back to the wall, like they did in old westerns.

Gareth sat at the center table with Janus and several of the Danes. At one point, he caught my eye and smiled. When he raised his tankard to me, I smiled back and blew him a kiss. That was a mistake. His whole table hooted and hollered.

"Slow down," Sargon warned "You're drinking too fast." He took my goblet.

Crap, I thought, I shouldn't be drinking so much. Not with the baby. First thing tomorrow, I would go to the kitchen to boil some water for drinking.

Kendra urged me to join her en route to the washroom.

Yes, even in Land's End we went in pairs.

Giggling, we exited the hall. Raucous laughter followed us through the hall. We stepped outside. It was a lovely night.

For privacy's sake, we headed for some bushes. I got to go first because I was "older and preggers," as Kendra put it.

When it was Kendra's turn, I waited around the corner, staring up at the stars. There were millions of them here—bright, twinkling, almost scary in their numbers. I never saw that many at home, not even in the desert.

Cedric came up behind me and pulled me into his arms. I was about to tell him he was crazy, when he turned me around and kissed me. His mouth came down hard on mine, and it was all I could do to keep standing upright. In fact, I couldn't. I'd drank too much. With a giggle, I fell back against his arm, which gave way. Then I was on the ground, sprawled like a starfish.

Cedric cursed. He gave me his good hand and hauled me up.

Gareth rushed down the castle steps. "Rowena, did he hurt you?"

Cedric frowned. "Norland, stay back. I've no quarrel with you. It's that wolf-fiend who does her evil. I'm not the one trying to eat her alive."

He pulled the dress off my shoulder to expose the wound, but his actions did more than that. My breast fell out.

Could I be more embarrassed?

Gareth swore in a language I didn't understand.

I shrugged out of Cedric's reach and adjusted my dress. "Ssstop doing that," I slurred. "Everyone's always pulling my bodice down and it's getting really, really annoying."

Kendra appeared. "Leave her alone. Both of you. Hasn't she been through enough today?"

"Yes, leave her alone," Sargon snarled, emerging from the shadows. "We've already had one beheading this eve."

His threat was palpable. I felt barely contained fury all around me.

"Come wife," Sargon said, grabbing my arm. "It's time you were to bed."

I looked over my shoulder. "Kendra?"

She followed a few steps until Sargon said, "Stop there. She has no need of you tonight."

I gave a little sob as he hauled me inside the castle. When I looked back, Cedric and Gareth were talking, while Kendra stared after me, a worried frown on her face.

When we reached the room, Sargon waited until I was inside before leaving me to return to the celebration. He locked the door behind him.

I slept like the dead that night. It hardly mattered that I was in a strange bed in a strange room at the top of the castle somewhere.

Sargon was elsewhere and I felt safe.

Chapter 28

At first light, I took stock of the new room. It was actually a suite with two rooms. The first contained only the bed I had slept in. The second held a single desk, a chair and an entire wall lined with doors.

I opened the first door and found a closet full of weapons. I closed it quickly. Then I went to the farthest door. Inside were my dresses, hanging neatly in a row. My vet bag was at the bottom. My pink backpack and cowboy boots as well. Kendra's work, no doubt.

This suite was sparsely furnished. It looked disused, for the most part. There were no draperies or tapestries on the walls. Windows opened to the front courtyard, toward the drawbridge. You could see for miles down the dirt path leading up to the castle.

Good for surveying all who might want to force the gates, I reckoned.

I dressed in the sleeveless lilac dress with the scoop neck. It had a filmy capelet off the back that attached at the shoulders and swept down to my waist, spanning the distance between day dress and evening gown. I wore a matching headband and the broach.

I went to find Kendra. She was in her room.

"Wear something nice," I said. "We'll be on the podium most of the morning."

Today was the longbow trials. I was rather excited. Thane would be competing. Probably Janus too. It was going to be a good day—a great day.

Shows how wrong a girl from the golden west can be.

We stopped in the kitchen first for something to eat. It was miraculously clean and showed no ill effects from our episode the day before. George was frying up bread left over from last night's feast. Believe it or not, bread fried in pork fat is one of the most delectable things on earth when you're starving.

I had a revelation.

"Hey, Kendra, I'm not throwing up."

This was the first day I hadn't started with the chamber pot as my best friend.

"That's a relief," she said. "I worry about you losing weight."

"I'm making up for it now."

George brought over scrambled eggs. I shoveled them in between bites of fried bread and drank a load of sterilized water.

When I was full, I rose. "Thank you, George."

I kissed his cheek and his face reddened.

Kendra reached down to pat Ralph, who was dining on leftovers she'd *accidentally* dropped.

"Let's walk around the castle to the main square," I suggested.

In the square, the men filed out the main gates to the fields beyond. There was great excitement everywhere. Groups of all sizes gathered, examining each other's weapons.

In the distance, I saw the jousters practicing.

"Where's Logan?" I asked.

"On the field practicing."

Sargon saw me from the castle steps. Approaching in his ceremonial black, he greeted Kendra and me with a smile. I had to continually remember to wipe the fear off my face when he was near.

"You look pretty today," he said with satisfaction.

I felt like a butterfly pinned to a board. "Thank you."

"Thane is practicing his longbow with the others. We'll go watch him together. Wait for me here. I'll not be long."

Richard materialized at Kendra's side. And I felt Cedric behind me. How was it I could feel his presence before I saw him?

I felt for the chain around my neck. The Roman coin was fastened though the pin on the back of the Tintegal broach.

"You shouldn't be standing with me," I whispered to Cedric.

We watched Sargon stride away from us.

"Watch this," Cedric said, all keyed up. "It happens now."

"What are you going to do?"

"Stay here." He sauntered into the center of the yard. "Sargon, I hear your wife is with child. Have you taken precautions to ensure it is your own?" His voice rang clear across the yard.

Beside me, Richard and Kendra gasped in unison.

Sargon stood stone still, his back to us.

"Cedric, no!" I cried.

Sargon turned slowly and faced Cedric. His face was cold with fury.

His hand went to his sword. He unsheathed it.

I ran across the dirt and grabbed his arm. "No! He'll kill you."

Sargon backhanded me across the face and I fell to the ground, stunned.

The whole courtyard was hushed.

"You strike your pregnant wife?" Cedric sneered. He spat on the ground. "I will not treat her so when she is mine."

He could not have said anything more incendiary.

Richard rushed forward and tried to haul me away, while a crowd of infuriated men gathered in the square. More spilled out of the castle.

Sargon's face was black with rage now. There was nothing human left in him. His teeth were bared. His eyes gleamed like hot coal, seeing nothing but his opponent. They became two beasts circling in the sun, the golden lion and the black wolf.

I wanted to look away, but couldn't. Cedric wordlessly willed me to watch. His power circled over me. Then it funneled up into the sky.

Sargon swung first.

The clang of swords echoed in the air. Overhead, dark clouds gathered, creating shadows on the ground. The swords hit again, and thunder cracked, clouds crashed against each other. Another clang. Then a yell, a blur of motion and the roar of thunder.

Sargon's sword arm hit the ground. Then his head sailed past me.

I screamed.

The courtyard exploded with shocked voices.

The earth raced up to meet me as I crashed to the ground, fighting the hideous vision burned in my retina.

"The king is dead!" someone screamed.

Then all around me, I heard, "The king is dead!"

Someone picked me up as easily as if I were a rag doll. He smelled of sweat and animal blood.

"Put your arms around my neck," Cedric said.

Obeying him, I buried my eyes in his shoulder. Silent sobs wracked my body.

"Stay back, Norland," Cedric commanded. "Rowena is my kin, not yours. You have no rights and you cannot win today."

Cedric turned to Richard. "Bring Kendra. Jon, get the men to pack up and follow. Be swift."

I was lifted on a horse—not Lightning. Cedric mounted in a sweep behind me and kicked us forward. He held me with one great arm. My head flung back against his chest as we set off.

I heard screams behind us, but could not utter a sound.

We galloped out the gates and to the east. The sky was growing blacker by the minute.

Ahead, I saw a mighty line of men on horseback. A thousand or more, all dark and featureless in the mist. We raced toward them and I thought for sure we would be slaughtered.

Cedric muttered something in a language I did not recognize.

The men on horseback parted in the middle so we could pass. Then they closed rank behind us.

"My men," he said. "From the south."

Or straight from hell, I thought.

We rode as though the hounds of Hades were after us. I swear the stallion never touched the ground.

Thunder chased us until we reached the river. There, we stopped and dismounted to water the horses. Richard and Kendra rode up beside us, while the others followed at a distance.

Richard leapt off his horse. "Cedric, you risk us all."

"You prefer to stay behind? They might decide to kill all from Huel. I would. I got us out of there. The defense will hold 'til tomorrow."

"But to kill the king—"

"'Twas the only way."

"But why?"

"That demented fiend nearly killed her."

One more time, he yanked the dress off my shoulder.

Jon caught up and gasped when he saw the wound.

"Next time it could have been her throat," Cedric said. "I sought to bring her home. The child is mine."

Richard went white. Jon cursed.

"The wolf would never let her go," Cedric said. "I *had* to kill him."

"This is evil that you do," Richard said. He had never seemed more like a man, the golden boy gone forever.

Cedric's eyes narrowed. "You will swear allegiance to *me*. Or die with them, cousin."

There was a nasty silence.

"I stand with Huel and always will. But don't make me do your evil."

Cedric stared at him a moment, then nodded.

Castle Huel was bustling. In the courtyard, a hundred hardened men stood by. I knew not one. More men from the south, no doubt. After Kendra dismounted, I took her hand. Eyes followed us all the way up the stone stairs.

We gathered in the great hall. Bone weary, I slumped into a chair. Kendra sat across from me with Richard. Cedric paced the floor.

Grandfather entered with Jon.

"Cedric, they tell me the child is yours," Grandfather said.

"It is."

"How do you know?"

"I know. I knew the second life took hold."

"Your dark arts…"

"He drugged her," Kendra blurted.

"For the pain," Cedric said.

"Pain doesn't explain why you came to the door naked," Kendra said.

Grandfather could not have been more appalled. "And Rowena?"

Kendra glanced at me. "She was in bed."

I hid my face in my hands. Could this day get any worse?

"First Ivan ties her like an animal," Grandfather said, shaking his head. "And now you drug her, Cedric. The very men sworn to protect her. Is there no honor in this house? Jon, do *you* have anything to confess?"

Jon went white.

"No," I called out before he could answer. "He stopped himself."

There was more stilted silence.

"By the river that first day, before he knew who I was. He was…a gentleman." Kind of. Eventually.

"Ivan tied her up," Cedric snapped.

"You're no better using drugs," Grandfather said. "There is evil in you. If you harm her—"

"I would never harm her! Never. How could you think it? I faced that band of brigands to keep her safe. I risked my life today. It drove me mad to see him strike her. I could not lose after that."

We would never be free of that memory.

"Think, Sire, a child," Cedric said seductively. "What you've always wanted. A true child of Huel, sired by me, and out of Rowena. Our very future. Is that not worth the risk?"

"You'll marry her."

"In a church?" Cedric laughed and crossed his arms. "Why not? That will be…interesting. But I have another ceremony in mind as well."

I felt cold through and through.

Grandfather gathered my hair in his hands. "My poor Rowena. This world of ours is hard on women. You alone give me hope, dear one. May this child you carry be our salvation." He kissed my forehead, then turned to Cedric. "We need to make plans. Take the women upstairs and return to the hall."

Cedric nodded. "Kendra, go to Richard and obey him. He will be your protector."

We all knew what that meant. He was giving her to Richard.

"I need her claimed," he told me before I could protest. "I can't have the men fighting."

Richard's face was fused with red. He nodded once.

"She can have the room next to Rowena's old one," Cedric said. "I'm taking Rowena to the tower."

He waited for someone to dare fight him on this.

"You're mad." Grandfather face was aghast, the deep lines clearly showing. "She lost her husband today. Have you forgotten?"

"I'm not letting her out of my sight. I can protect her there." Cedric's mouth hardened. "Come, cousins."

Grandfather took a step forward, but Jon caught his arm. From the stairs, I saw the two of them in a heated argument. Of all the men, Jon alone seemed to grasp the rising danger in Cedric.

We left Kendra with Richard on the second floor. At the end of the corridor, we climbed a circular stone staircase to the light at the top. Cedric took my hand and led me into the tower suites, which resembled something from a fairy tale.

The first room was square, with wardrobes, a table and tapestries lining every wall. It led to a second circular room with windows on three sides. A lone bed stood in the middle.

"These are my rooms," he said proudly. "As eldest, I got my pick. I love the view from here."

We stood at the northernmost window, looking out. You could see all the way to the river. I saw the forest in the distance, my path to the real world. One where flying severed heads wasn't the norm.

I found the courage to speak my mind. "Cedric, tell me…am I anything more to you than breeding stock? Do you like me or even my looks at all? You never say a word."

"I haven't?"

I shook my head. "Not once."

God, I sounded pathetic. But it had been a horrible day and I needed to know where I stood with this violent man, who now controlled my future. My safety rested in knowing my power over him—if I had any.

"Your hair is like a waterfall of autumn leaves. Your eyes are lovely, so like mine, but softer." His finger traced my mouth. "These lips call me closer. And your shape, good lady, your shape drives me mad. These beautiful breasts…" He cupped them.

I thought about Thane, wishing these were his hands on me.

"I nearly grabbed you right in the church that first time I gazed upon you," he continued. "This tiny waist, these ample hips that are made for childbirth." His hands traced down my hips. "I even love this brand upon your shoulder. It reminds me how you stood in the clearing like a goddess, with your head held high, defying them, even as they stripped you."

He grabbed my hands. "There is not one thing I do not love about you, Lady. And love you I surely must or I wouldn't be playing with hellfire like I am."

"What do you mean?"

He put his mouth on mine and kissed me gently, then more deeply. The ache in me was agonizing. I leaned into him.

He laughed and held me off. "Always, *always,* you surprise me. Keep your need warm. I'll be back before long."

When he left, I felt a void. It was like the room had emptied of life itself. For a long while, I sat on the bed.

Sargon was dead. I was safe from him.

Though it was a relief, the horrible way in which it had happened would always haunt me. But I couldn't be sorry. I had been an abused wife in a world where women had no rights.

Was there anything worse?

But life with Cedric wouldn't be much better. This strange link between us disturbed me. I knew it had to be magic in origin, and it seemed to be getting stronger.

I brooded until men arrived, carrying our belongings. I busied myself by hanging the clothing away in wardrobes. It looked as if all of my stuff had been collected—except for one thing.

The wooden chess set.

I smiled sadly. Thane would have something to remember me by. Would I ever see him again?

Much later, Cedric entered the room.

I was in bed, but still awake.

"Your grandfather says I'm an unspeakable fiend if I force you to have sex with me the very night of your husband's death." He sat down on the mattress. "There's a certain amount of truth to that, since I was the one who killed him."

This was new—Cedric acting rational.

I fought for control as an invisible power overtook me.

"I am grateful for that," I said.

Were those my words, my voice? The draw to him was almost unbearable now. A spell?

His eyes lit up."You didn't love Sargon."

"I hated him in the end. I feel like you've released me from prison. Can you imagine what it is like to have to submit to someone you hate?"

"Did he know that?"

"I'm sure he didn't. I covered it well."

"Because if *I* found out after all our lovemaking that you hated me, I would kill you."

Panic seared my throat. "Why? I don't understand."

"It's the betrayal. I give my love and you *pretend* to, and all the time you're despising me. It doesn't bear thinking about."

"Then don't."

I turned to the wall, hiding the fear on my face. Cedric pulled his tunic over his head and slid into bed. I could feel his eyes on my back.

"No," he murmured, "I think not tonight. Instead, we will wait until after the ceremony."

I was so relieved I nearly wept.

Chapter 29

I was getting married today. Again.

"You know, you might want to rethink this whole marriage thing," I said to Cedric when we were getting dressed. "I'm rather hard on husbands, in case you hadn't noticed."

He raised an eyebrow.

"They don't last long," I reminded him. "Remember? It might not be in your best interests."

Amused, he chuckled. "I have protections that even you can't sabotage."

"I wouldn't be too sure of that."

I'd been doing pretty well without even trying. One husband was dead; the other was as good as dead. Pretty scary for less than a month.

Two of Cedric's men had to go south for the priest, so the wedding was set for early evening. There was to be a small dinner after.

It was already noon when I made my way to Kendra's room. She was sitting by the window, brooding.

"What's wrong?" I said, plopping down on the bed.

"I don't know what's up with Richard." Frustration oozed from her. "He wouldn't come into the room last night. He wouldn't say a thing. He stood at the door, went all red and then left. When I got up this morning, I found him sleeping on the floor in the hall, lying up against the door."

I held back a laugh. "I expect he has some issues of loyalty to deal with internally."

She started pacing. "Maybe I got it wrong, but I thought Richard was supposed to be my protector, which means—well, you know. Doesn't he want to?"

A laugh escaped. "I'm sure he wants to very much, Kendra. That's why he's always blushing. But Logan is—or was—his friend. He doesn't know what to do the fact that you were Logan's girl."

We quietly mused about the men of this world.

"Do you miss Logan?" I asked.

"Yes! Of course I do. But I get this thing about families. You're my family, so I need to be here when there is trouble. I can't stay with Logan. We're not married."

"Do you love him?"

"I sure like him a lot. I mean, we had lots of fun together. He's a very physical guy. Maybe that's some of the problem. He's *all* physical." She sighed. "I may not look like an intellectual, but I am in the university taking some pretty demanding courses. And Logan? Well, he's more the apprenticeship type—if you get my drift."

I nodded. "You need someone to challenge you intellectually."

"Or at least be interested in something beyond weapons. I don't know. Maybe it was a good thing we never got to talking about marriage. I can't imagine people get divorced around here."

"No, that's pretty much not allowed. They kind of kill you for that." It was my turn to sigh. "Which reminds me...I'm getting married this evening. Again. Third time."

She groaned. "So soon?"

"Afraid so. Not that I have much choice about it."

"How do you feel about it?"

"Confused. Frustrated. Resigned. I hated this lack of personal freedom. I hate losing control of my own destiny." I gritted my teeth. Cedric takes it from me, as Sargon did, without a thought. On the other hand, he's kind to me, which is the most important thing right now. And he's awfully attentive."

"I'm getting the feeling that's important to you."

"Never thought it was. I mean, with Steve things were okay but rather ho-hum. I always got the idea he'd rather show me off than keep me to himself. Cedric makes it clear he can't keep his hands off me. It's sort of like he's been saving up for a decade, waiting for me to be his."

Kendra gave me a sad smile. "Wish I had that problem."

"Let me remind you that you are still only eighteen, missy, and a little young to be pining over lusty men."

"Nineteen next month."

"I turned twenty-five last month," I said.

What a nice day that had been. Dad had been in town and took me out for dinner at the Biltmore. I had lobster and the most wonderful dark-chocolate soufflé for dessert.

Oh crikey, I thought. *Dad.*

"Kendra, can I call Dad again on your cell phone? Mine doesn't seem to work from here."

"Sure. One sec."

She reached into her bag, found her phone and flipped it open.

"That's strange. I can't get any reception."

"Crap. Let me see that."

Sure enough, no bars. Yet, we'd had full reception at Castle Sargon.

"Guess we're out of reach."

Darn. I really wanted to hear Dad's voice.

"Cedric's a smart guy, isn't he?" Kendra said. "He knows I'm not going to leave you, especially now you're tied to him. And Richard will have to be loyal and stay on Cedric's good side by being with me."

"Oh, he's clever all right."

"Do you think you could ever love him?"

"I don't know. I feel something very strong when I am near him and it scares the daylights out of me."

"Why?"

I stared out the window. The green hills of Huel were shadowed by huge cumulous clouds.

"There are aspects to Cedric you don't know about. He has a dark side, and although he's only ever used it to rescue me, I know there must be more to it. I...don't want to get drawn into that again.

"Maybe you'll have a choice, Row."

"Maybe. I doubt it." I felt that chill again. "I don't seem to have much choice when it comes to Cedric."

"Can you look at things in a different way? Like the guy killed the creep, who was beating you up. And he rescued you before from those lecherous bandits. That's got to be a big plus. Besides, you seem to enjoy the physical part with Cedric. Are things really that bad? I mean, you have to be allied with some male guy in this world. It's just the way things are. I take it—from that whole kitchen food fight scene—that Ivan wouldn't be your top choice."

No, I yearned for Thane. I missed his gentleness.

But Kendra didn't know this, and I wasn't ready to tell her.

"No." I smiled. "Ivan and I fight like brother and sister. And this way, with Cedric, I get to stay with you, Grandfather and my family at Huel. So you're right. Things could be a lot worse."

Kendra patted my arm. "I'll go wherever you are, so don't worry about leaving me behind. You won't. You'll need me when you give birth."

Realization suddenly struck me.

Good God, I was going to have a baby!

I would have it in this primitive world, with no hospitals or doctors. And Cedric was convinced it was *his*.

What if it wasn't? How would he react? What if the baby had black hair and black eyes? Or blond hair and blue eyes? How would he feel if the baby was Gareth's? Or Ivan's?

Or Sargon's...

Of course, this assumed that I survived the birth.

"It does feel like we belong here," Kendra said, gazing out the window. "It's prettier country than Sargonia. Softer somehow. These rolling green hills remind me of Tennessee and Kentucky. I like it." She spun on one heel, facing me. "What are you wearing tonight?"

"Haven't thought about it. Could be a problem. I'm definitely running out of gowns again, and I can't wear the same ones I wore to my last two weddings. That would be creepy."

"Maybe we should go on a closet search through the castle."

"I need to find some bigger dresses. Or figure out a way to let them out."

Already, I was noticing a difference in the fullness of my breasts. My waist would be next. Oh joy.

"You need to learn how to look after your clothes," she chastised.

"I know."

She giggled. "How many dresses have you ruined so far?"

I tallied them. "The green silk, the ivory muslin, the light green, the white and pink...they're toast. The one from the ride yesterday needs some repair to the bodice. Oh, and the gorgeous one with the vest from the mud fight. You weren't here for that."

"Mud fight?"

"Ivan."

"Oh."

Time to change the subject.

"Let's go down to the stables. I'll help you brush up on your vet skills."

We spent the next two hours checking over the horses and meeting the grooms. The head groom here doubled as farrier. He was a huge man of about fifty years old with a jolly sense of humor. His name was Pip.

"Lightning's antsy again." I brushed her, trying to calm her.

"It's the palomino," Pip said. "He's a persistent brute. I'm keeping them well apart."

"There must be something in the air here. Where is he now?"

"The Lord has him out."

It was nearing the time of my wedding. I stood alone at the wardrobe trying to decide what to wear. My options consisted of four dresses. The blue sapphire, which was too heavy for this milder weather, the deep cherry off-the-shoulder, which I couldn't wear as it would display the wound on my shoulder and two dresses I hadn't worn yet. One was a fine ivory linen with gold trim. Not one of my best colors, but it was rather modest and very Grecian.

It would do well for tonight.

The other dress was black silk. It had the same empire waist with fully gathered skirt and scoop neck. At first, I thought it was a sleeveless mourning dress, but it was cut much lower in front. On closer inspection, I realized it wasn't sleeveless at all. Ribbons of fabric draped from the underarm and wrapped around the upper arms.

What an odd style. It almost looked Goth.

For fun, I tried it on. You would think it had been cut specially for me. I couldn't help but stare at my reflection in the mirror. Not mourning—oh no, it didn't give *that* affect at all. Far too sexy.

Who was this weird priestess?

The dress had come from the box room at Castle Sargon. Who had it belonged to? Sargon's mother?

I decided to leave it out to show Kendra. She'd get a kick out of it.

In the meantime, I dressed in the ivory. It made me look…innocent. If that was possible in my condition. I brushed my hair into a high ponytail and secured it with an elastic band. Then I draped a gold headband around my forehead.

Richard came to get me.

"Everyone's convened in the chapel," he said. "Cedric doesn't want to waste time changing. He'll change after the ceremony."

We continued down the corridor to the great staircase. I had to hustle to keep up with him.

"Why the rush?"

"Cedric's men tend to be simple. If you're married to him, then they will follow him without question in your defense. He knows that being without a husband is dangerous for you. Another man could make a claim—or at least a royal could. But no one wants to come between a man and wife who are married before God. The men may be loyal to Cedric, but if you were married to…say, Thane, now that he will be king, and Cedric ordered his men to take you back, their loyalty would be conflicted."

I nodded.

"It's a race against time," Richard said.

What the heck did he mean by that?

I thought about all that he'd told me. Cedric and everyone else obviously expected something terrible to happen. Soon.

I gasped, realizing I'd missed what he'd said earlier. "Thane automatically becomes king?"

Why had I not thought about this?

"He's next in line to the throne," Richard said.

We left the castle and headed for the small stone chapel.

Halfway there, I stopped. "Richard, what does that mean for my baby? I was married to Sargon when we found out I was pregnant. If my baby is a boy, what does that mean?"

Would my son be an heir to the throne, even though Sargon died before my child was born? I didn't want that. I didn't want my child to be burdened with any responsibilities.

Richard fidgeted with the buttons on his tunic. "I don't know."

The sky was gloomy and ominous as we stepped inside.

The first thing I saw was the scowl on the old priest's face.

Crap! It was the same fellow who'd married me before. He didn't approve of me then, and now that I was pregnant, his opinion sure hadn't changed.

I tried to give the priest a modest smile. But as Kendra said later, I couldn't look modest in a nun's habit.

With his hair tied back, Cedric looked magnificent, though he was dusty from riding. His arms were bare and the leather bands on his wrists were scored with cut marks from fighting.

He turned when he heard us enter the room. When he saw me, he beamed the most radiant smile, one I'll never forget.

Resigned rather than pleased, Grandfather took my arm.

Thunder rolled. Rain pelted against the lead windows and streams of water cascaded down.

I wondered if this was an omen.

The ceremony was over in a flash.

When Cedric kissed me, a crack of thunder shook the chapel.

"You look like a goddess," he whispered.

A rain goddess, no doubt, as I was soaking wet by the time we reached the castle. Rain continued to pour as we raced to the side door. I glanced up and saw sheet lightning sweep the sky in a spectacular display.

Did someone disapprove of this wedding?

We had a small, quiet meal in the great hall. Jon, who was absent for the wedding, joined us. He smiled at me, but looked grim when addressing Cedric. No one made speeches or uttered congratulations and best wishes. The men talked of interim defenses the whole time.

I was occupied with my own worried thoughts.

Toward the end of the meal, Cedric pulled me aside. "There are things I must do tonight. When you finish here, go to our suite and wait up for me." In a blink, he was gone.

I could hardly contain my fear. What was so important that it had to be done on our wedding night?

Sensing my mood, Kendra signaled me with her eyes. I shrugged, then shook my head and turned my attention elsewhere.

"Grandfather, I have a question of a rather legal nature."

"And what is your question?"

"This child I carry—"

"You want to know its status in our world," he said, interrupting me.

I nodded.

"To be honest, I don't know. If a son had been born while Sargon was still your husband, then he would be heir to the throne. Thane would be regent until your son came of age." He rubbed his chin. "But I don't know that this situation has ever happened before. There may be a legal challenge, especially if it can be proved that the child is not Sargon's."

I chill raced up my spine.

"But I don't want my child in line for the throne," I said. "I will certainly not seek that. And you're assuming it is a boy. What if it is a girl?"

"That would be best. I hope it *is* a girl. That would be safer. If you have a girl, then people would leave us alone. She will know Cedric as her father and we will raise her here in safety."

Until she becomes of marriageable age and she becomes another pawn in the marriage games, I thought bitterly.

"I'm not so sure people *will* leave us alone," I admitted. "Not now that I've proved fertile."

Grandfather was silent.

Not long after dinner, I claimed to be weary. The others made a small fuss over me. Leaving them, I climbed the long stairs to the tower.

In the bedroom, I removed the Grecian dress and donned the royal-blue dressing gown that matched my old Natori nightgown.

Crawling into bed, I slipped into a deep sleep.

Chapter 30

When I awoke, the night sky out the window greeted me.

I was still alone.

My eyes were drawn to the tapestry on the southernmost wall. It hung on a thick brass rod, and a matching rod balanced the bottom to keep it from swinging. It was the darkest tapestry in the suite, with blues, golds and greens interwoven against a black background.

In the shadowed room, the colors glowed as if lit from behind. It drew me out of bed. I touched the silk and examined the scene depicted—a night sky, stars, odd symbols and letters in a language unlike any I had seen before. I peeled it away from the wall so I could see the reverse pattern. But I saw something else, something that was completely hidden by the tapestry.

A door.

I'd heard of this sort of thing. Many old castles had hidden passageways to provide escape from enemies if the castle was besieged. Perhaps this led to the chapel. Or to an outlet beyond the castle walls.

I hesitated for only a moment.

The door started six inches above the floor and was only about five feet high. The handle lifted easily. The door swept inward easily, as if frequently used.

I ducked inside and found a narrow spiral stone staircase leading down. It had no railings. Half-melted candles illuminated the way as I started down the steps, which twisted round and round. I followed them carefully, watching my every step.

There were no windows in the stairwell. No one looking at the castle could possibly know it was there.

I shivered.

As I moved down several stories, the air grew colder. The walls were damp. I suspected I was underground. Reaching the bottom of the stairs, I followed a corridor around a bend.

I heard low voices.

Ahead, the corridor brightened and I stepped through a passage into a stone room. It took a moment for my eyes to adjust to the increasing light.

"She answers your call well, Cedric."

I didn't recognize the voice.

"Cedric?"

The air buzzed with electricity. I could feel his excitement.

"I'm here, my love."

Someone took my hand and drew me into the room.

At last, my vision cleared.

The cavernous room was lit by a dozen black candles.

Cedric wore a robe of black, gold and green that matched the tapestry. To his right stood another man, about forty, with curly black hair. He was more compactly built than Cedric and he wore a similar robe. A third older man stared at me. He reminded me of the wizard Merlin, except his head was bare. When he stepped aside, I saw a long wooden altar, draped with a beautiful tapestry similar to the one upstairs.

A single red candle graced the altar.

I looked into Cedric's eyes, which were blazing green, and felt my own will dissolve under their power.

"Rowena, these men are priests of my own faith. This man is my friend Drake." He nodded to the younger man. "And this is our high priest Manfred. They will perform a ceremony tonight that recognizes our marriage. Do not be afraid."

The priests' faces were kind—different from the elderly priest who disapproved of me earlier.

"I am hardly dressed for a public occasion," I said, embarrassed. I wrapped the blue robe around me tighter.

Drake handed me a goblet. "No matter. You are beautiful. And our Master loves beauty. We drink to your union."

I put the goblet to my lips, sipping the delicious, sweet wine.

"Drink more, my love," Cedric urged. "Drink it all."

I drained my goblet. Drake took it from me and refilled it from a decanter, which he placed on the altar.

That's when I noticed the dagger and the rope.

I must have started because Cedric drew me to him. "Rowena, have no fear. I would let nothing hurt you."

My head began to spin.

Damn, he had drugged me again.

I wavered on my feet and clutched his arm for balance.

"Her entry to this room signifies her consent," Manfred said in a gravelly voice. "We may begin."

Drake struck a bell. Three times.

Cedric kissed the top of my head and held me up.

"In nomine Dei nostri Ba'al excelsi," the old priest droned. "In the name of Ba'al, I call upon the forces of Darkness and the infernal power within. Consecrate this place with power and light..." His mesmerizing voice trailed on.

My head grew too heavy to hold up. I leaned against Cedric.

"We call upon the element of fire to come serve us. Flame the passion of Rowena and Cedric, and fill them with all consuming ardor and lust for each other."

My knees gave out. Cedric caught me, lifting me in his arms.

"We call upon the elements of air, earth and water to serve us..."

I drifted in a state of blissful consciousness. Even in my addled mind, this ceremony made sense to me. I could understand it more than the Christian one performed earlier.

"Bring her to the altar so that I may bind your hands," Drake said.

Cedric gently placed me upon the altar. It was cold, but I was glad of the tapestry on it.

"As this cord binds your hands," Manfred said, "so do your lives become joined." He took my right hand and Cedric's left, winding the cord around both. "Rowena, you bring the energy of Babylon—boundless, dark, intuitive and soft."

What a strange a thing to say. I felt no energy at all. In fact, I could not lift my hands to close my gaping dressing gown.

"Cedric, you bring the energy of Ba'al. Wield this blade as a symbol of your love."

Cedric took the dagger. "I pledge my blade, as I pledge my soul, ever to your service. Accept it, my beloved. And with it, all that is mine becomes yours."

He plunged the dagger into the goblet I'd been drinking from.

"Babylon and Ba'al, female and male, dark and light," Manfred chanted. "Neither has meaning without the other, but though their eternal interplay the universe is born."

Flames whirled around me, becoming larger. They illuminated the zealous faces that surrounded me. I sought Cedric's eyes. Even in my drugged state anxious, I was desperate to connect to something or someone real. Something I could understand.

The words from a song played in my mind.

"He prays like a Roman with his eyes on fire."

Around us, a circle of fire burned, but I remained ice cold.

No one said a word. The silence was so intense I could hear the hiss of the candles.

"We will leave now," Manfred said to Cedric. "You may consummate this marriage in the presence of our Master." He untied the cord that bound our hands.

I heard a door close.

My bleary eyes tried to focus in the dark. They had blown out all but one candle, the red one. Cedric removed his robe and leaned over the altar. He caressed my lips with his, the warmth of them breathing life into me, into my mouth, my lungs.

Then he was on the altar, hovering over me. One hand reached down, parting my legs and lifting my hips. As the candle danced, we were one again. Groaning, he repeated my name, then covered my mouth with his.

I whipped my head from side to side. He held me still, plunging into me with relentless power. We soared to a place of raging skies, intense heat and screaming pleasure that verged on pain. Forged together. One.

I awoke in the bed in the tower room.

Alone.

I could tell by the sheets and the soreness between my legs that Cedric had been with me last night. And that we had consummated our marriage bed.

I had only fleeting memories, but they disturbed me.

Chapter 31

I dressed in the trusty rose muslin and went to look for Kendra. She never ventured up the steps to the tower room. I didn't know if it was fear of heights or fear of Cedric.

She was reading a book in her room—an honest to goodness genuine fiction paperback.

"What are you reading?"

"*Dead Until Dark* by Charlaine Harris. It's terrific."

I groaned. "I know. I've already read it. Do you have any others? The next in the series? I would kill for something to read."

She shook her head. "Next time we go back through the wall, we load up with paperbacks."

"Amen. But I'll read that again when you're done."

I studied Kendra for a moment. She looked different. Younger, somehow. Then I got it.

"You've taken out your eyebrow ring."

"The piercings too. I thought maybe it turned Richard off." She snapped the book shut. "How did last night go?"

I wasn't sure how much to say. I was having trouble deciphering what was a dream and what had actually taken place.

"I don't remember much, except a lot of candles and two odd men. Friends of Cedric. They seemed nice enough."

I didn't tell her I'd been drugged again.

"How about you?"

She shrugged. "Nothing good. Richard is avoiding me as much as he can."

"That must make it pretty hard for him to be your bodyguard."

"Yeah." Her eyebrows drew together. "Sucks big time."

"Change is coming soon. You'll see. Nothing seems to last for long around here. Look at all that has happened."

Cedric appeared in the doorway. "Kendra, some privacy."

Nobody ever said please around here.

Kendra bounced up. "Meet you at the stables, Row."

I waited for Cedric to enter. He did so with hesitation. This was the first time I had seen him since the ceremony last night.

Or at least the first time I could remember.

"How are you this morning? How are you feeling?"

I met his eyes. "A little weary. But I'm fine."

With fire in his eyes, he gazed down at me. "You were magnificent last night. Everything I had dreamed of. I could not have asked for a more equal or courageous bride."

"Equal?"

"You have a pride in you that is like any man's. You never falter."

I can falter with the best of them, but this was probably not the time to bring that up.

"You made me proud."

A sudden, inexplicable power drew me to him. I tried as hard as I could to resist, but it was useless. I would have melted into him, but for a call from the hall.

I recognized Henry, a trusted, middle-aged archer.

"Sire," he said from the doorway. "There are two men from Sargonia at the gates. They are asking for parlez."

"Who?" Cedric demanded.

"The brother of the king and his cousin."

"Are their troops within sight?"

"No, Sire. I came from the parapet. It is only the two of them."

"Interesting." Cedric nodded. "Let them in."

I followed them to the front steps.

Outside, Thane and Logan were dismounting.

"Hail, Cedric. I come in peace." Thane looked resplendent in the purple and silver colors of his house. He bowed deeply to me. "M'lady, it is good to see you looking so well."

I grinned, ridiculously joyful. To my dismay, his face reflected none of my pleasure. Hurt, I turned to Logan. His expression was grim and uncomfortable.

Kendra rushed up behind me and gasped.

"State your business," Cedric demanded.

"I do not intend to avenge my brother's death. From what I have been told, it was a fair fight. He drew first, made the first swing, and—" His mouth twisted. "Perhaps you have done me a personal favor. I would not be ascending to the throne otherwise."

Cedric crossed his arms and nodded.

"I wish to speak to my brother's widow, the queen."

"The queen," Cedric said with a sneer.

"She remains the queen until my coronation. That is the law."

How odd. I was a queen without a king or castle. What did that mean exactly? And even more important, what would it mean for the child I carried?

"As queen," Thane said, "she will be required for the coronation ceremonies in three days hence. As earl, you are expected there, along with your house. You will need to arrive the day before. I anticipate that you will keep Rowena well guarded at all times. We will reserve a separate wing of the castle for your retinue. You may guard it with your own men."

"That seems fair," Cedric admitted.

I sensed he was excited at the prospect of more drama.

Thane took a deep breath. "There are some matters I wish to discuss with the queen. Matters of royal burial."

Oh God...

We were all uncomfortable, yet I had to admire Thane's cleverness. He may not have had the imposing physical presence of his brother, but he had a way of speaking that commanded a quiet authority.

"May we use your great hall?" he asked. "Allow us some privacy, but remain within sight, if you wish."

Cedric could hardly refuse. "And Logan?"

"Logan wishes to speak with Richard. He will remain outside."

That was a surprise.

Kendra squeezed my hand.

"Come then," Cedric said.

He stepped aside as Thane climbed the steps and entered the castle. Then he signaled me to follow.

Thane strode to the far end of the table and pointed at the chair across from him. Obedient, I sat down and fought to ignore the wild thumping of my heart.

Cedric guarded the door, a scowl on his face.

"I have already taken care of the burial arrangements," Thane said in a quiet voice. "I am not here about that."

My heart leapt. "I didn't think so."

"I could not get through his defenses before now. Has he made your union legal?

I couldn't meet his eyes.

"I thought as much. The man is not a fool. I would have acted just as swiftly." He gazed at me with steadfast blue eyes. "Rowena, I will not challenge him. I know he uses the dark arts and it would not go well for me. But should you come to find that you can separate yourself from this house in body and spirit, know that you have my full protection. Anytime, anywhere, you may call on me." His eyes drifted to my stomach. "I would raise your child as my own. You must know how I feel about you."

I looked him straight in the eyes. "Must I?"

"I treasure our time spent together in Scottsdale. I have thought of little else since. I have only one regret from that day."

"Regret?"

"That I did not lie with you on that bed when I had the chance," he whispered.

I was rocked to the core of my existence.

"Were you free, I would marry you now—this hour. If God and the future don't allow that ceremony, then still know that you have a place in my heart. Have I made myself clear?"

I flushed, then nodded. Sweet heaven, Thane *loved* me.

I realized something. I loved him too.

But we could do nothing with Cedric watching us.

"How beautiful you are," Thane murmured. "We would do so well together, you and me. With you at my side, we could bring in a new era of learning to this land. Imagine. A place where culture and high thought would take equal place with physical pursuits."

Tears filled my eyes. It was wonderful to hear the hope in his voice. But would knowing how he felt about me only make things worse? I tried to imagine lying with Cedric, while loving Thane in my heart.

We said nothing for a long moment.

"Take good care of yourself, Rowena. I will wait for your arrival in two days." He smiled and stood. "Save time for a game of chess with me."

"God bless you, Thane. You are the best man I know."

A spark lit in his eyes. I don't know what he would have done had Cedric not picked that time to stride up behind me.

Thane cleared his throat. "Cedric, I have a chest of things for Rowena at the castle. They come from Sargon's estate. She may collect it at the coronation."

Again, I admired Thane's strategy. Here was another good way to ensure that we attended the ceremonies.

Outside, I watched Thane settle in his saddle. As he bid farewell, I recklessly cried out, "King's pawn to e4."

His eyes lit up and he grinned. "Noted, m'lady."

Thane left with Logan, who gave Kendra a pleading look over his shoulder as they galloped away. I watched as they rode out the gates and through the fields until they were out of sight. With them, the sun disappeared behind a dark cloud.

"What was that all about?" Cedric asked, his voice deceptive in its calmness.

"A game we played. *Chess*. I'll teach you if you like."

He frowned. "I don't—"

"Cedric?" Jon said, rushing to his side.

While Cedric was distracted, it occurred to me that Grandfather had napped through the whole scene. Man, he would be angry.

Leaving Cedric, I searched for Kendra. I found her in her bedroom, distraught.

"Oh God, Row, it's too awful."

With her spiky black hair growing out into a tapered bob and her tear-filled gray eyes, she looked heartbreaking.

"What did Logan say to Richard?" I asked.

"I wasn't close enough to hear. I only know what Richard told me after." She glanced looked down at her hands, her voice quivering. "Logan said he would gladly die in battle tomorrow if he thought he would never get to see or touch me again. He said if he had to share me with anyone, he would choose Richard. He said that he would never challenge Richard, his one true friend. He would never kill Richard under any circumstances."

I reached for her hand. "Logan is a decent man."

"He asked Richard to treat me well. He assumed we were already sleeping together." She let out a sob. "I don't know why Richard didn't say anything."

"But Logan *does* want you back?"

Kendra nodded. "He told Richard he was sorry, but that when he had the opportunity to take me back, he would. He was giving fair warning." Tears streamed down her cheeks.

I squeezed her hand. "What did Richard say?"

"He didn't say anything. He embraced Logan."

Good Lord. It was almost too painful to imagine. Two friends, both good men, loving the same woman. Not wanting to hurt each other. I could almost hear the male duet from The Pearl-Fishers opera playing in my head.

"Richard told you all this."

"Yes," she said.

"You have two good men in your life, Kendra. How lucky you are."

"I never thought about it that way. I guess I am." She blew her nose in a handkerchief. "What did Thane want? A duel?"

I sighed. "No, he won't challenge Cedric. He couldn't win. We're to be at his coronation in three day's time. Funny how we keep bouncing back and forth between these two castles."

"Yeah, hilarious."

"You know, sweetie, you should be feeling better now. Logan has given Richard his okay."

"Maybe he won't be so shy now."

"And you're a smart girl. You can figure out why Richard didn't correct him about the sleeping together."

"I guess. He wanted Logan to think it was a done deal."

Kendra wiped her eyes with her sleeve and attempted a smile.

"Did Richard say anything about what was going on back at Castle Sargon?" I asked.

"He said most of the men are still there. They couldn't get through Cedric's defenses until this morning, so they had some kind of council of war and then couldn't agree on what to do. Oh, and they've postponed the tournament until after the coronation."

"That makes sense," I said.

Though the war council bothered me, I hoped our return to Sargonia wasn't some sort of a trap. Thane was a man of his word, but he wasn't the only one involved. Besides, he wasn't king yet.

I was worried for him. A lot could happen in three days.

Chapter 32

A formal schedule of the tournament activities and coronation ceremonies arrived the next day. With it came a message for me. The messenger managed to get past Cedric and present a note to Richard. He, in turn, gave it to Kendra, who hauled me into her bedroom.

The note read: *King's pawn to e5*.

"What does that mean?" Kendra asked.

"It means he has accepted my chess challenge."

Sometimes the smallest things could bring happiness.

"And how are things with you, Kendra?"

"Good," she said, blushing. "Great."

"You took Richard through the paces?"

Kendra grinned. "You could put it that way. He's still shy. And he's so afraid of hurting me."

"That's a good thing. Believe me."

My shoulder was still a mess. Until it healed completely, I would never be free of the haunting memories.

"So what's the schedule for the next few days?" she asked.

"We leave tomorrow morning, which means we'd better pack. There are trials going on right now for the tournament. These will determine who makes it to the finals in each category. They end tomorrow."

I thought of Thane. "The coronation is the day after. The actual tournament starts after that."

Like modern day car races, with trials on Friday and Saturday and the actual race on Sunday.

Kendra frowned. "This is more like Olympic Games than a medieval tournament."

"Why do you say that?"

"Well, in medieval times—from the time of the Norman conquest until maybe the 1400s—they had mock battle tournaments. The men divided into two sides and fought all at the same time. I think it originated in France. But those tournaments were very dangerous. A lot of people died."

"How do you know this?"

She shrugged. "One of the guys I dated in high school was really into medieval stuff."

"Well, don't mention this to any of the men here. It might give them ideas. We're a lot safer with Olympic Games, even if they do use weapons."

Kendra clambered to her feet and rummaged through her wardrobe. "I guess we bring every dress we've got—again."

"My packing will be quick," I said, envious of the clean, undamaged state of her garments. "I'm down another four dresses."

Things were getting desperate. I had to find more suitable attire, dresses I could breathe in as my waist expanded.

"The coronation will be a formal affair," I said, "so save your best for that."

"What are you wearing?"

"The off-white Grecian."

"What do you have to do at the coronation?"

I lifted my shoulders. "I have no idea. Maybe wear a crown and hand it over to Thane? Or pour tea? Pass around the cake plate?"

Kendra giggled.

We spent the afternoon packing. First, we stuffed her satchel and then I took her to the tower room.

"I've never been here before," she said, nervous.

"Nothing will bite you." I smiled. "The view is pretty from here. Look, you can actually see the river in the far distance."

We stared out the window in companionable silence.

"I've really come to love this place," she said. "The colors are so rich here. It's like seeing everything through a brighter filter. The greens are greener, the sky is bluer—"

"That reminds me," I interjected. "I have something to show you that I think you'll like."

I removed the black dress from the wardrobe.

"Oh my God, Row. That is too sick. Put it on."

I did. The dress fit well, unlike the sapphire blue, which was becoming too snug.

"Pretty, isn't it?"

Kendra snorted. "Hardly. You look gorgeous, but not a bit pretty, which implies innocence."

I swatted her arm. "Hey!"

"That dress is a knockout," she said with a laugh. "It's almost too black, if you know what I mean. Even black looks blacker here. Wear it tonight, why don't you?"

I twirled in front of the mirror. "Maybe I will. I'd planned to leave this one behind anyway. I've only got two good gowns left—the off-white Grecian one, which I was saving for the coronation, and the deep cherry."

God, what I'd do for a shopping mall right now.

We packed up the rest of my belongings and set them by the door. A page would move them later.

"See you at dinner," Kendra said.

"Where are you going now?"

"Richard is taking me for a walk outside the castle grounds."

"Oh really?" I winked. "Don't forget that people can see you from the turret."

She snickered. "Oh, I don't think Richard is the roll-in-the-grass sort."

Later, I made my way downstairs. When the men saw me in my little black dress, all talk stopped. The silence was distressing.

Kendra and Richard entered the hall. They too froze.

"Where did you get that dress?" Grandfather rasped.

"From a room at Castle Sargon. Is there something wrong?"

"It's not a dress for a virtuous woman," Jon cut in. "Not here anyway."

I put my hand to the bodice. "Is it too low-cut?"

Surely, no lower than others I had worn.

"What are you talking about?" Kendra said. "I think she looks grand."

"It's a witch's gown," Richard said quietly.

"I didn't know that," I said. "I'm running out of clothes that fit. This was in the closet."

No one said a word.

I let out a frustrated huff. "So I really shouldn't wear this?"

Grandfather shook his head.

"Nonsense!" Cedric said, arriving through the front door. "It looks magnificent on you. Pay them no heed."

"Cedric, don't be a fool," Grandfather said.

"I like it." Cedric moved behind me and draped his hands on my shoulders. "It's very fetching. She needn't wear it in public, of course. Might set some tongues wagging." He kissed my hair.

"Do not think to make her into something she isn't," Grandfather warned.

"We shall see about that."

"Cedric, I mean this. Do not play with her soul. I'll stop you myself, if I must."

No one could doubt the threat there.

"I would not bring her to harm," Cedric said, wrapping his arms wrapped around me.

I felt that familiar zing of electricity.

The tension in the room eased when Kendra offered me her sweater. I covered the dress as best I could.

"Will you be competing in any of the games," I asked Cedric.

"Wouldn't be fair," he said cryptically. "Though I might judge wrestling, if asked."

Jon frowned and Grandfather nodded approval.

I thought their reaction strange.

Later, Jon filled me in.

"Everyone knows Cedric is a student of the dark arts," he said. "They don't trust him to play fair."

Ah...so that was it. Cedric was a *student* of magic, not a master. It made me wonder about the amount of power he had and how far it extended. In the past, he'd been able to sense my distress and locate me. But maybe there were limits to his magic. Maybe, one day, his power would fade.

Cedric excused himself to do some nightly ritual. I was curious about this, but knew better than to follow him. Instead, I cornered Jon in the hall.

"I've been wanting to ask you for hours," I said. "How fares Ivan?"

"He is healthy physically. I am not so sure his mind is as well."

"What do you mean?"

"He has not left this land. I urged him to go, to fulfill the conditions of banishment. I even offered to go with him. But he refuses to consider it and has allied himself with ruffians. I could not stay with him under those conditions."

Jon's eyes strayed to the top of my dress.

Ever since our very first encounter by the river, he had been uncomfortable around me. At dinner, he always sat across the table. Sometimes I would catch his eyes on me, as if drawn by the memory of that first day.

He stepped closer, then caught himself and looked away.

I changed the subject. "Ivan risks death by defying the order. Why does he do this?"

"Cedric." He shrugged. "And you."

I groaned. "His hate for Cedric is far stronger than his love for me."

"'Tis both."

"How powerful is Cedric's magic?"

"I am not sure. All I know is he needs to be at the spot where he intends to do magic. He can't do it from afar. He needs to see it. When he set that defensive line around Castle Sargon, he had to be within sight to do it."

"So he can't do anything from a long distance. He couldn't, for example, cause havoc in Norland when he is here at Castle Huel."

"That is correct, m'lady. I also think he needs some time to plan. He often casts magic on special books or talismans. And I have noticed that he doesn't seem to be able to react fast enough to protect himself from danger."

Now I knew something that Jon didn't. The Roman coin I wore gave Cedric the power to follow me. This was beyond the powers that Jon described.

He proceeded to the window, then faced me from a safe distance. "All this could change. I don't know how powerful he is capable of becoming."

A shiver swept up my spine. "Please don't think me disloyal, Jon, but I hope he doesn't become too strong. We have a saying where I come from. 'Power corrupts. Absolute power corrupts absolutely.'"

"A wise saying, m'lady. I expect you are right, not that we will have much influence. Still, 'tis good we stand with him and not with his enemies."

I had one last question. "Do you think he will harm Ivan if given the chance?"

Jon's brown eyes met mine. "That is my one great fear."

Cain and Abel, I thought.

"Rowena, they were always at each other's throats, even before you arrived."

He said it to relieve my guilt, but I remained uneasy.

When Cedric joined me that night, he was thorough and possessive. But every time I closed my eyes, I saw Thane in my mind. When Cedric plunged inside me, it was Thane I dreamed of—Thane's hands and lips that caressed me.

Thank God Cedric could not read my mind.

"I'm disturbed," he said afterward. "Something is going to happen in the next few days. I can feel it. It involves you, but you aren't hurt—never fear. Keep wearing the broach."

"Maybe we shouldn't go to the coronation."

He shook his head. "We must. Not to go would be shameful. An act of cowardice."

Heaven forbid he ever acted in a way that wasn't courageous.

"Don't venture out from the castle courtyard without me or Jon," he ordered. "Or Richard. I think we can count on Thane to be honorable, but I wouldn't trust any of the others. Norland probably doesn't recognize our marriage. They have strange customs up north."

Neither of us got much sleep that night.

Chapter 33

We set out the next morning under a gray sky. The mood was oppressive and I couldn't shake the feeling of impending doom. We moved like a convoy and the noise of animals and men was deafening. I could hardly stand the rich and overpowering odor of so many beasts. Cedric's troops had swelled from forces arriving from the south. At the river, Drake met us with his own entourage of elites—at least two hundred men.

It took much longer to reach our destination. As we neared Castle Sargon, excitement built among the men. From several miles out, we passed camps of troops, a sea of tents. Friends separated by time and loyalties greeted each other along the way. Excited, they slapped each other's backs and knocked one another down.

I smiled at their joy and tried to check my own angst.

We left most of the men at a field encampment to the south. Our immediate family and a few trusted men proceeded to the castle grounds.

Thane was waiting on the steps when we rode in. He did not move to help us dismount, but waited for us to come to him. He watched me dismount. He observed the others for a second, then his eyes came back to me.

"Don't act subservient," Cedric hissed, pushing me forward. "You still outrank him."

Thane smiled as we drew close. "Welcome, Huel. Welcome, m'lady. I've reserved the rear wing of the castle for you. Come with me."

I took Thane's offered arm. Touching him was like Valium to me. My heart calmed, my breathing slowed and the air had more oxygen.

Cedric hung back a few feet so he could yell orders to the men. This gave me an opportunity to slip Thane a note.

Knight to f3.

Thane raised a brow."Your next move?"

"This opening I have used is called the Spanish Opening," I told him. "It is complete in five moves. The opening, that is, not the game. There are countless ways to start a game. I am keen to see if your next move will follow suit."

"You shall have it tonight."

The suites at the back of the castle were well placed. There was only one entrance, which could be easily guarded. Thane led me to the last room at the end of the hall, a large bedroom with a double bed in the center, ringed with wardrobes. Faded tapestries lined the walls, and one large window let in light.

"This was my mother's room," he said. "I'm told she liked the view from here.

I stood beside him and we gazed out the window.

The back of the castle stood against a dark cliff that rose almost straight up. This window faced the edge of the cliff. The view had the effect of looking down a long, dark corridor to a place of brilliant light beyond. It was not a normal pastoral view and it made me wonder about his mother.

"This trunk was Sargon's." He pointed to a small wooden box with leather straps. "I thought you might like to have it."

"Thank you."

"I haven't looked in it. If you like, I could stay here with you while you do so."

"No. Cedric will be here soon."

He nodded in understanding.

I would inspect the trunk in private, without Cedric nearby.

"I have Sargon's sword, if you would care for it."

I shivered. "You keep it, please."

"Then I will leave you now. By the way, I've arranged a quiet meal for your family tonight in these quarters. We will all be together tomorrow."

He raised a hand to touch my cheek and a wave of emotion washed over his face. Before I could move forward, he left the room.

A great commotion signaled Cedric's entrance. Our belongings followed and we spent a quiet night unpacking.

Late in the evening, a messenger arrived with a note addressed to me. *Knight to c6.*

Alone in my room the next morning, I dressed in my faithful rose muslin. I planned to head to the stables, since Kendra had gone to see the caber toss trials with Logan. It surprised me that Richard was cool with this, but I guess he really did trust the two of them. What a difficult triangle.

I only dealt in pentagons.

Today was going to be a great day. I didn't feel sick, the sun was shining warmly and Lightning waited in her stall.

The square was busy. There seemed to be a lot of men wandering around—men I didn't know.

Then I spotted Gareth. He was talking to Janus. It was the first time I'd seen them since arriving. When Gareth caught sight of me, he grabbed his brother's shoulder. I was about to join them, but something in Gareth's face warned me off. Not far from them, Richard and Cedric were deep in conversation.

Strange...

Thane greeted me at the doors to the stable. "Rowena, I—

"Che Ghiell!" someone bellowed.

My heart leapt to my throat. What was happening?

The mood of the crowd changed instantly. There were yells and a blur of action. Without warning, the yard was full of Norland men with their daggers out. A swarthy looking man threw Richard to the ground and pinned him with a sword. Gareth cornered Cedric, his broadsword pointed at his chest while Janus held a dagger to Cedric's throat from behind. All this time, everyone had thought Gareth helpless with his wounded right shoulder.

Little did we know that he was left handed.

The tension in the yard was unbearable. I felt like we were all standing on the edge of a precipice, arms linked together, waiting for that one small move that would pitch us all over the cliff.

"Rowena!" Gareth called. "Come here now. We'll get your things later."

I gaped at him as if he had grown three heads. "Are you out of your mind? We're in the middle of a tournament here and everyone has pledged *no* violence."

"I've got it under control," Gareth yelled. "You and I leave now. My men will follow. No one else." He aimed his broadsword at Cedric's heart.

"Gareth, stop! Don't kill him. No killing."

I used my classroom "stop-a-riot" voice. It worked.

All eyes in the courtyard were on me now.

"Okay, I am totally fed up. Gareth, I'm not going anywhere. This has got to stop. You can't go tossing me back and forth like I'm some sort of prized toy. Did anyone ever think to ask me what I might want?"

No one answered.

"Don't you realize I'm going to have a baby? We need to come to an agreement. Maybe I spend six months with you and six months with Cedric. Maybe I stay here with Thane until we get this sorted out. We can work something out. But I am *not* going anywhere today. And this violence is going to stop right now."

"Negotiate?" Cedric said in disbelief. "To share you? Are you mad?"

My lips pursed in anger. "I am still queen until the coronation. That means I'm the highest-ranking person here. Gareth, order your men to back off with the knives. You will not challenge Cedric. Or get Janus to do it or anyone else." I strode toward Gareth and the crowd parted. "Let me make this absolutely clear. If Cedric dies, you will never see me again. And if you die, ditto. As a matter of fact, if a single person dies today in this yard, I'm outta here. Believe it."

Whispers could be heard from the gathering men.

"I'm the queen," I said in my firmest *Alice in Wonderland* Queen of Hearts voice. "You *will* obey me."

Gareth frowned. I think Cedric actually sniggered.

Thane emerged from the crowd and stood before me. "Rowena…Norland's men won't obey you over him, and my men won't take orders from you, even though you are their queen. A queen doesn't command troops here. She is owed protection."

Oh hell. He made it sound like a bloody beehive, where the queen was just guarded in some back honeycomb and had no life of her own. What a bunch of male chauvinists.

"What are you talking about?" I fired back. "What about Boadicea? What about Queen Elizabeth the first, who ruled over the entire British Empire, including all the colonies?"

Again, there was a wave of baffled mumbling.

Too bad. I was on a roll.

I jabbed a finger into Thane's chest. "I've read more battle strategy than the whole freaking lot of you. I can shoot a gun as well as any man. And I can do it from horseback. So don't give me any chauvinist crap about being a woman."

More mumbling again.

Maybe it was the word *gun* or maybe I lost them all at *chauvinist*. I don't know. Get a dictionary, people.

"Perhaps these times haven't happened yet in our world," Thane said gently.

He reached out but I backed away.

"No!" I said, furious. "This is too much. Where is the rule book here? I need to see a job description. What is the point of being queen in this piss-poor world if it doesn't come with any power?"

Cedric burst out laughing. "Isn't she magnificent when she's angry?"

Several others joined in the laughter, which I'll admit was a good thing. It's hard to kill somebody when you're laughing at someone else.

But I was beyond furious. If I'd had a rifle, I would have shot them all—including Thane. And believe me, I wouldn't have missed.

I stomped my foot like a five-year-old, then fled up the steps to the castle. They could bloody well kill each other for all I cared now. They could slice each other's throats and throw the bodies to the wolves.

"Bunch of primitive Neanderthals," I yelled to the empty hall. "I'm not staying in this miserable place one day longer."

I strode through the hall and out to the kitchen. George was kneading bread dough and he gave me a big smile. I bent down to pat Ralph, then picked up my fanny pack from a nail on the wall. Inside was a pen and pad. I wrote a quick message to Kendra and placed it under a tankard.

"Can you make sure Kendra gets this note, George?"

He gave me a puzzled nod. "Yes, m'lady."

I kissed his cheek and calmly left the kitchen, the fanny pack in my hand.

Lightning was too far away in the stables. I didn't want to go past the men. With any luck, I would never see any of them again.

I opened my mind to find another equine soul.

The connection was quick, intense.

Around the corner, a pretty mare was tied to a post. She was quite happy to let me mount. I took her around the back to the postern gate. It was guarded by an elderly soldier with only one arm. He was leaning up against the wall, fast asleep.

I had no trouble sneaking by him.

The mare was eager to run, so we did. As our minds met, I told her I was escaping from some randy male. She seemed to get the gist of my predicament. She galloped even faster.

Since everybody saw me go into the castle, I figured I'd have a decent head start. They would think I was upstairs, sobbing on my bed.

I smiled into the wind.

Nobody would expect me to leave by the back way. They would be incensed when they found out. Good for them. I hoped they beat each other silly.

Eventually someone would start looking for me. Probably Kendra, who would find my note in the kitchen. But she'd never tell anyone what I'd written. And no one else could read English.

By evening, Cedric would wonder why I hadn't turned up for dinner. I figured I had two hours at the most. At least I could be to the river before anybody started following. That meant I had two full hours to think about the men I was leaving behind.

There was Gareth, who had started it all today with this ridiculous, very public attempt to carry me off—again. The man had spent time and money to find me on the other side of the wall. He had given me his magic jewel, the one I carried in my pocket now, to keep me safe. If this wasn't a token of love, I can't imagine what else would be.

I thought of Ivan, my first lover here. He had vanished to who-knows-where. We couldn't be together for more than twelve hours without fighting like cat and dog. But it was hard not to feel something for the man who had risked his life and lost his liberty for me.

And Cedric, who seemed to have a physical power over me that surpassed even my darkest dreams. He professed to love me, but had laughed at me today in front of the others. I wasn't about to forgive that any time soon.

And lastly there was Thane, clever, kind and the man I wanted more than anyone I'd ever met. He had never made love to me. I felt a tug on my heart for what we had missed. Who would play chess with him now?

I would miss Thane the most.

Loneliness swept through me. I felt like Dorothy saying goodbye to the Scarecrow, the Lion and the Tin Man.

I was almost to the river when the guilt started. Real guilt. Not about the escape so much, but because I hadn't waited for Kendra. In the note, I urged her to follow me as soon as she could. I said I'd wait for her on campus. To be honest, I wasn't sure what she would do.

I took the mare up the hill and into the small clearing that had been so well used in the past month. I slipped off the horse and hit the ground with a thud. I walked along the familiar path until I reached the split oak.

I glanced over my shoulder for one last look at the valley. How beautiful it was with the river running through it and the azure sky above. I would miss the orange sun. I would miss a lot about this world.

A tear trickled down my cheek.

"Enough of this."

With determination, I strode through the trees, heading toward the portal for the very last time. Closing my eyes, I took three steps in.

I opened my eyes. What the hell?

Instead of the walls of the classroom, I was surrounded by trees. I was still in the forest. Frowning, I retraced my movements and stepped toward the portal. *Still* in the forest.

I walked around the split oak, hoping to see if something had shifted. Everything looked as it should. Holding my breath, I started over again and marched forward.

Nothing.

I could scarcely breathe. I leaned against the tree trunk and tried to figure out what to do next, where to go. I was alone in a very dangerous forest.

Even worse, the portal was gone.

Chapter 34

I raged and I cried. When I got the self-pity out of my system, I sat down with my back to the tree and considered my options.

There was no going back to Castle Sargon. I'd left there in a huff and a girl has her pride. Okay, maybe that pride was stupid, but I couldn't help it. Sometimes, for a sensible modern girl, I'm just plain stubborn.

Huel was the closest castle, but it was vacant and the way there was quite exposed. After what happened last time with Willen and gang, I was leery about even moving into the clearing, let alone wandering about on my own in the open.

I could go north to Norland Fortress, but that was almost a day's ride. And wasn't that what got me in this mess in the first place, refusing to go to Norland with Gareth? So nix that idea. Gareth was the cause of my current misery. I could hardly forgive him for that. The bloody nerve of him, making decisions without consulting me.

I went over my choices in my mind, circling them until I was emotionally wrung out. Maybe the portal would open again. Maybe there was some sort of cosmic interference that would clear in a bit. Maybe if I waited an hour or so, I could try it again.

I waited, sobbed a little more and lay down on soft moss.

I fell into a deep slumber.

Through the pale mist of a dream, I saw my mother as she had been before she died—smiling, reaching out to me. She turned to Grandfather, who embraced her with joy, and the three of us stayed clasped in each other's arms. We were finally together.

The mist grew darker.

My mother drew back and started to fade.

"No!" I cried, reaching for her, desperate to keep her with me.

Her eyes filled with sadness.

Fading...

"Here she is!" Kendra called out in the distance. "Thank God."

Footsteps approached and I opened one eye.

Thane knelt in front of me, gazing down with concern.

"Thane," I said.

Sensible, steadfast Thane. How good he looked, with those brilliant blue eyes and curly black hair.

"You gave us quite a scare, Rowena."

His gathered me in his strong arms. He didn't even scold me.

"Are you okay?" Kendra asked. Logan stood beside her.

"I guess." I paused. "The portal's gone."

"Oh, no. That's why you're lying here. I figured we'd have to go back through it to talk some sense into you. So I brought along these two."

That made sense. Logan and Thane had been already through the portal with me. It wouldn't be such a shock next time. And Kendra knew where I lived.

"I don't deserve a friend like you, Kendra." There was shame in my voice. "I left without telling you. I'm so sorry. I'm an emotional mess and I feel so guilty. I'd cry some more, but I'm all dried out."

"Of course you're overwrought. All this happening today—and you're pregnant too. All those hormones racing about."

"Remind me to use *pregnant* as an excuse for my natural stupidity in the future," I muttered.

I looked into Thane's eyes and saw only love and relief.

"What happened after I left?"

"General chaos," Thane said with a shrug. "But they all backed down. No one was injured. There was much confusion." He brushed my hair away from my face. "Kendra found your note and came to find me. Everyone else thinks you're still in the castle. We sought to keep this as quiet as possible."

"And...Gareth?"

"He is not welcome at Castle Sargon. I've sent him and Janus away. They'll return to Norland."

"That's good of you." I said.

He could have done much worse. His brother would have.

"The moment of danger had passed, Rowena. He violated the agreement, so he forfeits all future invitations." He took my hand. "Did you mean what you said in the courtyard, about staying with me in Sargonia?"

Now was the moment to tell him the truth. "I—"

"We should go," Logan interrupted. "I feel uneasy here."

I gazed across the valley, noting the fine mist that was rising.

"We left the horses in the clearing," Kendra said.

I groaned. Not that clearing again. I hated that place.

Holding my hand firmly, Thane led the way and we walked single file out of the trees.

Immediately, I noticed something was missing.

"Where's the sorrel mare?"

I entered her mind. Why was she so upset? I gasped as a dozen horses filled my mind. I opened my mouth to warn the others.

Too late.

A haughty voice rang out behind us. "Ah, Thane, you return my wife to me. My humble thanks."

"Ivan!" I whispered.

He stood not ten feet away, with at least a dozen men around him, all armed. They moved so swiftly that Thane had no time to pull either of his weapons.

We were surrounded.

"So easy," Ivan said to Thane. He shook his head and smiled with satisfaction, towering over everyone, including Logan. "I have scouts everywhere between your castle and Huel. All I had to do was follow you to see where she would run to."

Thane cursed.

"Don't move and you will live," Ivan said. "I only want what's mine. What your brother stole." There was hatred in his voice.

Thane glanced at me, shaking with anger.

"Thane, please don't do anything." I begged.

I turned to Ivan. "I'll come willingly."

"I'll come too," Kendra said, moving to my side.

"No, Kendra, it's too dangerous. Stay with Grandfather. Ivan, let her stay with Grandfather. Please."

"But you need me," Kendra said, tearing up.

Did she have any idea of the fate that could befall her?

"I'll call for you when I need you," I said. "When it's time."

"She is Richard's lady now," I pleaded with Ivan. "You know it's too dangerous for her with your men." Men that reminded me of Willen's band, rough and unwashed. But I didn't say that out loud.

Ivan frowned. I could almost see his thought patterns. Richard was his beloved kin and he had no quarrel with either Richard or Grandfather.

"Agreed," he said finally. "Thane, you may return to your castle. I want you to live. It serves my purpose. Go back and tell my elder brother that I have won. Go back and tell Cedric that I have taken his prize. That even his rotten magic didn't help." Hate spewed from his mouth and he spat on the ground.

Ivan grabbed my arm. "Rowena, come now. Mount."

I twisted from his grasp, ran to Kendra and hugged her.

"This is so unfair!" she cried. "You're doing it again. Sacrificing yourself to save me."

"Take care of yourself, little sister." I stroked her black hair. "I love you dearly. I'll find a way to see you soon."

I released her and met Thane's eyes. "Bishop to b5."

He jerked as if hit. Then he nodded.

"Come now," Ivan ordered.

I swung up into the mare's saddle and glanced at Thane. He stood like a granite statue, staring at me with a mix of sorrow and self-loathing.

Astride his horse, Ivan grabbed the reins of my mare and we rode into the mist. The rest of his band followed.

I looked back once, but the mist was too thick.

We rode a long time before I had the courage to speak.

"Where are we going, Ivan?"

"To a place they'll never find us," he snapped.

Completely hidden by mist, we followed the river south.

I fingered the Roman coin at the back of the Tintagel broach, the coin that linked me to Cedric.

The coin that would lead him to me.

We rode south for hours, stopping once to water the horses. I did not know this land. It was very green and fertile, with rolling hills. We passed burned-out farms and razed stone houses. I saw no one. I don't know if it was the pounding hooves that scared people off or if there was simply no one to see.

At dusk, we came to a castle ruin. Stone rubble marked the placement of the ancient walls.

"We stay here for tonight," Ivan said, dismounting.

"You mean we're going farther?"

He laughed. "Oh, yes. Even Cedric can't follow us across the sea."

My breath caught in the back of my throat. If Ivan took me on a boat, my rescuers would never be able to follow.

And besides, I got seasick something awful.

The light was nearly gone. The men made a fire in the ruined courtyard and roasted wild game. Ivan pointed to a spot in the grass and I sat down. He brought me meat and hard tack that was so tough, I couldn't eat it. Afterward, he went to talk to the fellow tending the fire.

Eyes watched my every move.

A quiver of fear trickled up my spine.

These men disturbed me. Two were missing arms. All were filthy. They watched me with furtive eyes. Ivan hadn't introduced me to any of them. He was the only one who stood between me and these rough men, who most likely were criminals.

I wondered if Ivan had thought about that. Exactly how much loyalty did they feel for him, especially if they knew his plans to leave the country?

A gray-haired, bearded man glanced over at me whenever he thought Ivan wasn't looking. His eyes gleamed with madness.

I swallowed hard and looked away. Closing my eyes, I curled up on the ground. There was little I could do but trust in Ivan, and I was so tired, I couldn't find the energy to be scared.

I was half asleep when Ivan nudged me.

"Come," he said, helping me to my feet. "We have our own quarters."

Again those eyes followed us. Ivan led me into the ruin and down a flight of stone steps. It was so dark I had to keep both hands on the wall to either side of me to keep from falling. We descended into a small basement room with no windows and only candles for light. The walls were bare, the room cold. Like in Norland, there was a pile of furs on the floor. In another corner, there was a pile of clothing.

I was so exhausted, I could no longer stay standing. The next thing I knew, I was sliding beneath the furs.

Ivan returned, carrying two tankards.

"This is a problem," I said. "I can't drink too much ale. It's bad for the baby."

"We can boil water for you tomorrow. This much won't hurt. My mother drank nothing but ale and I turned out fine."

We might disagree on that, I thought.

I took a cautious sip and set the tankard down on the ground. I yawned. "I'm so tired." I closed my eyes.

He was beside me in an instant, his mouth on my cleavage and his fingers working the laces.

"I'm too tired for this tonight," I pleaded.

"You don't have to do a thing."

"Please, Ivan, wait until morning."

Lifting his head, he sighed and moved away.

Hours later, I woke up. I opened one eye. Small rays of light shot through the wooden boards that made up the ceiling. I looked over at Ivan. He was asleep on his back. I cuddled down into the furs and slept some more.

A scream woke me.

I jerked to my feet.

Cedric stood over Ivan, his sword inches from Ivan's chest.

He drove it in.

I screamed.

I heard the death gurgle and saw the blood fly. Ivan's eyes were open, staring at me as though I'd betrayed him.

I rolled away, gasping. I hid my face, unable to utter a sound.

"Get up," Cedric ordered.

He was cleaning his sword on a robe. Dear God, he was humming, wiping the blood away, his eyes flat, opaque disks.

Emotionless.

He grabbed me and hauled me to my feet.

"Don't look back," he ordered, still humming tunelessly.

I wanted to scream, but couldn't even find air to breathe.

Cedric carried me up the flight of stairs. I kept my eyes closed until we reached the sunshine. Jon and Richard were there, plus a dozen men on foot, including Drake.

Bodies lay scattered on the ground.

I tried not to look at them.

"My child," Grandfather called out from his steed.

I was shocked to see him there.

"She's unharmed," Cedric said. He set me down. I teetered and fell to my knees.

Grandfather frowned. "Where's Ivan?"

There was a pause.

"I've taken care of him."

"You've killed him?" Grandfather said, his eyes flaring in disbelief. "You've killed your own brother?"

Cedric ignored him and readied the horses.

"Can you ride?" he asked me.

I was numb and couldn't reply.

"We need to leave," he insisted. "There may be more."

"Cedric!" Grandfather shouted. "Answer me!"

Cedric turned, his bloody tunic catching the light. "Yes, I killed him. I struck him through his black heart. The cretin was taking her to Port Town to catch a ship, with none but himself and these vermin for escort. Do you know what she would be worth down there?"

Grandfather's face went white. He opened his mouth to say something and choked on the words. Resigned, he signaled with a hand. "Jon, Richard."

They hurried down the steps toward him.

"Do up your bodice, Rowena," Grandfather said, unsmiling.

I turned away and hastened to the task.

"We'll take him back," Grandfather said. "Jon, wrap him in something. Richard, help Jon."

"I'll go south with Drake," Cedric said.

"Until we learn the penalty for your crime, you'd better."

Cedric turned to me. "Rowena, mount up."

"Not with her, you don't." Grandfather's eyes were daggers. "She comes with me back to Huel."

"She's my wife!" Cedric yelled.

"You may have her back when you resume your duties at Huel. She will wait for you there. For once in your life, be unselfish. Think of the child."

Cedric paced the ground, furious. I was frozen to the spot.

"Would you kill us all as well?" Grandfather roared. "First the king, now your brother? Where does it end?"

Silence filled the air. Even the birds stopped singing.

I held my breath.

"Go now," Grandfather said tiredly. "Before I order your death myself."

Cedric swung up onto his horse and cantered off. Drake followed with several of the men.

Grandfather released a long sigh. "Come with me, Rowena. The others will follow."

I followed, ever dutiful. Anything to get away from the horror.

We rode for several miles before my grandfather spoke again.

"This was not necessary. This was evil."

Silent tears worked their way down my cheeks. Grandfather caught me wiping them away.

"I'm sorry, dear one. I can imagine what you saw. Can you be brave until we reach the castle? Then you may weep, as much as you need. But for now, we need to travel."

I nodded and sniffed a bit. "You all came to find me."

"Of course," he said, as if that were only natural.

He kicked his horse to a gallop, and mine followed suit. We rode to the east and then north. At least I'd had slept last night and was able to keep up.

When we reached the stables at Huel, I held back and cornered Richard. "What did Cedric mean, how much I'd be worth?"

Richard's face went scarlet.

"Tell me," I implored. "I've got to know for my own safety."

"The few women who survived the war four years ago live in the coastal towns to the south and east. They are mostly over fifty and along with some young men, they serve a certain…function."

"Ah," I said. I got it now. "We call that 'the oldest profession.'"

"So I am told." He coughed. "Though I've never been there."

He was alone in that, I thought.

"I am also told," he said, "that there are boatmen along the eastern coast who go raiding to other lands."

Oh Lord, what a frightening thought.

"I must warn Kendra," I said.

We walked across the courtyard to the castle steps and went inside to the great hall where Kendra joined us.

Before anyone could mention funeral arrangements, I said, "What is the punishment for killing a brother?"

An uncomfortable pause ensued. Either they were shocked by my blunt language or the fact that I had spoken first.

"At best, banishment," Grandfather said.

I held my breath. "If Cedric goes, must I?"

"Not legally. But this is Cedric. He'll probably force you, kidnap you."

My stomach churned in rebellion. "I won't go. I can't leave all of you. I've had a long time to think about this on the ride back. I'll go to Thane tomorrow and bargain with him for Cedric's freedom."

"What are you talking about? What can you do to force a king be lenient?"

I looked him in the eye and his white brows drew together in outrage.

"Don't tell me he'll want to play chess, girl. I'm not a fool."

It was my turn to be angry. "What would you have me do, Sir? If there is price, I must pay it. I'm not even sure there is a chance I can do anything, but I must try. For my sake more than Cedric's. I cannot be chained to him in some foreign country. He terrifies me." My voice rose in near hysteria.

Kendra trembled and tears welled in her eyes. Richard reached out to comfort her and I was envious.

There was no one here to comfort me.

"Every time Cedric uses magic, he becomes more inhuman. Like Sargon was. If you could have seen him in that room..." I couldn't finish. "Surely you have thought of what Cedric might do if he is banished?"

The vertical grooves in Grandfather's face deepened.

"Think of it," I said. "He would bide his time and then bring all the black magic he could to retaliate. We would be enveloped in it and never be free. You *know* Cedric. He would grow stronger and stronger until none could oppose him. Hundreds would die." My voice dropped to a bare whisper. "I can be a whore for less than that."

Grandfather cried out in anguish.

I didn't care. Why mince words? I was tired of it all. Tired of always having to figure out the best way to survive. Tired of being the one to make the sacrifices when I was treated as so much less than others. Dammit, I wasn't the one who got us into this jam.

"You continually dismiss me because I am a woman, and yet here I am bailing us out when I can, doing what I can to protect us all." With all the pride of Joan of Arc, I faced my Grandfather. "Cedric has killed twice now. He killed the king and now his own brother. In cold blood."

"It is beyond belief," Grandfather said. "Our house is doomed."

"Would you not do anything you could to save this family? Of course you would. But you can't help us now." I pointed to Jon. "He can't help us either. Only I can."

Grandfather gave a defeated nod. "I would rather die than have you disgraced."

"Are you are prepared to sacrifice Richard and Kendra, as well as yourself? Jon and me too?"

He shook his head.

"I can give Thane what he desires to keep him content, whatever that may be," I said. "I'll figure it out. I'm good that way."

"Do you not see, Rowena? The way you are, as you so plainly put it, is exactly why you are in such danger here. If you were a simpering fool, they wouldn't want you."

My heart skipped a beat in dismay. "So I should leave? I should go back to where I came from?"

"No, no!"

"The portal is closed, Grandfather. I couldn't go back if I wanted to."

"You can't go. What would I do here without you? I'd worry every minute." Grandfather paced the floor. "I need to think how to keep you safe. Why is it so hard to do?"

We stared at each other.

I loved him—I loved them all. But they made it difficult.

"I'll leave for Sargonia tomorrow," I said.

Chapter 35

We buried Ivan in the morning. My heart was heavy with shock and despair. I forgave him everything on that misty morn. Ivan, my kin—so full of life. How could he be gone now? I had lain with this man. He may have fathered my child. If I could have wished him back, I would have with all my heart.

Once more, I felt the naked horror of Cedric's action. To take a life is a monstrous thing. To kill a brother is heinous.

I dressed for my trip to Sargonia with care. The white Grecian dress was demure, yet regal. It would suit for today.

Kendra watched me prepare.

"Before you say anything," I said," this is something I must do alone."

She nodded and hugged me hard. Of them all, she understood.

The trip to Castle Sargon was a somber one. Jon went with me, as well as two of his men. We reached the iron gates in early evening. Thane's men were silent as we passed.

Our tragic news had traveled fast.

I realized then that we had missed the coronation. As well, it seemed the tournament had never taken place. Our recent turmoil had left everyone on edge and the warriors had dispersed, the camps empty.

Something else occurred to me.

I was no longer queen.

Thane watched from the balcony as we rode in. As we reined in, he turned and disappeared from sight. Moments later, he materialized on the castle steps. He wore the royal broach. It meant he had been crowned.

My heart flipped.

Thane's eyes blazed when I drew near. He noted the others and gave them a nod.

"This is a sad day for you," he told me. "I am sorry."

I sucked in air to keep my voice steady. "I've come to bargain for Cedric's freedom."

He frowned, placed one foot up on the stone masonry and leaned his arm on one knee. I was reminded of *The Thinker* statue by Rodin.

"What do you plan to offer in return?" he asked.

I was acutely aware of the others witnessing our conversation.

"Whatever it takes," I said.

He straightened. "This is best discussed in private. Shall we retire to the library and think about this over a game of chess?"

I nodded and followed Thane into the castle.

Once again, I found myself in the library. It should have put me at ease, but I was oddly distressed by the familiarity of it—and by Thane.

"Sit," he said.

He reached for a decanter and poured two goblets of wine. He handed me one, then drank his down completely, refilling it.

I only sipped the wine.

"Let's play." He watched me, measuring. "Do you enjoy gambling? You win, I grant your request. I win, you agree to meet my terms."

I licked my dry lips. "That's fair."

More than fair. He had never won a game yet.

He straddled a chair. "You will notice I have been playing our game on this board. I have set the pieces as we have played them thus far. Shall we continue?"

My heart leapt to my throat.

It was as he said. The pieces were ready for play. Our game played from afar had meant something to him. But I had cheapened that by coming here today with my request.

"Your turn, Lady," he said, draining his goblet once more.

As he refilled his goblet, I looked at the board. The next move was so obvious I played immediately.

He took no time and played his next.

I stared at him, dismayed. How had he responded so quickly?

I contemplated various strategies. My hand shook as I placed the piece.

Again, he moved without taking any time.

"You've been practicing," I said.

"Daily. I wanted to be worthy of you."

I almost broke down then. I looked at the pieces. My eyes watered and I couldn't concentrate. Flustered, I stood and stared out the window. Mist was rising up the hill. I reached for my goblet, took a drink and touched the knight.

Why couldn't I think?

I hesitated, let go of the knight and moved the bishop.

"Check," Thane said.

My eyes flashed from the board to him.

Thane had won.

"I've played your side of the chessboard as well as my own every day since you've been gone," he said. "I studied every possible combination of moves you might make."

My Lord, Thane was clever. Much more so than his brother.

I pushed away from the table. He stood up as well.

"Your terms?" I said, finding it difficult to talk.

"You. Here. One night every month."

I swallowed hard. "And Cedric goes free? You will not banish him?"

His expression hardened. "He would take you if I did."

My eyes never left his. "I don't know how this could be managed."

"Manage it. Those are my terms."

We stared at each other for a long moment.

"Agreed," I whispered, looking away.

I heard something hit the floor. When I turned, I saw his belt lying at his feet.

"Take off your dress," he said in a hoarse voice.

I couldn't move. My heart was in a vice.

"Take off your dress and get on the bed."

To my horror, I started to cry. With shaking hands, I undid the front laces and lifted the dress over my head. I held it in front of me, walked like a zombie to the bed in the next room and sat down.

Thane followed, stripping off his tunic and britches.

He terrified me, this stranger looking down at me with the stone face. Where was my Thane?

"Why are you crying?" he snapped. "You agreed to this."

"It has been a very bad two days and...I'm mortified," I said between sobs. "I never thought I would mean only *this* to you."

I thought he loved me.

He cursed and slammed the bedpost with his fist. "You think I hold you in contempt? I *love* you! With all my heart. I am furious that you would do this for Cedric. I hate him."

We stared at each other across an abyss of emotion.

"But I'm not doing this for him," I cried. "I'm doing it for me. I don't want to be dragged off to some foreign country." Away from you.

He growled and spun on one heel. "Give me a moment to cool down." At the window, he leaned against the frame. "I am sorry, Rowena. This is not what I had planned." He held onto the window frame for support.

I sniffled. "Kings never say they're sorry."

"This one does." His voice was gruff. "I had planned to make love to you, not punish you like this. But the anger I feel—the unbearable need to possess and control you—is intolerable. There must be something of my brother in me after all."

"You are *not* your brother," I said softly.

"The light is going." He released a tortured sigh and faced me."Will you do something for me? I want to see you before the light goes." He moved toward me, his arm outreached. "Let me take your dress, Rowena. Let me see you. Indulge me this one thing. I have longed for it, dreamed of it."

I understood this yearning.

When I stretched out on the bed, he took the dress from me. His eyes caressed every inch of my skin. Every freckle and dimple.

I had never felt so exposed.

Ever so lightly, he touched my stomach. I arched automatically and moaned. This had an instant effect on him. He went rigid.

He slid into bed beside me. "Let me do this properly. Let me show you how I feel."

His hand moved to my breast and I hissed in a breath.

"Why were you really crying?" he asked. "Tell me. I need to know you better. You are more tenderhearted than I thought."

I thought about lying, but what more could I lose by telling the truth?

"It is horrid when your dreams are dashed," I whispered.

"You have dreamed of this too?"

I gazed into deep blue eyes and saw the man I loved. "Yes."

His hands touched me everywhere, the hollow of my waist and the rise of my hips, lower…

"Do you have any idea how much I have wanted you?" he said hoarsely. "For days and weeks you have haunted me. I turned to books to learn everything I could about what I could do with you. To you. I longed to know your scent, to taste you. You are beautiful, so lovely, so much more than I imagined."

There was something close to worship in his eyes.

"The beast is gone, I promise you. I won't let him back. Go back with me in your mind. To that day in Scottsdale. Remember what you saw in the bedroom? It was me. Look."

He took my hand and placed it on his chest, the same chest that had lit my desire before. The black hair was soft beneath my palm.

"This is my heart," he said. "You hold it in your hand. Don't crush it, I beg you." One finger traced my eyebrow. "I love your eyes. They are windows to your mind and soul. I could not be a man and not love your body. But, Rowena, it is your mind that captures me most. How could there be such intelligence in one so beautiful?"

His words mesmerized me, flooding me with hope.

He moved over me and kissed my mouth. He licked the tears from my face. "Sweet and salty." His finger moved to my mouth. "So many times, I've heard words from this mouth and wondered what it would be like to be this close. Let me in, Rowena. Taste me."

His mouth came down on my parted lips and I melted, welcoming his tongue. That warm caramel feeling flowed through me, working its way down. His mouth left mine and went down to my neck. He kissed, tasted and licked.

"What is this small indentation here called?"

"The suprasternal notch," I whispered.

"I love it." He trailed kisses from there to between my breasts. "So much to choose from. But I need to be closer."

In a flash, we were as close as two people could be. We moved in a slow, lingering dance. He groaned, his teeth grazing my breast. I moaned as we rocked together, bathed in moonlight from this world's two moons.

"It's me, Rowena," he said. "Not the beast. *Me.*"

His mouth came down on mine.

Sweet, sweet love. He held me until I was flying, my eyes closed, lost in his scent, in his arms. I felt a rush of warmth surge through me as he moved inside me, stroking, sending heat waves in every direction. Then the power arched and bridged to something calmer.

I drifted...

Thane kissed my lips. "I will devote my life to this pursuit."

I felt sweeping joy, unlike anything I had felt before.

I grinned and kissed him back.

"And wilderness is Paradise." He cocked his head to one side. "How does the rest of it go?"

I snuggled closer. "You remembered."

"I fell in love with you that day. And yes, I kept remembering parts of that beautiful verse. Say it again."

"'Here with a loaf of bread beneath the bough, a flask of wine, a book of verse—and thou, beside me singing in the wilderness—and wilderness is paradise enow.'"

"How true." Thane spoke softly. "This poet, he knows of what he speaks. 'Tis in my heart, these very words."

"Soon I will be heavy with child and you will tire of me."

He laughed without mirth.

"That won't happen. Remember, I crave the knowledge of it and will cherish every step along the way. Besides...I love you, Rowena from Scottsdale."

I smiled. "And I love you, Thane from Sargonia."

We slept then, curled into each other.

When I awoke, light was streaming in.

Thane stood by the window.

"What's wrong?" I asked.

"It's dawn."

My heart sank. Soon it would be time for me to go.

I reached out to him. "Come back for a bit."

He turned and stared.

"What is it?" I asked, feeling a warning chill.

"I've made a decision. I'm changing the terms."

My mouth went dry. "What do you mean?"

"Cedric may keep his freedom, but not you. I'm keeping you here. What kind of man would I be if I let you go after last night? Tell me that?"

"He'll kill you, Thane! He killed his own brother."

"It is *your* safety that concerns me. I will not let that demon near you." There was steel in his voice. "You may think me bookish, Rowena, but I am still a warrior. And king. My word is law. You stay with me."

He reached for me, kissed me savagely, and in that brief moment I knew his iron will.

Thane left me mid-morning to meet with his war advisors, while Jon rode in a frenzy to carry the news back to Huel.

I stood on the balcony overlooking the courtyard. Already I could hear the sharpening wheels spinning, honing the blades of war.

Chapter 36

The problem with falling through walls into alternate worlds is a person usually doesn't have time to pack a suitcase.

"I haven't anything to wear," I grumbled. This was true. After weeks in Land's End, I badly needed a wardrobe overhaul. Actually, I needed a wardrobe, period.

It was mid-morning in the castle at Sargonia. I was in the royal bedroom.

"I like the white dress you rode in wearing," Thane said.

The white dress—it was ivory actually, but what man would know that?—was in a heap on the floor. Sometime during the night it had been stepped on. Maybe rolled on. Most would call it ecru.

"I like it too, but that's all I've got. Wasn't expecting to stay the night, let alone the month."

"I'll get you more dresses. Anything you like."

Thane was in that lovely post-coital state where men promised women anything. In his case, I had no doubt it was true. He would move the earth if he could, this man.

"But it's no use. You'll just wreck them all." He laughed, a wonderful sound that did something to my heart. "The food fight was my favorite."

"It wasn't my fault," I insisted. "People are always trying to rescue me, and frankly, it's getting tiresome." It was also hell on clothes.

"You do present a problem. If you would only stay in one place."

"Listen, buster. It wasn't me who started the whole Texas brawl thing at the tournament last month. I didn't *ask* to be kidnapped. And I don't go about beheading people who get in my way, unlike some people."

Thane put his hands behind his head. "You use the most fascinating idioms. What is a 'Texas brawl'?"

"And another thing!" I was on a roll. "This change-the-terms rescue of yours could be interpreted as another kidnapping. So you're no better than the rest of them."

"Surely, I am better in bed." He grinned.

"Don't call me Shirley," I muttered from habit. But it was hard not to grin. This verbal sparring with Thane was unique among my lovers.

Life sure was different beyond the wall. I was stuck here, without a bank account, without a single charge card, and to top it off, I was a teeny bit pregnant. And I had no clothes.

The castle walls were made of stone and kept out a lot of noise, but even I could hear the commotion in the hall. Men were yelling and footsteps pounded.

A breathless page appeared in the doorway. "Eight riders coming, wearing Huel colors."

Thane jumped to his feet. "Have them wait in the courtyard until I give the word. Guard them." I watched him don breeches and tunic, then sling on his belt and sword. I, in turn, reached for the dress and whipped it over my head.

"Is Cedric with them?" I asked with trepidation. Would this happen so quickly? I had only been at Castle Sargon two days.

"I don't know," he said. Those deep blue eyes looked straight at me. "Come with me. They'll demand to see you."

We left the royal suite and moved down the corridor. When we reached the great hall, Thane went to his desk of office. He motioned for me to sit in the chair to the right. I obeyed, sitting up straight and nervously smoothing the wrinkled ivory skirt over my legs.

"Let them come," he told the page at the door.

I watched and waited, measuring Thane's mood. He seemed cool as usual, his muscled torso leaning back in the chair. I loved to watch him, the way his dark hair sprang back from that strong forehead. He had a Roman nose and carved lips and the only sign I saw of his discomfort was the way his hands clenched and unclenched.

Grandfather and Jon came into the room. I was relieved not to see Cedric. I rose to my feet, ready to embrace them, but something in the old man's stony face held me back.

Grandfather looked at me hard, seeming to check that I was well, then turned to Thane. "I have come for my Granddaughter."

Thane contemplated this for a moment and then shook his head. "She came to me to bargain. She met my terms. Cedric's freedom for hers."

A wave of horror crossed Grandfather's face. "You know Cedric will never stand for this. You hold his wife hostage here. That will mean war!"

"Are you here to declare it?"

Rage was building in Grandfather. "You make my Granddaughter a whore!"

Thane vaulted to his feet and shoved the table with both hands. It toppled forward with a crash. Grandfather yelled and reached for his sword. I was paralyzed with fear, knowing what this would mean. Jon leapt forward and seized the old Earl's right arm before the sword left the scabbard.

"Don't!" Jon pleaded. "You know what he will have to do."

I knew myself. One didn't pull a sword in Land's End without being forced to use it. Honor demanded it. Especially when this was the King, in the King's own castle.

My eyes switched to Thane, who was fighting for control.

"Get out," he said. His voice was gravel.

They glared at each other, the two men I loved. I began to move forward, but Jon caught my eye and shook his head. This was a silent battle between Titans, the older, venerable one and the strong new King. There was no way Grandfather could win this now.

Finally, he seemed to realize this. Grandfather set the sword back in its place, abruptly turned and left the room without looking at me. Jon followed.

I had never seen Thane so angry. He clenched his fists and his whole body shook. I kept my distance and waited for him to shake off the fury.

He turned to me. "Do you feel the same?"

"No!" My response was immediate and self-preserving. "In my world, women choose their mates and they can leave a marriage if they want to."

Thane looked unconvinced. The rage was changing to something equally powerful and just as scary.

"I've shamed you." His voice sounded appalled.

"I choose you, Thane. I choose you." What else could I say to defuse this?

"I've shamed you. He's right. I've dishonored you. And the damnable thing is I won't stop. I can't." Thane moved toward me. I held out my arms and he gathered me into his. "The second it's possible, I'll make you my wife. You must believe that."

"I do," I said with all the conviction I could muster. What I really felt like saying was, 'Who the hell cares?' I'd been married three times and none had worked out too well. But I understood the conventions here and the need to appear to respect them.

"You may want to reconsider that plan. I'm pretty hard on husbands." I tried to sound jocular, but it was no joke.

"Cedric will not kill me, Rowena. You underestimate me."

I felt a chill descend upon the room.

He reached for me and kissed me savagely. When he released me, his sapphire eyes looked into mine. "My dear, sweet Rowena, I am a scholar and my mother was a sorceress. Did you not suppose I had been well-schooled in the art of magic?"

My heart skipped a beat.

He laughed when he saw my face and drew me close against his chest. "Yes, I hid it well. A wise man keeps his greatest weapon cloaked until he needs it."

I felt his heartbeat, strong and hard, against my cheek.

He kissed my head. "It is ironic. I am King and my word is law, but the one thing I want more than anything I cannot have. As long as he lives, we cannot marry."

Uh oh, this didn't sound good. Warning signs were going off big time.

Thane relaxed after a moment, then released me. He walked to the door to signal a page. "Stop them leaving. Bring them back. I'll speak to the old Earl privately."

To me, he said, "Leave us for a while, Rowena. I need to speak man to man. Wait in the library."

I left as he requested. I felt the world spinning around me, out of control, and I was a mere dust mote in it.

Later, Grandfather walked into the library and sat down across from me at the chess table. His expression was pained and his body weary.

"This is the game you both play with such devotion," he stated. "Will you teach me one day?"

"Of course," I said. "You will like the strategy in it." I glanced up at him and my eyes filled.

Grandfather sighed. "He tells me that he loves you and desires to marry you. He says he wishes nothing more than to grow old with you."

I sat up straight. This was such a clever thing for Thane to say.

"The obvious way in these circumstances is for him to challenge Cedric and be done with it. I've asked him not to do that. Does this upset you?"

I answered quickly. "No! I don't want another fight."

Grandfather exhaled loudly. "Thane won't let you go. This means you must suffer as his mistress. I understand it is not your choice to make, but it pains me just the same. Would that I were younger and could defend you as I should."

I could see self-loathing and defeat in his face.

"Also, I do not know what Cedric will do. I don't know the extent of his attachment to you."

I shivered. "I think it is more his pride that we should worry about."

"'Tis true," Grandfather said. He shifted his weight on the chair. "I have more dilemmas. Thane offers us a place here. He has asked that your cousin Kendra return here for your sake. I have agreed to this."

I let out a sigh of relief.

"As for us all, I must return to Huel and meet with your cousins. We will get word to Cedric. I can't predict the outcome of our meeting, so I ask you to be patient."

I nodded. I could be patient. It was the future that I dreaded.

"I don't want to go back to Cedric, Grandfather. I'm terrified of him."

"I know that, Rowena. I know." Grandfather sighed. "But I fear Thane underestimates Cedric. His command of magic grows daily and he loves a fight." He rose.

I jumped to my feet and ran to hug him.

"There, there, my dear girl. I think you will be safe here, at least. Thane seems to care for you. I do trust that. Can you abide him?"

I nodded. "We are friends."

He hugged me hard. "I do not think he would be entirely satisfied to hear that."

Perhaps not, but Grandfather would be equally distressed to learn how I really felt about Thane.

That night Thane was especially attentive. He gathered me in his arms and as I moved to reach for air, he held me tighter to him.

"There will be war," he said, his lips grazing my hair.

I shivered. "Must there be? Surely, we can come to some compromise." The last thing I wanted was to be the cause of more violence.

Thane shook his head. "Not just Huel and I. Norland has been making treaties all along the northern coast. My scouts are reporting large movements of troops."

I raised up on one elbow. "You have spies?"

He smiled and pulled me down. "We all have spies. I happen to have very good ones. They are extremely loyal to me and well-placed."

I wondered at that particular wording. The question must have appeared on my face.

"My brother was not very imaginative."

"You had spies separate from Sargon?"

He kissed my hair. "Always."

"Did he know?"

Thane laughed.

I thought about that. Thane was indeed more cunning than I had thought.

Chapter 37

I had the next afternoon to myself. Thane left to meet with his war advisors, with orders that I was not to leave the castle proper. That was okay. I was looking forward to a nap.

"Rowena! Row? Are you here?"

Kendra. I jumped to my feet and raced to the door.

A dark-haired sprite of a girl with large brown eyes skipped down the corridor toward me. Her slender body literally bounced down the hall. 'I'm here!" she proclaimed. "They wanted me to wait for Gramps, but I knew you wouldn't be coming back, so I packed up all our duds and—"

I had my arms out and around her before she could finish. She hugged me hard.

"Clothes! You brought my clothes. That's almost as good as bringing you."

"Figured you'd think that." She grinned. "Good thing I came. What did you do to this one?" She poked at my dress.

I looked down at the ivory-slash-ecru. "It got drop-kicked. And maybe stepped on."

"By the whole Prussian army, looks like. It's totally wrecked, Row. It'll never come clean. Good thing I brought reinforcements."

"You rode out this morning?"

"Knew you wouldn't be going anywhere. Richard tried to stop me, but—ha! He soon realized he better ride along to keep me safe. I left him at the gate." Her voice changed then. It softened. She moved back and patted down my shoulder.

"He wouldn't come in?"

She shook her short black hair. "Didn't want to run into Logan. Where is he, by the way?"

I shrugged. "Somewhere with Thane, making war plans. Kendra, this time I've really gone and done it."

She grabbed my hand. "Not your fault, although you do cause a lot of trouble. But nothing you could have done about this. Of course, I told Jon that Thane would never let you go. Silly men. Can't see past the nose on their face sometimes."

I pulled her into the bedroom and gestured her to sit down on the bed beside me. "Tell me the important things. Did anyone else come with you?"

She shook her head.

"Richard has gone back," I said. "Okay, tell me about Cedric."

She frowned. "Don't know. Jon says he's down in that area where they found you and Ivan. He's got friends. You know those strange guys who were here for your wedding? The Druid types."

Oh yeah, I knew them. Hard not to shiver at the memory of a Satanic wedding in all its midnight glory.

"He'll blow a gasket when he hears, of course," Kendra said. "I wouldn't want to be Thane."

Or any of the men who got in the way. My turn to frown. How the hell was I going to keep them both alive? Or rather, how would I keep Thane alive and my dreaded husband away from me?

Kendra's eyes spotted something on the night table. She lifted a silver bracelet encrusted with flashing stones of amethyst, topaz and garnet.

"Row, look at the size of these stones. Where did you get it?"

"Isn't it gorgeous? Thane left it for me this morning. Said it was my mother's, and his mother's before that."

"Try it on. Here, let me help you." She struggled to spread it apart. It took a bit of work because the hinge seemed heavy from disuse.

I couldn't see the clasp from this angle. But jewelry is jewelry and it was a gorgeous thing. I held out my left arm and she closed it around me. There was a burst of yellow light, then *zzzap*. A shock ran up my arm. "Ow!"

Kendra's eyes were huge. "What the hell was that?"

"I don't know, but it hurt. Get this thing off me!"

She fiddled with my wrist, turning it over. "That's strange. Do you know where the clasp went? It doesn't appear to be here. Or at least, I can't find it."

"Not a clue."

"I don't think this is coming off easily. We'll have to ask Thane about it." She shook her head, puzzled. "Does it hurt? It's rather large."

"Not at all. It looks heavy, but honestly I can hardly feel it on me."

"That's weird. Oh well, you can hide it under most sleeves if it worries you."

My jewel-encrusted bracelet was the last thing that worried me. I had a war to prevent.

I awoke that night sometime before dawn. Moonlight streamed in from the open window, calling me, pulling me. I lay still for a moment and willed myself to stay put. But it was no use. His call was silent but insidious, seeping into my mind from all sides and enveloping all other thoughts.

I moved out of bed so as not to disturb Thane and reached for the royal blue silk dressing gown—the one I had brought from Scottsdale on that first fateful trip through the wall. I found suede slippers on the floor and put them on.

I took one last look at the bed. Thane was in a deep slumber on his back with one arm flung out. His black hair curled like a child's. He looked peaceful and content. I left him, knowing he would be safe.

The night sky was brilliant with stars as I left the castle by the secret door in the library. The air was cool and I pulled the dressing gown around me. I followed the moons to the postern gate. I lifted the secret latch and let myself out. The moonlight pulled me, drew me down a path on the side of the cliff to a clearing out of sight of the castle.

Cedric was there, alone, waiting. The moonlight lit his features so that all was clearly visible. The red-gold hair, the eerie green eyes, and the huge warrior build that always gave me shivers. His arms rippled with muscle and his wrists were banded with leather. I would have known him anywhere merely from the way he stood.

"Why are you here? Why have you come?" I slowed my feet, fighting the draw.

Cedric waited for me to come to him. He knew I would. He had designed it so. The draw to him was inescapable and that reinforced the terrible truth I had surmised.

I inched forward, fighting it as hard as I could. "You've put a spell on me, haven't you?" I was breathless. "I felt it that first night when I was drawn to the tapestry."

"Do you feel it getting stronger?" He smiled with cool excitement. "Each time you see me, it grows. Eventually it will work over longer distances. When I call, you will come."

I had managed to stop about ten feet from him and now the need was compelling, the need of an addiction.

"Then I'd better not see you again, so it can't grow stronger," I said warily.

He covered the ground between us in two seconds. "Don't be a fool."

I was in his arms and then his mouth was on mine, drawing life from me. His arms around me formed a cage I couldn't escape. My fingers traveled up through his hair, trapped in there, and when he pulled my hips against him, I closed my fist hard. His whole body went rigid against me, abruptly, solidly.

"It works both ways," he said hoarsely, releasing my mouth to look down at me. "That is the supreme irony of spells like this. Your need feeds mine."

I pulled back with some effort. "You mean this isn't real? What you feel for me is just a spell and nothing more?" I was almost insulted. But at the same time, maybe this would work in my favor. It could give me an out. If I could figure out a way to break the spell, maybe Cedric would let me go.

He laughed lightly. "Hardly. The spell feeds from emotion. It merely allows emotion to win over reason. If I was indifferent to you, it would repel you rather than draw you in."

The pain of being so close and not closer was almost unbearable. I lay my head on his chest and the pain instantly turned to relief. "How do we break this spell?"

"We don't," he said, almost growling. "I don't want to. You won't either when you get used to it." He lifted his head. "You smell of him."

He frowned, momentarily distracted, and I found the strength to fall back out of reach. He moved forward to grab me with one hand.

I backed up again. "No. Stay back just for a moment. Please. We need to talk." I was breathless, fighting the draw with every ounce of energy I could muster.

He stood stiffly in front of me and folded his great arms across his chest. "So talk."

I licked my lips. "I made a bargain with Thane to save you. My freedom for yours."

His eyes softened. "I know that."

It would war in him, the fact that I had sacrificed for him, the fact that I had lain with another man to free him. He would love that I seemed to care enough, yet he would hate that I had done it.

I turned to the cliff wall, hoping the draw would lessen somewhat and it did. "I can't welch on the deal or you will be killed. You've got to let me see this out, for your own safety."

Cedric smiled in disdain. "He won't kill me. I'll get him first." He moved closer.

"Don't!" I begged.

He ignored me. His hand grabbed my wrist and then just as suddenly let it go. He gasped and his face flashed with anger. Or was it fear? He touched the garnet stone in my bracelet and sprang back as if the thing had been on fire.

The oddest thing...the red stone was glowing.

"Where did you get this?" he demanded.

"W-what?"

"This witch's bracelet. It channels magic. Where did you get it?"

I gulped. "I found it on my night table."

"More likely it found you. The bracelet chooses whom to give its power to. It's chosen you for some reason. I can't fathom why. Have you tried to take it off?"

"It won't budge. I can't even find the latch anymore. It seems to have vanished."

Cedric cursed. "Why? Why would it have chosen you?"

I could think of only one reason. I withdrew my hand and hugged myself with both arms. "Sargon's mother was my great-aunt. Did you know that? Not from your side. From the other."

He swore again. "And you are the last remaining female of the line. That's why."

Why was he so upset? This bracelet seemed to scare him, yet it didn't seem to have any power that I could detect.

"I must find a way to control that power," he muttered.

He was silent. I could sense his deep, churning thoughts.

"I know you don't want to leave Castle Huel, Cedric. Don't risk banishment, please."

"If it comes to battle, I'll be ready soon. But this witch's bracelet is a mighty complication."

"You can't do battle with Thane until I am free of it? Why?"

"I daren't risk it. You can't control it. It could channel my magic to support the house of Sargon."

He stared at me and I was lost in the brilliant green of his eyes. "I must consult with someone who will know how to master the bracelet. I need my freedom to do that."

Thank God! He would leave me be for now.

He cursed. "I loathe this, leaving you here." He stood and pulled me to my feet.

"It's best. I'm safe here and so is the babe."

Cedric's eyes burned into me and I felt the draw come back to life. He reached for me and kissed me deeply, thoroughly.

"Our child," he said with wonder. "You will be with me when it is born, I promise you."

"Go now. Quickly. Be safe." Don't kill anyone else, I silently pleaded.

He grabbed me once more, kissed me, and then just as suddenly, released me and blended into the night. I felt my whole body shudder from the pain of separation, and then—abruptly—release.

Thank God.

The night sounds followed me as I hurried back to the castle. It was trickier to open the postern gate from outside, but I managed. Very quietly I made my way back to the library door and slipped into the royal suite. Thane was as I had left him, sleeping soundly. I slipped off my dressing gown and wondered what I could possibly do next to postpone the inevitable battle of the Titans.

Chapter 38

Next morning Kendra and I decided to gather wildflowers. I could see from the library window that the meadow adjacent to the castle was ablaze with color.

"This place is so vibrant," Kendra exclaimed. She bent over to snap off a buttercup stem.

"It's not like the desert, is it?"

I was happy. The orange beams of sunlight were dazzling. I left Kendra picking flowers and leaned back against a stone wall, closing my eyes to better drink in the sweet scents.

Someone close by whispered my name. *"Rowena."*

I opened my eyes and saw no one. Was it the wind?

I peeked around the wall.

A great big bear of a man stood not five feet away.

"Collin!" I smiled in recognition. "What are you doing—"

A hand came round behind to cover my mouth. "Shhhh," a voice said in my ear. "It's just us."

Janus?

"Gag her," another man snapped. "Don't take a chance."

I knew that voice. I friggin' knew that voice. Anger rose in me. I started to struggle and several more arms came from nowhere to hold me still. I counted Collin and Roderick, who looked apologetic, and a red-haired man whose name escaped me. Janus removed his hand and before I could even squeak, a rolled up cloth was shoved in my mouth secured with a gag.

"Get the bag," Gareth said harshly.

I tried to scream, but it came out muffled. They had the bag over my head and tied in no time. I tried to kick and connected once. Someone yelped and swore.

Gareth picked me up and threw me over his shoulder. I knew it was him by his body, his scent.

"I'll take the bag off when we get out of sight," he said.

They walked quietly and no one spoke. I could sense several horses eager to run.

"I'm putting you on astride. Put your left foot in the stirrup here and I'll help you up. Don't even think of kicking him forward. I've got four men holding him in place."

It was the strangest sensation, mounting a horse blind-folded. Someone held my skirt up so it wouldn't rip. This was a taller horse than I was used to, a man's horse. Gareth jumped up behind me and his arms reached around for the reins. We moved ahead at a cautious pace.

"I've played the idiot long enough," he said. "I let your bastard cousin live because you wanted it and I was a fool. I'm not giving in to you anymore. You're coming with me and that's the end of it."

I screamed a whole bunch of things at him, but they all sounded like muted cotton.

"Wait a few minutes and I'll take that off."

It was hot in the bag and my eyes pooled. When he finally slowed to untie the bag, tears were running down my cheeks.

"Don't be like that," he said roughly. "No feminine wiles. I'm at the end of my patience with you."

As my nose got stuffy, I started to choke.

"Great Gods," he cursed. "Janus, hold up there." He undid the knot at the back and took off the gag. I reached in quickly to remove the cloth, nearly gagging in the process. I coughed and gasped about six times.

Then I found my voice. "You son of a bitch!"

"Odin's breath! Back on it goes." He tied the gag and I elbowed him in the chest once, not too hard because I didn't want to be roped up. He cursed again. I was still trying to catch my breath as he kicked the horse forward.

Gareth headed north along the cliff edge. Eventually he would have to turn east to reach Norland, which was a half-day's ride from here. I lay my head back on his shoulder and closed my eyes.

Could I have been more careful? Was this inevitable?

Poor Kendra. No doubt they had her roped up and I was responsible for it all. Surely Gareth would keep his men in line. He wouldn't let them hurt her.

Thane would have a fit when he found us missing. And the Earl—poor old Grandfather—all I ever did was bring him angst. What a sorry turn of events.

I took stock of my possessions. Just the one dress again, the newly washed rose muslin. My fanny pack. The bracelet, though it wouldn't come off. The Tintagel broach was around my neck on the chain, but I hardly needed it to keep me safe. Gareth was the one who had given it to me, after all. Thank goodness I had on my cowboy boots, although I would miss having soft leather slippers for daytime.

I slept for some time, lulled by the sway of the horse and Gareth's familiar scent of hay, leather and something thoroughly masculine.

It was nearly dusk when we came to a small encampment in the hills. Four tents were pitched in a field and several men stood by a fire on the rocks. There were shouts and greetings. They all looked over and a few came forward to take our horses.

Janus slid off his mare and came to help me down.

As soon as I hit the ground, I tore the gag off. "You son of a bitch! How dare you kidnap me!"

Gareth dismounted and strode forward. "Kidnap? I rescued you!"

"It's not rescuing when you gag and tie me like a hog." I whacked him across the face with my open hand. "Ow!" I cursed and cradled my right hand. "That hurt like hell."

Behind me, Janus laughed. I think the rest of the men were in shock.

"You're crazy. I was only taking you home to Norland where we belong."

I stood with my mouth open. Hells bells. In Gareth's eyes that would be true.

"And don't give me any of that innocent business," he continued, "because I have a right to be mad." His arms flailed in the air. "That whole debacle at the tournament? That was your fault. I had it all worked out. Days of planning, calling in allies from all across the north. My men were in place and Cedric under my sword, helpless. One lunge and he'd have been dead. Then you pull that stunt in the courtyard and I have no idea where you are. I can't find you and the whole south is in chaos." His voice grew bitter. "And now Thane puts in a claim. I should never have given in to you. Never."

This shook me. I was raised a liberated woman and had always prized my independence. Then why was I finding this confession of his so moving? There was primitive stuff at work here that went well beyond my understanding. The man had raised an army, for pity's sake, and if that wasn't humbling...

"Oh...well," I mumbled. "Sorry about that."

His jaw unclenched. "It won't happen again, I assure you. I've risked my men enough."

"Gareth, you can't keep me chained to a wall."

"Why the devil would you need to be chained? I just want to keep you safe with me up north where I control things."

"Well, maybe if you had told me what you guys were planning to do..."

"You're impossible. Had I told you, would you have allowed me to kill Cedric? Of course not. You're far too kind-hearted. But he's a fiend and he needs killing. I'll manage it next time."

I was distracted by another fear.

"Kendra?" I spun in a panic, searching.

"Here!" She dashed forward in a whirl of energy. I was nearly knocked over by her hug. A familiar figure moved up behind her.

"This is Roderick," she said when she let go of me.

"I already know Roderick." I nodded to him. "The bloody nose is new. Did you do that?"

"Well, I didn't know he'd be nice, at first," she said.

Someone snickered.

"Shut up, Janus," Gareth ordered.

But Janus was all-out howling now.

Kendra turned to Gareth. "Oooo, Row. It's Thor from the movie."

I remembered then that Kendra had never met Gareth before.

"Kendra, Gareth. Gareth, my cousin Kendra."

Gareth nodded but his face stayed hard.

I decided to stay equally firm. "Tell your men that if any of them touch her, I'll kill them. Actually, what am I saying? She'll kill them herself."

"No I won't," Kendra said, smiling. "I like them."

I sighed and closed my eyes. How was I going to keep this girl safe in a place like Land's End? Too much had happened and I was weary.

"Gareth, can Kendra and I have a tent for some privacy? We have some things to discuss."

He nodded curtly and I was relieved. We had a truce, but we weren't exactly on good terms yet.

I thought back to our time together. Had it only been three days? You can pack a lot into a few days. Maybe this interlude wouldn't be a bad idea after all. I had to think strategically. I would miss Thane, but at least he would be safe from Cedric.

I turned to the Janus and the others. "It's good to see you." I reached my arms around young Roderick. They had to go a long way up. "You too? I swear you've grown." He blushed.

"And Collin, dear Collin." He gave me a big bear hug. It felt good. His beard tickled my forehead.

"Rowena, behave!" Gareth growled.

I turned to snap something back, but was caught by a shiver.

"She's cold," Collin said. "No wonder. That gown is nearly threadbare."

Roderick leapt forward to put his cloak around my shoulders.

"I have no clothes," I said with a sad frown.

"So like a woman to worry about her clothes." Gareth shook his head. "I'll dress you in a hundred gowns, never fear. And your cousin too. But first I need to talk with my men. Janus, show them to my tent."

Janus led us to the tent furthest away. He held the flap open and signaled for us to enter. I hesitated and let Kendra go first.

I'm not a tent sort of girl. In my experience all sorts of critters like tents. I didn't *think* there were rattlesnakes and scorpions in Land's End, but I still had a lot to learn about the place. Including how to get out of it.

The tent was a kind of canvas and it smelled musty. There were a few fur rugs thrown on the floor, but that was it.

"We'll be safe here with them," I told Kendra with no confidence at all.

"You weren't kidding when you said Gareth was a Viking. He looks right out of a movie."

'Movie, yeah. That's what this adventure reminds me of. An extremely poorly directed, low budget film."

Kendra laughed. "I've never had such fun in all my life."

I sighed and sat down on the furs. Clearly, she was hopeless.

So here we were again in a place we hadn't planned to be. At least the natives were friendly. Too friendly, but I was learning how to deal with that. In the last few weeks, I'd had to adjust my feelings about what was right and wrong.

"You know, I'm not nearly this permissive back home."

Kendra stared at me, one brow arched.

"No, really," I insisted. "I'm a one-man kind of girl. It's just..." I searched for the words.

"I understand what you mean," she assured. "In this place the safest thing to do—actually, the only safe thing to do—is go with the flow."

I fiddled with the chain around my neck and took if off. "That's better. This thing is heavy." I rubbed the back of my neck and looked down at it.

The Tintegal broach was lovely, with blue and green stones in an ancient setting. It hung like a pendant on the heavy chain, along with something else. Weeks ago, Cedric had left a Roman Coin in my hand to keep me safe. Later, I had attached the coin to the broach as a way of keeping track of both and they had somehow become fused. In theory, the combo worked to keep me alive. But in practice, I was noticing that Cedric seemed to know where I was at all times. Maybe it served as a magical homing device?

"You know, this kidnapping might not be such a disaster as I originally thought. Remember, Gareth was the guy who originally walked through the wall of our classroom. He once told me that he was the one who hired a wizard to build the portal into our world."

"You mean—"

"Yes. He must know where this wizard-guy is. If I can find him, I'm sure I could get him to open the portal again." Okay, not *sure*, but like the ant and the rubber tree, I had high hopes.

"Then we could go home for a visit," Kendra said, her brown eyes sparkling. "And bring back more chocolate."

Then we could go home for good, I thought. But why ruin the mood?

"So," Kendra said, "all you have to do is...?"

"Sleaze it out of Gareth," I finished.

"So the plan is you find out where the wizard is from Gareth. We go for a ride and accidentally on purpose get a little bit lost and end up where the wizard is. He sets up the portal again so we can take a quick trip through it. Then we bring back something fab, pay off the wizard with it and head back wherever we want."

"Yeah, that's kind of it." She was actually ahead of me. I was proud of her. "I haven't worked out the details yet."

Kendra continued to speak, but I couldn't hear her anymore. My head was filled with thoughts of animals panicking. Horses were transmitting fear, birds were lifting and soaring away, smaller animals scurried into the dense underbrush.

I vaulted to my feet, but before I could say anything, the tent flap whipped open. Janus stood in the opening and his face reflected what I already knew.

"Cedric is coming," I said before he could speak.

He nodded once. "There's a line of riders on the other side of the rise. A hundred or more."

"He's after me, Janus. You've got to let me leave. Gareth won't be able to do a thing."

Janus's mouth gaped. "I—"

"Let us have horses. We'll get away and that will stop the bloodshed. *Please*, Janus! I don't want Gareth to die in this small encampment when he can't even call his own troops to battle."

It was the way to appeal to Janus and Gareth would be mad as fury when he found out I'd used the young man.

The cries of men were audible. I could feel the tension in the camp.

"Come quickly," Janus said. "There are horses tethered nearby. Keep to the forest. Head north until you come to the fork. Gareth is speaking with the scouts. He won't see you if you go that route."

I didn't hear the rest. I was out the flap and around the back in seconds. Kendra was right on my heels. It was easy to follow the trail of fear to the row of horses lashed together. We took no time to choose, but untied the last two steeds at the end closest to the forest trail.

I adjusted the stirrups of the first beast and then mounted in a ghostly whirl. The forest trail was right ahead. I coaxed the big animal forward and silently disappeared into the woods. The forest was deep, but opened up to mix of trees and grasslands only a few minutes into our escape.

In those first few minutes it became apparent to me that I had not been lucky with my horse. The one I'd chosen was a horse with no manners and no inclination to speak to me. When I tried to read its mind, it said something very bad in horse talk. Not that I am fluent, but the inference was not at all nice. It wouldn't even tell me its name, so of course I kept thinking of it as Horse. Or more accurately Damned Horse, which probably annoyed it further.

Damned Horse had a tendency to veer under very large tree branches with the express purpose of knocking me off. I countered by whacking said animal in the rump with my not so gentle boots. In fact, I had a good notion to tell this beast that it could be dropped off at the very next glue factory, except I was unsure if Land's End *had* a glue factory. To my chagrin, I needed this beast of burden to take my sorry hide away from the violent stand-off behind us.

Hopefully, Cedric would back down when he realized I wasn't there. If the past was anything to go by, he would. The man seemed to have a one-track mind and he didn't waste any energy or magic on things that would not contribute to his immediate goal.

I pulled Damned Horse to a dead stop. "Kendra!"

She pulled her mare up beside me. They were both out of breath. "What is it?"

"How's your horse?"

"Fine," she said, stroking the mare's mane. "Rather sweet really. Why?"

"Mine is the spawn of Satan."

Damned Horse had the nerve to snigger. Yes, horses snigger. It may *sound* like a whinny, but it's much more degrading when you actually know what they're thinking.

"Kendra, I left the Tintegal broach back in the tent."

She shrugged. "Maybe you'll get it back later."

"I don't want it back. The broach is magic and it keeps the wearer safe. But more important, it has a coin on the back that I think Cedric has been using to track me. Sort of like a homing device."

"And you left it back there? That's a good thing, isn't it? Cedric won't be able to find you now."

"Yup. That's what I've been thinking."

For once, things were going my way. Not that I could take any credit.

"Just hope it doesn't make him really angry when he finds *it* and not me."

"You're thinking he might kill Gareth?"

"I'm thinking he might annihilate the whole western seaboard. Then again, maybe not. He doesn't tend to waste magic."

Was his magic a finite resource? No doubt about it, I needed to learn more about the way things worked in this world.

Damned Horse jerked on the reins and kicked up its front legs. I think the cause was Kendra's mare. Wouldn't you know it? Another randy male in Land's End.

"We'd better keep going," I said. "Slow your pace a bit. I think this horse from hell is wearing down."

A few minutes later we came to the fork in the forest.

"What do we do?" Kendra asked.

"Let me think…"

As I said this, I noticed a strange thing. The garnet stone in my bracelet was glowing. Just a faint glow, but definitely something I could see. What could it mean?

"Wait here," I said to Kendra.

I guided Damned Horse down the path to my right for about ten paces. The stone continued to glow. I stopped, turned the animal around and continued back to Kendra. The glow became more faint. Then I steered Damned Horse onto the path to the left. Nothing. We walked for about twenty feet down that path. No glow at all. I maneuvered my horse back to Kendra.

"So cool!" I said. "This bracelet is showing me the way."

Her dark eyes watched me, skeptical. "What do you mean?"

"Look at this. When I start down this path, the stone glows." I showed her.

"Okay, so the stone glows."

"I'm thinking it may be attracted by other magic. Maybe it'll show us the way to the wizard."

The mare jolted skittishly as Damned Horse tried to sniff her butt. Kendra pulled the female away. "You sure you want to trust an assumption?"

"It must have some reason for wanting me to go this way. I'll bet there's a source of magic at the root of it all. And we need magic to get back through the wall. Besides, it is a witch's bracelet."

"Oh great," Kendra muttered. "So it's going to lead us to a bunch of witches. That makes me feel a whole lot better."

"Don't be silly. They wouldn't be witches because there aren't any witches left in Land's End. They burnt them all."

Except for my great-aunt, I remembered. Thane said his mother had died in childbirth. That would have to be with his birth because I hadn't heard of any other younger siblings. It was a sorry fact that before 1920 fifty percent of women died in childbirth.

"Okay," Kendra said with a huff. "We'll let the bracelet signal the direction we take. I mean, how far can it be?"

Two hours later grew into three.

"Stop!" Kendra cried. "I can't take it anymore. Doesn't this wilderness ever end?"

"Hold on. I see blue up ahead."

At last we came to the river.

I slowed and signaled for Kendra to pull up beside me.

"What do we do?" she asked. "It's too deep for the horses, isn't it?"

I scanned left then right. "We look for a narrowing and we jump. I've done it a hundred times in Arizona. Well, not jumping water exactly, but jumping over cacti the size of garbage cans. And cacti will do a whole lot more damage than water, believe me."

I could feel her eyes on me.

"You're kidding. Tell me you're kidding."

"Look, Kendra. We'll keep going until we find a reasonable approach. It'll be easy, I assure you. The horses will know what to do." I paused, wondering if Damned Horse would agree. " I'll go first and your horse will follow."

She shook her head. "We could go back. Or we could just follow the river north. Maybe we'll end up back at Gareth's castle."

I sniffed. "It's a fortress, not a castle, and I'm not going there. Honestly, Kendra, you aren't missing anything. Drafty old thing with no proper beds. The bracelet is telling me to go this way so that's what I'm doing. Don't you see? If we can't get to the source of the magic, we may never find our way back to the States. I've got to go back. My Dad will be frantic."

"Row, you don't plan to stay, do you?"

"Don't worry," I said. "I'm only suggesting a visit. Only a day or two, so that I can see Dad and explain things, maybe pick up more supplies. We need supplies. We're out of chocolate." I grinned, knowing I had her at *chocolate*.

We walked our mounts for twenty minutes until we came to a place where the river narrowed.

"Here's a good spot," I said. "I'm sure we can make it across."

The gap was about six feet and the bank on the other side was grassy.

"Are you sure?" Kendra frowned. "The water looks rather deep. And fast moving."

"That always happens when a river narrows," I said. "All the water gets pushed into a smaller space, so it moves faster." It sounded like it could be true, but I was from a desert state, so what did I know?

"I don't think you should do it, Row."

"Nuts. I've jumped this distance in my bare feet. I can certainly do it on horseback." I pulled Damned Horse about twenty feet back from the bank and then kicked him hard. "Go, dammit!"

Damned Horse galloped like a bat out of hell, then lurched to a stop at the edge of the riverbank. I, however, did not. I flew over the beast's head.

Splash!

"Row, are you all right? Row?"

I came to the surface, choking on water. "I'm okay. I can stand here. It isn't deep. "Damn, but it's cold. This m-must be a m-mountain stream." My teeth chattered.

"Um…" Kendra paused. "I think your horse is gone."

"Sonovabitch!"

I saw Damned Horse trotting off in the distance. I could hear the equine snickering in the wind.

"Here, let me help you out." Kendra dismounted, moved to the edge of the bank and stretched out her hand.

"Thanks. This bank is—oh crap! There goes your horse."

Sure enough, the mare decided to follow Damned Horse. Off she trotted without a care in the world.

Kendra hauled me up. "Bloody hell. What now?"

I shook like a dog and got her all wet. "We go north, I guess. Unless you want to walk across the river."

She shivered. "Nope. You look freezing."

"It's nothing," I said nonchalantly. "I'll dry in the sun."

"Your dress is ripped."

I looked down. The skirt had a slit running up the side to my thigh. I sighed. "Another one bites the dust."

"I don't know how you do it." She shook her head. "I haven't wrecked a single one."

We continued north, walking single file along the riverbank. The hot sun dried my clothes, then slowly sank over the horizon.

Kendra moved up beside me. "I'm beat. Can we stop for a while?"

"Thought you'd never ask." I went down on my knees like a camel and then rested on my butt. "I'm starved. What do we have left?"

She plunked down beside me, then opened her fanny pack. "One granola bar and a handful of almonds. The almonds are old."

"I don't care." I held out my hand. "I could eat a horse."

Actually, I wouldn't have minded eating Damned Horse, but he was probably all the way back to Gareth's camp by now. Gareth, who would be wondering what the heck had happened to us with our horses returning alone. That is, *if* he were still alive to care.

I didn't want to think about that.

"So…do you think Gareth will come searching when our horses return without us?"

"Maybe. We should stay right here in the open where they can find us."

Kendra stretched out in the long grass "I'm glad you're here with me, Row. I'd be scared without you."

"Nothing to worry about. I've been in worse jams than this."

Dusk had drifted into night.

I was thankful the bugs weren't too bad. Better here than in the forest.

The stone in the bracelet pulsated. Why was it glowing again?

My wrist ached beneath the bracelet.

"The ground is hard," Kendra complained.

"I'm so tired, I hardly care," I said, yawning and massaging my wrist. "What I really want is a long sleep in the nearest warm bed."

There was a bright flash of light.

Kendra screamed.

Then the world exploded around me.

Chapter 39

Birds chirped. That was the first sound I heard. I opened my eyes. It appeared to be just before dawn. I was warm and comfortable, lying on my side in a soft but completely unknown bed. Furs covered me. There was a goblet and a dagger on the table beside me.

Where the heck was I?

An interior stone wall stood directly in front of me. Light filtered in through a long narrow window meant for defense by bow and arrow.

So this was a fortress?

I squeezed my eyes and recalled the last thing I could—wishing for the nearest warm bed. I guess *this* was it.

Holy hell, the bracelet! I had rubbed the stone and it had thrown me into the very position I had asked for.

But where was Kendra?

A strange sound came from somewhere close by. I shot up to sitting position and looked to my right.

"Yikes!" I said, scrambling to get out of the bed. "Who are you?"

A man lay on the bed beside me, and what a man. He was very tall, with white-blond hair to the shoulders, and his cheekbones were unusually high. His facial hair was confined to a mustache and goatee. There were lines on his face. I put his age around forty.

When he sat up, I saw that his eyes were a pale gray, very light, and his skin was pale. His teeth were good and he seemed quite clean. He was smiling the sort of smile a greedy child has on Christmas morning.

"A gift from Odin," he said, his eyes widening. "Bless the Gods, I will give sacrifice to their honor today." His accent was thick and foreign.

I grabbed for my dress, which was at the end of the bed. How in blazes had that come off in the night?

"Oh no." I groaned. "Not you too." Bloody hell, I couldn't go anywhere in this world without an armed escort.

"How did you come to be here?" he asked.

If he didn't know the answer then we couldn't have…

"You are a gift. Which of the Gods should I thank?"

A gift? Oh Crikey. How could I answer that one?

"Um…I think there might be some mistake here. Wrong bed. You know, that sort of thing." It sounded lame even to me, but the truth was even more unbelievable.

The man snorted. "The Gods don't make mistakes! You are a sweet gift for a lonely warrior. Bless the Gods. Who sent you? Freya or Sjofn?"

I swallowed hard. "What we have here is a classic misunderstanding. The Gods made a mistake. I simply got sent to the wrong bed. Sorry. Wasn't my fault. Honest."

He frowned. "You were meant for another? I don't believe it. They would take you back if t'were the case. Go then! Leave me now if the Gods command it."

Apparently, they didn't.

He grinned. "You see, my sweet one. You are a gift. Look at you. Every curve just made to set me afire. Come closer."

I backed away. "Can we maybe negotiate something? I wasn't planning to be here." And there didn't seem to be any way I could get out.

"Think not to escape. My men guard the door."

The blasted man was reading my mind.

"However you came to be in my bed, it was meant. You are here and you will need my protection. Take your chance with my men or cleave to me, Lady. Your choice."

I pulled the dress around my hips, tucked it at the waist and rose to my feet. My hand reached for the heavy goblet from the bedside table. "Stay back."

His mouth curved into a strange smile. He swung from the opposite side of the bed and rose to his feet. Damn. He wasn't wearing any clothes.

I gulped and went red in the face. "Don't come any closer."

"I must work for you? So be it. Do your worst, fair Lady."

I threw the goblet at his head. He caught it with one hand in a lightning move and tossed it on the floor. How had he done that?

His smile held. "Be reasonable, woman. You land in my bed and you do not expect me to take advantage of the situation? Am I made of stone?"

"It was a mistake. I was as surprised as you are."

The man moved to the great wooden door and closed it. He stood there blocking the only exit. I made a quick move back to the side-table and lost my dress in the process, but came up with the dagger in my hand.

"Stay back," I said again. "I'll use this."

I would, too. I was sick and tired of having no control over my own destiny.

"Well done," he said. His eyes went bright as he gazed upon my body and he made a lazy move to the center of the room. "You might get in one swipe. But my arms are long. Do not think you can overcome me. The male is always built stronger to overwhelm the female for breeding."

"So this is about breeding?"

I moved sideways to the middle of the room. We were almost circling each other, like two combatants.

"Not always." His arms were out, ready to move. "This is, I think, about power. And pleasure." He licked his lips. "You are a very beautiful woman."

For a brief moment we stared at each other across the room.

Then I felt fury.

Hadn't I learned anything in my weeks in Land's End? Two could play at this game. I was learning how to control men through sex. Give them a taste and make it good—damn good. They would fight to come back for more. I would control this man and make him my slave if that's what it took.

I smiled. There were two ways to do this—play the victim or run the show.

His eyes were brilliant and I felt the power burn in me. I stamped my foot on the floor and threw the dagger into the corner where it bounced off one wall and rebounded off another.

"Okay, big boy. Hit me with your best shot. Let's see what you can do." I fairly spit the words.

He hesitated a second in disbelief. "You are mad."

I laughed, a good old-fashioned hysterical cackle. "I'm good and mad. Sick and tired of being pushed around. First Gareth does this ridiculous rescue thing and then mucks it all up when he gets within sight of a battle. Then I end up riding for hours and hours in the middle of nowhere, scared to pieces." Oh yeah, I was on a roll. "I haven't slept well for days, my clothes are in tatters, I'm pregnant and hungry as—"

"You are with child?"

"Yes."

"Norland's?"

I hesitated. Then I nodded. "Yes, Norland's." Instinct told me it was the right thing to say. It might even be true. I hoped it was true.

The tall man straightened. "I would not hurt an unborn child."

I stared in disbelief. "You're kidding me, right?"

Sex doesn't hurt a fetus. But I wasn't about to mention it now.

"I would never take such a chance. A child in Land's End? And a son of Norland? Do you not realize the significance?"

I did, but who was to know this barbarian would have any code of chivalry?

"Well, this is awkward," I said. "What do we do now?"

He scrunched his face. "Why would the Gods send me a gift if I cannot use you?"

Oh brother. I thought fast. "Perhaps it is some sort of test? Or maybe they needed you to protect me?"

The big man frowned, then nodded. "It is a test. So be it. I shall protect you well. And your child when he is born."

"It could be a girl."

He nodded again, only this time with a smile. "That would be even more preferable." He stretched, raised his arms above his head as far as he could. His whole body arched in response. "Come let me hold you. It has been so long since I have held a woman." He pointed to the bed.

I hesitated a moment, then shrugged. It seemed harmless. We had one bed to share and a need to keep warm.

I moved self-consciously over to one side of the bed and sat down on the covers. The big man did the same and then reached over for me. I nestled my back into his chest to make us like two spoons in a drawer. It seemed safer when I couldn't see him. I heard him sigh deeply into my hair.

What a beautiful moment. This strange man holding me so sweetly, caressing me but not forcing anything else. I cannot explain the sensation of being held by a powerful man who swears to guard you and your child. It was almost fatherly, his warmth against mine, the strong male scent.

After a while I rolled over to face him. "Who are you? What is your name?"

"I am Lars."

"My name is Rowena."

"I know who you are. I saw your cousin take down Sargon the King."

"You were there?" I had not seen him, but that was not surprising. The impromptu battle had been a horror.

"I am allied with Norland." He rolled on his back and looked off in the distance.

"You are Gareth's ally?"

"Norland puts great stock in you, calling in his allies to raise an army. I wanted to know why."

"Gareth would kill you if he found out you tried to…bed me."

"Are you going to tell him?"

I shook my head.

"I thought not. Nor shall I. Besides, Norland needs me. My men like a battle, but even so, I wanted to know why I should risk their lives. I have a dilemma . Two, in fact." He put his hands behind his head. "I should return you to Norland, for that is what allies do. And I value his allegiance. It would not serve me well to go against the huge army he has raised."

This confirmed what I had been told. The troops from the several ships landing in the north were allied with Gareth. The north was stronger than any of Thane's advisors had anticipated.

"But I have another choice. Your cousin has approached me."

I sucked in air. "Cedric?"

Lars nodded. "He wants to make a deal for you and form a new allegiance in the bargain. It is tempting."

Ice invaded my blood. "And you want to hear my appraisal of what that could mean."

He turned to me and frowned. "How interesting. Why do you think that?"

Oh heck, this old-world chauvinism again. I'd over-anticipated.

"Sargon always sought my advice re battle strategy," I said. "I studied the great historians in school, Tacitus and others. The Greeks and Persians. He called me Minerva."

His eyes flared. "And your cousin? Does he so name you?"

I smiled at the memory in spite of myself. "No. He calls me Valkyrie."

"Why ever that?"

"Because I ride like a man."

"That I would like to see," he said with a chuckle. "And I shall. I have your pretty little filly with the strange saddle in my stables."

"Lightning is here? How very strange..." Then it hit me. "Oh, I get it. Gareth planned to make a stop here before moving on to Norland."

Lars nodded.

"Lightning was a gift from Gareth," I told him. "The saddle is my own design."

He stared at me in appraisal. "How things become clear. Anyone can measure your looks, but Norland kept this part of you a secret. It explains the King's regard. He could never suffer a fool. Yes, Lady, tell me your ideas about where I should place my allegiance. You have my ear."

I sat up. "I'm cold. Do you mind if I pull this up?" I reached for the fur rug bed cover.

A knock sounded at the door.

Lars growled a command.

A pause. Another voice answered and he sat up. This time he yelled several words in that weird, guttural language I couldn't understand.

Footsteps retreated.

Back in bed, Lars wrapped his massive arms around me. "Why do you wear a witch's bracelet?"

I fingered the bracelet. "It was my great-aunt's. It won't come off and I don't know how to use it right."

"Minerva. Valkyrie. Witch. You have complicated my life immensely this day." He rolled away onto his back. "Tell me why I should ally with your cousin."

My mouth was dry. "You shouldn't."

Another pause. I could feel his surprise.

"Why ever not?"

"Cedric terrifies me. You should fear him too."

"Rowena—what a pretty name, I have never said it before. Rowena, Cedric claims you are his. Is this not so?"

I sighed. That annoying custom of ownership. How far back should we go here? "Gareth claims the same and he has the prior claim. But it was not done in church as is required in the south. So Cedric does not recognize it."

"Why should I fear him?" There was confidence in Lars's. "I fear nobody."

"You asked if I were a witch. I'm not, but Cedric is a master of the dark arts and he is getting stronger every day. He has me under his control and I can only stay free of him by keeping distant. If you send me back to him, I will lose my freedom forever."

Lars scanned my face. "This is a bad thing for you?"

"Would it not be so for you? Women are no different. And another thing…Gareth may accept this news that you have only protected me and nothing else, but don't ever tell Cedric I was here in your bed. Not if you value your life."

Lars raised up on one elbow. "You really are afraid of this cousin of yours."

I shivered. "I know what he is capable of. I've seen the alter he worships at. I saw him kill Sargon and his own brother Ivan. I was there, lying beside Ivan when the sword pierced his heart. He'd kill you without a thought."

"And that would bother you?"

"No man is an island," I mumbled.

"So you would have me continue to ally with Norland."

"For my sake, certainly. But to be honest, I don't know if it will make a difference. In the long run Cedric will win. I don't know a man who could stop him. I thought maybe Sargon could, but I was wrong."

"He is not that powerful," Lars said with disdain.

"You don't understand." Tears pooled in my eyes. "It's not a physical thing, although he is a powerful man and I think you underestimate him there. You saw what he did to Sargon and that was natural enough. But now that he has magic at his disposal, he doesn't care about fairness. He never did." My voice broke.

"Rowena." Lars gathered me up in his arms. "Calm down. You are safe here." He kissed my forehead and held me tight.

We stayed like that for a minute or so. I felt warm and safe in his arms. Oh, what a day this had been, a day spun on its head.

"I'm so thirsty," I said, sniffing.

He cursed, let go of me and leapt to his feet. He pulled open the door and spoke to someone. Lars returned with two goblets. He gave one to me and I drank it. He took some of his, then passed it to me. I finished his off too.

"Now sleep," he said. "We have some time yet."

I slept in the arms of this warm, gentle giant.

Sometime later I awoke with a start. The sun was high in the sky.

I sat straight up in bed.

"What is it?" Lars asked.

"Cedric's coming." I replied. "I can feel him calling." I covered my face with my hands. "It's too soon. I didn't think it would be this soon."

I heard a sharp intake of air beside me. "Tell me what you feel."

At least he took me seriously now. I tried to describe what was happening to my mind, but it was hard to break free enough to do so. "He's close. He's sending out—I guess you would call them *feelers*—to locate me. He knows I'm here in this dwelling, but he can't see where exactly. Yet. He's trying to pull me out."

Lars sat up. "What do you mean, pull you out?"

I rocked back and forth. "Give me a moment. I need to concentrate." I pressed the base of my palms to my eyes as Cedric's magnetic pull increased, and a little line of pain with it. "He's trying to pull me out of this building, into the open. He doesn't want to encounter you if he can help it. He thinks you might interfere." I stared at him. "How does he know that?"

Lars snorted. "He is no fool. It is my land. I have a reputation."

I gasped. "It's getting stronger. He can't be more than a mile away. I have to leave." I swept back the covers, rushed to my feet and threw on my ripped muslin dress. Where were my boots?

Lars jumped out of bed. "You cannot leave. That would be foolish. A woman alone in these parts, you'd be dead in a day. Be reasonable."

I stopped long enough to meet his eyes. "You don't understand, Lars. He'll destroy you to get to me. I've got to ride out for the sake of your men. Please help me."

He cursed and threw on his clothes. His weapons were on the floor. He grabbed them and swung open the door.

I was through it, then sprinting across a room filled with men still lying on pallets. I didn't stop, but shot out the main doors. The stables were to my left. I ran for them, calling to Lightning in my mind.

Behind me, Lars yelled for his men. There was a noisy commotion.

"Riders coming," yelled the guard on duty. Men poured from the fortress, shouting orders and gathering arms.

I had Lightning by the bridle and was leading her out when I felt the triumphant call. I cried out and fell to my knees.

Lars was to me in a second. He pulled me up and held me to him.

"Hold me tight." I begged him. "Don't let me free. I can't control this."

Screams erupted from the courtyard. An unusual hush followed.

I looked out the gates and saw riders, hundreds of them dressed in black, riding black horses. As before, their features were indistinct. They surrounded the walls, forming a solid line with no break, but did not enter the yard.

Then I saw Cedric. He looked bigger than ever and as strong as a lion as he cantered through the gate on the giant palomino. He came alone. He wore green and gold, the ceremonial colors of Huel. His eyes found me immediately and I cried out. Lars wrapped his arms around me from behind, locking them in front, holding me firm.

Cedric stopped and dismounted. He took one step and shifted his eyes to Lars. "You have my wife. Release her."

"I take orders from no one," Lars replied with derision.

Cedric smiled, his eyes that brilliant green color again, with no depth to them, no soul. "I take it you do not accept my overture for allegiance then."

There was a dangerous silence all around us.

Cedric's expression changed as his eyes moved from Lars to me, gathering in the way I was being held.

"You have my wife!" he yelled, the fury barely checked.

"And I mean to keep her," Lars shot back, his eyes gleaming.

Oh God, these males and their macho egos. Would it ever end?

"Then prepare to fight," Cedric said in an icy voice.

Lars reached for his sword. That was a mistake. As his right arm released me, I was jerked forward by Cedric's power. I screamed and fell to my knees. An invisible curtain had fallen behind me, a bubble of power that surrounded Cedric and me like a force field. Lars tried to reach for me, but his arm hit an imperceptible wall. I could hear the men cry out as their weapons bounced off it.

Cedric waited for me to come to him. He folded his arms and smiled, ready to enjoy my humiliation. I fought it with everything in me, staying on my knees, avoiding his eyes.

He beckoned me once more. I resisted, turning around on my knees and facing Lars, who was yelling instructions to his men, frantic to find a way to get through. I sensed Cedric's impatience and I hated him for it, hated that he would force subservience on me. The pain in my head was so excruciating that I curled up in a fetal position on the ground, unable to move or think.

Cedric strutted forward, closed his huge hand over my wrist and roughly yanked me up. The pain in my head released the instant he touched me. I opened my eyes as he swung me up into his arms and carried me to the horse as if I were no weight at all. The bubble shifted behind us, but protected us still. Men fell in behind, though they could not breach it.

My wrist hurt from being pulled. The bracelet had made an imprint in my skin . I held it to my chest and massaged my wrist.

Cedric drew the palomino closer. Soon he would lift me onto it.

I wished with all my heart to be somewhere else, my favorite place.

The air turned bright yellow around us.

"Lady Rowena!" I heard Lars cry out.

There was a snap and I was tossed into the sky.

Chapter 40

I landed in a heap on hard floor. It wasn't a graceful landing.

The sky was still spinning and my stomach fought nausea. I lay on my back, looked around and tried to take in what the hell had just happened.

I was in the library at Castle Sargon. Alone. But not for long.

Kendra dashed in from the adjacent bedroom. "Thank God! Are you alright?" She reached down and pulled me up. Then she hugged me hard.

"I'm fine. Let me sit down for a moment in the next room."

I was still light-headed.

When we reached the bed, I plunked down on it. "I don't ever want to do that, ever again," I said with conviction.

"Tell me what happened. I've been worried sick."

I told her most of it. I left out the Lars gift-from-heaven part.

She shook her head, then filled me in on her story. "After you vanished, I didn't know what to do. I called your name over and over, and started walking south down the riverside, retracing our steps.

"You must have been scared."

"Terrified. It was pitch black. Then Logan and a search party found me. Thane had sent them out looking for us."

I smiled.

"They brought me back to the castle and I went right to bed," Kendra continued. "When I awoke this morning, almost everyone was gone. Even Logan. George says Thane is already at the battlefield with his troops. I didn't know what to do so I waited for you here. Figured it was the first place you would go."

My heart caught on one word. "Battlefield? Kendra, we have to stop this."

"I thought you would say that. But how?"

I scrambled to my feet and dashed toward the wardrobe. "Not sure yet, but we've got to find them. I'll figure something out when we get there. But first, help me find something to wear."

She leaped to her feet beside me and rummaged through the wardrobe.

"Find anything?" I asked.

"Nope. You've wrecked everything."

My eyes landed on the dark cherry dress. "It might fit."

"Isn't it rather fancy for riding?"

I shrugged. "Thane is going into battle. I should probably attempt to look regal for the sake of the men. Besides, everything else I have is ripped or dirty. I don't want to join his side looking like a tavern wench."

"A tavern wench after a big brawl."

I scowled. "Help me into it."

It was a struggle, but we succeeded. Kendra laced the dress loosely.

"Your hair will cover the back," she said.

"Now to the stables." I picked up my skirt and ran.

Ten minutes later we were saddled and leaving through the front gates.

"Good thing these two fillies were left behind," I said. "Two small for the men, I guess. Do you know where they are?"

"George said they would likely meet on the border with Huel, by the river."

The river...Thane at war with my family from Huel.

My stomach twisted. How would this day turn out?

"Let's go," I called to Kendra as I kicked the horse forward.

We rode hard for some time. Like most young horses, ours were anxious to run. I felt their excitement and tried to caress their minds with reassurance.

As we traveled, I scanned the horizon for any sign of troops. None yet, but the evidence of recent footprints—male and equine—were everywhere. I knew this landscape well. Many times, I had traveled between Castle Sargon and Huel. For some strange reason, this felt like it would be the last.

A chill ran down my spine.

As we neared the river, I saw soldiers far in the distance. We were close to the clearing, just a ride up the long hill to the forest edge.

I motioned Kendra. "Keep close."

When we crested the hill, I pulled the filly to a stop. From this vantage point, I could see for several miles. "Holy hell, Kendra. Look at this."

Thousands of men milled around on our side of the river. White tents sprouted like mushrooms on the verdant meadow that had been my first sight of Land's End. Colored pennants flanked a row of tents midway.

I forced my eyes to look beyond them.

Across the river, a line of Cedric's demon horsemen flanked the shore in both directions as far as I could see. Beyond the wall of ghostly black, ten thousand men or more made camp. Cooking fires dotted the landscape. To the south I could see more troops and men on horseback marching closer, in serpentine trails like ants.

"God help us," Kendra whispered.

I knew Gareth's allies would be moving down from the north.

I gazed to the left. Nothing yet.

I pointed down the hill to the flying banners. "There. That's where Thane will be."

"Should we join them?"

"I think we should stay here. Thane has scouts. He'll know soon enough that we are here."

As we stood watching, a thunderous roar rose from the troops beyond the river. Huel colors were carried into camp by a line of mounted warriors. No question what that signaled. Cedric had returned.

I shivered and wondered if we could be seen from the distance. "Kendra, I'm nervous. We should dismount and hide the horses."

We both swung down and walked our animals to the clearing.

"Should we stay here?" Kendra asked.

I shook my head. "I want to see what's coming."

Better to face it full on than shrink like a coward.

I led the way back to the forest edge. Below, a single rider made his way up the side of the hill. Thane. I could tell by the colors draped across his horse. Silver and purple—the colors of Sargonia.

My heart pounded as horse and rider pulled over the crest.

Thane vaulted off his mount and strode over to face me. "Great Zeus, are you all right?" He reached down, his tender embrace holding me as if I were more precious than gold. "Like a gift from the Gods."

I chuckled at the irony of his words.

His mouth covered mine and he kissed me passionately. When he drew away, I gulped for air.

"What happened, Rowena?"

"Cedric was about to throw me on his horse. We were in this magic force field—like an invisible bubble—and Lars couldn't get through it to help me. None of his men could."

"How did you escape?"

"Cedric grabbed my wrist and it hurt so I rubbed it. Then the sky burst open. There was a big yellow flash and I landed in the castle."

There were a million questions in Thane's deep blue eyes. I had a few myself about the 'how' of what had happened, the science or magic of it, which is why I was unprepared for his next question.

"Who is Lars?"

My mouth shot open, then closed. "Lars is one of the Dane leaders, an ally of Gareth's."

"You were that far north? I've had scouts all over our lands, but not there. I've been mad with worry."

And you were quite right to be worried, I thought. But I didn't say it out loud.

"Cedric followed me after the whole Gareth kidnapping thing, so Kendra and I took horses and went east. I ended up in a fortress and could feel him drawing closer. It's a long story." I glanced at my wrist. "Thane, how could this happen? I wished to be with you and rubbed your mother's bracelet."

"You wished to be with me?"

I nodded. "I remember thinking that I fervently wanted to be back in the library. That's the last thing I remember before the yellow flash of light."

He pulled me to him. "It is worth it then. It will all be worth it." His arms were comforting, his scent was soothing, everything about him was reassuring—except for those words.

"What will be worth it?" I demanded.

"We are ready. My troops are amassing to meet Cedric's forces."

"No!"

Thane caught my shoulders with both hands. "I must, Rowena. There is no other way."

But there was another way.

Thane dropped his hold and stood back. The fingers of one hand raked through his hair. "We'll meet on the field at dawn tomorrow unless the fiend defies convention and attacks tonight. How to keep you safe though. That is what disturbs me."

I gazed over the battlefield below. Tens of thousands of men would be hurt or killed. Thane and Cedric would fight to the death. There would be no victor. In my heart I knew that. They would destroy each other.

I turned to Kendra. "We've got to leave. It's the only way. You know that, right?"

She stared at me, her eyes two pools of liquid chocolate. "Yes, I know. There'll be a bloodbath if we don't."

I spun back to Thane, who seemed to have turned to stone. "If you love me, tell me the truth. How much magic do you know? Can you open the portal for a brief time?"

He hesitated. "I don't know. But I think *you* might be able to."

My jaw dropped. "What?"

"The bracelet. It was your mother's. You never asked how it came to be in my possession."

Bugger. How had I missed that? "Tell me."

He paced the ground, stroking his chin. "Sargon found the bracelet in the forest by the split oak tree. He recognized it as the one that was willed to your mother by our own. I think it broke away from your mother's wrist when she slipped through the portal to your land."

My brain's synapses were working fiendishly to figure this out. "You're saying magic doesn't work on the other side of the wall? Did you test it when we were there?"

He stopped pacing. One eyebrow lifted. "I am always astonished by your quick intelligence. That is exactly what I meant. Magic doesn't exist in your land. I tested it. The bracelet chose to stay on this side rather than relinquish its power."

"Like a living thing," I murmured.

Maybe that was it. Magic was a living thing in Land's End.

"Before it separated," I said, "the bracelet gave my mother the power to open the portal."

The headache came on like a siren this time. Before I could say anything, I was on my knees, gripping my head and moaning.

"What is it?" Thane cried.

"Cedric's here." I closed my eyes to concentrate better. "He's calling me. Trying to draw me into view so he can better focus the spell."

I gasped. The tendrils had found me and were reaching in.

"We've got to leave now," Kendra wailed. "If Cedric gets close enough, she'll have no will left."

I heard nothing after that but the call. Soft, sweet words took over every space in my mind, owning it, filling every crevice with yearning and desire for him alone.

I screamed in frustration.

Thane raised his arms and chanted to the sky, words I'd never heard him say before—ancient words. The air seemed to shimmer before us. The dark magic released and slowly faded as my mind cleared.

"I've set a magic shield in place. I don't know if it will hold." Thane shook me. "Rowena! Can you hear me?"

I nodded. "See if you can open the portal."

He hesitated.

"Please, Thane! If the shield doesn't hold, I'll use the bracelet to escape back to the castle."

He freed me.

Kendra was already dashing toward the split oak.

"Go with her, Thane," I said. "She'll show you exactly where."

He stepped around me and ran for the tree line, while I backed up to the edge of the path.

This was *my* time. I would face my greatest test of courage.

I waited, my arm stretched out. The bracelet twinkled in the sun and I watched the jewels start to glow, first softly and then shimmering.

Magic was building all around me. I could channel it.

Two riders pounded up the hill. Cedric and Richard. They stopped about fifty feet away.

I felt Cedric's siren song and willed it back with the bracelet.

It worked! A jolt hit my wrist and ricocheted.

Cedric jerked in shock. He leapt from the palomino and moved forward, sending waves of magic in my direction. I pushed them back with equal force and his body jerked with each hit.

His face was black with anger. He raised his massive arms and chanted words to the sky, the devil's own words. The ground shook, but nothing could touch me. The bracelet reinforced the invisible shield Thane had created and every magic arrow boomeranged off it with increasing force.

Cedric roared like a lion in agony.

Beside me, Kendra gasped. "What the—" She stared at Richard, who had dismounted and moved to her side. To *our* side.

The significance of that hit me. Cedric would be furious. I had to do something to keep him from following us.

I used my other weapon—words. "Cedric, your magic won't work beyond the wall. Magic doesn't work there."

I felt a slight drop in his power. Then just as quickly, it surged. I was nearly flung off my feet as spears of lightning ricocheted off my bracelet. Still, I held my wrist firm.

"Think of it, Cedric." My voice dropped to seduction. "No power, no wealth, no title. You will be nothing more than an ordinary man if you walk through the portal. Cedric, a common peasant."

His fury fed the magic. A blast of force surged against me, nearly knocking me over.

For a second I panicked. Until I felt Thane's presence beside me, reinforcing the shield.

"It's open," he said. "I don't know for how long."

I nodded in comprehension. "Kendra, you go first."

Her eyes caught mine, then turned to seek Richard's. For a shocking second they stood locked in gaze.

Richard? She loved Richard?

Before I could say a word, she walked through the wall.

The next thing happened so quickly I barely saw it.

Richard stormed after Kendra. He raised one arm at the portal, then vaulted through it and was gone.

A deafening growl came from Cedric. Then a battle cry boomed from far away.

There was no time to spare.

I turned to Thane. "How much do you love me?"

"More than my life."

"More than your kingdom?"

He didn't hesitate. "Yes. I'm coming with you."

"I don't know if we will get back."

"It matters not." His sapphire eyes searched mine. "Wherever we go we'll be together, Rowena."

Desperate to break through the barrier, Cedric threw arcs of pure destructive power. The shimmering force field held, though I knew it would dissipate the moment I touched the wall.

With one last breath, I grabbed Thane's hand and pulled him toward the split oak. The air sizzled as our combined magic dispersed at the portal. There was a sudden tug and an earsplitting roar.

The bracelet fell from my wrist. The earth shifted from forest to classroom.

With one final step, we walked out of the past…and into our future.

~ * ~

If you enjoyed this book, please consider writing a short review and posting it on Amazon, Goodreads and/or Barnes and Noble. Reviews are very helpful to other readers and are greatly appreciated by authors, especially me. When you post a review, drop me an email and let me know and I may feature part of it on my blog/site. Thank you. ~ Melodie

mcampbell50@cogeco.ca

Message from the Author

Dear Reader,

Do you crave a short escape from real life at times? One day, when I was feeling overwhelmed with work, family and parental caregiving, I thought to myself: I wish I could walk right through that wall into another world.

That night, *Rowena Through the Wall* had her start. I hope you too have enjoyed escaping through the wall with Rowena, and will look forward to the second book in the series, *Rowena and the Dark Lord*.

Please follow my blog: www.funnygirlmelodie.blogspot.com

Thank you again for reading!

Yours in escape,
Melodie

About the Author

By day, Melodie Campbell is a mild-mannered association executive; by night, she transforms into a fevered scribe of comedy and suspense. Melodie has a Commerce degree from Queen's University, but it didn't take well. She has been a banker, marketing director, comedy writer, association executive and college instructor. Not only that, she was probably the worst runway model ever.

Melodie got her start as a humor columnist, so it's no surprise her fiction has been described by editors as "wacky" and "laugh-out-loud funny." With over 200 publications and five awards for short fiction, Melodie's work has appeared in Alfred Hitchcock's Mystery Magazine, Star Magazine, Canadian Living Magazine, The Globe and Mail, The Toronto Star, The Hamilton Spectator, New Mystery Reader, Mysterical-E and many more.

Melodie is now the General Manager of Crime Writers of Canada. She lives in Oakville, Ontario, with husband, two kids and giant Frankenpoodle.

www.melodiecampbell.com

IMAJIN BOOKS
Quality fiction beyond your wildest dreams

For your next eBook or paperback purchase, please visit:

www.imajinbooks.com

www.twitter.com/imajinbooks

www.facebook.com/imajinbooks